MW01002402

AVALON TOWER

FEY SPY ACADEMY

C.N. CRAWFORD

ALEX RIVERS

PROLOGUE

*A*lix glances at the top floor of an apartment building, staring at the couple shagging against the window. Even from here, she can see the pleasure on the man's face, his breath misting the glass.

That would be an infinitely better way to spend the day than the mission she has planned. She can imagine Agent Rein holding her like that, gripping her as he kisses her throat.

But it will never happen. Love is strictly forbidden for the spies of Avalon Tower. The problem is, banning desire doesn't douse the heat. If anything, it fuels it. Sometimes, Alix thinks all the Avalon spies are unsatisfied, obsessed, lost in fantasies. Today, especially, her head isn't in the game—even though Fey soldiers probably lurk all around this place, waiting to run their swords through agents like her.

Distraction is death, she reminds herself.

She turns away, scanning the street for signs of her Fey enemies. She doesn't see anything amiss. In fact, it all looks perfectly calm, picturesque and quaint. Wrought iron balconies overhang the cobbled alley. Here, in the south of France, the scent of lavender mingles with the brine of the sea. The streets of this coastal town are ancient, stony, labyrinthine. At the bottom of the sloping road, wisps of fog curl over the Mediterranean. A cafe overlooks the sea—Café de la Fôret Enchantée. The meeting point is by the back door.

She peers out across the outdoor tables, where a pretty woman with raven hair is eating cake and flirting with a waiter. Alix feels a pang of jealousy. For normal women—those who aren't spies trying to save the world—love is always a possibility.

Focus, Alix.

Still a picture of serenity around her. No sign of the Fey soldiers. But no sign of Rein, either.

A church bell tolls, making her heart skip a beat. Rein should be here. He's usually early.

She takes a slow, calming breath. She's always thinking of him, which is exactly why love is forbidden in the first place. It takes your mind off the mission and leads to stupid decisions. She's never told him how she feels, how she seems to always be looking for him. Every time she sees a reflection, she checks the glass to see if *he's* behind her, hoping to see his boyish smile instead of looking out for the enemy. Whenever she walks into the dining hall at Avalon Tower, she scans the room for his slender form.

She's always coming up with excuses to get close to him, but she can never quite tell if he feels the same about her.

The clouds slide over the sun, and she feels a chill. She should stay at the beach, alert for any sign of the Fey, those terrifying soldiers in royal blue. But she's not going to leave here without Rein. He's late for the rendezvous, and her mind spins in a million horrible directions.

Pulse racing, she climbs back up the hill. Her skin tingles with the hum of the veil emanating from the streets nearby, the misty barrier that separates this world from that of the Fey. In theory, it's a boundary that keeps them on one side and humans on the other, but it's not that simple. For one thing, you can never be sure exactly where the veil is. Sure, the Fey control it, but sometimes, it seems to have a mind of its own. The magical boundary roams a bit, shifting its location ever so slightly. It's a hungry thing, and if it consumes you, you die. Every few weeks, it leaves a curious tourist dead on the winding streets of southern France. Alix is one of the few people alive who can actually control it, who can stop it from killing those passing through.

Casually, she checks her watch, and dread skitters up her spine. Rein was supposed to be here six minutes ago. He's *never* late, especially not for an exfiltration operation. The fugitives should be just beyond the veil by now. She feels like she can hardly breathe.

Spies are taught to suppress emotion, to maintain complete control of themselves, even when danger lurks in the shadows of every alley. But now, Alix feels her training fail as the terrifying possibilities race through her mind. What if he was slaughtered already? What if the veil shifted location and killed him? She'd lose her mind if anything happened to Rein, if she never got to see his brown eyes again or had the chance to wrap her arms around him.

She grits her teeth so hard that she nearly bites her tongue. *Get it together.*

She masks her feelings with a wistful smile as she crosses the road to the gold- and salmon-colored shops on the opposite side. She pretends to look in the windows at the madeleines and croissants, the slices of cake. Anyone watching her would think she's just a hungry tourist on vacation, a cute blonde in a sundress.

Fog drifts across the street.

Eleven minutes late now. Alix's blood roars. Something is *definitely* wrong. She starts to march back to Café de la Fôret Enchantée.

At last, she hears the whistle that is their signal, and she heaves a sigh of relief. It's coming from behind her. Did she miss him somehow?

The signal is coming from a narrow lane, and Alix hurries over to it.

She turns the corner, and the world tilts beneath her feet. Now, she's face-to-face with a towering Fey. Silver hair flows down his back, and he wears the dark blue velvet of a Fey soldier. There's something about his eerie stillness, about the sharpness of his gaze that sends fear ringing through Alix's bones. It's the metallic sheen in his green eyes that's so disorienting, otherworldly. His lip curls, exposing one of his sharpened canines.

Alix reads nothing in his eyes except loathing.

We've been compromised. Alix's heart slams, and she turns to run.

But her path is blocked by a second Fey soldier, and Alix is caught between them. She reaches for her dagger, but it's too late.

A blade plunges into Alix's stomach, and pain rushes through her. Her training takes over, and she tries to pull her dagger, to dodge, to parry, to run, but her limbs don't obey her for some reason. She falls to her knees.

Strange. Her wound doesn't hurt that much. She hardly feels it at all.

Thoughts of Rein flicker through her mind as she bleeds onto the stones.

CHAPTER 1

S   *even minutes earlier.*
        I breathe in the scent of the ocean, a fragrance tinged with cypress, and sip my coffee. It's hot for early spring, and it almost looks like steam is rising from the sea. From my spot at Café de la Fôret Enchantée, I see the cloud of shimmering mist shearing across the landscape.

My vacation has been heaven so far. The breeze rushes off the water and leaves a faint taste of salt on my lips. This place is good for my asthma, I think.

The atmosphere in the south of France feels different than California. Here, the light is soft, honeyed, not the glaring, overwhelming harshness of the LA sun.

Nearby, the magical veil rises to the sky like a wall of fog. It's eerie and undeniably beautiful. It moves sometimes, but I'm at a safe distance here. Just beyond the tables of the outdoor café, waves crash over the white rocks. This might just be my favorite place in the world.

I manifested this trip with positive thoughts and vision boards. Also, many hours of minimum-wage labor and eating cereal for dinner instead of going out to bars. This two-week vacation is my destiny.

Sure, I feel a twinge of guilt at leaving Mom behind, but there's no way I could pay for us both. And it *would* be better to have my friend Leila with me, but she's scared of going anywhere near the Fey border. She thinks they might still leap out of the veil and murder you at any moment, even if the guidebooks from our bookshop and the U.S. State Department *clearly* say it's safe.

I pick up a sprig of lavender from the vase on the table and inhale.

I'm still enjoying the lovely scent when a dark-haired waiter slides a slice of a blackberry cake onto the lace tablecloth before me. "Bon appétit."

I definitely ordered the *lavender* cake, but cake is cake. "Thank you."

As I take a bite, the fruity flavor bursts on my tongue. This slice costs the equivalent of three hours of work at the bookshop, but I try not to think about it. Fifteen years ago, the war made prices soar, and they never went down again. Luxuries like cake are stupidly expensive. *Vacation*, I remind myself.

Another bite. The sugary, tart flavors coat my tongue. Mom would be horrified. *So many carbs, darling.* She lives on vodka and boiled eggs.

The waiter watches me take a bite and smiles. With his bright blue eyes and square jaw, he reminds me of someone, but I can't quite put my finger on it.

"Is delicious, yes?" he asks. He must have pegged me as a tourist because he's speaking in heavily accented English.

I nod. "C'est délicieux."

His shoulders relax as he shifts to French himself. "I'm glad. Are you here on holiday?" He wears a flat cap over wavy brown hair.

"I arrived a week ago. Only one week left." My chest clenches at the realization that my trip is already half over. For five years, I've looked forward to this, but I can't spend the other half of my vacation mourning the end of it, can I? "I wish I could stay."

Sure, it's a teensy bit lonely having my birthday cake at a table for one, but it's probably better than what I'd be doing at home.

"Where are you from?" he asks.

"The U.S. west coast. LA."

"LA, as in Hollywood? Are you an actress? A model?" He lowers his eyelashes, then looks up again. "Your hair is very striking. So unusually dark."

Is he flirting with me? "Thank you. No, I'm not an actress."

I glance at the veil again. I can't seem to keep my gaze off it. What's happening on the other side?

"Have you seen any?" I turn to him and whisper, "Fey."

He blanches. It's almost like saying the word out loud

9

sends a ripple of terror across the café, and for a moment, I regret it.

I catch the brief tightening of the muscles around his mouth until he softens them into a smile. He shrugs. "Sometimes, they patrol the border on our side. But most of the south of France remains independent. We're safe here, and there's nothing to worry about. King Auberon has no interest in claiming more of France than he already has."

That's what I told Leila. Except I'd sounded convincing, and when he says it, it sounds distinctly rehearsed. What is he *not* saying?

What I do know is this: fifteen years ago, the Fey invaded France. When it first happened, the world was stunned. Until that point, no one even knew they existed. And then, suddenly, they were marching through Paris, commanding the boulevards. Their dragons circled above the Eiffel Tower. The Fey were beautiful, otherworldly, seductive...

Lethally violent and hell-bent on conquest.

The French military fought back and managed to keep some of the south free and under human control. Unoccupied. It's supposed to be safe.

But as the clouds slide over the sun, I feel the atmosphere suddenly grow tense around me. It's hard to put my finger on it, but there's something sharp and grim in the air now, replacing the soft ambience.

I glance at the waiter, who still lingers by my table.

Maybe there *is* more danger here than the tourist boards are willing to admit. Maybe Leila had a point.

The night before, as I ate bouillabaisse in a restaurant by the sea, I overheard a man arguing with his wife, telling her that an anti-Fey resistance was fighting King Auberon. A magical cold war that played out behind the scenes, one with spies and secret missions. He made it sound like these spies had legendary skills, that they could kill a Fey in two seconds flat with their bare hands. That a highly skilled, elite force was our only hope if we wanted to stop the evil king from taking the rest of France.

His wife called him an idiot and told him to stop talking.

But there's a tension here that makes me want to know more...

I flutter my eyelashes. "Have you heard anything about the secret resistance?" I whisper.

The waiter smiles, a dimple in one cheek. "Ah, that." His smile is patronizing, and he rolls his eyes theatrically. "Rumors only. How would they fight the Fey in their lands? You cannot cross the veil into the Fey realm, and even if you did, the Fey would spot you as a human instantly. And anyway, they have magic. We don't. I really doubt such a resistance exists."

I glance at the veil again. Misty shades of faint violet and green twist and spiral, plunging into the ocean and rising up to dissipate in the clouds.

If cell phones still worked, I'd be snapping photos like crazy. But electronics fizzled out with the arrival of the

Fey. For whatever reason, Fey magic destroyed our most modern technology.

The waiter sighs wistfully. "The veil is beautiful, isn't it? Is that what you came here to see?"

Something about this waiter makes me uneasy, but I'm not sure what it is. He reminds me of someone I hate, but that's a completely irrational reason to dislike someone. "I did want to see the veil," I admit, "but also, I used to come to France, years after the Fey invasion. Starting when I was fifteen, my mom would take me here. We stayed at a château in Bordeaux during the summers."

He flashes me a smile. "I've been. Amazing vineyards, of course. Shame that we lost half of them to the occupation."

My stomach tightens as I remember those summer vacations. Our days were spent with my mom drinking all the wine in the vineyard. Then, when she was properly wasted, she'd urge me to flirt with rich French guys who "could do a lot for me." I remember she was so loud and drunk one night—

Oh. That's why he looks familiar. He resembles the dark-haired, aristocratic demi-Fey who broke my heart when I was a teenager. What a great example of a memory that should have stayed repressed.

The waiter is nearly as handsome as that demi-Fey, but not quite. Humans rarely have the shocking, heart-breaking beauty of the Fey.

I stare at him over the rim of my coffee cup. "What's your name?"

"Jules." He seems to think this is an invitation, and he pulls out the chair across from me. He stares at me dreamily across the table. "And yours?"

"Nia."

"I'm finishing my shift soon." This is clearly suggestive. But what does Jules have in mind, exactly? Maybe he wants to whisk me off to a beautiful hidden bookstore full of rare volumes. Or maybe he wants a quick fumble in a hotel room, in which case the answer is no.

I take another bite of the cake, tasting the confiture, and dab at my lips with the napkin. I still haven't satisfied my curiosity, so I lean forward and whisper, "What do you think it's like now? In the occupied regions? In Fey France?"

His eyes dart furtively to the left, then the right. He leans forward on his elbows and quietly says, "I try not to think about it. I hear things I wish I could forget." He keeps his blue eyes locked on me, as if suggesting I should do the same.

I wait for him to go on. When he doesn't, I ask, "What sort of things?"

"I see them coming through here, sometimes," he says. "Fugitives."

I stare at him. This *definitely* wasn't in the tourist guidebooks. "What fugitives?"

"The Fey king, Auberon, hunts anyone who doesn't support him. He accuses scores of people of treason and slaughters them. I think he particularly hates the demi-Fey. He suspects them of disloyalty, and he demands

13

complete fealty. The police here are supposed to report any demi-Fey they see escaping. Otherwise, Auberon might invade the rest of France." He straightens. "I mean, he won't. He knows he can't win. Even if electronics don't work, we have guns and iron bullets. And we help to keep things under control. We protect what we have."

A shiver runs over my skin. "I see. And how do you do that?"

"We report any fugitives we see. No one is allowed to help them. It keeps the status quo intact." He opens his hands and shrugs again. "What can we do? We have to keep the peace. We can only enjoy life and keep things the way they are."

A tendril of guilt twines through me, and I try to push it away.

"Is there a special reason for your vacation?" he asks.

"It's my twenty-sixth birthday."

He grins. "Well, Nia, we must celebrate. Has it been a good birthday so far?"

Church bells toll, and the sound echoes across the stones and out to the sea. The air grows colder, grayer. "Probably one of the best. Definitely far from the worst."

My worst birthday was when I was fifteen, back in LA. Mom promised to throw a huge party. This was when we still lived in a house in Laurel Canyon with gorgeous views of the city, and it felt like my one chance to impress the rich girls from my school. But she started drinking champagne early and fell through a glass table while the DJ was playing an ABBA song. She kept laughing hysterically as she bled all over the hardwood floors.

The girls from school never spoke to me again.

Oh, good. Another memory that should have stayed under the surface. I muster a smile.

Jules turns to look behind him, and I realize that a cold hush has fallen over the outdoor café. The sea no longer sparkles. It's churning under a gray sky.

Then my gaze flits to a pair of Fey marching over the white rocks. Actual, real-life, terrifying Fey, the kind that slaughter people for being disloyal.

Fear flutters through my chest.

I've never seen full-blooded Fey before. I find myself staring at their towering, godlike physiques. But it's the eerie, otherworldly way they walk that holds my attention. With every graceful movement they make, my mind screams that danger lurks between me and the roiling sea, a primal fear that dances up the nape of my neck and makes it hard to breathe.

They look so out of place here—warriors from another time, draped in dark cloaks that seem to suck up the light around them. Long hair flows down their backs, silver and black, and their bright eyes send alarm bells ringing through me. Not to mention the *swords*.

My mind flicks back to the stories of what happened when they first invaded Breton. The burned homes, the corpses left in their wake...

One of them glances at me, bright emerald eyes with a metallic sheen. He looks *lethal*. My stomach flips. I'm not even doing anything wrong. I'm a tourist, legally here on vacation, but I suddenly feel like I'm about to die.

My pulse races as I look down at the cake again, trying to go unnoticed. I stare at it, gripping my fork.

When I look up again, the two Fey are gone, and I exhale slowly. Around me, the café conversation resumes.

Jules turns back to me, frowning. "It's unusual to see the Fey patrol here. They must be looking for someone. A fugitive, perhaps. A demi-Fey." He narrows his eyes at me. "The demi-Fey are very beautiful. Like you." He stares at me, his eyes narrowing. His words linger in the air. "And they don't *always* have pointed ears, you know. You said you are from America?"

I can feel his suspicion, and a shiver runs down my spine. Suddenly, I desperately want to get away from this guy.

"America, yes." I clear my throat. "Do you have a phone here I can use?"

With a clenched jaw, Jules points inside. "It's by the back entrance."

I drop some money on the table and stand. Head down, I cross into the café. There's a back door, I think, in case I need to run out of here.

Am I being paranoid that the waiter suspected me? Or was Leila right about coming here? I'm not sure which idea I dread more—the actual danger I could be in or the gloating *I told you so* I'd get from her.

I find the phone by a door that looks out onto a side street. Like most phones these days, it's a refurbished antique, the only kind that still works. It's beautiful, really, with a copper body and ivory handset. I pick it up and put it to my ear, blinking at the loud ringtone. I dial my mother's number, turning the old rotary dial, then wait as the line crackles.

There's a metallic tang in the air that sets my teeth on edge. I close my eyes and inhale.

"Hello?" My mom's voice sounds strange, distorted by wires and distance.

"Hi, Mom! It's me." I try to control my wavering voice.

"Nia," she says heavily. "I'm glad you finally decided to call."

"I called three days ago," I remind her brightly.

"It's been at least a week."

"Okay." There's no point in arguing. "How are you doing?"

"I'm broke again. And my feet are *aching*."

"Soak them in a plastic tub of water, Mom. Just make sure to turn the water off before it overflows." I listen distractedly to her as I stare outside. "Don't leave the water running unless you're there."

She's overflowed the sink so many times.

"Well, I can't remember everything when it's just me on my own."

"Please try to eat well," I say. "I left out tons of healthy groceries for you."

Something catches my eye outside. There's an alleyway across from this café, and a bright crimson smear streaks across the ground. What *is* that?

"It's my birthday," I say, trying to focus. "You were in labor for ten hours, remember?"

It's her favorite thing to say on my birthday.

"*Today?* Nia, you keep getting older." She makes it sound like an accusation.

"Well, it's better than the alternative, right?"

I'm staring at that bright streak of red, but my view is blocked by a group of tourists who walk by, dressed in costumes like the Fey—sheer materials in rich colors, burgundy and chartreuse. One of them drops a bit of jewelry—a blue crystal pendant—but the woman doesn't seem to notice.

"My little Nia, all grown up," Mom is saying. "You know, I was already doing modeling jobs when I was—"

"Fourteen. You're still so pretty, Mom." I tap on the glass to try to get the woman's attention, but she doesn't seem to hear me. She keeps walking, and her beautiful blue jewel gleams on the sidewalk.

A heavy sigh from Mom. "Well, I have crow's feet now."

"No, you don't. You don't look a day over nineteen. Mom, I have to go. I'll call you soon."

"You'd better. Because you *left* me here, all by my—"

I hang up and push out the back door of the café. I pick up the jewel from the sidewalk and glance at it. It's beautiful, otherworldly, and it gleams in the sunlight.

"Excusez-moi!" I call out.

The woman turns around, and I hurry closer to the group, smiling. "You dropped this," I say in French.

But as I look closer at them, my smile starts to fade. They're not wearing costumes, I realize. They are actual *Fey*, and some of them have delicately pointed ears.

Or more likely, they're demi-Fey. Are they fugitives? Their gossamer clothes are ripped and dirty.

My pulse races. The Fey soldiers aren't far from here. Did Jules say they'd be slaughtered on the spot? Or dragged back across the veil?

They aren't wearing shoes, and the fear in their expressions is clear. It's the same look that Mom gets after too much coke. One of them even looks like her, with dark hair and gaunt cheeks. A blonde woman staggers next to her, hugging herself. Her eyes look haunted, too.

If someone like Jules catches them, he'll send them straight to their deaths.

One of them is just a bony little boy with haunted eyes and emaciated cheeks.

Children need looking after. The thought screams in my mind.

I glance back to that alleyway. With sickening clarity, I can now see that crimson smear of blood brushed over the stone—as if someone had dragged a dead body backward. My stomach turns. What's going on here?

I quickly hand the jewel over to the woman. "You dropped this."

She grabs my arm. "Alix? Rein?" Her accent is one I don't recognize.

I stare at her in confusion. "No, that's not me. I'm sorry."

I glance past her. A woman is leaning out of her doorway, glaring at us. She wears a pinched expression. "Who are you?" the woman barks in French. She's glaring directly at me. Now *I'm* under suspicion.

Am *I* about to be turned in? Am I about to be a blood smear on the pavement?

Fear drags its claws though my chest. Leila was right.

CHAPTER 2

We're just out of sight of the café's outdoor tables, and there's another lane off to the left. The angry woman is staring at us, waiting for an answer.

I glance at the little boy again, who looks up at me with big brown eyes.

I could turn and run, but two things stop me. One is purely selfish. I've already been seen with them, and Jules suspects me entirely on the basis that he thinks I'm too cute to be human.

But the other reason is that I cannot stomach the thought of this little boy becoming another pool of blood.

I smile and wave at the woman who's staring at us from the doorway. "Tour group!" I yell in French. "Fey themed. Pretty good costumes, right?" I give her a cheerful smile, then turn back to the group. "Bonjour à tout le monde!" I call out to the haggard demi-Fey, beck-

21

oning them toward the road that cuts off to the left. "Nous pouvons commencer la visite. Bienvenue à la ville frontière magique!"

I grin at them, and they all stare at me, fear etched on their faces. I just told them that we could start the tour and welcomed them to the magical border town. They don't seem to understand what I'm trying to do.

"On the beach," I continue in French, "we will have a view of the incredible veil, the barrier to the Fey kingdom. Until fifteen years ago, most people didn't even know they existed. They lived in another dimension, one created by magic long ago—Brocéliende, the Fey realm. Auberon's own kingdom was withering, so they invaded our dimension, and he occupied France for more territory. Now, the Fey have two regions: Brocéliende in the other dimension, and Fey France in our world. The French fought back valiantly, preserving some of the south."

The stone road gives way to hot, white sand.

At least on the beach, all the bare feet will make sense.

I give a speech that makes war sound dramatic and heroic. The truth is, of course, horrific, rife with senseless deaths and violence. But tour guides don't dwell on that. War tourism is supposed to be *fun*. I frantically gesture for them to follow me to the beach, over sand and short shrubs that smell like thyme. When they don't follow, I grab the blonde woman by the hand and pull her along. The others reluctantly shuffle after her.

They all look so thin, so terrorized. What *happened* to

them in the Fey realm? And what will happen to me if someone decides I'm one of them?

"After the peace talks," I go on, "King Auberon promised not to claim any more territory, and we have now established the status quo." Lowering my voice, I quickly ask, "Est-ce que quelqu'un parle français?" I switch to English. "Does anyone here speak English?"

Blank stares.

Maybe I should try the Fey language? "Mishe-hu medaber áit seo Fey?"

"Stop trying to speak in Fey," one of the women whispers in English. Her eyes are strangely bright, an otherworldly violet. "I understand English. Your Fey pronunciation is painful."

Ouch. I've been trying to learn from a book, but the pronunciation was never clear on the page.

"Okay," I answer softly, beckoning them closer. "Listen, you all need to get off the streets. Now."

"Why would you say that?" She flicks her hair behind her shoulder in what looks like an attempt at a casual gesture. "We're ordinary English citizens on holiday." Her Fey accent makes every word twirl beautifully, and she doesn't sound remotely English.

"Sure," I say dryly. "Listen, anyone can see what you are." Someone in the group gasps, and the violet-eyed woman turns to run. I grab her by the arm. "No! Don't run. It will only call attention to you."

Her lower lip juts out. "Are you an agent?"

An agent? Are those the spies I heard the man talk

about yesterday? The secret resistance? Sadly, I'm no hero. "No. I'm not an agent. My name is Nia. What's yours?"

She hesitates for a few seconds, looking as if she regrets her earlier words. Finally, she sighs. "I'm Aleina. We were supposed to meet a contact, but he never showed up. He had a secret way through the city to the docks. Disguises. Counterfeit passports. Weapons to protect ourselves. He has everything we need. But he's not here."

"I don't have those things."

"Can you protect us if we get attacked?" she asks desperately.

If we were attacked, the only thing I could do would be to distract the attackers with a terrible Fey accent. "Um...no."

"Then you can't help us." Her eyes mist with tears. Up close, I see that there are flecks of gold in the violet of her pupils. Her fingers are delicate. Even with her ears covered by her black hair, these are telltale marks of a demi-Fey. "I'll have to try to summon help." She lifts the blue jewel.

"Summon?" I glance at the crystal. It seems to pulse with an unearthly light. "What does that do?"

"It's a magical cry for help," she says, her voice tight. "Once I break it, it'll erupt with a very loud noise and bright light. It might summon the resistance here. It's a last resort." She tugs at the pendant.

"No!" I grab her fist before she can yank it off. "The streets are patrolled by Fey soldiers today. You'll get us *both* in trouble. The Fey will be here in seconds if you use that. Listen, I have a better idea."

She releases her crystal. "What?"

"People here are used to tourist groups," I say. "The south coast has lots of visitors who come from all over the world to see the veil. Some of them dress like Fey. We'll pretend to be a tour group, and I'll be your guide, okay? That's what I was doing before, acting as if I were your tour guide. It'll explain why you're all grouped together and why you're dressed like this."

She nods. "Okay."

"Good. But you don't quite look right." I scan the group again. Twelve of them. Some of them don't look Fey, but others are obviously so. I point to a man whose ears are more noticeably pointy. "Put on that woman's hat. We need to hide those ears. And you, miss? Hide that pendant. It's clearly Fey. Anyone with long hair, use it to cover your ears." I had to make them seem human.

The group quickly follows my instructions. They seem reassured by my presence, which sends a pang of guilt twisting through my chest. They have no idea how badly I'm out of my depth.

But I'm deep in this now, so I plaster on a smile and march forward.

On the beach, tourists are sitting out with picnics and under umbrellas. The light radiates off the sea, and the marine wind toys with my sundress. The sand's heat warms my soles through my sandals.

I settle into my role as a tour guide, projecting my

voice and speaking in French. "If you all follow me, ladies and gentlemen, down this way. Back in the year of the invasion, a number of people fled the Fey realm. Luckily for us, these days, there's peace between us and our Fey neighbors. The local police work in tandem with the veil guards to maintain law and order, and to keep the status quo intact." We stand out on the beach, and I lead them toward the town's streets, where other tourist groups usually roam.

The group follows me obediently across the sand. Some of them still look frightened, but others look curiously around them.

"Any idea of where you have to go at the docks?" I ask Aleina in a low voice.

"I think just northeast of here."

I swallow hard. That would be the dock directly next to the veil. "Okay, we'll have to go up that street. I think."

"You *think*? You don't know?"

"I don't live here. I arrived this week."

Aleina mutters an unfamiliar word in the Fey language. It doesn't sound very nice.

"Over here, ladies and gentlemen," I holler. I didn't realize how difficult it was to be a tour guide. Talking loudly while marching, constantly turning around to address the group. My asthma is starting to act up, my breath coming in wheezes. "That statue over there commemorates the French peace treaty with the Fey. Over a hundred thousand humans and Fey died when the Fey army first appeared in our world. King Auberon ripped through the magical barrier between the Fey realm and ours, shocking us all with the existence of mythical beasts and powerful magic, as I'm sure you remember. The Fey magic destroyed the advanced technology of the French military. The human army was defenseless against magic, and the Fey quickly took over the north of France and the Channel Islands. To save part of the south, the French resorted to old-fashioned cannons that used a scattershot of iron nails. Iron saved the south, thanks to the Fey aversion to iron."

The demi-Fey aren't even acting as if they're listening to me anymore. All of them are looking up toward wisps of fog coiling off the eastern veil. I follow their eyes, and my stomach plunges.

Two large red beasts swoop through the sky high above the town, wings flapping slowly. *Gods save me.* Dragons.

I'd seen one, three days ago, a tiny speck in the distance. These two are much closer, flying just above the town, their scales glimmering in the sunlight. Their heads pivot as they search the earth.

My gut tells me that they're looking for these very fugitives, and they could spot them from above, a group of magical beings. They say dragons can smell fear from far away...

I try to slow my breathing.

If the dragons spot the demi-Fey, it'll be over for them. They'll simply dive and scorch them all, turning them into living torches. It's what they did during the war. The smart thing for me to do would be to bolt, to put as much distance between me and this group of demi-Fey as I can.

I look at them huddled, eyes wide and locked on the dragons. The little boy with dirt on his cheek clutches one of the women's legs, and she strokes his shaggy blond hair absentmindedly.

Shit. I can't leave them. My heart thunders.

With a racing heart, I glance around. On the beach, people are sitting up and pointing at the sky. Some are smiling, marveling at the beauty of the dragons. Drinking champagne. After all, the dragons aren't after *them.*

That means my tour group shouldn't look scared, either. They should look relaxed but excited, getting a glimpse of not one but two dragons. Real tourists would delight at the chance to tell their friends about this back home.

"We are incredibly lucky!" I call out gleefully. "Ladies and gentlemen, in the sky, you can see *two* red dragons. Those majestic beasts work with the Fey to keep our borders secure. Everyone, wave at the dragons to thank them for keeping the border safe!"

I begin to wave enthusiastically, a deranged grin plastered on my face, smiling as if my life depends on it. Which it does.

This is my M.O.: act like everything is fine, blast people with positivity, and hope for the best.

Except the fugitives are frozen in place, not moving.

"Aleina," I mutter through clenched teeth, "wave at the damn dragons. Look happy."

After a second, she starts waving, a rictus grin stretching her lips. Then others follow suit. The dragons glance our way, then turn their heads in disinterest. My chest unclenches.

"Okay, folks, the tour continues," I shout, my heart in my throat. "Come on, we still have a lot to see on this glorious day."

I lead them up toward the winding stone roads, and the dragons recede into the distance. My pulse is roaring, and I can hardly breathe. I turn back to the demi-Fey. They're scared, all looking to me for guidance, and—

Hang on. There's one missing. That blonde woman I'd grabbed by the hand earlier.

"Where's the woman who was with you?" I ask Aleina urgently, trying to recall how she looked. "Um...the one with the golden hair and the green skirt?"

Aleina blinks and turns around. She looks at one of them and says, "Ei-fo Vena, le-an chuaigh sí?" *Where is Vena, did she get lost?*

He shakes his head helplessly and answers in Fey that he's not sure. She was there just a few minutes ago. He thinks she might have run.

You've got to be kidding me. "Okay, wait here," I say.

I hurry up the road by the restaurant, searching for Vena on the narrow lane. When I turn a corner, a shimmer of green draws my attention. She's there, racing up a winding road. I take a step after her, then freeze.

Two Fey soldiers round a corner, and they're marching

toward her. I slip back behind the corner, watching from the safety of a stone wall. Fog curls over the stony street.

One of the Fey draws a sword. The wind picks up his white-blond hair, toying with it. His dark, velvety cloak billows behind him. He's speaking in Fey, but I can't hear exactly what he's saying. She looks so tiny there, dwarfed by the colorful buildings and the imposing Fey soldiers.

She's shaking her head, trying to tell them that she doesn't understand what they're saying, that she can't speak the Fey language. I chance a step forward. I can tell them she's on my tour. *Sorry, officers, those tourists would lose their heads if they weren't attached—*

The pale-haired soldier swings his sword. A crimson spray spatters on the nearby wall. She topples onto the street, blood gushing down her green skirt.

I gasp and slink behind a corner, tears springing to my eyes. The world feels unsteady beneath my feet. *Shit, shit, shit!* Are there no laws here? Southern France is supposed to be *un*occupied, but apparently, the Fey can kill in the streets, without a trial, or even a good reason.

I risk a look back, but don't see anyone following me. My breath is ragged in my throat. Either the soldiers didn't see me or they thought I didn't look like much of a threat.

I walk down to the beach, the image of her murder playing on a loop in my mind. She didn't look much older than me. And it was the way she collapsed, just folding onto herself...it all seemed so casual. A lazy swoop of the blade, an arc of blood. A job done.

I clamp my eyes shut and bite my lip. The seaside air no longer smells fresh. It feels like I'm inhaling brackish rot. My lungs whistle as I inhale. I'm running out of breath, and this could be a panic attack or my lungs collapsing. Probably both. My airway is narrowed to a single point.

I focus on my senses and the feel of the ground beneath my feet to calm myself and ignore the seaside scent of decay. I smell thyme and brine, the faint whiff of lavender. I feel the kiss of the breeze against my skin.

My chest is practically caving in. From my handbag, I pull out my inhaler. Two puffs. Within moments, my airways start to open.

I shove the inhaler back into the bag and hurry back over the brush, onto the sand. I shield my eyes and find the group huddled on the beach.

"Where's Vena?" Aleina asks.

My heart clenches. I can't lie to them. "Dead," I say. I can't let them linger for someone who's never coming back, or they'll end up bleeding out, too. "We have to go." Raising my voice, I call out in French, "Okay, everyone! Let's continue our tour." The cheer in my tone borders on hysteria. "We need to get to the docks, where the French navy fought the large sea serpent."

I walk forward, then glance over my shoulder and motion for them to follow me. Aleina's eyes shine, and she follows me resolutely. The rest follow suit.

I lead them across the beach, and the sun dips lower in the sky. Twilight stains the clouds with red. As I plod along, I try to keep a smile plastered on my face, though my body is trembling like leaves in the wind. I take them on a grim procession into a network of alleys, a spiderweb of cobbled streets that spread out over the seaside town. While I rattle off random historic facts, my mind is still on Vena. It was the ease with which the Fey soldier had swung his sword, like a bored teenager swinging for a baseball. I've seen a few dead people before, but they were all at funerals, neatly in their coffins. Never a murder. Never such casual violence.

Wrought iron fences and brick buildings crowd the road. As dusk darkens the sky above us, I lead the demi-Fey up the hill. "As you can see, the gutter runs through the center of the road, a relic of the medieval era..."

I know no one is listening, but it doesn't matter. I keep going, trying to look casual.

Between buildings, we get glimpses of the sea and the coils of mist from the veil. The fog seemed like a fascinating curiosity when I first arrived. Now, it's horrifying. *All* of this is horrifying.

Sweat trickles down my temples. There's no one around, so I drop the tour guide act—until I catch a glimpse of Fey soldiers at the bottom of the hill. We're close to the veil here, and it hums in my ears.

My tour group still looks terrified, and I wish they'd stop clinging to each other.

"We'll turn right here," I call out, and move to turn back down the street—then realize that a couple of patrolling Fey are marching on that road, too. "I meant left, of course."

But now, we're also getting pinned in by the Fey soldiers. I clench my jaw, my mind whirling.

I turn toward them, marching backward, beckoning for the group to follow me. "Our tour continues down by the beach!"

I take another step back, and Aleina shouts my name in a panic.

Violet-sheened fog snakes around me, and my stomach plummets. The misty veil has roiled closer, and it's drawing me in.

Magic thrums over my skin, making my teeth chatter.

My thoughts go dark, my body cold. I'm inside the veil. And that means I'm about to die.

CHAPTER 3

*L*ike the nightshade flower, the beauty of the veil hides its deadly nature. Fey magic isn't particularly stable, and the results of touching it vary. Some people die of a heart attack. Some scream in agony as their insides melt. Some turn to dust or freeze solid. But the end is the same. The veil is hungry, and it feeds off death.

And yet—

Despite standing in the midst of it, I'm still alive. Unless—as some people say—the dead don't realize they're dead?

Through the coils of fog, I stare down at my hands. The mist shifts and slides over my wrists, strangely sensual in the way it moves like a living thing.

I'm still breathing. I don't feel any pain. How long will this death take? I inhale humid air tinged with sea salt. I feel fine.

I can't even hear the mist's buzzing or feel the prickling of magic on my skin.

Strange. Maybe the magic doesn't work in this part of the veil.

From here, I can still see the others—silhouettes in silver and violet beyond the veil. From my ankles up, the fog slides under the white lace of my dress like a lover's caress.

"Aleina?" I ask.

"You're still alive?" she asks, shocked. "I can't see you."

Hope lights in my chest. "That's perfect, then," I tell her. "This part of the veil is fine. We can hide here, I think. It's not lethal."

"No!" she mutters, terror in her voice.

"It's an in-between space," I say. "I'm fine, and it's the perfect place to hide. And the soldiers are blocking us in right now."

The seconds tick by as my anxiety grows. I understand her reluctance, but those soldiers will end up noticing them, and I can only imagine what will happen then. I'm about to urge her to move when I see a silhouette nod and step forward. Aliena's hand comes through the fog, and she takes a deep breath as she sidles up next to me. "Come on, everyone," she whispers in Fey.

One by one, the demi-Fey slip into the veil, and instead of draining them of life, the mist seems to welcome them in its embrace. I gesture, and the little boy grasps my hand, joining me.

Through the whorls of fog, I can still see the stone

alley beneath my feet. But everything's different here beyond the veil. For the past few years, no one has come here at all. Garbage has accumulated in this no-man's land, and the air smells of rot and decay. I swallow. I shouldn't be here. Outside the mist, I see the silhouettes of Fey guards pass by, swords drawn. They don't notice us at all.

"How did you get through the veil the first time?" I ask Aleina.

"We had a...I don't know how you say it in English. An orb? A *Cosaint* orb. But it shattered." She swallows. "We lost two people when that happened."

A shiver runs along the back of my neck, but I push the fear away. I count to ten, giving the guards time to walk away, then emerge from the mist. Aleina follows me. Then the rest.

Creeping to the edge of the alley, I peer out. No veil patrols. Good.

"Okay, we're clear," I say. "Let's do the same as before. We're just a group of tourists, okay? It's crucial that you all give the appearance of being calm, even if you don't feel it."

Leading them out, I begin hollering inane facts, trying to look as if everything is fine. The temperature drops sharply for some reason, and my teeth chatter. The cold bites at my skin. What *is* that icy wind? Perhaps it's my body's reaction to the trauma of it all. I just saw a woman executed in the street, her blood drenching her clothes. I accidentally stepped into a magical veil that through sheer luck didn't destroy me.

My heart thrums in my chest, but I keep talking, giving the tour. I smile, rattling off facts about the heroics of the French army during the invasion, still explaining how lucky we are to have the status quo to protect us. I lead them down the hill toward the dock. My breathing is becoming more labored, wheezy, a constant eerie whistle as I inhale and exhale.

"Are you all right?" Aleina asks. "You don't sound so good."

"I'm fine," I pant. "I have...asthma. Stress induced." With every word, I try to inhale, get just a bit more oxygen into my lungs.

"You don't know the city, and you get sick if you exert yourself," Aleina mutters. "Why did you think you're the right person to help us?"

"Well...I didn't see...anyone else...stepping up." My head is spinning. I'll have to take a break soon.

"I'm thankful you did," Aleina says.

I raise an eyebrow. "Thank me when I get you to the docks."

Where are we? I've led this group down a meandering, unfamiliar street. I've never been this far east before. And when they turn to me, they're all looking at me with expectant faces, trusting me with their lives. Me. The person who once got lost in the neighborhood she lived in. The person who can't read a map to save her life.

C.N. CRAWFORD & ALEX RIVERS

I look around, desperately searching for anything familiar on the crowded street. Tourist shops line the road —some selling crêpes or ice cream, others Fey-themed and magical, beribboned floral crowns and hazel wands in the windows. A gold-lettered sign above a shop reads CHÂTEAU DE LA FEÉ.

I pause, leaning against a wall to catch my breath. At least I'm starting to warm up again a little. The twilight-streaked sea sparkles under the sun. Thank God. Once we get to the sea, we can figure out which way the docks are.

"Follow me to the beach," I call out, breathing in the salt. "We are going to see where the French prepared for the final assault on the Fey fleet, armed with—"

I pause at the sight in front of me. We've reached a wide, paved road that leads to the docks. Two French policemen are checking people's papers as they pass through.

Shit.

They can't risk the status quo by letting demi-Fey fugitives through. In fact, that's probably why they're here—searching for these very fugitives.

"They're just human," Aleina whispers in my ear. "Only two of them. We can fight them. Some of us can make it."

"No!" I blurt. "The police have guns. And they will call the Fey soldiers to help them. It's all part of their agreement. You'll die."

"Then we'll die free," Aleina says.

"That's a nice sentiment, but dead is dead." I think of Vena. "You've come too far to give up."

I notice that the cops don't check everyone. There's too much traffic, too many passersby. There are only two of them. They'll definitely stop us, though. Sure, my tour guide act was good enough for the occasional glance, but not for cops who are actually searching for fugitives.

"We'll wait for an opportunity," I say. "I'll create a distraction. You go through doing what I did. Act like the group's tour guide."

Aleina pales. "I don't even speak French."

"English will be fine."

She shakes her head. "I don't look anything like a tour guide."

She isn't wrong. While the tourists on the beach might not have noticed that her clothing was off, the police would be looking more closely. They'd see the velvet, the silk—the exquisite tailoring mixed with frayed edges and dirt smudges, the long limbs on display—and they'd recognize a group of demi-Fey refugees.

I wish I had a proper disguise for her. Something that would make her inconspicuous. But I can't think of anything—

My gaze flicks to the shops, and an idea pops into my mind.

"Wait here," I say, and hurry across the road into Château de la Feé.

It's a crowded shop of strange curiosities. Statues of Fey with real butterfly wings glued to them. Round bottles of brightly colored syrups labeled as potions. Decks of fortune-telling cards with skulls and snakes.

Leather-bound books in the Fey language. Antique maps of their realm.

But none of that is what I'm looking for, so I press on until I find what I need. I grab it, then rush to the front of the desk. A woman with a tidy gray bun peers at me over her glasses, then demands seventy Euros. I pay her, trying not to calculate how many hours working in the bookshop that is. I have more important things to worry about. She stuffs my things into a paper bag.

Outside, I hurry back to Aelina and hand her the bag. "Put all this on."

She peers into the paper bag, and her lip curls. "But...why?"

"A demi-Fey would never dress in fairy wings because it's stupid." They look cheap and ridiculous, and they're the perfect disguise. "I've seen a bunch of tour guides wearing wings like those. Some tourists here expect props, you know? They want the whole Fey experience. And if you put it on, you won't look Fey. No one will think you're Fey if you have those wings on. There's a flower crown, too."

"Okay. Fine." She snatches the bag from me and pulls on the glittery pink wings with two straps over her shoulders. When she crowns herself with flowers, I breathe a sigh of relief. The costume completely shifts the perspective. Her strange clothing and pointy ears look like part of it now.

"Okay," I say. "Let's wait for the right opportunity. For

now, start doing your tour guide act. I'm going to create a diversion. Go through once I start."

She takes over for me as a guide, speaking in broken English. "Ladies and gentlefolk, this here is the house of a French general. He used deadly iron weapons. He blew up the wicked Fey, leaving them in bloody pieces on the road."

Worst tour guide ever, but it would do. Her voice fades as I hurry down the hill toward the docks, where sailboats and yachts bob in their moorings. I wait for a few minutes until a policeman starts arguing with an old woman who has forgotten her paperwork. That just leaves one cop.

"Excuse me!" I shout at him. "Ex-koose-moi! Monseer? Common ça va?"

I'm abusing the French language, and the cop visibly winces.

"I speak English."

My first instinct is flattery. "And you speak it so well! Mais je voudrais, uh...pratice mon français maintenant. Vous êtes très fashionable," I say in mangled Franglais.

His eyes grow hard, and I can tell this tactic isn't working on him. In fact, it's only raising his suspicions. Europeans expect Americans to be loud and obnoxious, and maybe I'd need to turn up the dial on that.

"I'm looking for, like...do you know where...je voudrais, like, a McDonald's or something?"

"No, move along please." He waves me out of the way.

This is too important for me to shrink away, and I

need his attention on me. And what better focuses a person's attention than loathing?

"Is there any decent chocolate in this country?" I ask. "The food in France isn't what it's cracked up to be. No offense, but I thought you were supposed to have good chocolate. Have you tried Hershey's Kisses? Because those are delicious."

His face goes red, and he gestures to his left for me to go. "If you please," he says in a clipped accent.

From the corner of my eye, I see Aleina walk past, leading the group and talking about the French navy like a tour guide. The cop's attention flickers to them for just a moment, and I wave my hand in his face.

"Ex-koose-moi, garçon? Do you know McDonald's? Do you have any in this country? McDONALD'S," I shout up at him. "I can't stomach more of your French crap."

He shoots me a withering look. Whoops. Overdid it.

"Not here." He purses his lips and points west. "There are plenty of better restaurants in Marseille. And American chocolate is not even real chocolate, legally."

I fold my arms. "You must be joking. Have you even tried real pancakes? Not like the weird, thin kind you have here, but like a big, fluffy pile of *real* pancakes? Because in America, you can buy frozen ones that have a sausage in them and maple flavor already in it. You just heat them up, and boom—there's your breakfast. And that kind of innovation is why America is the greatest nation in the world. It frees up extra time for more work hours. Amazing, right?"

By the time he shoots a pleading expression at the second cop, Aleina's group is already gone.

"Anyway, thanks." I turn away from him, relieved I can drop the act.

"Mademoiselle, can I just see your passport?" he asks from behind me. He sounds pissed.

I turn back to him and clear my throat. "Sure, officer, is there a problem?"

"No. Just a routine check."

Thankfully, I have my passport with me. I reach into my bag and pull it out. He stares at it so long that my heart pounds.

"Nia Melisende?" he asks.

"I'm American," I say hopefully.

He flips through the passport, then hands it back to me. "Have a pleasant day," he says, sounding bored.

"Mer-si boo-koo." I start walking toward the docks.

"Mademoiselle, the restaurants are the other way."

"Oh, yes, thank you. I just want to take a photo of the pretty French boats." I smile at him and turn away.

When I'm sure he's no longer looking, I break into a little run, my boots creaking over the wood.

It takes me a few minutes to locate Aleina and the rest of the group, who are standing by a large clipper ship. Aleina is talking to a man on the deck—another demi-Fey. His pointed ears rise out of wavy, dark hair that falls to his sharp jawline. The sleeves of his white shirt are rolled up, exposing tattoos that snake around his muscled forearms. As I take a step closer, my heart skips a beat. The moment he cuts me a sharp look, I recognize those eerie silver eyes, the straight black eyebrows. And yet, he seems a million times bigger, towering over everyone else, shoulders as broad as a door frame.

So *that's* what happened to Raphael Launcelot, the beautiful demi-Fey who broke my heart.

CHAPTER 4

J stare at him, mouth ajar. I spent so long trying to forget about him and that night in Bordeaux, when the stars shone so brightly and the air smelled heavy with ripening grapes, and now Raphael is standing before me, looking like a damn demigod.

We met at a château during our summer trip. And after we kissed, he never spoke to me again. I *also* remember hearing him call me trash after Mom fell down the stairs drunk one night.

He is, in fact, a million times better looking than Jules the waiter, which is endlessly frustrating. You can tell by his bearing that he knows how beautiful he is, too. Sun-kissed skin, muscular physique, the piercing silver eyes...

I loathe the man.

From the top of the gangplank, he glances at me for a fraction of a moment, but if he recognizes me, he doesn't let it show. A woman in a blue dress stands by the main

45

mast, demanding the names of every fugitive. She has peaches-and-cream skin and wears her wavy blonde hair in a messy bun. Her large diamond earrings gleam in the setting sun. She looks delicate in every way except for the sheathed sword slung around her waist.

My gaze trails over the deck, which is fully stocked with an arsenal of spears and harpoons. An old-fashioned fishing ship, maybe? Here, the smell of the sea mingles with the woodsy scent of the ship and a hint of tar. Crew members dressed in blue jackets are climbing up the rigging to unfurl the sails.

There's another woman on the deck, too, this one unarmed. She wears a flowing yellow gown and a dreamy expression.

As I step closer, I can hear Raphael arguing with Aleina in Fey. "I don't understand," he tells Aleina in a clipped voice. "Where's our contact?"

"I told you, he never showed up," Aleina answers impatiently.

A muscle clenches in Raphael's jaw. "What happened to him?"

"I have no idea. We had to get here by ourselves."

"How did you even make it this far?"

"We had help," Aleina said, gesturing at me. "From a tourist."

From high above, Raphael shoots me a cautious look. His otherworldly eyes narrow as he takes me in, but I don't see any flicker of recognition. "You told *this woman* about us?" He injects the words *this woman* with an impressive amount of disdain, suggesting he might remember me after all. He isn't calling me "trash" out loud, but it's certainly implied.

"We didn't have much choice." Aleina casts a worried look back toward the policemen at the entrance to the port. "I can explain it all later. We need to get underway."

The blonde woman saunters forward and touches his bicep. "We're not going with this group. The names don't match our list."

"None of them, Viviane?" he asks.

I stare at them. Are they out of their minds?

"Some of them," Viviane clarifies. "There are three missing who were supposed to be here, and three more who are *not* supposed to be here." She points at the little boy. "Him, and those two ginger ladies."

A woman with the same shade of fiery hair wraps her arms around them. "They're my daughters. I'm not leaving them in either of the Fey controlled territories. Of course I'm not."

"We told you," Viviane snaps. "Only people who were approved. We were very clear. You're here because of the information you possess. *They're* of no use to us."

Aleina holds the boy's head as he cries against her leg. His tears left streaks on her pale gold dress. "His parents were killed on the way here. He's only four. Do you have children? What kind of person leaves a four-year-old behind?"

"His parents were warned. We can't take everyone," Viviane shot back. In the setting sun, her diamond earrings glitter. "We vet everyone who comes, and we have finite resources. Do you know what will happen if word gets out that we're taking care of *every* demi-Fey who straggles up to the docks? I'll tell you what'll happen. We'll lose the war."

And here I thought the war was over.

Aleina still strokes the little boy's head. "His parents were two of the people killed on the way here. Their names are on the list. We can't leave him. They'll arrest him. Or…"

Or kill him.

"So, stay and look after him," Raphael says quietly. "Your choice. There are thousands of demi-Fey and human fugitives. We cannot take everyone."

The little boy's face crumples, and he turns to Aleina, crying into her thigh. "I'm sorry, Malo," she says. Her voice cracks.

I feel a twist in my chest as Aleina climbs the gangplank to the deck. I reach out for Malo's little hand. Now that he's with a stranger, he's trying to stifle the sound of his crying. He must be terrified.

I understand they can't take everyone, but a little boy who just watched his parents die? Clearly, Raphael is as much of a prick as always.

Raphael catches my eye and runs a hand through his hair. "Look, we have limited funding and space. Every person on our list was handpicked by the resistance. If we start making exceptions because of sentiment, anarchy will drag us into ruin. We have no room for stragglers, no provisions to help them. We are fighting for our lives."

"So is this little boy," I say.

"We don't have time to argue with you," adds Viviane. "We leave these three behind."

The demi-Fey will be slaughtered in the streets. Just like Vena, they'll bleed to death on the cobbles. Would they spare a little boy? I doubt it.

Then again, I'm not sure Viviane really cares.

"I'm not leaving without my daughters." At least the redheaded woman is seeing sense here. She folds her arms, glaring up at the ship.

With the five of us on the old dock, Raphael nods at Viviane. "Fine. We need to go."

"You've got to take them, please. Please." Desperation rings in my voice. Malo is clinging to my hand.

Raphael shakes his head. "The resistance is doing its best to help the fugitives, but we have to prioritize. We stick to our plans. These people on our list need to be extracted before anyone else. And with respect, you have no idea what the fuck you're talking about."

"I understand you're abandoning a child who just watched his parents die," I snap.

Raphael grits his teeth. "Not that I need to explain myself to a tiny American pixie princess on a fun holiday jaunt—"

"Did you just say *pixie princess*?"

"—but these are the people who can help us fight Auberon. They have information and knowledge we need to win. And *that* is why we are taking them. We're an army, not a charity. Now, why don't you go back to drinking champagne on the beach and chasing after rich men?"

My cheeks flush. Oh, wonderful. Apparently, he remembers my mother. Chasing after rich men is her favorite hobby and the entire reason we had those summers at the château.

Behind me, the two young women are sniffling. At least they have their mom, unlike Malo. Now, he only has me.

I squeeze his tiny hand. He's crying against my leg now, too.

I'm desperate. I need some kind of leverage to stop the ship from setting sail. Unfortunately, confrontation is not one of my skills. I'm generally a people pleaser.

And yet, Raphael *really* brings out the fire in me.

One of the crew is already starting to release dock lines. Panic tightens my chest.

I clear my throat and venture, "Well, I *do* hope the French police over there don't find out about this. They tend to cooperate with the Fey army to preserve peace. What will they do if someone alerts them?"

"Stop!" Raphael holds up a hand, stopping the crew from untethering the ship. His body tightens with anger. I can almost feel the cold fury rippling off him. "Is that a threat?"

Of course, I would never risk these people's lives by calling the authorities. But at least I got his attention.

I hold his gaze. "I'm just wondering out loud. Would they even let your ship leave the port? They're truly terrified Auberon will take the rest of France."

Viviane leaps onto the dock, and the damp wood creaks beneath her feet. In the next heartbeat, she has her blade at my throat. The sea breeze whips at her blonde ringlets. "I'm taking her out."

I freeze, unable to breathe. I've never been threatened with a weapon before. My head spins, and my knees grow weak, but I force myself to meet her gaze.

"No!" Aleina calls out.

"Don't, Viviane," Raphael barks. "Too messy." He leaps down, too, and steps closer. In the dying light, his pale eyes pierce me.

I should be stepping back. Turning away. But for some reason, I'm standing my ground. My gaze flicks to Raphael. "They're just three extra people. The boy hardly takes any space."

With his hands on his hips, he stares back at the dock. "Fine. Viviane, lower the sword. Everyone comes aboard. I don't have time for this."

I exhale in relief. After a few seconds, Viviane drops her blade.

The redheaded mother looks at me with tears in her eyes. "Thanks," she whispers. "For everything."

I swallow hard. "Sure. I'm glad I could help."

One of the young ginger women scoops Malo into her arms and carries him up the gangplank.

Raphael's head is turned, and he's staring intently at

something. I turn to see what he's looking at, and my heart skips a beat. One of the policemen is running for us, his feet thundering over the wooden dock. "Nia Melisende!" he shouts from the distance.

"How does he know your name?" asks Raphael icily.

"He checked my passport."

Raphael pulls on a cap, covering the curved tips of his ears. Then, smoothly, he leaps onto the dock. To my surprise, he slides his arm around my shoulders, and turns me to face the other direction. He points out to the sea, like he's showing me a sunset. "Follow my lead and play along. Stay relaxed. Calm."

My breath slows, my thoughts zeroing in on the warmth of his arm around my shoulders. Bizarrely, I find myself actually staying calm, as if his words are a command I can't ignore. His masculine scent triggers a long-buried memory, but the last time I saw him, he wasn't nearly this muscular.

"Nia Melisende!" the cop calls again from behind us.

With his arm still wrapped around me, Raphael turns, a calm smile on his face. He raises his eyebrows. "Looking for my wife? She's not feeling very well, I'm afraid."

We make a ridiculous pair. I'm short as hell, and Raphael towers over me.

The policeman is still catching his breath, one hand on his chest. "My colleague said"—he gasps and breathes in deeply—"there were others who walked in with you. Unaccounted for." He waves at the boat. "Those lot. We never checked their papers."

Raphael frowns. "Ah, no, it's fine. They had their passports checked earlier." He pulls his arm from me, coughing into his elbow. "Bloody hell, Nia. I told you that you were going to give me that fever. Have your blisters gone?"

I stare at him for a moment, but only *just* a moment. I can always figure out what people want and give it to them. It's one of my greatest skills. And right now, I know exactly what role I'm supposed to play.

I wince, touching my side. "No. I must have caught something terrible."

Raphael grimaces. "I tell you what. It's the mongrel flu, is what it is. Do you know how bloody contagious that is, Nia?"

"Well, it's not like I did it on purpose. If you weren't manhandling me all the time, you might have avoided catching the chancres."

"Chancres?" asks the policeman. His mustache twitches.

I shoot him a forlorn look. "In all the places the sun don't shine. They're in my throat, too, and if I cough…" I start to cough.

He pales, then glances at the boat. "Perhaps I needn't worry about their passports, then."

I nod, still coughing. "I hope it's not fatal. They all have it, too."

The cop casts another worried look at the boat. He starts to turn and walk away, and my chest unclenches. But before he takes another step, he freezes. As he turns back to the boat, his brow furrows. The wind skims over us. Slowly, a look of fury crosses his features. I turn to see who he's looking at—Malo, his little pointed ears showing through his dark curls.

The cop opens his mouth to shout, but Raphael jabs him in the throat. It all happens so quickly, I can hardly register what he's done.

The cop falls to the ground, choking and gurgling. My heart gallops in my chest, my eyes wide with horror. Raphael reaches down, grabs the cop's head and jaw, and swiftly twists. There's a sickening crunch, and the policeman's body sags.

I stare, shocked. Just like before—one minute, someone was standing there alive, and the next moment, gone. I had no idea someone could kill a person that silently and efficiently with only his bare hands.

"Quick," Raphael says. "Grab that net there."

Out of reflex, I follow his instruction, grasping a tangled, weighted fishing net and numbly handing him the edge.

"Help me." His voice is crisp, impossible to argue with.

He wraps the net around the body. I try to help him, my fingers trembling. What am I doing? When the cop is wrapped up, Raphael kicks him into the sea. With the weights tied to the net, the body instantly sinks.

My heart is still racing when Raphael grabs me by the bicep and drags me up the gangplank.

I stumble onto the deck. "What's happening?" I ask, stunned by the sudden turn of events.

"He knew your name," Raphael says tersely. "Which means the other cops might know your name. You can't stay here to get interrogated."

I have a million more questions but no time to ask them. I lick my lips, tasting salt. What am I going to do in this situation, fight off the lethal, armed spies with my purse?

Already, Viviane is sidling up to him. "How long until they find his body?"

"There's a strong westerly undercurrent here. He'll be dragged a mile away, but we need to go now." His glance darts back to the beach. "The nearest police station is just two hundred thirty yards away. They might come looking for him. I reckon we have about seven minutes to get out of here."

"I'm not going with you," I say with as much confidence as I can muster. None of this is part of my plan. I have a ticket back home in a week; all my things are back in my hotel. I'm not someone who deals with stress well, and I'm barely functioning. At this point, I have no desire to throw myself into more danger.

Viviane raises her sword, and the blade nicks my throat. "The thing is, we're not asking."

My stomach *drops*. I stare at her, my thoughts racing. Wisps of her blonde hair lift in the wind, and she watches me with pale eyes.

Usually, I'm good at figuring out what people want and using that to get what I want, too. But right now, my mind is drawing a blank because this woman is not about to back down.

"Cast off!" Raphael calls out. "Everyone's on board."

The world seems to dim as people bustle around. The boat's engine roars to life, spewing black smoke.

My stomach twists in knots. Where the hell are they taking me?

As we set off, the marine wind whips at my hair. Finally, Viviane lowers her sword. Her jaw is clenched, and she's looking at me with disgust.

I look back at the dock. It grows smaller and smaller. This is a horrible mistake, something I never should have jumped into.

And yet, what else could I have done?

CHAPTER 5

The ship rocks with every wave, the horizon tilting left and right, up and down. Seawater mists my face, and the ship's timbers groan and creak.

I stand by the stern, clutching the railing, my stomach roiling with the movement. I'm not very good with boats. I can get seasick just looking at the water. And right now, I'm regretting the berry cake I ate earlier. In fact, I regret getting out of bed this morning. The bed didn't go up and down. The bed was great. So steady and reliable.

"Hey!" someone calls from behind me. "You."

Nauseated, I turn around to see Viviane glaring at me. The Mediterranean wind whips loose strands of her curls. "Raphael wants to see you."

"Okay," I say faintly.

"He's waiting for you in the captain's quarters." She points emphatically.

"Right." Maybe inside, where I don't see the waves, I'll feel better.

I keep a tight grip on the rail as I cross the gently sloping deck. How long is this journey going to last? I climb up a narrow set of stairs to the quarterdeck. An ornately carved door leads to the captain's quarters.

The moment I step inside, I instantly feel worse, the movement of the ship even more pronounced belowdecks. Raphael, however, is completely unbothered by it. He's standing over an enormous table, staring at a map. In here, everything is burnished mahogany or brass, and the scent of the wood feels oppressive.

Only now do I realize that Viviane is behind me, practically breathing down my neck. I lean on the other side of the table, trying not to vomit.

Even though Raphael supposedly wanted to see me, he ignores me and looks at Viviane. "Everything in order?"

"Looks that way. Aleina is taking care of the rest of the group."

"Good. Did you check on the TTCB?"

"I did. No alerts."

"Check again. I don't want any surprises."

Raphael was clearly in command here.

"On it." She steps outside.

"Close the door." He doesn't even look up from the map when he gives me the order. His skin is so tan, I wonder how much time he spends out here on the sea.

I close the door behind me, trying to breathe deeply.

Nausea churns in my stomach, and I wonder what he'll do if I bring up that cake all over his map.

"What's, uh...TTCB?" I ask.

A quirked eyebrow. "None of your concern."

Right. Okay. I suppose I don't need to know what it is. I don't really need to be anywhere near this ship, or near Raphael and his attitude.

I shove my nausea and my hatred down and flash an attempt at a charming smile. Though given how I feel, I suspect it looks cadaverous. "My name is Nia. Lovely to meet you. Such an impressive ship you're commanding."

He cocks his head, frowning. He lets the silence hang in the air, just to let me know how much he hates me.

I've got news for you, my friend. The feeling is mutual.

I quickly abandon the plan to charm him. Something about him makes my skin prickle with heat, and I can feel my nostrils flaring.

I take a seat across from him at the table and clutch my stomach. "Well, I wasn't expecting to run into the *Prince of Bordeaux* here." My voice twists with the intense dislike I feel. I'm shocked at the words that tumble out of my mouth.

Really, I'm usually nice.

"Yes, I remember you, too. *American.*" I'm not sure if the last word is a description or a derisive nickname.

Ice spreads through the air between us, and he leans closer to me across the table. So close that I can see that his silver eyes blend to a bright blue just at the edges, eyes fringed with long black lashes. I wonder if Viviane is his girlfriend. They'd go well together. Gorgeous exteriors, insufferable personalities.

"I remember you." His expression is unreadable. "And your mother."

My stomach tightens, and I feel a sudden urge to jump off the boat. The memory of him carrying my drunk mother up the stairs rears its ugly head, and my urge to throw up is back again in full force. "I'm surprised you remember."

"Hard to forget."

"Okay. So, we don't like each other." I glare at him. "And just so you know, I usually like almost everyone, and I don't like upsetting people. So, it's—"

"A high degree of loathing for me, got it." He drums his fingertips on the table. "I don't understand how someone like you could pull off getting these fugitives to the city, or why you would even bother."

Someone like you. Cold fury snaps through me, making me grit my teeth. "I was going to say the same for you because you seem prone to making snap judgments about people you know very little about. And that can't be a great quality in a leader, can it? Not to mention it would make you a shitty spy." Something feels good about letting it all out. Is this why people argue? Is this why people get drunk and scream in the town squares? I get it now.

He takes a seat in a high-back leather chair and folds his arms. "Why don't you report in detail how you helped the fugitives reach us?" He still sounds like he doesn't believe me. After all, what could garbage like me possibly know?

I sigh, growing flustered. "I was having birthday cake at a restaurant. I ordered lavender, but they brought blackberry—"

"I mean report the relevant details."

"Fine."

He lifts a finger. "Hang on, you were celebrating your birthday by yourself?"

I glare at him. *That's right, I'm a giant loser on top of everything else.* "I'm on vacation by myself, yes. Not that it's any of your business—"

"From what I remember, you spend a lot of time on holidays," he murmurs.

"Do you want me to report or not?" I say sharply.

I suppose I don't need to tell him that my days of having luxury vacations are over, that I spent five years eating store-brand cereal to save up the fare. And tempting as it is, I will not tell him that he ruined five years of careful planning by kidnapping me. "If you must know, *Raphael*, I saw the demi-Fey through a restaurant window. By the time I realized who they were, someone was watching us, and I was guilty by association. There were Fey soldiers marching around. The fugitives looked terrified, and I hate when people are scared." My mind flickers with a memory of Mother screaming that bugs were crawling on her skin. I clear my throat. "So I pretended to be a tour guide and that they were my group. And I led them to the docks."

"And that was it? You just jumped in and brought them to me?"

"It wasn't that easy," I snap. "A member of the group panicked and ran. Vena was separated from us, and the Fey soldiers slit her throat. That's why I didn't want you to leave the others behind. They're executing people in the streets."

His expression doesn't change at this news. "There were fourteen when they left Brocéliande. Eleven got to us, plus the extra we didn't want. That's a seventy-eight percent success rate. Above average."

My throat tightens. It seemed so cold to refer to Vena as a percentage. I didn't know her at all, but somewhere, her family would be mourning her death.

His pale eyes are locked on my face. "I know what you're thinking, but it's a war. People die. We need to focus on the living. And right now, I need to know *exactly* what happened. Every little detail might be important. So, start at the beginning. Where did you see them? Why did you even approach them?"

I go over it, racking my brain for every single detail. The jewel. The woman who stuck her head out from her house. The two red dragons swooping overhead. The way we hid in the veil—

"Stop right there." He raises his hand. "What do you mean, you hid in the veil? The veil is lethal to anyone without an orb, and there's only a handful of those in the world."

I shrug. "This part of the veil wasn't lethal."

He stares at me, his face an expressionless mask. "I understand how the magic works, and you obviously don't. There are no parts of the veil that are safe. *None*."

I spread my palms. "Well, I'm still here, so I guess there are."

Darkness slides through his eyes. "*All* of it is lethal."

I've contradicted him, and he doesn't like it.

"You asked me to tell you what happened, and I'm telling you. The veil shifted over me like it was hungry. It enveloped me. But there was no humming once I was inside it. There wasn't any prickling on my skin, like there usually is when I get close."

His expression tightens. "No...humming. You hear humming near the veil?"

"Yes, because it hums. Anyway, the others joined me inside the veil, and they were also safe, and it was quiet. No humming."

His expression is so cold, I practically get goosebumps. "And if I go ask the others, they'll verify that's what happened?"

"I'm not imagining things," I say with a touch too much force. Because the truth is I do imagine things, and I'm sometimes confused about what's real and what's not.

"Right. Give me a minute." He stands, and I suddenly remember how ridiculously tall he is. He has to duck his head to leave the cabin.

I wait, replaying everything he said to me. His skill for condescension is really unparalleled.

Someone like you...

I remember you...and your mother. The disdain in his tone.

I stand, clutching my stomach, and make my way to the door as quickly as possible. I'm afraid the cake is about to make an appearance for a second celebration. I swing the door open. The fugitives are sitting on the deck, and the clouds have darkened to a purplish gray. I rush for the boat's rail, pushing my way through the group.

A high-pitched voice, loud and terrified, echoes in my mind. *"We're gonna die, we're gonna die, there's no escape, they'll catch you. WE'RE GONNA DIE!"*

Oh, hell, no. It's happening again. This is the entire reason my doctor told me to avoid stress. I'm not avoiding stress, and now the voices are back.

I whirl around, checking to see if it could be real screaming. But no one's lips are moving.

The voice shrieks in my skull, laced with hysteria. I can tell myself it's not real, but the fear is infecting me anyway. My heart lurches.

"WE'RE GOING TO DIE!"

"No, we're not," I mutter, clamping my hands over my ears and shutting my eyes. "We're not! Please be quiet. I'm not." The nausea and screaming are overwhelming me. "Stop screaming in my skull!"

The voice stops. Totally quiet now.

When I open my eyes again, everyone is gawking at me. Raphael stands nearby, his eyebrows drawn together. I'm sure his opinion of me didn't improve much in the past twenty seconds.

Viviane glares at me. "Is she on drugs?"

Ah, if only it were that simple.

I want to get away from their stares. I make my way back to the captain's quarters. Yanking the door open, I clutch my stomach. Of course, this was bound to happen. It's been a few weeks since I heard the voices, and I was getting really hopeful that maybe *this* time, they were really gone. I've never had a diagnosis or anything because the voices are the only symptom I have. Apart from them, I have no disordered thinking. My doctor believes ten percent of the population hears voices, and that it's something to do with the subconscious and human evolution, and it's not necessarily a bad thing. It's just that while others might hear gentle guidance, my voices are *very* loud.

The only thing that guarantees silence in my mind is being under no stress at all—just lounging in my room, reading—which makes the bookstore a perfect place for me to work.

I drop into a chair in the cabin, dreading Raphael's return. I was hoping the next thing he would say to me would be something like, "Apologies, you were absolutely right about the veil, and you are clearly completely rational," but I'm not sure that's in the cards now.

The door creaks open, and I turn, expecting Raphael. Instead, it's the woman with the yellow dress who saunters in. The warm cabin light washes over her coppery skin, and she's holding a delicate porcelain teacup with a saucer. Her dark brown ringlets are a halo around her pretty face.

She flashes me a disarming smile, and the scent of bergamot reaches my nose. My stomach revolts again.

She peers at me over her teacup. A strange, intricate tattoo of a vine decorates her neck, disappearing into her collar. She sips her tea. "Good evening."

I'm still trying to calm my beating heart, but when I focus on her, a little of the nausea goes away. Her eyes are large, with mismatched colors: one hazel, one brown.

"I'm Tana," she says airily.

"I'm Nia."

"Oh, you poor thing, that's it. Let it all out."

Another wave of nausea crashes over me. "Let all what out?"

"Oh, sorry." She smiles. "I got confused. That hasn't happened yet."

I desperately need a nap on still land. "Do you work for Raphael?"

"I guess I do." The thought seems to surprise her. She sits across from me, sipping her tea and staring at me over her teacup.

"What do you do here?" I finally ask her.

She frowns, and the steam curls in front of her face. "I need to look out for pursuit. Or any other dangers out here. My job is to keep us safe."

"Is that something to do with the TTCB?"

She laughs brightly. "Spy boys and their acronyms. I guess I am the TTCB. It stands for Tea, Tarot, Crystal

Ball." She leans forward and whispers, "I don't really use the crystal ball. So tacky."

My eyebrows raise. "Is that…is that really…" I want to ask, *Is that actually reliable, because it sounds like nonsense,* but I can hear how condescending that sounds.

"I can sometimes see things." She takes one last sip and flips the cup onto the saucer. Then she removes the cup and shoves the saucer across the table toward me. The tea leaves lie on the saucer in dark, damp clusters. "See? The leaves say there's one patrol ship. It's far to the north." She pauses. "Actually, it could also be foretelling a rainy day tomorrow. No, *definitely* a patrol ship, like I said before."

"You read the future in tea leaves…to look for patrol ships?"

"It's not a perfect system." She sighs. "But I've got us out of a few near scrapes."

A sudden wave rocks the boat, and the nausea crashes over me. I slam through the door, bursting onto the deck, and make it to the rail just in time. Gripping the wood, I unleash my birthday cake into the angry sea.

I hang over the rail, wiping my mouth on the back of my hand. I rest my head for a moment, and then feel a hand on my back.

"Oh, you poor thing, that's it. Let it all out," Tana says.

"Oh, gods," I moan, straightening. I feel slightly better.

"Here." She hands me tea in a porcelain cup. "It'll make you feel better."

I take a sip, closing my eyes. To my surprise, it starts working almost immediately. I take another sip and already feel my stomach calm. I clutch the teacup and look at her. The wind whips her curls.

"You predicted that." Though I suppose it wasn't exactly hard to predict.

She nods. "Back in Brocéliende, I used to tell people whether they'd find love in their life." Her eyes sadden. "Then, suddenly, all I could see in the future was death. Tens of thousands slain, the demi-Fey hounded. I had to get out. So, I did. The cards led me here to train for MI-13. Luckily, I have a skill they need."

I down the rest of the tea and hand the cup back to her. "Thank you. I think I really am better."

Only now do I realize we're sailing west, and I can see the last arc of the molten sun dip beneath the horizon. Already, the moon is out, a curve of silver in the indigo.

She takes the cup from my hand and flips it onto a saucer, just as she did before. As the boat rocks, she examines the pattern of the tea leaves, and her eyes widen. "Oh, Nia," she says breathlessly. "You don't even know."

I swallow. "Know what?"

"How extraordinary," she whispers.

My eyes widen. "What do you see?"

"We'll have to do a card reading later," she says, her voice sharp with excitement. "This is a lot for tea."

She glances over my shoulder with a smile. I turn to see Raphael approaching.

I marvel at the way he's able to move so gracefully, like a cat, even on a rocking ship. He looks perfectly in control of himself at all times, a born leader. I have to remind myself of what he did all those years ago.

"There he is," Tana says, "the captain of our lost vessel."

"We're not lost," Raphael says.

"We're lost in time," she murmurs.

He sighs. "Tana, did you see anything?"

"One patrol ship, far to the north."

He shrugs slowly, sliding his hands into his pockets. "We'll avoid it. Can you give me a moment alone with Nia?"

With a smile, she glides away.

Raphael leans back against the rail, looking far too casual, given we're out at sea, evading the Fey army. His gaze cuts to me. It's dark now, but his eerie pale eyes burn in the gloom. "I talked to Aleina. She says exactly what you said about the veil."

I flash him a half-smile. "Told you."

No, I'm not above saying I told you so.

"But the veil doesn't hum, Nia. It doesn't make anyone's skin prickle."

I blink at him. "It does. Like bees. You haven't heard it?"

"Only you can hear it humming like that. Because it resonates with your magic."

I frown at him. "No, you're confused," I say slowly, as if talking to a little child. "I don't have magic. I'm fully human. My dad is a boring finance guy named Walter, and my mom...well, you've met my mom."

69

"But you do have magic. A rare form of magic. You're a Sentinel."

I turn, gripping the rail again, and stare out at sea. "No, listen. I haven't seen Walter in a while, but..." Walter was *definitely* human. No one so boring could ever be Fey. "Anyway, I'm fully human. I've never in my life used magic."

One of his dark eyebrows shoots up. "A Sentinel can disable the veil. That's what you did. You disabled the veil's magic with *your* magic. Sentinels are the only ones who hear the hum of the veil."

I shake my head. "It must be one of the fugitives."

"It's *not* one of them. Sentinels are extremely rare, and it's not them. Only a Sentinel can feel the magic on the veil prickle their skin. Exactly like you described. None of the fugitives heard the veil hum. Only you did. And now, your vacation days are over because MI-13 currently has only two Sentinels, and we need another."

My eyes widen as his words sink in. When I think about it, Walter and Mom cheated on each other all the time. I suppose my dad could be anyone...

Oh, hell, no. I won't be getting out of this easily, will I?

CHAPTER 6

y jaw drops. "You can't be serious. *Me?*"

The briny wind whips at the dark waves. "For reasons that are beyond me, you've been born with a gift," he says. "You have a responsibility to use it."

"You've got the wrong person." The truth is, I'm barely functioning.

He nods at the others. "Not that long ago, you were the one insisting that we leave no one behind. Are you all done caring about others now?" A note of mockery rings in his deep voice. "Let me guess. It was a good story before. But now? It's interrupting your luxurious vacation a little too much, right?"

"I'm not trained. I'm not qualified. I'm asthmatic." *I can't handle stress. I hallucinate. I hear voices. I am fundamentally broken.*

He stares out to sea. "Well, I can't say I'm surprised the little pixie princess would rather not get her hands dirty."

Prick. Blood rushes to my face. "It's not that I don't care. I just don't want to be a liability."

"Why are you even trying to talk her into it?" Viviane sidles up to him, standing so close their arms touch. "The girl was covering her ears and screaming at shadows just a few minutes ago. We can't have someone like that on a mission. She's cracked."

I clench the railing and stare out to sea. I hate the fact that she's right.

"The American doesn't need to be a fully trained Agent of Camelot," says Raphael. "All she needs is to get a crew through the veil using her magic."

Did he say *Camelot*? "You really think I'm half Fey?" My brain is still scrambling to keep up.

Viviane ignores me. "You'd enter the veil knowing that your life depends on *her* abilities?"

They're really talking about me as if I'm not right here. I'm about to speak up when Tana rushes over.

"Raphael." Her voice has a sharp edge. "The cards are warning of danger."

"From where?" Raphael asks, turning to look at the horizon. "The patrol ship in the north? Or are they coming from France?"

Tana shakes her head. "From below."

For a second the words just hang there, no one saying anything. Then Raphael shouts, "Battle stations!"

"What's going on?" I ask.

"Get inside the cabin," he commands.

Screams ring out as the boat dips sharply to the left. I

slip, slamming into the rail. As the boat pitches, I frantically grip the wet rail. The sea is directly beneath me now, and I find myself staring at the churning waves. The water is darker, much darker than it should be.

Suddenly, it erupts, knocking the boat back in the other direction. I'm clinging to the rail for dear life, but I lose my grip and slide back across the deck. Seawater washes over me, and I'm sure that I'm about to topple over into the waves. A powerful arm wraps around my waist, holding me tightly.

Raphael secures me against his enormous body, one hand on the rail, the other curled around my drenched white dress. I can feel the steel of his muscles through his clothes as I hold on.

"Hang on," he shouts over the roar of waves, then releases me. I grab the rail, and he charges up to the main deck.

My stomach flips as I follow Raphael with my eyes. An enormous serpentine coil rises above our boat. Thick as a ship, it's covered in metallic scales that gleam silver in the moonlight. Rising high above us, it blocks out the sky. I can't figure out where it starts and where it ends—or maybe it's everywhere.

A sea serpent.

I've only seen one in a blurry photo before, from the battle of Mont-Saint-Michel, when the Fey and their serpents destroyed most of the French navy. But terrifying as that photo was, it didn't do this creature justice. My heart plummets as it opens its jaws, exposing rows of jagged teeth. It screams like a banshee, then snaps down toward the deck so quickly that I feel the rush of its speed whooshing past, and the smell of rot fills the air. When it rears up again, I see someone's legs sticking out of its mouth, frantically kicking. People hurl spears, but they bounce off the monster's scales.

"Aim for the throat!" shouts Raphael.

The scales there are thinner, its flesh exposed, but the angle and the creature's horrifying speed make it almost impossible to hit.

Screaming erupts around me. The boat tips to the right, and I'm tossed against the ship's wheel. Pain explodes at the side of my head. I scramble to my feet and turn to follow some of the fugitives, who are trying to get to the relative safety of the cabin. And then I notice something from the corner of my eye.

Malo, huddled by the railing, up on the main deck.

The boat keeps rocking, but I grab the rail and force myself toward the wooden stairs. The beast shrieks, and the sound rumbles through my marrow. I make a run for the stairs. As I struggle to climb them, sea spray washes over me, robbing me of breath.

It's chaos. Wires snap free and wood splinters around us. Blood streaks across the deck, mingling with the seawater. Raphael is barking orders. A few uniformed crew members are thrusting spears at the beast, trying to hit its throat. Aleina and some of the others are clinging to whatever they can. Malo's grasping the railing, petrified, screaming into the wind. The serpent looms above him, ignoring the spears bouncing off its scales as its malevolent red gaze finds the boy.

"Malo!" I shout, but there's no way he can hear me in the chaos.

The serpent rears back, unlocking its jaws. Those sharp teeth will be carving through the little boy any second now. I need to distract the beast, but there's no way it'll notice me, even if I lunge at it and strike it with my fists.

A desperate idea sparks to life in my mind, and I rush over to Aleina. I grip one of the thick wires for steadiness, and with a sharp tug, rip the crystal pendant off her neck, the shimmering jewel she told me makes noise and light when shattered. I slide across the deck and smash it on the boat's iron rail.

A sharp, keening cry rips across the horizon, so loud that it drowns out the other noise. Blinding, colorful lights burst from the pendant. The sound slides through my bones, overwhelming me.

As the lights fade, the world dims to a haze, and there is a ringing in my ears. I hang on tightly, and a wave crashes overboard, drenching me again.

When I look up, I see that it worked. I distracted the serpent from Malo. Unfortunately, it's now staring in my direction, its eyes searing through me. It hisses, and it sounds like it's speaking Fey. As it lunges for me, Raphael knocks me to the deck. We roll out of the way as the serpent strikes, the snapping jaws inches from us. Raphael scrambles to grab a discarded spear, and just as the beast starts to raise its head, he thrusts the spear into its thinly protected throat. Shrieking, it rears back, the spear jutting from its neck. The monster looms like a tidal wave, and I wonder if it's going to crash down on the boat. Then it disappears beneath the water, leaving a dark stain of blood shimmering under the starlight.

I stare at the rippling waves. "Did you kill it?"

Raphael grips the rail. Seawater slides down his golden skin and drips from his dark hair. "Not quite." His tone is perfectly even, like he's talking about flowers blooming in his garden.

As soon as the words are out of his mouth, a furious shriek rends the air. The serpent shoots from the water, mouth gaping.

From behind, a hollow *thunk* sounds, and a harpoon soars through the air. It sinks into the creature's eye, turning it into a red crater. The serpent keens in torment, then slides into the waves. I whirl to see Viviane bracing an enormous harpoon gun against her shoulder. Raphael pulls out another harpoon and hands it to her. She loads it, and it clicks into place. As she scans the water, tension coils around us.

All of us wait, half expecting the beast to surface again. But now, the waves have calmed. Viviane lowers the harpoon gun, then returns it to its mount. She wipes her hands on her dress and crosses back to the quarterdeck.

I stare after her. Godsdamn it. I didn't want to have to admire her, but I do.

Aleina scoops up Malo and turns to follow Viviane.

She pauses, leveling her violet gaze on my face. "That's twice you've saved his life. He's been through a lot. Auberon has been hunting us in Brocéliende, then in the new territories in Fey France. And now this."

I tremulously smile at him, and a glow spreads through my chest.

Malo reaches out for me and touches my arm, just a soft brush of his fingers. Then he lowers his head against Aleina.

I wipe the streams of seawater off my face and look down. My white dress, I discover, is now virtually transparent. On most days, I'd be red-faced with mortification, but given what just happened, I don't think anyone is really paying attention to my nipples.

With a tight throat, I look up at the glittering stars spread out above us, relieved that most of us survived.

I walk down the stairs and step back into the captain's cabin, my legs shaking. Raphael and Viviane are standing by the table. Viviane's blonde hair drapes over one of his broad shoulders. She doesn't seem to notice me, but Raphael's eyes flick my way the moment I walk in. His jaw tightens like he's annoyed by the interruption, but he did just offer me a job, didn't he?

For a second, I think of stepping out again. Better than what I'm about to do. I shouldn't make such a decision so rashly.

But the emotion that washed through me when Malo touched me in thanks doesn't ebb away. This is real. Realer than anything I've ever done.

"Fine." I drop into a leather chair, dripping seawater all over it. "I'll be your Sentinel."

I can hardly believe I'm saying it.

Viviane sighs and rolls her eyes, but Raphael's silvery gaze studies me. Droplets of seawater cling to his long black eyelashes. For a moment, I think he's going to change his mind and say no. His gaze dips, and his entire body seems to go still, the muscles tensing. I watch as his fist flexes. Is he regretting asking *someone like me* to join him?

After what seems like an endless silence, he looks up at me again. "Good. We'll drop the fugitives at a safe house, and then we'll carry on to Camelot. You'll be at our spy academy."

"A spy academy?" I frown. "How long has this academy been around?"

He leans back in his chair. "About two thousand years —since the Romans. And now, we're a secret part of the British government. If you look over the list of the British military intelligence services, you see MI-1, MI-2, and so on. MI-5 and -6 are the most well-known."

"Right. James Bond."

"They go all the way up to MI-19. But all public lists skip MI-13."

"And that's you? In *Camelot*? As in King Arthur?"

"That's where we train spies. Avalon Tower in Camelot," he says, "and I think we could use you."

"You think I could hack it in a spy academy?" I absolutely cannot. "I was terrified just now. I don't really need any more terror in my life."

He leans back and shrugs. "Well, fear is normal. It's an ordinary response."

"You didn't look scared. You didn't appear to show any emotion whatsoever when we were nearly killed by a sea monster."

You know who else doesn't have fear? I wanted to say. *Psychopaths.*

He sighs. "Right. Well, I didn't say being scared serves any purpose—it's detrimental in most cases. I said it's ordinary. Anyway, despite your fear, I think maybe we can teach you how to be an agent. I think you can learn to be a spy if you can master your emotions."

Ordinary.

I brush a strand of damp hair out of my eyes. "Does becoming an agent involve spending time around you? Are you the person who would teach me to *master my emotions*? Because I don't love that idea."

Something unreadable flickers in his eyes. "Trust me, I don't want to spend time around you, either."

I glare at him. Usually, I tell people what they want to hear. But Raphael brings out something completely different in me, and I'm not sure I can stop it.

CHAPTER 7

J lean over the guard rail, staring at the choppy sea. The medicinal tea wears off about every half hour, and I'm retching. It's a really charming cycle of swallowing tea and bringing it up again.

After the sea serpent's attack, we all spend the rest of the journey teetering between exhaustion and slightly hysterical fear. Everyone, that is, except Raphael. As far as I can tell, the man never tires or experiences emotion.

Hours ago, we dropped the fugitives by the towering white cliffs at the south of England, but the journey just seemed to stretch on. And on. And on.

With a broken ship, we've been moving along the southern coast all night at a snail's pace. If my geography is correct, we're sailing around Cornwall.

Seagulls squawk and swoop overhead. I wipe a shaky hand across my lips, my gaze on the horizon. The first blush of dawn tinges the sky, and the fiery curve of the sun rises above Cornwall. At last, we're heading toward land, the foggy mouth of a river. Even now, hours later, my dress is still damp, and I'm chilled to the bone. The garment is ripped in several places, and there's a wooden splinter in my forearm. Serpent blood stains the white fabric.

Raphael steers us into the river, and rickety wooden piers rise up on either side of us. An empty iron cage hangs from a post on one of the docks. I blink at it. Did we travel back in time? The ominous metal box looks like something they once hung pirates in.

Tana hands me another cup of tea. "Almost there, love."

"To Camelot?"

She nods. "It was once part of Cornwall, you know, until the king of Wessex invaded. The rulers of Camelot used magic to hide it. Some say it was Merlin himself, protecting Camelot from his oak tree. Some say he doesn't die."

Goosebumps rise on my skin.

Around us, the river narrows. On either side, stone and timber frame buildings crowd the riverbanks. A thin fog hangs over them, tinged by rosy morning light. Gas lamps lend an ochre glow to the mist. This place really feels like stepping back in time.

"How come no one knows about Camelot?" For some reason, I'm whispering.

"It's secret, of course." She smiles at me. "That's what makes it a perfect place for spies. Only permitted ships can enter." She sighs. "This river is haunted, you know. I can feel it. A long time ago, the Fey used to cut off people's heads and throw them in the river, and now, I can hear their spirits whispering."

A shiver runs through me. "Oh." I can almost hear their whispers myself. "I didn't know the Fey once lived close to humans."

Tana smiles faintly. "Oh, yes, in peace for a while." She cocks her ear at the water, as if listening to something, then shrugs. "They named the tower after the old Fey kingdom, Avalon." Tana smiles wistfully. "In some parts of Camelot, you can still find the roads and temples built by the Pendragon kings long ago. The Pendragon walls encircle the city, hundreds of feet high. A few hundred years ago, we stopped putting severed heads on the city gates, you'll be pleased to know. At least, I'm pretty sure we stopped."

I clear my throat. "I'm glad to hear it." That's twice now she's mentioned severed heads.

"Our academy dates back to the Roman occupation of Britain. You'll learn all about it soon enough."

We drift past stone buildings that stretch up into the morning sky. As the wind skims over me, I take another sip of warm tea and stare as we slowly drift toward a white bridge. My heart flutters. The remaining mast and the engine's tall pipe will never clear it.

No sooner does the thought cross my mind than the bridge splits in the middle with a metallic groan, the two halves lifting into the sky to make room for our ship. Once we clear the bridge, we glide further east, where the river widens into a glassy lake. In the distance, a castle towers over the river.

My breath catches, and I stare at it. *Camelot.* The stone has an almost golden tinge, the towers cloaked in wisps of fog. Part of the castle stretches out into the lake, shrouded in mist.

"Avalon Tower, Camelot's oldest castle," Tana whispers, pointing to the right. "In the days of Arthur, Avalon was out there, occupied by the Fey and ruled by the evil Queen Morgan. She's dead now, defeated by the Pendragons. For fifteen hundred years, Avalon has been lost in the mists of the lake, and no one can find it."

"And Merlin was a Fey?"

"Oh, yes. A Fey ally to the humans, but things fell apart."

I turn to look at Camelot again, and my jaw drops. Tana said the castle was called Avalon Tower, but it's a city surrounded by walls and gates, turrets and spires, connected by high walls that rise over the river. Moss climbs the stone, the growth so dense that it makes the walls seem to blend with the natural world around them. The fog thins, and the rising sun washes the golden stone in a rosy shade.

Our ship glides into a narrow canal and bumps into a wooden dock. On the main deck, I can hear Raphael barking commands to the crew. Tudor-style timber frame houses line one side of the canal, and apple trees grow on the other.

My bleary eyes take in the activity all around us, burly

men unloading cargo from ships, others pulling ropes to moor us to the wooden dock. A mixture of scents assaults my nose—spices, apples, the sweat of the workers. Finally, the ship is moored, and I close my eyes, thanking the gods that we've arrived at last.

I'm in a daze as I follow Tana down the gangplank. Even here on steady earth, the ground seems to still move beneath me.

Dressed in a dark peacoat, Raphael leads us off the ship toward a stone archway. He shoves his hands in his pockets, not even looking at me. Viviane glides along next to him.

But when we're in the archway, she stops abruptly, blocking my path. She stares down at me, cocking her head. "May I see your passport?"

"Why?"

"I want to see exactly what the French soldiers read."

I retrieve it from my leather bag. It's streaked with water in a few places but readable. I hand it to her, and she turns and walks away, little pieces of ripped paper fluttering in her wake.

The torn pieces of my passport.

Panicking, I hurry after her. "What are you *doing*?"

She whirls and grabs me by the throat, pinning me to the wall. "I don't want you here," she says through gritted teeth. "You're weak, you're impulsive, and you threatened to inform the French soldiers about us. I think Raphael is making a bad decision because of a pretty face. Do you know how much that infuriates me?"

I don't answer. Hard to talk when you can't breathe.

"Lucky for me," she goes on, "you're unlikely to survive even the first weeks of training. It's brutal and dangerous, and the Pendragons will cut you down in a heartbeat. You'll be dead before you can betray us."

She releases me, and I gasp for breath, my hands going to my bruised throat. Little does she know, Raphael thinks I'm an idiot, but something tells me I'm better off if she believes someone powerful is on my side.

"If you don't want me here, then why the hell did you rip up my passport?" I croak.

She quirks an eyebrow. "Do you really think I'd let you leave, now that you can expose our location?" She's still boxing me in. "You're not leaving. And if I get even the faintest hint that you're going to pull another stunt like threatening to inform on us, I will end your life. Maybe your dinner will be poisoned. Maybe I'll slit your throat in your sleep. Maybe I'll simply bash your pretty little head against a rock. Understood?"

She hurries away into the narrow streets, and as much as I have *no* desire to follow her, I have no choice. Most of my money is in the spa hotel in France. I no longer have my passport. Without the help of someone powerful, I'm stuck in Camelot.

I touch my neck, wincing as I catch up to the others.

Raphael apparently didn't see a thing. He looks relaxed as he leads us through a narrow network of cobbled streets. Timber and brick buildings nestle on either side of the lanes, and smoke coils from chimneys above us.

Bloodstained and tattered, with dirt smeared on the back of my dress, I look like one of the fugitives I just rescued. Except here, in Camelot, no one notices. Who *are* all these people?

It's not long before the alley opens up to a large thoroughfare, where horse-drawn carriages race over the stones. Is this really where I live now? Camelot? I have no idea how long I'll be here, or how I'd get out if I had to. Mom will miss me bitterly. Or at least, she'll miss that I bring home money and pay the rent. What on earth is she going to do without me? I guess maybe it's time she figures that out. And in any case, it doesn't seem like I have much of an option to get out of this.

No more bookstore. No more one-bedroom apartment shared with Mom as she binges coke and alcohol. A distinct silver lining.

We walk down a gently sloping hill toward the castle that looms over the lake of Avalon. From here, I can see that Avalon Tower is a vast construction, with two sets of walls surrounding a number of central buildings. Raphael leads us to a gatehouse set into one of the walls. He still hasn't uttered a word to me. I suppose we *did* declare our hatred for one another.

A line of guards stands outside the gatehouse, their smart red cloaks vibrant against the stone and oak. As Raphael marches up to the gate, the soldiers part without a word, like leaves drifting on a lake. Above the arched door, the words AVALON TORR are carved in the weathered stone. Old English, I think. That carving must be over a thousand years old.

The heavy oak door groans open, and I step across the threshold. A strange thrill flutters over my skin. This place feels important—ancient, powerful.

Across the courtyard, a central castle stands on a gently rising hill. It's made of ivory stone, and its spires loom over us, four stories high. The sight makes me dizzy, and, unbidden, a nursery rhyme floats through my thoughts: *Avalon Tower, the Midnight hour, bury his head in the raven's bower...*

Strange rhyme, definitely not something Mom would sing to me. Maybe a nanny?

Tana yawns and points at the ivory castle. "That's Merlin's Tower, and it's sort of the central location. Offices, the dining hall, the training halls. A top floor that none of us are allowed to visit. The dorms are in the other towers."

Viviane is waiting for me at the door to Merlin's Tower. She still looks furious, and Raphael is already inside. "Are you coming?"

"Sorry!" Tana says, touching my arm. "I'm bloody starving. I'll meet you for breakfast in a few, yeah?"

Tana takes off and breezes past Viviane, Into the tower. I hurry up the stairs after her. Viviane tuts and opens the door, and we cross into a vaulted stone hall. Candles in sconces illuminate the stone walls and arched ceiling. Raphael peers into an office by the doorway, one crammed with books and papers, and a burning fireplace.

A man with a blond beard sits at a desk. He's wearing a dark blue suit and something around his neck that looks like a silver collar, with an opening at the front.

"Ah." He peers at Raphael over his glasses. "Who have you brought with you, Raphael?" His booming voice echoes in the corridor. This man could be an opera singer.

I'm just relieved that everyone is speaking in English and not Fey, since my accent is apparently terrible.

"A new recruit." Raphael glances at me for a fraction of a second. "She's going to work with us."

The man pulls out a large silver ring made of twisted metal, like the one he's wearing, and hands it to Viviane. She slides it around her neck.

"Thanks," she says. "I'm going to get out of these filthy clothes!"

I stare after her. That's exactly what I want to do—bathe, change, sleep for ten hours—but I'm still here with Raphael.

When I turn back to him, I see that he's wearing a similar collar, only in gold.

"Did you find the fugitives?" the bearded man asks.

"Most of them," says Raphael. "But they said their contact wasn't waiting for them. Amon, do you have any idea what happened? Their contact, Leia, was supposed to—"

"She's dead," Amon said. "The Fey forces caught her. And Alix. And Rein."

Silence stretches out. Then Raphael whispers, "Damn.

We lost three crew members to a sea serpent attack." He runs a hand through his hair. "The Fey must have found out about the exfiltration op."

"It's a terrible loss," Amon says heavily. "But worst of all is Alix. Without her, we're down to one Sentinel. MI-13 can't function with only one."

Raphael levels his pale gaze on me, the torchlight gilding his beautiful features. "That's where *she* comes in."

Ah, there it is, that note of disdain again, like he resents everything about this.

I wave and smile at Amon.

"Nia was simply on holiday in France," Raphael goes on, talking about me as if I'm not there. "She brought the fugitives to us by hiding them in the veil. It turns out she's a Sentinel, and she had no idea. She apparently didn't even know she's demi-Fey."

Amon's eyes widened. "The gods must have sent you to us."

A wave of dizziness washes over me, and I lean against a cold stone wall. "At your service."

"Well, for heaven's sake," Amon huffs, "get her something to eat before she faints in the entryway. Don't you travel with snacks, Raphael?"

Raphael points to the end of the long hall. "You can get breakfast. Head down this hall and take the stairs on the right. I need to debrief Amon."

My eyebrows rise. "I'm allowed to wander around a spy academy by myself? Just stroll in and get breakfast?"

"Eight guards already saw you walk in with me," Raphael replies, "one of them a telepath. If you weren't supposed to be here, you'd already be dead."

CHAPTER 8

*M*y gaze roams over the Gothic ceiling as I walk. This place looks like a grandiose version of Oxford or Westminster, with soaring arches and ornate carvings from centuries ago. It's like a medieval monastery on a scale fit for gods. In any case, it's intimidating, and with every step, I feel even more certain that I don't belong here.

Someone like you...

I notice a bathroom door by a staircase and slip inside. A mirror hangs over a porcelain sink, and I stare at myself. My black hair is a mess, and I try to smooth it down, then knot it into a bun. I take a bit of time to just breathe, inhaling the woodsy scent of the mahogany walls. Then, as ready as I can be in a dress stiff with seawater and stained by serpent blood, I exit and walk up a narrow, spiraling set of stairs. The steps are wildly uneven, and if I remember anything from my history classes, it's a trick they used in the old days to trip up invading forces.

At the top of the stairs, I turn right through an arched doorway into the dining hall and hesitate, realizing that I'm completely underdressed in my mud-smeared, blood-stained white sundress. Almost all the women present sport ethereal, gossamer gowns, elegant garments that display their perfect bodies to advantage. The men are a bit more casual in button-down shirts and trousers that show off their athletic forms. Holy crap, everyone here is gorgeous. Many of them wear metallic neck rings, most copper and bronze, but some silver. Torcs, I think they're called. It takes me a moment to realize the diners are mostly grouped at separate tables by color: bronze, copper, and silver.

My gaze sweeps around the room. The occupants are garbed in a rainbow of stunning colors—sky blue, indigo, cerulean, and emerald—and they sit at tables laden with great platters of fruit and baked goods. Bright murals line the walls of the dining hall, and at the far end of the chamber are twelve-foot-high portraits of a man and woman with gleaming blond hair. They're dressed in rich blue fabric and wear golden crowns. Arthur and Guinevere, I presume.

Sunlight streams in through long windows. Washed in the morning light, richly dressed and confident, everyone in this room looks like royalty. I glance down at myself. My dress is tattered and bloodstained, my cheap handbag is smeared with mud, and I'm wearing dollar-store plastic sandals.

The hall falls silent as the others notice, and within moments, all eyes are on me. I swallow hard and step inside. Never in history have plastic sandals sounded so loud, echoing off the high ceilings as I walk across the wood floor. Deafening. Why is everyone *staring*? Why are they all listening so intently to my sandals squeak?

A young woman at the silver table eyes me, then leans over and whispers something to her friend. The other woman lets out a small laugh, and for a moment, I'm back at my fifteen-year-old birthday party all over again, watching the cool girls laugh at my drunk mom.

But I'm not fifteen anymore, and whether or not these fuckers know it, they actually need me here. At least, Raphael seems to think so.

I raise my chin and scan the room. Someone is waving at me, and my chest unclenches when I recognize Tana in the back. Even after the trials of our journey, she looks fresh somehow, her yellow dress pristine.

I walk over to her through a narrow gap between seated cadets, brushing against a few of them as I walk. As I do, more people start whispering and muttering to each other, and I hear snippets of their discussions.

"—heard she talked to herself during the entire trip—" a woman says as I go by.

"—tried to kill a sea serpent with a distress crystal—" I hear another one say.

"—threatened to call the military to blow up the mission—" a man in green says, and sniffs.

A loud, vehement voice in my head joins in. *You don't belong here*, it chides. *You're weak. A risk. You need to leave, leave, LEAVE.*

I stumble, swallowing the urge to retort aloud. I grit my teeth and keep going. Apparently, word has gotten out about our misadventures. That was fast. Whoever talked didn't paint me in a very flattering light.

I circle the table and sit across from Tana. At this table, no one is wearing a torc.

"Nia, so glad you're joining us." Tana grins at me. The sunlight catches her hoop earrings. She gestures at the girl to my left. "This is Serana."

"Nice to meet you, Nia." Serana smiles at me. There's something wild in her smile, half joyous, half predatory. Even sitting, she's one of the tallest women I've ever seen, and her red hair drapes down her back. She has an eerie beauty, with pale white skin and a smattering of freckles across her cheeks. Her bright green eyes mark her as unmistakably demi-Fey. She gives me a single nod of approval. "Tana told me about what happened on the boat. Fair play. Very gutsy move, that one with the crystal." She drums her fingernails on the table. She's wearing chipped black nail polish.

"Oh." I clear my throat. "I got the impression that people here don't think that."

"Eh." She waves her knife in a circular motion, the

blade nearly nicking the ear of the guy on her other side. "Bunch of wankers. They don't like strangers."

"And I'm Tarquin," the guy to my right interjects. He has a long, bony nose and nostrils that seem to stay flared. "Tarquin Pendragon?"

He looks at me expectantly. He has smooth auburn hair, combed neatly sideways, and thin lips pressed into a tight smile.

"Very nice to meet you," I offer.

He clears his throat. "You know of Arthur Pendragon, I presume. *King* Arthur of the Round Table?" He points at the towering portraits. "That's him and Queen Guinevere. I'm the spit of him, they say. The absolute spit of him."

He looks nothing like the chisel-jawed, tan man in the portrait. Tarquin's skin is the color of milk. "Quite."

He grins uncertainly. "Yes. Arthur founded this place and built most of Camelot. His blood runs in my veins."

"I see. You're a descendant of Arthur?" I can see he wants recognition for this. "Very impressive."

His grin fades. "Yes. Well, I'm descended from his sister, Morgause." His expression brightens. "But some say the Pendragons in those days had incestuous relationships, so really I could be..." He clears his throat. "Anyway, since you're new here, I can show you around. As a Pendragon, I feel it's my duty to look after lost young women who are new to our academy. Of course, I can show you around the rest of Camelot, too. Outside the Tower. I've lived in the city my whole life."

There's something false about his smile that sets my teeth on edge, but I murmur, "Thank you."

So he's one of *those* Pendragons that Viviane referenced, someone who might cut me down just weeks into training.

But he doesn't seem to hate me so far.

My stomach rumbles, and I turn to a platter of food. It looks like something from a fairytale—fresh bread pudding, jams, fruit, cakes decorated with dandelions, entire baked salmon and potatoes, all resting on a bed of wildflowers. Teapots stand on the table, along with a golden liquid that might be beer or whiskey. I immediately grab a small dandelion cake, then a piece of salmon and a potato, then bread and blue cheese, and dive in. It's possibly the weirdest and most delicious meal I've ever eaten.

As I eat a buttery potato, I pour myself a cup of tea. "This is incredible," I mutter. "Salmon for breakfast? Is this some sort of celebration?"

Serana's eyebrows raise. "Celebration?"

"It's Nia's birthday," Tana says. "So, we are celebrating."

"Is it really?" Serana says. "Happy birthday!"

"My birthday was actually yesterday." I frown. "I mean, is the breakfast always like this?"

Serana nods. "It's just breakfast, love. But it's Fey breakfast."

Marvelous. My gaze flicks around the room. "Why, exactly? Are many of the demi-Fey here from the Fey realm?"

"No," says Tana. "Most of us aren't, and that's exactly why we do it. I mean, for one thing, most of the people here are human, like Tarquin."

Tarquin snorts. "Not exactly like *me*, but yes. Same species."

"But even most of the demi-Fey have never lived in the Fey realm. And that's why all this is part of the training," Serana says. "Most of us didn't grow up in the Fey culture. We've always hidden among humans."

"I see."

"These meals and the clothing are very important," said Tana. "Four years ago, we had two undercover agents in the Fey realm. They had a good cover and perfect disguises. It should have been an easy mission."

"They were demi-Fey but raised in England," Serana adds. "One fellow buttoned his shirt all the way up, and the girl wasn't used to wearing all the sheer dresses, so she had a jacket over it. It didn't take long before they attracted the unwanted attention of a bastard Fey soldier. He followed them around, and then he noticed that they refused mead in the morning. And that's the thing, isn't it? Fey *always* have a glass of mead with breakfast and one at dinner."

Tana picks up the bottle of mead and pours it into a small glass. It sparkles amber in the sunlight.

"The two spies were captured, tortured, and executed," Tana says, her voice soft. She hands me the little glass. "Drink."

Alcohol in the morning. Mom would fit right in, then.

I take a sip and wince. I never drink alcohol, and this tastes too strong and too sweet.

Serana grimaces at me. "You'll need to get over making that face. That's exactly why they decided to incorporate the food and the clothing into the academy." She spears a piece of salmon with her fork. "But it's not exactly a hardship. Our cooks are from the Fey realm. They're brilliant."

"*I've* been training since I was a little boy in Camelot," Tarquin says. "My dad realized that we'd have to get acclimated to the Fey culture thoroughly in order to carry on the family tradition, even if it's not in our nature to act like the wild beasts of the Fey world. But a hunter must understand his prey, yes? Like wearing antlers and the scent of musk to hunt a stag. It's common sense, really. If those two demi-Fey agents had done the same, they'd still be alive instead of slaughtered like pigs."

"That's right," a large guy sitting next to him says around a mouth full of food. "You're totally right." A piece of meat spatters from his mouth into his mug, but he doesn't seem to notice, or care.

"What, exactly, is your family tradition?" I ask. "How is this related to King Arthur?"

Tarquin shrugs. "The Pendragons destroyed the bitch queen Morgan. We had to. Her son tried to kill everyone in Camelot, you know, and the Fey kept shooting our soldiers with their arrows. Morgan sent her son to murder Arthur out of sheer bloodthirsty rage. Barbaric. Pendragon strength rid Camelot of that scourge. Arthur and his knights had it all in control back in those days.

And now, we've gone soft. That's why I think Avalon Tower should be focusing on ancient Camelot families with heritage and means, with the strength of character to fight them. Like we did before." He sips his mead. "Of course, I'm not saying you all don't belong here, but people need to know their role. Do you understand what I'm saying, Nia? They say you're a Sentinel, so I guess you'll do your part by getting teams across the veil. I think it's commendable of you to volunteer, knowing as little as you do. But you'll need someone from the knight class to command you. Particularly one with a gold torc. We can't expect every American off the street to make the decisions of a knight, or even a squire." He laughs at the concept, and for the first time, I think I see a genuine smile.

The knights, I assume, are all nobles like him. "Of course," I say, sipping the mead. It's growing on me. "I don't have the right breeding for complex thinking."

"Exactly, you get it. We all have to do our part." Tarquin clears his throat. "We always manage to get gold," he blurts. "The Pendragons," he adds. "We're the only ones who score high enough to get gold."

"What do you mean?" I ask.

Serana sighs loudly. "We'll all be tested in a few months. It's called the Culling because half the class will get kicked out. Sometimes, people get hurt. Even die. For the humans like Tarquin, they'll be tested on languages, spy skills, things like that. We do the same tests, but we also have to demonstrate magic. Those who pass the Culling are all ranked according to our levels."

"And that's where the torcs come from?" I ask.

Tarquin nods. "The gold classes have their own dining hall. They're all knights. So, in a while, I'm afraid I won't be able to eat with you anymore. This is the hall for the squires and the silver knights, the men-at-arms, and the cadets." He wrinkles his nose apologetically.

I raise an eyebrow. "So, Raphael is a Pendragon?"

Tarquin's cheeks go red. "No," he says sharply. "He's demi-Fey, of course he's not a Pendragon. Well, we *were* the only ones to get gold until he came along. Anyway, someone like you may need a more experienced hand to guide you."

His friend leans over, grinning. "And his hands are very experienced."

"Fascinating, you two. Really fascinating history," Serana says. The way she smiles at him makes me draw away. She's like a cat grinning at her prey. Her strings of metal necklaces gleam in the rays of light. "Fucking inspiring."

But Tarquin is refilling his mead, looking as if his point has been made.

I try some bread with a slice of blue-veined cheese. "Oh, gods, the food."

It's one of the most amazing things I've ever eaten, and for a few seconds, I can't focus on anything but the flavors in my mouth. I shut my eyes, chewing blissfully.

"I know, right?" Tana says, her voice seeming to come from far away. "It makes me want to go back to the Fey realm. Apart from all the murder."

"This is actually subpar in comparison to the food I have at home," Tarquin says.

Everyone ignores him.

"Did you try this cheese?" I ask Tana.

She shudders. "I can't eat cheese. Sometimes, I glimpse dark visions of the future in it. I don't like that."

"We all know what that's like." Serana nods sagely. "It's a problem."

Tana sighs. "I'd be eating a fine French cheese, and suddenly, I'd see a broken heart in it. Or a flood. You can't enjoy cheese if it has a flood in it."

"I usually take mine with a bit of strong mustard," Serana says.

"So, you don't eat any cheese? Ever?" I ask.

"I can have butter," Tana says. Her expression is deadly serious. "Butter transcends time."

"I think we can all agree on that," I say.

"Nia," says Serana, "will you join the rest of us in our classes? We only just started."

"Why would she need to go to our classes?" Tarquin asks sharply. "She's not going to be in MI-13. She won't be a real Agent of Camelot with a torc. She's just getting the real agents in and out. Like a taxi driver. Transportation."

My head throbs. "I think Raphael wants me to have some basic skills."

"Well, you'll find it very difficult," Tarquin says. "I mean, I grew up in Camelot, and I trained to go to this academy for years. There are feeder schools to prepare us. What have you done these past years?"

"I work in a bookstore," I say.

"A *store?*" He sounds scandalized. "Right. What—like, you stand at the till and take people's money, and give them change? Coins and that sort of thing?"

"Have you never been in a shop before?" I ask.

"Not really." His eyebrows are near his hairline. "And I've certainly never had breakfast with someone who worked in one. We have all sorts here now, don't we? Interesting times. Stay with me, and I'll help you get through those classes—because they are quite complicated." His thigh is a little too close to mine. "Oh, dear. You're using the wrong fork right now."

"Honestly," his friend adds, aghast.

Tarquin points. "That's a salad fork. And we don't change hands with the forks and knives here. That's out of the question. Listen, they usually get rid of people who can't keep up or who make buffoonish mistakes, but the Pendragon family is very well integrated here. My father is on the board, and my uncle is a professor."

I inch away. "That's nice of you to offer, but I think I'll be fine. I've never had a problem with learning from books."

He leans in closer, and the muscles around his mouth tighten. "This place can get really overwhelming, especially if you aren't cut from the same cloth. But you seem like you might have some hidden potential, and I could help you bring it out. I could tutor you in my room. I have a legacy room in the Green Knight Tower."

His arm brushes against mine.

"Aren't you lucky," I say, my tone flat.

"Just tell him what you actually think, Nia," Serana snaps. "Here, let me show you how it's done."

She leans over and slams her knife down into the table. The blade thunks into the wood, half an inch deep, between me and Tarquin. It wobbles, staying deeply lodged in the oak.

"She's not fucking interested, Tarquin," she says. "She isn't going to sleep with you for favors."

Tarquin's eyes widen. "Are you implying that's what I was asking for? I was merely being chivalrous. We've all heard about her screaming at imaginary people, so I figured I could offer her a hand." He turns to me, narrowing his green eyes. "But obviously, you're not interested in the help of a *gentleman*." His jaw works. "Good luck with some of the other men here if you think I'm not good enough for you. Did you really think I was trying it on? I have much better offers than someone who works in a *shop*."

The guy next to him leans forward. "She's a septic. It's rhyming slang from London, you know? Septic tank. Rhymes with Yank."

"*Septic*," Tarquin repeats acidly. He stands abruptly and throws his napkin down, then marches away from the table. Tarquin's friend blinks, staring slowly around him, as if he's not sure how to react. Then he gets up and hurries after his friend.

Right. Now Tarquin hates me. I haven't had enough sleep for this. "So, they'll be the Pendragons Viviane mentioned when she said she hoped they'd cut me down fast."

"Did she really say that?" asks Tana.

"They're all absolute tossers." Serana glowers after the retreating men. "Tarquin and most of the gold torcs are an insufferable bunch of twats, but they can't be avoided in this place. Nor can Viviane. The thing is, Tarquin and his lot don't even deserve the gold. It's just that the people in charge of Avalon Tower make sure the Pendragon family stays happy. The Pendragons think they run Camelot."

"But they're destined for mediocrity," Tana says with a sigh.

I raise my eyebrow. "Did you see that in your cards or something?"

"No." Tana shrugs. "They're just absolute bellends."

Serana looks me over and frowns. "Look at the state of you. Finish your food. We need to get you some proper Fey clothes."

CHAPTER 9

Serana leads me through a maze of interconnecting halls, our footsteps echoing around us. Avalon Tower is even larger than I'd first thought, and it's hard to keep track of where we are. Serana's legs are much longer than mine, and I struggle to keep up as we climb four flights of crooked, winding stairs. On the top floor, rib-vaulted arches stretch high above us. Diamond-pane windows overlook the court-yard, where wildflowers grow among the tall grasses and apple trees.

I turn to look at some of the paintings on the wall. They're mostly portraits, though some depict ancient battles or mysterious castles. One of the portraits sends a ripple of dread up my neck. A towering Fey man dressed in black is running his sword through the body of a naked woman. The corpses of more women lay strewn over the grass by his feet. I stare at it, catching my breath. The man wears a dark, spiky-looking crown and a cruel smile on his lips. "That's a bold choice for a decorative image."

Serana turns to look at me. "Ah, that sadistic bastard is Mordred Kingslayer. He was an evil Fey from thousands of years ago. The one Tarquin was talking about, who killed Arthur. Back then, the Fey had real, primal magic. Even some of the twisted ones like him. He broke in here one night and murdered King Arthur, along with hundreds of innocent people. He's dead now, but guess who that fucker's son is?"

I stare at her. "Auberon?"

"The very one. They're descended from Queen Morgan. They say the House of Morgan will burn Camelot to ash—that's Auberon, and his son, the prince. Let's hope that particular prophecy is wrong."

I pull my gaze from the disturbing image. There's still at least one more set of stairs to climb into a tower.

My lungs rattle when I breathe. "What do you think of Viviane?" I ask through labored breaths. "I'm afraid I've made an enemy of her."

Serana glances back at me. "The silver queen? I think she's probably fucking terrifying to have as an enemy. A real piece of work, you know?"

"Great."

"If I were you, I'd try to avoid her as much as possible. Though you'll meet her again soon enough, no matter what you do. She teaches combat. But there are plenty of other classes. You've only missed a few weeks."

"How long does it go on for?" I wheeze.

"Training for an agent? It used to be for a year, then the Culling. Maybe a year or two to specialize."

My heart skips a beat. "A year?"

I can't leave Mom on her own for a year. Can I?

"I know." She sighs. "Not nearly enough, is it? And it's even worse now. We've lost a lot of people in the field, so they want to start active missions in just six months. People are barely ready at six months, but that's when they'll test us."

My head is still reeling. I can't imagine I could actually pass the Culling, and Mom will lose it if I don't return. But who needs me more, my adult mother or the fugitives hunted by a maniacal king?

I still have a million more questions. "Serana, Tarquin said his family has prepared him for this since day he was born—"

"Tarquin is an egregious twat." Her words echo off the stone stairwell.

Right to the point. "Sure, but it's wild to me that he grew up with all this. Learning to fight the Fey before the rest of the world even knew they existed. And this whole place... How long exactly has it been here?"

She stops on the stairs and turns to look at me. "Ages. It started with the Roman invasion. Have you ever heard of the Ninth Legion?"

I frown. "I'm not up to speed on my Roman invasion trivia."

"Basically, an entire legion disappeared in Britain, up by Scotland. That was the Fey, trapping them in trees and

107

stones. Some soldiers were taken captive and dragged into Avalon to toil for Queen Morgan. But a few survived. They made it their mission to understand the Fey, to get their friends back."

I touch the wall's bricks, thinking of those loyal soldiers trying to recover their friends more than two millennia ago.

"That's how this place started, I guess," Serana continues. "As a place to figure out the weaknesses of the Fey. They never found their men, though."

"Oh," I say heavily.

"I suspect that's how the first demi-Fey turned up. Children of those early soldiers and the Fey. Anyway, in time, relationships between Fey and humans became peaceful. Avalon Tower even invited some of the Fey here, like Merlin, obviously."

"Merlin was Fey?"

"Of course. Humans have no magic, and he was one of the most powerful magicians ever."

"But...things changed, right? You said that this guy killed King Arthur." I point at Mordred's painting.

"Yeah, exactly. He was sent by Morgan. After that, Fey and humans became mortal enemies. For centuries, demi-Fey like us were not allowed in Avalon Tower. Not until recently. Now, they're desperate enough to take us in."

I stare at her, and the words *like us* roll around in my mind. "I never knew I was demi-Fey. Not until yesterday. I'm still not convinced, to be honest."

She shrugs. "Like I said, humans have no magic. So, you must be demi-Fey."

The world feels unsteady beneath my feet as I follow her further up the stairs. Just a week ago, I was ordinary little Nia, quietly shelving books in a shop. And I can't quite escape the feeling that perhaps all of this is a mistake, that I'm in over my head and don't belong.

My lungs shriek, and my airways narrow. I reach into my satchel, pull out my inhaler, and take two puffs. This thing is nearly empty.

Serana watches me shove it back into my bag. "Asthma?"

"I thought it might be better by the seaside."

"Does the sea air really work?"

I consider that for a moment. "Not really."

"Right. Anyway, let's get you dressed." The stairwell opens up to a landing, and she stops before a large oak door.

"Where are we?"

Instead of replying, she knocks. When there's no answer, she knocks again.

"This is the wardrobe?" I ask.

"Who is it?" A deep voice pierces the oak.

"It's Serana and the recruit. She has no proper clothes."

For some reason, I wasn't expecting a man to oversee the wardrobe, but maybe I needed to reexamine my assumptions.

"Give us a minute." A woman's voice this time.

I feel as if I'm interrupting something, and Serana turns to me, raising an eyebrow.

At last, the door opens, and a woman crosses out, the door slamming shut behind her. She's tall, with platinum hair, sun-kissed skin, and a golden torc. She's exquisitely dressed in a sheer, silvery gown and diamond jewelry. As her gaze sweeps up and down my body, her lip curls, and her nose wrinkles. "Oh, dear." Then she walks past us, her hips swaying.

"Ignore her," whispers Serana. "Her name is Ginevra, and she's a Pendragon agent from MI-13. Direct descendant of Arthur and Guinevere. Awful snob."

The door creaks open, and Raphael is standing there, looking stunningly, frustratingly hot. I'm utterly unsurprised that he was spending his time with someone described as an *awful snob*.

But I'm also unable to stop staring at him. Towering windows let in morning light behind him, gilding his body, illuminating the dark waves of his hair. He isn't wearing a shirt, and my gaze lingers over his carved V-line, his thickly corded muscles, the whispers of shadow against tanned skin...gods, what would it feel like to be pinned against the wall by this warrior's body? Ginevra probably knows.

My fingers curl into fists, and I pierce my palms with my nails. *Remember, Nia. He's an absolute dick.*

But also, I shouldn't think of the word *dick* while I'm staring at his absolutely godlike bare chest. I raise my eyes instead to his golden torc.

"Mr. Launcelot," says Serana. "Your new cadet needs clothing for her training." Her tone is suddenly a lot more clipped, respectful.

His gaze cuts from Serana down to me. "Ah. Didn't see the little pixie princess down there."

So much for respect.

Still, I can't stop staring. Sinuous vines are tattooed on his golden skin, following the lines of his carved muscles. On one of his large, athletic shoulders, he has a tattoo of grapevines that sweep over his collarbone and chest. They wrap around a nautical star, a ship, and a swallow.

I can't tear my gaze away. Apparently, all it takes for me to forget about how much I hate him is for him to take his shirt off.

And he's *watching* me looking at him, and I cannot even begin to interpret his expression. The man is a cipher.

Why did he answer the door half-dressed? Was it to show off?

"Come in." He turns and pulls on a crisp white shirt.

I realize my jaw is hanging slack and snap it shut. Mortified, I force my gaze away from his body.

His room is nearly as stunning as he is. The space is ringed with towering mullioned windows twenty feet high. A desk stands against them, set with plants, candles, and books. Mahogany bookshelves are stacked with gold-lettered spines. Of course he lives in a place like this—a place fit for a king.

"I thought we were going to the wardrobe person," I whisper.

Raphael's muscles look tense, his expression glacial. "I'm one of the few people here who has lived in the Fey realm. I know how they dress."

Serana looks at me strangely. "Yes. It's a very important job. Mr. Launcelot will get you set up." She leaves me alone with Raphael, and I survey the room again. His chamber windows overlook the entire city of Camelot to the north. From here, I can see a bridge beneath the tower connecting two buildings, as well as the monumental walls that enclose three sides of the city.

"Nice place you have here." I turn back to him. "It's not the sort of room *trash* would live in, is it?"

One black eyebrow raises. "Listen, pixie. I understand you think very highly of yourself, but we're not in the vineyards anymore, you know. You're at Avalon Tower, and I'm a knight of the Round Table."

My eyebrows shoot up. "Is that really a thing?"

"Yes, that's a thing. Don't get too comfortable here. We're going down one floor so you can try things on. I don't know if we have anything for someone so ridiculously short, but I'll see what I can find."

He reaches behind me to open the door, and I inhale a rich, earthy scent like wood-smoked barrels, a heady musk swirled with the whisper of fertile soil. Immediately, my mind flicks back to the sun-drenched vineyards in Bordeaux, the way the grapes looked in the morning sun. The things he'd told me about them, thirsty and aching for life. I feel nostalgic for something that was never real.

Those holidays always have a dark undertone when I think about them now.

I must have a strange look on my face because Raphael pauses with his hand on the doorknob. "What's wrong?"

"Nothing."

"You don't disguise your emotions well. Obviously, something is wrong."

There's something intoxicating about him, and I scramble to think straight. "Am I going to be alone with you? Undressing?"

He stares at me, and his expression betrays little emotion. "What, exactly, are you worried that I'll do?"

Nothing. I hate him, but he isn't creepy. It's more that the idea of being alone with him seems dangerous, and it makes my chest flush. And that's particularly confusing when I know that he thinks I'm trash. "I don't think you'll do anything. Mostly, I just think you're an emotionless robot."

A line forms between his brows. "What the fuck is a robot?"

I grow flustered. They no longer exist, and he never saw one in the Fey realm. "It's like…a person made from metal. They used to make them before the Fey invasion fried modern technology. I guess most of them didn't look like people. Some were like…vacuum cleaners? I think we had one at home. A Roomba."

Silence stretches out between us.

"Never mind." I take a long breath to steady myself and smooth my hair. "You said we wouldn't be around each other, and here we are." My voice comes out sounding tinged with hysteria, and I wish I could rewind several minutes.

"Perhaps I'm starting to regret bringing you on, pixie," he says softly.

He pulls open the door, and I follow behind him.

"Ah, but you need a Sentinel," I remind him. "You need me."

And maybe—just maybe—I needed to get away from home as much as they needed me here.

* * *

BEHIND A CURTAIN, I slip into a dress made of filmy scraps of silk. I feel like I need a PhD to figure out how to put it on, but eventually, I reach a situation where my breasts are covered with crisscrossing swaths of fabric, my belly is exposed, and a skirt with a thigh-high slit sweeps down to the floor. It's a gorgeous lavender color, and the material is semi-transparent but thick enough around my breasts and hips to cover my nipples and underwear. It's pretty hot, to tell the truth.

And if Serana and Tana were on the other side of that curtain, I'd have no problem at all strutting out, head held high.

It's just that around Raphael, I feel acutely aware of every inch of my skin.

I take a deep breath, steeling myself. Closing my eyes, I imagine that I'm fully clothed and the cotton sleeves and long hems are my armor from his piercing gaze.

I step out from behind the curtain, the cool castle air whispering over my bare skin. I might as well be naked.

Raphael is sitting, watching me, his body completely still. Honeyed light spills in from the tall windows, casting half of him in gold. In the large wooden chair, he almost looks like a king.

He doesn't say a thing. He must be concentrating hard on the clothes because there is something intense in his gaze that I can't read. It's not the coldness he seems to reserve for me. On any other man, I'd assume it was desire. But on Raphael? Probably quiet loathing.

"It fits well." His voice sounds husky. "I got your size correct, but you look uncomfortable. The Fey don't walk around with their arms folded in front of their chests, grimacing."

I run my fingers over the delicate fabric. "I don't usually wear anything like this."

"Well, that's why you're here, to get used to it. Do you mind if I adjust the back a bit?"

"Do whatever." My voice comes out sharp and angry, but I lift my black hair to give him access.

He stands behind me, tightening one of the straps.

"You breathe with a slight wheeze." His voice thrums over my bare shoulders.

"Asthma," I say. "My inhaler is running low."

"We'll get you a new one." A little brush of his fingertips sends tingles over my skin, and my muscles tense at the sensation. Oddly, the wheeze in my lungs goes away, and my airways open up.

"You're going to need to relax," he says quietly. He steps in front of me again. "It fits perfectly, but your body looks as supple and relaxed as the stone walls behind you." He cocks his head. "This will need a lot of work. The Fey will immediately identify you as a spy. So, your job is to relax."

I clamp my hands on my hips. I am fucking terrible at relaxing, especially when someone tells me to relax. And *especially* when that person is Raphael, the gorgeous man who once broke my heart.

"You look like you hate everyone around you," he adds.

"Oh, that's because I do."

He drops into the chair, appraising me with those piercing eyes. "Okay, pixie. Close your eyes for a moment. Breathe in deeply and focus on your breath. Think of the place where you feel most comfortable, where you feel completely yourself. Somewhere in your home, maybe. A place you would be right now if you could."

For a moment, my mind is blank. I've never felt comfortable at home. Home is a place of chaos. Home is a place where my mother screams at night.

The bookstore, maybe.

But then my mind blooms with maroon grapes, plump with sunlight. There was a time there, before it all turned sour, when that Bordeaux vineyard felt like a perfect, golden idyll.

With my eyes closed, I hear Raphael moving behind me again. "May I touch your shoulders? They're hunched up."

I nod.

I feel his fingertips at the base of my throat, then the brush of his skin on my shoulders. Heat follows in the wake of his touch. He keeps his hands on my shoulders. "Your shoulders need to be down here, not up by your ears."

He touches the base of my spine. "Shift your hips forward. There. Fey women lead with their hips when they walk, chins held high."

Warmth is radiating off his body, and it's infinitely distracting. Maybe if I pretend he doesn't hate me, I can relax. I pretend he's Jules, the reasonably handsome waiter.

"Good," he murmurs. "Take deeper breaths, fill your lungs. Then I want you to walk across the room. Fey movements are fluid, relaxed. Imagine that rivulets of water are flowing down your skin, dripping down the curves of your body."

My pulse is racing for reasons I *really* don't want to explore.

"Walk across the room," he commands me quietly. "Toward the window."

As long as I'm not looking at him, I can relax a little more. I ease the muscles in my shoulders and picture water running down my body. Except as I walk, I'm picturing myself completely naked and Raphael's hand stroking up my spine...

At the window, I turn back to him. My lips part, and my cheeks flush, but I feel a magnetic pull toward him. I hate this man, but he's godsdamned seductive, and I might as well not lie to myself.

When I'm only a few inches from him, I stop and look up at his face. This close, his silver eyes are hypnotic, so striking against the black eyelashes. Something about his expression is searing. Is that *still* loathing?

"Good." He licks his lips.

Then, abruptly, he turns from me. "You've used up enough of my time. Pick out a few more things if you want, but I'll send the rest to your quarters. I have more pressing concerns."

My brow furrows. "I don't need to try everything on?"

He's already at the door. "Go find Amon. He'll get you a room."

Raphael, as usual, cannot wait to get the hell away from me.

The sound of the closing door echoes in the hallway.

CHAPTER 10

J'm trying to follow Amon's directions to my room in Lothian Tower, but at this point, I'm too sleep-deprived and self-conscious in the transparent silver gown to function normally. As I clutch my new clothes, I'm pretty sure I've been going in circles.

Where is the damn room?

At last, my gaze lands on it—number 333—a wooden door inset into an ornately carved stone arch. A brass lion juts from the door with a circular door knocker in its mouth.

I knock twice. Moments later, the door swings open, and Serana beams at me. "There you are!"

Light floods the room through tall arched windows, illuminating three beds with headboards carved to look like interwoven vines. Round tables stand between the beds, and plants grow in pots on the large stone windowsills.

This place looks amazing, cozy and grandiose at the same time. It even has two sets of bookshelves that display old tomes and flickering candles in jars.

Tana sits on one of the beds with a book in her lap. "No classes today. We can rest, and I bloody well need it." On the table next to her is a gold-engraved black teapot and several matching cups.

I turn to look at Serana's bed. On her side, the vibe is very different from Tana's tidy corner of the room. Senara's bed is chaos incarnate, the bedsheets tangled and knotted. Half a dozen outfits are discarded on and around the bed, and books litter the nightstand, stacked in a precarious tower. The hilt of a sword peeks from beneath her pillow. Yellow stains—which I can only hope are from tea—streak her duvet.

"Welcome to our room," she says. "The three of us will be sharing."

One of the books topples off her bedside table, and I rush over to catch it. I start stacking the books neatly, my eyes darting to the third bed. Mine, I presume. I'm so tired that it's drawing me closer like a magnetic pull. "I hope you forgive me if I just sleep all day."

"I'll pour you some mugwort tea," says Tana. "It will give you soothing dreams when you fall asleep."

Serana cocks her head at me. "What are you doing, love?"

I belatedly realize I was trying to untangle her sheets. "Your bed looked uncomfortable."

"I'm a fucking mess." She shrugs. "I'm fine with it, though."

"Right. Of course." I pull the sheets over my bed, making it neatly.

Once it's made, with the pillows piled up, I drop onto the mattress with a relieved sigh and accept a steaming cup of tea from Tana. "Ah, thank you."

I sit up, glancing at my roommates over the rim of my mug. It's an unusual feeling for me, being looked after, and it warms my chest along with the tea. I take another long look at their room—no, *our* room. Over Tana's bedside table hangs a portrait of a man with a long white beard. He wears blue robes with silver crescent moons and a torc around his throat to match. He holds a gnarled wooden staff, and the gold placard beneath it reads MERLIN.

My breath catches. I still can't believe all this is real. "A silver torc?" I ask. "Do you mean to tell me that Raphael has achieved a higher level than Merlin himself?"

"Ah, no," says Tana. "Merlin wears Avalon Steel. It's a special sort of metal made by dragon fire and cooled in the lake, granted to him by the Lady of the Lake when she was alive." She grins. "He loves wearing it because Nimuë made it for him. I mean, he *loved* wearing it. Past tense. Only Merlin, Arthur, and some of the most powerful Fey of Merlin's court had those. It doesn't exist anymore because all the primal magic is gone from the world. Primal magic disappeared when the Fey left for Brocéliande."

When I look closer, I can see that the torc does have a warmer tone than silver, a rosy sheen.

"I need to let everyone at home know that I'm here," I say after a few seconds. "Do either of you know how to get a letter quickly to the U.S.? Or is there a phone here?"

"No phones for us." Tana nods. "I can help you with a letter. It's a very speedy service. But of course, you can't let them know you're *here*. No one can know Camelot exists. They vet all the letters."

I blink as it sinks in. "Right."

"You'll need a cover story," says Serana. "You fell in love, and you're staying for your new fella. Raphael." She snorts. "No, I'm only joking. He obviously hates you."

I stare at her. "You picked up on that?"

"It's a bit obvious, darling." She shrugs. "Well, he either hates you or wants to shag you, or both. But you cannot shag him. Absolutely not allowed at Avalon Tower."

"Tarquin didn't seem to care about that rule," I say.

"Oh, those rules don't apply to the gods-chosen Pendragons, of course. Just us commoners. Don't worry, there are plenty of options outside the tower." She shrugs. "If you have the energy for that sort of thing."

"I'll keep that in mind."

"Is there a story between Raphael and you?" she asks. "Have you met him before?"

"Nothing interesting," I mutter. "Anyway, I'll just tell my mom I found work in an amazing bookstore."

"Whatever it takes." Serana flicks her red hair behind her shoulder.

"Are you still in training, Tana?" I ask. "I thought you were already an agent."

"I'm back for more training," she says. "I've been helping MI-13 for a while, mostly on boats, like the one where we met. But they want to send me into Fey France, so I need a whole bunch of new skills. I'll be in the fighting class and the spycraft classes."

My stomach tightens. "They won't expect me to go into Fey France right? I'll just help crews across the veil barrier and stay on this side, I'm assuming. Tarquin was sort of right. I'm not at all prepared to be here."

"Tarquin is a wanker," Serana says. "You don't need life advice from him. Missions never go as planned. As a Sentinel, you'll have to know how to react and improvise when the time comes. And yes, that could be in Fey France. Maybe even Brocéliande."

"Wanker. It's a funny word," Tana says dreamily. "Wanker. Say it enough times, and it feels weird. Wanker. Waaanker. Wan*ker*. Wanker."

Serana massages the bridge of her nose. "Tana, I think you drank too much mugwort tea."

Tana clutches her mug. "Waaaaaaanker."

"Were you ever there?" I ask Serana. "Brocéliande?"

She shakes her head. "I'm from the Isle of Man. But Tana comes from Brocéliande."

Tana's eyes are drifting shut. "Did you know that in the ancient days—in the time of primal magic—when the Fey were still in Avalon, they would build a large wicker tower and put humans inside it and burn them? And they'd spill

123

human blood to fertilize the soil, where mistletoe grew. I wonder if they still do that."

Serana rolls her eyes. "Tana, you're going to scare our new roommate."

I'm desperate to sleep, but I have two days' worth of grime on me, and my nails look filthy. "Is there a bath somewhere?" I ask.

"Ah, we're lucky." Serana grins. "Tana was able to persuade them to give us a good room with our own bath." She points at a door just between the bookshelves. "Right there."

I sigh with relief. "Thank you." I pull out some of the new clothes—a red dress with no sleeves—and head for the bathroom.

I open the door to a narrow stone room. Light streams in, forming diamond-shaped patterns on the flagstone floor. Candles and soap rest on wooden shelves, and burgundy towels are stacked neatly on a cushioned stool. A copper clawfoot tub stands on one side, and I turn on the tap. As the bath fills, steam curls into the air. I slip into the tub as the water rushes in, and my muscles start to relax. After the long journey here, this feels amazing.

For the last seven years, we've been in an apartment that has a bathroom down the hall, shared with strangers. It has a single shower stall that always has someone's hair in it.

This? This is luxury.

I scrub the grime and seawater off my body. I don't stay in the bath too long because I'm in danger of falling asleep. But as I step out and the water trickles down my bare skin, I hear Raphael's voice.

Imagine that rivulets of water are flowing down your skin, dripping down the curves of your body.

I wonder if he remembers that he kissed me once, out there in the vineyards all those years ago. Or if he has any idea that the kiss ruined me because I think nothing will ever top how it made me feel.

I really need to stop thinking about him.

I dry myself off aggressively, then I pull on the red dress. The material is exquisite and silky against my skin.

I cross into the bedroom again and freeze. An unfamiliar man is sitting in the room, nestled next to Tana on her bed.

"Oh, sorry," he quickly apologizes. He has a wave of raven-dark hair, brown skin, and large eyes. He wears a white, frilly shirt with the buttons open and a top hat. Strings of silver necklaces gleam on his neck, and his eyes are lined with black eyeliner.

He smiles at Tana and me. "You have a new roommate?"

"This is Nia," Tana says.

"She's joining the academy." Serana is carving a piece of wood with a sharp blade, and wood chips are scattering all over the floor and her bed. "Just came in today after single-handedly killing a sea serpent and smuggling an entire crowd of fugitives through the border."

I huff a laugh. "That's not even remotely true."

"I'm Darius." He waves. "Nice to meet you. I'll get out in just a moment. I just came for a quick reading."

"Darius is addicted to Tana's readings," Serana explains. "You know drug addicts? He's like that, but for cartomancy. He's here every night, asking about love. Tana, where is my soulmate? Tana, is the fella I met today the one? Tana, does this devil on the card mean I stop following my old lovers through the streets of Camelot, or am I destined for a gorgeous bad boy?"

"I *also* ask about weightier subjects, not just my love life," Darius snaps.

"I don't mind either way." Tana is shuffling her cards. "But before we do *your* reading, I promised one for Nia."

Darius scoots to the corner of the bed and gestures at me. "Ladies first."

"It's not necessary," I say warily.

"Oh, let her get on with it," Serana says. "Or she won't stop harping about it."

I sit down between Darius and Tana, and she hands me the deck of cards. "Shuffle and think of the future."

I shuffle the cards, but thinking of the future seems impossible. I used to have everything planned years in advance. But now? I have no idea what's happening.

I finally hand the cards back to Tana, and she flips the first one. I peer down to see what it is, and a chill sweeps over my skin. I don't know a ton about tarot, but this one is obviously ominous. It looks like a tower struck by lightning, with silhouettes of bodies falling from it. Flames rise from some of the windows, and dark storm clouds surround it.

"The Tower," she says.

"Like...Avalon Tower?" I ask.

"Perhaps. The cards shouldn't be taken too literally."

She frowns and flips another card, which she places across it. This one was The Lovers. A naked couple are in flagrante. I don't think the tarot cards in America are quite this racy. These two look to be on the verge, and I find myself staring a little too hard.

"Huh. The Lovers." Tana sounds puzzled.

"What? I never get The Lovers," Darius says. "Serana told me that you don't even have that card in your deck."

"I was just trying to spare your feelings, hon." Serana gives him a sympathetic smile.

Tana runs her fingers on the card. "This one's both in the past and the future. A lover from the past."

My chest flutters. I've only had two real boyfriends, and they worked in the same bar. One of them was obsessed with getting women to do body shots off his abs, the other with his terrible glam rock band. I hope neither of them is in my future.

"And The Tower interjects in between," says Tana. "Pulling them apart, drawing them together."

"Pulling and pushing, huh?" Serana makes a really crude, unmistakable motion with her fingers. "Some good stuff, Nia. The readings here don't usually get that saucy."

"You know, this should really be done in private," Tana says sharply.

"Well, it's my room, too." Serana sticks her tongue out.

"Just imagine I'm not even here," Darius says. "I want to see what happens."

She places the next card below the first two. It sends another chill over my skin—a man sitting on a throne decorated with large ram's horns, the general appearance of an evil god. The card reads "The Emperor."

"Your parentage," she mutters. "Something about it puts you in danger."

That one is easy. "My mom. She has issues." Mom has fallen asleep drunk on the sofa with a lit cigarette on many, many occasions. She once drove a car into a building when I was in the passenger seat. Nothing could be less surprising to me than the idea that she puts my life in danger on a regular basis.

"Well, *that's* not your mother." Tana jabs a finger at the card. I feel like the card reading isn't going to her liking.

My stomach tightens. Mom raised me to believe Walter was my father, a boring, very human man with a large bank account. But obviously, he wasn't. I had some questions to ask her. Specifically, what Fey did she bang?

"I don't think I know who my dad is," I say, "but I suppose being demi-Fey is what puts me in danger."

She flips over more cards—The Moon, then Death, a skeleton riding on a horse beneath a stormy sky. Lightning cracks the clouds above him.

A shudder dances along my spine. "Sometimes death isn't bad, right? In the tarot cards? It just means a change or something?" I ask hopefully.

But Tana seems like she can't even hear me anymore. She flips more cards, almost in a frenzy. More swords and blood, a card with coins. The Wheel of Fortune. Then she pauses, puts the deck aside, and takes a long breath.

"Tana…" I swallow. "Am I going to die?"

She raises her eyes and meets mine. "Yes."

I blanch. "What?"

"We all die someday, but demi-Fey live much longer than humans."

"Right, but what did you see in the cards?"

She shakes her head. "Usually, the cards are much clearer. But with you, there are so many forces involved that the future fractures. There are almost endless possibilities. I see…duality. Struggles inside you and out in the world. Impossible decisions. And a lake. *The* lake."

A silence settles in the room.

"You know," Serana finally says, "normally, when you get a new roommate, you should invite her to a party, not scare her half to death."

"Oh. Right." Tana collects the cards miserably. She raises her eyes to me. "Um…do you want to go to a party?"

"Not today, thanks."

"Good." She looks relieved. "I haven't been invited to any."

"I was going to go next," Darius said. "But with your current mood, you'll probably see only death, destruction, and plague in my future."

"No, let's do your reading now," Tana says brightly. "Your readings always make me feel better."

I get up from Tana's bed and lie down in mine. Even with Tana's terrifying card reading, exhaustion settles over me, and I can already feel my eyes shutting. I lie on my side, watching Tana and Darius as he shuffles the cards.

"Why do my readings make you feel better?" he asks.

Tana flips cards onto her bedsheets. "It's nice to see love in the cards instead of patrol ships and death."

"So you see love in the cards?" Darius perks up.

"No, but it's nice to think about it."

Darius clears his throat. "And the man who works at the Seven Stars pub? We bonded over an adorable cat wearing a lace collar who kept sitting in his lap."

"He's not the man for you," Tana says softly. "He's a rake, and he snacks on anchovies all day."

"Oh, well, that's a dealbreaker." Darius sighs. "The anchovies part, not the rake. I suppose that's why the cat liked him so much."

"You can see that the barista likes anchovies in the cards?" I ask sleepily.

"Yes," Tana says. "I mean, it depends on the reading. But in this case, it's The Devil again, with the seven of swords across it."

"Well, it figures that anchovies would be signified by The Devil," Darius mutters.

"I like anchovies," Serana interjects.

"You *would*," Darius snaps.

She glares at him. "What does that mean?"

Their voices sound muted. Sometimes, when I'm tired

like this, I hear another voice, one of my many hallucinations.

But unlike most of my hallucinations, this one happens
when I'm alone, and I actually like it.

This one started when I was around eighteen, a man's
voice, deep and melodious. Sometimes, the words felt
poetic, like a dark lullaby. Sometimes, they were downright violent. Often, a dark note of sadness runs through
his thoughts. But mostly, there's an undercurrent of a
velvet-tinged voluptuary. Beautiful, vulgar, seductive, and
dripping with pleasures I've never experienced.

*Two women in my embrace, two heavy breaths on my chest.
I cannot remember their names. The unruly sun pierces the
calm, and birdsong heralds the night's end. I will lie in bed all
day, wrapped in the limbs of bright, glaring strangers. But my
home is the night and the soft meeting of lips to lips.*

My eyes drift closed, and with the man's beautiful
voice in my mind, I dream of a starry sky.

CHAPTER 11

"*A*n agent should never be caught without a knife," Viviane barks.

Morning light spills through the tall windows. I slept so much in the past twenty-four hours that everything still has a dreamlike haze.

We're standing in a large hall with wood floors and vaulted stone arches. Weapons gleam on the walls. Twenty-two cadets stand dressed in fighting clothes— sheer, Fey-style dresses for the women, tight clothes for the men.

We're here to learn how to kill.

As my terrible luck would have it, my first class at the academy is self-defense, taught by the woman who threatened to slit my throat in my sleep. She's wearing a short black dress with long sleeves, a belted knife holster, and tall boots.

"A knife is an agent's best friend," Viviane says. Her

heels clack over the wooden floors as she paces around the room, scrutinizing us. "As you all know, I'm a very friendly person."

Someone chuckles. She pivots and gives him a cold, piercing stare. The chuckle dies.

"That's why I keep a lot of my friends on me!" Her voice echoes off the vaulted ceiling. "A knife in my belt, a knife in my sleeve, a knife in my boot. When I'm on a mission with no boots, or belt, or sleeves, I keep a knife in my knickers."

Some people shuffle uncomfortably. The image of Viviane walking around with a knife in her underwear is a vivid one.

"Sometimes, a particularly stupid student asks why we bother with knives and swords. After all, guns still work. The British military has them. And the answer is because we are not bloody soldiers, we are *spies*, you absolute fucking moron. Your job is to blend in, not to go into battle. The Fey use arrows, swords, and knives, so *we* use arrows, swords, and knives. So, listen carefully when I tell you what you need to know about knives." She shifts her arm, and a long blade slides from her sleeve into her hand. She flicks it in the air. It twirls a few times, and she catches it, pointing to the tip. "*This* is the pointy bit, and you should stick it into your enemy."

Her gaze slides around the room to make sure we grasped that.

"I'll divide you into pairs, and I want to see how you implement this complex technique I just outlined," she finally says. "You'll be using rounded knives so you don't accidentally murder each other." She points at a wooden block by one of the walls with a bunch of hilts jutting out of it. "At least, in theory, you won't murder each other, but we have had accidents before. Join your partners when I call your names. Serana and Darius. Liam and Clara."

I listen to the names attentively, hoping to be paired with Tana. It would make sense, after all. We're about the same size and—

"Nia and Tarquin."

Godsdamn it. She matched me with a Pendragon on purpose, didn't she?

My muscles tense as I walk to the wall and pluck one of the training knives from a block. I test the blade, reassuring myself that it's dull. When I turn, I see Tarquin smirking at me. Today, he's wearing his hair slicked back and shiny. His friend from the banquet leers at me.

"Horatio." Tarquin's slick auburn hair gleams under the chandelier light. "How long do you suppose it will take for me to bring her down?"

Horatio snorts. "She seems like the sort who will let you do whatever you want."

"She's going to get us in and out of the veil. That's her role, isn't it? The transportation. A public bus," says Tarquin, his pinched expression brightening. "That's what she is. A public bus. Everyone gets a ride, don't they?"

Gritting my teeth, I cross over to him. I won't let them get in my head. "Okay," I say, as I stand in front of Tarquin. "We should—"

He lunges forward, his dulled blade smashing into my stomach. Although it isn't sharp enough to cut, the force of the impact steals my breath. A second later, the pain blazes through my abdomen.

I double over, holding my stomach.

"Wait," I wheeze.

He rams the knife at me again, this time jamming it into my collar bone. The impact makes my teeth snap shut. I taste blood.

"Killed you twice, public bus," Tarquin hisses. He turns with a crooked smile. "I don't know why we let all these commoners in. Do you know, Horatio? Reeks of desperation."

Somewhere nearby, Horatio guffaws.

"They're trying to prove a point about equality, but it's nonsense, isn't it?" Tarquin adds. "Letting in the unqualified and unskilled just to seem modern."

His gaze flicks back to me. "What is your parentage, exactly? Did your mother walk the streets? Is Camelot so inclusive now we've got whores' children walking through our hallowed halls?"

He swings again. I shift to the left out of reflex and desperation. The blade whistles by my ear. Tarquin is momentarily out of balance. But I have a knife, too. Frantically, I lunge and try to stab, but by the time I do, he jumps back.

I'm panting, already feeling the crushing wheeze in my breath. Serana gave me tips before we stepped into class, and I'm trying to follow them. Stand ready. Watch my opponent's eyes. Wait for an opportunity.

He lunges at me clumsily, and I jump back. He swipes again, and I move.

Sure, he's strong, but I'm small and probably faster. That's how you beat someone like him, I imagine. Tire him out. Shift out of reach. Wait for the moment.

A cry rings out to our left, and Tarquin glances that way, distracted. This is my chance. I leap forward—

He pivots and grabs my wrist, bending it. Pain shoots up my arm. With a grunt, I drop the knife. In a smooth movement, he shoves me to the floor. Before I can push myself up, he's sitting on top of me. Adrenaline crackles through my veins, and my heart flutters. He wasn't distracted, nor was he slow at all. That was a trick.

He's pinning me down, gripping both my wrists in one of his hands. A strand of his slick hair comes loose, and his cheeks go red, eyes wild with glee. At the end of his long, thin nose, his nostrils are more flared than ever. With his free hand, he presses the knife against my throat. I can't breathe.

"Got you where I want you."

A voice, angry and venomous, echoes in my mind. *You need to be put in your place. You should have been nice when you had the chance, and now look at what you've done. Whore.*

I can't answer the voice. Tarquin leans closer to me, a drop of drool glistening on his lower lip. "Killed you again," he whispers. "And again. And again. I told you. You're not meant to be here. They're letting you in because you're the transportation. You're just a cheap ride."

His face is so close to mine that I can see every pore. I struggle, but I can't push him off. I try to knee him in the back, but my leg hardly moves. My lungs burn, and my vision darkens. My chest feels as if I might explode with the pressure. I need to breathe—

Suddenly, he's off me. I inhale a long, ragged breath, the world swimming into focus. I cough, gasping for air. I feel half dead.

This has been a disaster.

But somehow, Tarquin is injured, too. He's lying on the floor, groaning, blood dripping from his lip.

I turn to see Raphael standing above us both. "That wasn't going well."

I rasp, "It really wasn't."

Raphael's frigid gaze slides to Tarquin. Sighing, he slides his hands into his pockets. "If you kill one of our only two Sentinels, Pendragon, I will end your life." He flashes a dark smile. "And I don't give a fuck who your great-grandmother was."

"You'd better give a fuck, demi-Fey." Tarquin dabs at his bloody lip. "And how does this mongrel expect to function out in the field if she can't even take a bit of training?"

"Mate, mate," Horatio brays. "Why is she even here?"

"It's her first day of training," says Raphael coolly. "Murdering someone isn't education."

"Raphael." Viviane's sharp voice echoes in the room.

Everyone has stopped practicing, and they are all staring at Raphael, Tarquin, and me. Looks like we've put on quite the show.

I hate being the center of attention.

"This is my class," Viviane says. "And I think I can manage on my own."

"It didn't look like it." Raphael's pale eyes glint. "It looked as if we were about to lose one of our Sentinels."

Viviane folds her arms calmly. "I saw what happened, and it looked fine. I didn't see any good reason to interfere with her training. Nia was learning a valuable lesson."

"Viviane, if you suddenly find yourself with the rare skill that Nia possesses, then you can be a bit more careless with her welfare."

Viviane narrows her eyes at him. "Get out," she says through clenched teeth.

Raphael gives me a curious look, then turns and stalks gracefully from the room.

Viviane whirls, her cheeks pink. "Okay," she says, "that's enough for today. Put your training knives back and get out of here."

She stands by the knife block, arms folded.

I let Tarquin and Horatio go first to avoid looking at them, and then I return my training knife to the block.

"Nia, are you okay?" Serana asks me.

My chest feels bruised and crushed. "I'm fine," I choke out. "No worries."

"No worries?" She cocks her head, peering down at

me. "Tarquin better pray not to be paired with me next training session."

I smile at her. "Yeah."

Darius crosses over to us, his eyes wide. "I cannot believe Raphael did that. He just ripped Tarquin off you. Tarquin practically flew in the air like a posh little rag doll."

"I wish I could have seen it," I say ruefully.

Viviane clears her throat, and her expression looks furious. "Nia, I want a word. You two, piss off."

Darius grimaces at me, and he and Serana cross to the door.

Viviane glares down at me. "What was that today?"

"Tarquin lost it."

"I don't care about Tarquin." Viviane narrows her eyes. "He can take care of himself. He's a good fighter. I'm the self-defense instructor, and it's my job to make sure that out in the field, you'll be able to take care of yourself and your allies. And right now, Nia, it doesn't seem likely."

"I've never trained for this," I protest. "I work in a bookstore."

"Really? And when you're on a mission, will you ask them for mercy because you're just a harmless little reader of books?" She shakes her head. "I've never seen such a pathetic display of survival instinct. Tarquin is a big man. How do you beat a big man?"

I raise my eyebrows. "I need to be faster?"

"Don't be absurd. You can't be faster. He's been training from a young age, and you're weak."

I bite my lip "So...I should tire him out. Keep my distance until—"

"Aren't you asthmatic? The longer the fight is, the worse your chances are."

"I should use his weight against him?" I ask desperately.

"How? Scare him with diet tips?"

"I don't know. Why don't you tell me the answer? How do I beat him?"

"With everything you've got!" she snarls.

"Sorry, what does that mean?"

"Why didn't you bite his nose off?"

My jaw drops. "You want me to bite his nose off?"

"He was on top of you. Inches away. All you had to do was lunge forward and bite his nose off. Really grip that nose with your teeth and gnaw at it until you rip it to shreds. Or distract him, then gouge his eye out with your fingernails."

"You wanted me to blind him?"

"I want you to try!" she shouts. "Why didn't you stab him with your hidden knife?"

My eyes widen. "What hidden knife?"

"The one you should have on you." She raises her arms in frustration. "You're small and weak. You should always carry a hidden knife. And some poison. Don't be an idiot, Nia. Raphael is right about one thing. Whether I like you or not, you are one of our only two Sentinels, and you have to stay alive. That means doing *whatever* it takes."

I clear my throat. "Then you won't try to kill me?"

"I will if you prove yourself to be a traitor. Otherwise, no. I dislike you on a personal level, but we can use your skills. And for that, you need to stay alive."

"I do plan to stay alive."

She looks me up and down. "From now on, I'm training you. Classes start every morning at eight, so I want you here at six before breakfast. We'll do one-on-one training."

"Sounds wonderful." The idea of waking up every morning to get yelled at by Viviane sounds like my own personal hell. "For how long?"

"Until. I'm. Satisfied." She turns away.

My heart is thumping as I hurry out of the hall. To my relief, Serana is waiting for me in the stone hallway. "What did she want?" Serana asks.

I sigh. "She wants me to do extra training."

"That's not too bad."

"Every morning at six."

Her jaw drops. "That is literal torture."

"Better than dying, I suppose." I pause to consider it. "Slightly."

* * *

BY THE TIME we arrive at our Fey language class, the rest of the cadets are seated in benches that line a long hall. The stone ceiling is etched with Fey words and gorgeous carvings of vines and flowers. Serana and I slide into some seats.

Amon, the man I met the day before, steps in through a wooden door and walks down the center of the hall. He strokes his blond beard, rings gleaming on his fingers.

"Good morning," he says, his deep voice echoing off the ceiling. "I hope you all did your essays from the last lesson."

"Oh, bollocks," Serana mutters. "I forgot."

"Let's see." He looks around the class until his gaze lands on a student with white-blonde hair. "Moira, if I were to say, 'Sliha, ma an bealach lasifria,' what would you answer?"

"Um…" She gives a frozen smile. "Smola?"

He purses his lips. "That would do. For now. And if I say, 'Tavoi iti chuig an féasta,' what would you answer, Serana?"

Mentally, I translate that he's just invited her to a banquet.

"Uh." Serana fidgets. "I'd say…"

"Le pléksiúr mo stór," I whisper at her, hiding my lips with my hands. *I'd be happy to, sir.*

"Le pleksisigur mo sotror," Serana shouts.

Amon frowns. "I don't know what my uncle has to do with it, and he would never do *that* to a cow. Nia, since you seem to know the answer, what would you say?"

I clear my throat. "Le pléksiúr mo stór. Ani rak gúna nua de dhíth."

He raises an eyebrow and asks me in Fey, "You already know some Fey?"

"A bit," I answer back in Fey. "I've been told my accent

isn't great. I learned from books, and it doesn't have much similarity to other languages I know."

"How many other languages do you know?"

I start counting on my fingers. "English, French, Italian, Spanish, and some Arabic. I like languages, and there were so many language books in the shop where I worked."

"Language is the cloak of the gods," he says.

It's a line from a Fey poem, and I answer with the next line, doing my best to make my accent sound like his. "But silence is their true form."

There's a hint of a smile underneath that beard of his. "Well," he says, "I don't know if you were told, but this is a very basic class. I think you belong with my more advanced students."

CHAPTER 12

I've been summoned to see Raphael. My nerves flutter as I stand outside the aged oak door to his office. It's true that I have magical skills MI-13 needs, but for the past week, something has become clear: I don't have the knack for almost any of the spycraft skills.

I'm only good at one thing: languages. Everything else is a disaster. I can't follow someone without him noticing, or pay attention to specific signals, or plan complex subterfuge missions. When physical strength is required, I get crushed. After every self-defense class, bruises cover my ribs and thighs. During obstacle course training, I almost broke my leg. By this point, most of the cadets are wondering what I'm doing here.

So, the moment Raphael summoned me, I knew what it was about.

Standing outside his door, I'm gripped by a growing certainty that I'm about to be kicked out of the academy.

I hadn't wanted to join the academy at first. And I've spent the past week getting screamed at by Viviane every morning at six. Tarquin and his band of Pendragon bootlickers make a point to leer and mock me at every chance. *There goes the transportation, everyone gets a ride...* And now that I've proven myself bad at everything, everyone agrees I don't belong here.

I should be delighted at the prospect of getting out of this place.

But honestly? I like it here. I have new friends, *plural*. Not only that, but I have the chance to be someone important, to change the world for the better.

And besides that, I get to live in a literal castle.

Here, I'm not just Nia Melisende the lonely, broke bookseller anymore. I have the chance to become a gods-damned *Sentinel*.

And now, standing outside the door, I imagine leaving. Returning to a one-bedroom apartment to live with Mom, lacerating, soul-destroying loneliness my only companion as I watch her pass out every day and take drugs all night, then get sick in the living room.

I really need to knock on his door at this point, because I've been standing here like a weirdo for ten minutes.

Even the entrance to his workspace seems intimidating. Leering gargoyles are carved over the gothic arch, and a metal knocker in the shape of a hand hangs on the door. I force myself to grab the knocker and bang it against the wood.

"Come in." His deep voice penetrates the door.

When I step inside, I find him sitting in a leather chair before his mahogany desk. A fire crackles on the hearth, and light slants through the narrow windows in the stone wall. It's cozy in here, with the warmth from the fireplace and candles burning in a candelabra. The light seems to caress him, highlighting his muscular form and rolled-up sleeves.

I absolutely will not think about what he looked like without a shirt.

He's frowning at a paper on his desk.

"You wanted to see me?" I ask.

There's a strange hum in the room, a ringing in my ears that sets my teeth on edge and prickles my skin with goosebumps.

He looks up, and the firelight flickers in his pale eyes. "My favorite pixie princess, have a seat." He gestures at a high-backed wooden chair across from his desk, and I drop into it. My muscles ache, and I can feel them melting, even against the hard oak.

"I really think I can do better," I blurt. "I know what you think of me. I know I haven't done the best. And I know everyone reckons I shouldn't be here. But I actually believe it's my calling now to help MI-13—"

"What are you talking about?" Raphael stares at me. "Why are you hitting me with this wall of anxiety?"

"I thought you were going to tell me to leave."

He shakes his head. "Not yet."

I swallow hard. "Good. Because I could actually be

quite good at this, you know." I say this with much more confidence than I feel.

"I know. That's why I want you here. I'm not shocked you're behind the others. You've only just joined and already missed two weeks of training. I didn't recruit you because I thought you'd be an amazing fighter. You're here because you're a Sentinel. But we only have a few months before the Culling. And while you have teachers who will teach you to master the basics of fighting, spycraft, and Fey lore, there's no one to teach you how to use your magical powers. Nivene, the only other Sentinel, is too busy in the field to offer you instruction."

I swallow. "So, what will I do?"

"I'm going to teach you."

"*You?*"

His expression is impossible to decipher. "Our personal feelings toward each other are irrelevant. As a spy, your feelings *in general* are irrelevant, and you should ignore them. Only facts matter."

I nod. "You're lucky not to be cursed with feelings."

"We need a Sentinel, and you need training," he goes on. "And I'm the best person to do it."

I take a deep breath. It's a relief to know he'll be able to ignore his hatred of me. "Fine."

Leaning down, he lifts a wooden box off the floor. He places it on the desk, and the hum I'd been hearing grows louder. He tips the box so that its contents face me. A shimmering mist whorls inside the box, its colors constantly shifting. Within, I can barely glimpse the silhouette of something spherical. A ball, perhaps.

I frown at it. "That's the veil."

"It's a very weak imitation of the veil. It won't kill you if you touch it, but it will hurt. Can you hear it?"

"As soon as I came in," I say with a nod. "There's a hum and a slight prickle on the back of my arms."

"Good. Now you need to take the ball out of the box. You'll need to use your magic."

I take a deep breath. "I'm not sure how I did it before."

"Summon your power to disable the veil and grab the ball. Focus on the feeling of the magic. The sensations. Think about the noise and the prickle on your skin."

He makes it sound so simple. Closing my eyes, I focus on the hum in my ears and try to clear my mind.

The vibration fills my body, and the hair rises on my arms. I open my eyes and relax my muscles, trying to channel all of my thoughts into that small swirling surface, to the feel of the magic thrumming over my skin. The world fades around me. Is it working? When I reach for the ball, my skin buzzes, and the magic seems to slide toward me. As I stare, I can see how it all ties together, strands of magic woven into a net. A web of delicate strands that could be untangled. And if I just lean forward—

As soon as my fingers touch it, an explosion of agony runs up my arm. I scream and pull back.

Raphael watches me, a line between his eyebrows. He

stands and moves closer to me, sitting on the edge of the desk. "Give me your hand," he commands.

I comply, and he traces the skin on my fingers, then brushes his fingers over my wrist. "Does this help?"

Sparks trail in the wake of his touch, and heat pulses through my muscles, making my breath catch.

"Healing magic," I whisper, flushing. His magic feels disturbingly pleasurable, radiating through my body. I like the way his hand feels against mine more than I should. I want to close my eyes and lean back in the chair. I want his hands—

I stop the thought before it goes any further.

I glance up at his silver eyes, and for a moment, it feels like he can read every one of my secrets.

I yank my arm away. "I'm *fine*. I don't need your magic."

"Your expression says otherwise." He draws back.

"Okay."

"You're obviously in pain. I can read it easily in your grimace. Are you aware that your words are often at odds with your body language?"

I tense. "What are you talking about?"

"And now you look like you want to kill me."

"I'm perfectly calm," I say through clenched teeth.

"You tell everyone what they want to hear. It's not the worst skill for a spy. You're good at knowing what people want you to say. Your language is curious and relaxed with Tana. You reassure Serana and help her stay organized. With Darius, you flatter him because his insecurity demands it. You interpret what people need, and you give it to them. That's good. But you will need to control your facial expressions in order to be convincing, be aware of your emotions and master them."

Surprise flickers through me. "You've been watching me awful closely, it seems."

"It's my job to watch my cadets. I'd imagine that when you're with your mother, there was yet another version of Nia, wasn't there?"

My nostrils flare. "What does that have to do with anything?"

"With your mother, you are more accommodating. You assure her that you'll take care of her. You're the parent. You never argue, but can she see how much you resent her deep down? That you're tired of being someone who picks up the pieces of her chaotic life and tries to put them back together?"

"Can we go back to training?" I say acidly.

He leans back in his chair. "This *is* training. Emotions get in the way of your concentration and disrupt your magic. Besides, in any situation undercover, you will need to understand yourself and control your emotions. You don't want the Fey to know what you're thinking. You need to be aware of what you're conveying to people. Understand your true self, then hide it from the world so it can't be used against you. And once you understand yourself, you can also master your emotions." He sighs. "Okay. Let's back up. When you entered the veil with the fugitives, what were you thinking?

"I was scared."

"Okay, but it seems like you were able to suppress your fear enough to summon your magic. Try to close your eyes and remember that moment. Did you sense your magic as you went into the veil?"

I shut my eyes and try to remember, recalling the fear and sorrow. My chest tightens. "No. I mostly felt fear. And regret. I was trying to look after the fugitives, and I missed Vena running away. The patrol was about to grab us, and I already saw what they'd do if they caught us. They were so brutal, and I was frightened of them."

"And you don't remember feeling a connection to magic?"

"Not at that moment."

Rage—when I think of the Fey hunting down little barefoot Malo, I feel a stab of rage.

When I open my eyes, the hum is gone, the prickling on my arms has faded, and my chest is flushed.

I stare at the box. The veil is still there, but its power is gone. I lean forward, bracing myself for pain, but my fingers easily pass through the mist. I grab the ball.

My hand still in the box, I look up at Raphael for his reaction.

Just as a smile ghosts over his lips, a torrent of agony blazes through me. I yell, releasing my grip, and drop the ball. It crashes to the floor. In the next heartbeat, my hands are in his, and his magic is whispering over my skin, sending heat pulsing through my muscles. My heart races, and I let out a long, shaky breath. "Thanks."

His eyebrows lift. "It was a good start."

I pull my hands free and hug myself. I shiver, chilled to the bone, and my teeth start to chatter. It feels as if the cold is biting at my skin. "Why is it so cold here?" I glance at the fireplace, where the flames are still blazing.

"Using your magic drains energy from your body very rapidly," Raphael says. "That means it steals your body heat. Didn't it happen last time you used your powers?"

Thinking back, I vaguely remember the icy wind, the sharp drop in temperature. "Yes, it did, actually."

"It was a good first try," Raphael says. "Your powers are unstable, but we'll work on that. Any idea why it stopped working?"

"No."

It's a lie. It stopped working the second I looked at him. My power worked through fear and anger, and when I looked at him, I felt something else. As much as I hate to admit it to myself, I wanted to impress him. Long ago, he dismissed me. And now, I only want to prove him wrong.

CHAPTER 13

Our professor, Wrythe Pendragon, stands at the front of a stone room wearing the long black robes reserved for instructors and a gold torc. His sleeves are embroidered with what looks like an unsettling family crest—a shield with a crown and a severed head in the center. He's not *just* our professor, but he's also Avalon Tower's Seneschal—the headmaster here and a knight of the Round Table. Along with Viviane and Raphael, he comprises the most high-ranking members of MI-13 who meet in secret to plan our missions. And unfortunately, he seems to hate me.

I lean my chin on my wrist and watch the other cadets file in, taking their places on benches on either side of the hall. Light spills in through diamond-pane windows and streaks across the floor.

Wrythe's shoes clack on the flagstones as he strides between the benches. He pivots, and his extravagant blond mustache twitches. He adjusts his monocle and stares up at the ceiling. "Magic. The Fey's biggest advantage over humankind. And, as my brilliant niece Ginevra says, the gravest threat to us as humans."

Ginevra, the gorgeous woman who'd been in Raphael's room. My mind starts to wander as I obsess about what he and Ginevra were up to that morning.

I try to concentrate, but I'm exhausted. This morning, Viviane was particularly brutal, putting me through a series of exercises aimed at strengthening my lungs. With my sessions with Viviane, regular classes, equestrian training, written assignments, and memorizing France's geography, I've scarcely slept in the past three weeks. On top of that, I had three training sessions with Raphael where he kept telling me to ignore my emotions. I was genuinely trying to ignore them around him because his alluring scent and powerful, sun-kissed forearms make me feel crazy.

Slowly, day by day, I'm becoming better. Now, I can disable the tiny training veil for almost ten seconds—as long as I don't look into Raphael's deep silver eyes and get distracted.

My knowledge of the Fey language is growing by the day, and my accent doesn't make Tana visibly wince anymore. As for my fighting skills? Well, they're still rubbish. I'm weak and small, and bruises cover my body.

I blink, realizing I haven't been listening to the Seneschal. Instead, I've been staring at one of the gargoyles above the doorframe.

Wrythe is pacing, his hands behind his back. His robe is open, and he's wearing a velvet waistcoat and a blue, star-flecked cravat. "Once, the Fey possessed primal magic, a godlike power that threatened the human world. The ancient Fey could perform the deadliest of sorceries. And what were the five primal powers that the ancient Fey used to possess?" He looks around at the raised hands, squinting into his monocle. "The five *primal* powers, anyone?"

I don't even bother raising my hand anymore. Wrythe never calls on me. He's Tarquin's uncle and apparently shares his nephew's distaste for me. When his stare occasionally meets mine, he wrinkles his nose as if he smells something rank.

He points to a ginger man named Valen, who immediately flushes red. "The ancient Fey could polymorph other creatures. Turn people to frogs or ants, or whatever. They could conjure items into existence, which they mostly used to create fool's gold that would later disappear. They could control minds, pushing people to act without their consent. They could make people fall in love with them. And...uh..." His eyes widen as he forgets the fifth legendary magical power.

"*Uh*, Valen?" Wrythe's mustache twitches. "What sort of power is *uh*? Is it very dangerous, the magical ritual of *uh*?"

I hear sniggering from Horatio, Tarquin, and his gang on the other side of the room.

Wrythe shakes his head in disgust. "And the fifth primal power is"—he pivots—"Tarquin?"

Across the room, Tarquin folds his arms. "Aeromancy. Control of the weather."

"Exactly." Wrythe nods in approval. "Aeromancy, amoromancy—also known as love magic—polymorphism, mind control, and conjuration. Those were the five primal powers. Merlin, for example, could reputably control the weather. As an aeromancer, he received the top rank in Avalon Tower. But after he died, the Fey powers began to fade. King Auberon blames the humans for it. Progress and technology. That is partly the reason for the Fey invasion, according to him. No Fey has been able to use any of the five powers for over a millennium."

Darius mutters to me, "Except the Dream Stalker."

Wrythe whips around. "Mr. Merton, was there something incredibly important that you had to share with the group?"

Darius clears his throat. "The Dream Stalker, grandson of Queen Morgan. There are rumors that the Dream Stalker can not only control dreams, but also the weather."

Wrythe blanches. "We don't speak of the Fey prince. Are you a *moron?*" His words echo off the vaulted ceiling.

Darius shrinks in his seat.

"Don't ever think of him," Wrythe continues. "Don't speak about him. Don't bring him up. If you think about him, you might dream about him. And once you dream of him, you invite him in. Then the Dream Stalker will turn your world into a nightmare. He will torture you in every way imaginable. Everyone here knows this should be avoided. Except, apparently, you and your friend, Ms. Melisende."

Tarquin turns around to look at us, his eyes twinkling with clear joy.

A cold shudder spreads over my skin like webs of frost. I want to ask more about this Dream Stalker, but obviously, that isn't allowed.

"Most magic these days is a fragment of the Fey's early powers." Wrythe resumes pacing the class. "Simple illusions. Glamour. Mild telepathy. Some agents in MI-13 have these powers as well, now that we allow...all sorts. All sorts." He repeats that last phrase incredulously, then huffs an awkward laugh. "It is important to note that the Fey should only have one power at a time." His voice booms off the arched ceiling. "When a Fey has more than one power, the magic becomes weak and unstable. Muddled. Diametric magic is magic that interferes with itself. In the Fey realm, those with diametric magic are treated with contempt, as they usually are driven mad. They become dangerous and deranged, ravening idiots who will attempt to feast on humans and Fey alike. Cannibals."

He turns, pacing in the opposite direction. "Now that the Fey powers have weakened, the Fey are beginning to rely on human technology. What is the best example of that reliance, Tarquin?"

"The train of Gobannos," Tarquin says with a half-smile.

"That's right." Wrythe nods. "The train of Gobannos is part of the status quo agreements. A train that connects the independent, human-controlled south of France with the occupied north. Fey sometimes use it to import human goods. And a few rare times, we've smuggled agents onto that train, gaining access to the heart of occupied France."

He turns around and looks at me, his eyes narrowing. "Ms. Melisende. Since you've been paying such close attention, I would be happy to hear your opinion. Suppose you were an agent on that train, on your way to a gala. How would you present yourself to anyone who starts talking to you? What identity would you adopt?"

Shit. I clear my throat, trying to recall the texts I'd read two nights ago. "I would present myself as a baroness of one of the distant Fey isles in their realm, such as Saxa or Collibus. The majority of Fey aren't closely familiar with those two families, so they wouldn't question it. To fortify my cover, I'd come with at least two additional agents, one masquerading as my footman and the other as my personal secretary. They would be able to gather additional information from the common areas."

"A detailed cover." Wrythe raises an eyebrow. "And for the additional agents, perhaps you could use your friends, Ms. O'Rourke and Mr. Merton."

"Sure," I say warily. Serana and Darius shift uncomfortably. I'm starting to sense a trap.

"And then you would find that those from the Fey regions of Saxa and Collibus are almost never invited to the big galas. And in fact, Fey from Collibus *never* ride the train because they are backward, unsophisticated, and distrust human inventions. Your cover would instantly be blown. Not only have you got yourself captured, but your friends are now being tortured to death, and it's all your fault. How do you feel now, when you are being forced to watch your friends carved up to betray our secrets? They would break Ms. O'Rourke's fingers one by one. Shatter Mr. Merton's teeth with a mallet. Slowly flay the three of you alive until you told them everything you knew about Camelot. All because you had better things to do than to pay attention in class. Oh, *dear*. Not very good, is it?"

I feel nauseated, fixing my eyes on the flagstones. When Raphael asked me to join the academy, he didn't mention the possibility of torture.

"And this is why we have this class." Wrythe's voice booms over the hall as he addresses the rest of the room. "It doesn't matter that Ms. Melisende is barely paying attention to the lives of her friends. Her job, *thankfully*, is only to get a skilled agent through the barrier. But if the rest of you don't know *every little detail* of our enemies' culture, you *will* be found out. And your friends will suffer with you on the rack."

Everyone in the hall is staring at me like I just murdered someone.

The Seneschal puffs his chest. "Now, Ms. Melisende, please tell me—"

The large oak door at one end of the hall groans open, and Raphael and Amon enter the classroom. Wrythe bustles over to them, and Raphael leans in, speaking to him quietly.

Serana exhales. "That absolute bellend. Your answer was much better than anything anyone else could have come up with right now, and you're still new here."

"I missed some important details," I admit miserably.

"Only because you're stretched so thin! You're barely sleeping, Nia."

"Nia Melisende." Raphael's voice echoes over the room, and his piercing gaze bores into me.

Amon looks worried, and Wrythe's face is red with fury, jaw clenched.

Raphael nods at the door. "Come on. You have a mission."

CHAPTER 14

*T*he evening breeze is cold and whips at my hair. My horse, Dickinson, trots through the main street of a tiny village in the south of France, not far from the veil. Gas lamps cast warm light over stone buildings lining a cobbled road. Around us, colorful wood shutters are closed to the night.

This morning, Raphael received an urgent signal. A contact in occupied Fey France sent word about a possible invasion into South France, but the detailed intel had to be delivered in person.

In enemy territory.

The other Sentinel is off on another mission and can't be summoned back quickly enough. And that's how I ended up here, staring at Raphael's crisp white shirt and broad shoulders as he rides in front of me.

Two other agents flank him. On his right is a man

named Arzel, with long, flowing black hair and pale skin. Arzel wears a hunter's cap and a bow and quiver as part of his hunting disguise.

And on his other side is a demi-Fey woman named Freya, dressed in a Fey-style hunting jacket like mine, trousers, and tall boots. The moonlight streams over her bronze skin and wavy auburn hair. Like Arzel and me, she's also armed with a bow.

Graceful and sophisticated as she looks, she spent the boat ride next to me, vomiting over the side. We are sisters in nausea now. The past twelve hours blended into a series of rushed, nerve-racking moments. It began with a quick briefing in Raphael's office before the mission, then seven hours on a boat, during which Freya and I bonded between heaves. After horseback riding through the south of France for two hours, we're nearly at the veil, and nerves are making my heart race.

Up ahead, the three agents guide their horses past a fountain in a village square. The sound of the fountain's burbling mingles with the buzz of the nearby veil. The closer we draw to it, the more nervous I become.

When we reach the end of the village, we guide our horses out into fields. From here, I have a full view of the veil, and my heart speeds up. Sunflowers sway gently in the night breeze, bathed in the glow of the magical mist. At night, it shimmers like moonlight with an eerie violet tinge. So beautiful, so deadly.

Raphael pulls his mount to a halt and looks back at us.

Beyond him, the fog swirls, and magic buzzes over my skin, raising the hair on the back of my neck. I still have no idea if I can control the veil in person like I did before. What if that was a one-off?

My stomach flutters as Raphael's gaze lands on me and he guides his horse closer. The shimmer of the veil sparks off the hilt of his sword. A wayward lock of dark hair falls before his eyes. "You understand your role here, right? Open the veil and nothing else," he says quietly. "Wait just on the other side for us to return from Allevur."

"I know."

"Under no circumstances should you leave your spot. You must be ready to escape back through at any moment —with us, ideally, but without us, if necessary."

"Raphael, I know. Do you honestly think I'd want to wander around occupied Fey France by myself?"

He studies my face carefully, and my cheeks heat with the intensity of his scrutiny.

At last, he says, "The glamour is remarkable."

Serana was the one who glamoured me—that, it turned out, was her magical power. My irises had been glamoured to shimmer with golden flecks. The spell left my eyes dry and stinging, and they keep tearing up. Serana also lengthened my ears, disguising me as a full-blooded Fey.

Raphael's gaze brushes down my body, inspecting my disguise for any flaws. When he nods, I assume he approves of the tight trousers and riding boots, and the tight jacket that binds my ribs. I've also got a knife holstered around my thigh—used by the Fey to clean the deer they kill.

"Now, let's try it one more time," he says, then asks in Fey, "What are you doing here?"

I take a deep breath. "I'm part of a hunting party."

"No hesitating. That little pause means you will die. Again. Why are you here?"

"We're hunting," I say again, this time rushing it. The Fey have excellent night vision. To them, a hunting party is a perfect night out. "There are four of us."

"Don't give more information than they ask for." His silver eyes narrow. "What are you hunting?"

"Red deer in the Broc Forest."

"And your name?"

A short intake of breath. "Cyrania Gallowen."

"You hesitated again. Now you're hanging from the gallows or being tortured in the dungeons."

"Is this supposed to help me relax?"

"Where are the others in your hunting party?"

My heart races, as if this is a real interrogation. "I lost track of the rest when they went off chasing a deer. My old horse couldn't keep up."

Raphael frowns. "Fine. But avoid speaking at all if you can. Your accent is still flawed."

My nostrils flare.

He looks around us, scanning the field for activity. Seemingly satisfied, he guides his horse toward the veil. I follow after him, and the barrier's immense power thrums and crackles over my skin.

My stomach drops. All of this suddenly seems like a huge mistake. I'm supposed to disable this huge wall of magic? At this point, I've done it once by accident in real time. Sure, in Raphael's office, I can pretty consistently disarm the veil-in-a-box, but this isn't a tiny little practice barrier.

This is *the* veil. The god of barriers.

If I lose control over my power, I could kill myself and everyone on my team.

My heart thuds hard against my ribs. Raphael is absolutely certain this mission is necessary—that we're retrieving vital information that might save thousands of lives. But am I really the best option here?

Up ahead, the veil whorls, iridescent. The buzzing is so loud, it's like a banshee screaming in my ear.

A few feet from the veil, Raphael halts his horse. I urge Dickinson forward and join him. Wisps of the veil whip around us.

"I do hope you're ready," he says.

"Of course I am," I lie. "We've practiced this."

He nods at the barrier. "Go on."

I slide off Dickinson. Before me, the shimmering mist swirls, deadly and beautiful, stretching as far as the eye can see in both directions. This wall was woven by a group of powerful veil mages, and I feel the skill of their magic washing over me.

My heart races as I try to summon my magic. In

Raphael's office, I've discovered it has a slight warmth to it, like hot honey moving through my chest. I associate it with the color red. Sometimes, I see it in my mind.

But now, nothing is happening. No heating of magic, no silencing of the hum, no burst of red in my thoughts.

Raphael said we needed to be aware of our emotions and how they interact with magic. He thinks I need to suppress my emotions, but I'm not sure that's what works for me. I think my emotions make it happen.

I glance at the three agents staring at me. Raphael's expression is inscrutable, but the other two look worried and impatient. Freya is basically grimacing. Of course they're panicking. They're putting their lives in the hands of an untrained cadet who didn't even know Camelot existed a few months ago.

I look again at Raphael's perfect face and remember how he ghosted me. How he couldn't wait to get away from me. *Isn't she trash, though? She and her mother.*

Anger slides through my blood.

I turn back to the barrier and breathe. Doing the opposite of what Raphael taught me, I focus on my feelings. Even when he saw me in France, Raphael still thought I was just a champagne-swilling shit-show like Mom. Trash.

The veil still hums, stronger than ever.

All those feelings are layers. Thoughts that I disguise as emotions. I need something pure, raw. I peel the thoughts away, searching deeper. What do I *feel*?

I'm scared of failing—but I'm also scared of succeeding. I want to help fight the Fey. I want to help these people so that there's actually a point to my life.

Not good enough. The barrier keeps humming. I shut my eyes, searching even deeper, where my emotions are at their most visceral.

There's a certain constant heat, a pulsing need that I can't put into words. An anger roiling beneath the surface.

I'm always the one who picks up the pieces. I take care of things when everyone falls apart around me. I live in the shadows, trying to make things go smoothly. And who comes to help me in the night when I'm sick and can't breathe? When I'm calling for help, and there's no answer?

The humming goes silent.

I open my eyes. "Now." My voice is calm and commanding. I walk over to Dickinson, take his reins, and lead him through the silent veil. Seeing me move, the other three follow.

Together, we pass through the pearly mist of the veil, and I let out a long, slow breath. I close my eyes, inwardly thanking the gods. When I open my eyes again, we're on the other side. Fields spread out around us, and a few abandoned, roofless houses dot the moonlit landscape.

I relax my hold, and the barrier begins to crackle and buzz again behind us. Cold runs through my blood, replacing the magic's buzz, and ice slides through my bones. I hug myself, shivering, teeth chattering. This always happens after I use my magic.

"Well, that was bloody impressive." Arzel smiles at me. "Well done, Nia."

Shivering, I rub my hands together, trying to warm them. The air stings my cheeks. I mount Dickinson again, hoping that some of the horse's heat will warm my body.

"We have to move." Freya looks up at the sky. "We need to get to Allevur in a few hours, and we have a long way to go."

"I'll be here," I mutter.

Raphael shakes his head. "No, this location is too exposed." He points to a grove of trees on a hill. "There. You can take cover between the trees. We're heading that way. And we'll be gone several hours, so that will provide some cover if it rains."

The night wind whips at my hair as we ride toward a gently rolling hill and the grove at the top. In the distance, a darkened village looms in the shadows. Probably abandoned, like so many after the war. But if I remember correctly, there are some people who still live around here.

Just as we're reaching the base of the hill, Raphael mutters, "Bollocks."

My heart skips a beat. A group of horsemen gallops out of the grove toward us, wearing the blue cloaks of Fey soldiers.

My first reflex is to turn my horse and ride away as quickly as possible, but that's exactly the wrong impulse. We are, after all, prepared for exactly this kind of scenario. We're just a group of Fey on a hunt. In my bag are forged papers declaring that my name is Cyrania Gallowen. As the border patrol nears, I repeat the name in my mind until it becomes a strange jumble of meaningless syllables.

"Good evening," Raphael calls out in pristine Fey. He looks perfectly relaxed, smiling. "How goes the night?"

"It's good enough," the Fey in the lead says gruffly, scrutinizing us. His long ears poke through black hair, and his dark eyebrows are knitted together. Flecks of copper dance in his eyes as he scans us. His uniform is slightly different than the rest—the buttons larger, three golden patches on his shoulder instead of two. The old Nia wouldn't have even noticed it. But after a few weeks in Avalon Tower, I already know what it means. He is a sergeant, and he's probably been in King Auberon's army for decades. Full-blooded Fey live hundreds of years.

"My cousin was thinking of joining the army," Raphael says, gesturing lazily at Arzel. "I told him that you don't accept just anyone. That the king's army has standards. Isn't that right?"

"I'm old enough and large enough to join," Arzel snaps.

Raphael snorts. "He is barely fifty and has never slept with a woman."

Two of the other patrol officers smirk. The sergeant's face, however, is stony. "The king's army needs every volunteer at this time of trial to exterminate those without loyalty. We must protect ourselves from our enemies within and without. May his light shine brightly."

His voice is deep and melodious. There's something in it that sounds ancient, something that sends a shiver of dread up my spine.

"May his light shine brightly," Raphael repeats.

The sergeant's gaze flicks over us, taking in our outfits and weapons. "Hunting?"

"With nothing to show for it so far," Raphael says ruefully. "I don't suppose you've spotted red deer?"

"And why would you be hunting with a sword, pray tell?" The sergeant prods his horse closer to us, his coppery eyes locked on Raphael.

"He can't aim to save his life," says Arzel with a yawn. "More risk of killing us than a deer. So we allow him to slit the deer's throat after we catch it. He does like to feel useful, poor chap."

"I see." The sergeant's eyes flick to me. He stops as close to me as possible, leaning closer. His dark hair hangs down to a square jawline, giving his face a gaunt appearance. "I've been searching for demi-Fey vermin. You haven't seen any, have you?"

Can he hear the way my heart is beating? Does he see the hairs on the back of my neck rising? He inspects me as if the glamour spell is slipping. Does he know I'm demi-Fey?

"None at all," Raphael says. "Thankfully."

"You are a beauty," the sergeant mutters to me. "A Fey rose."

My eyebrows flick up with shock. *What?* I nervously smile, hiding my fear.

He bites his lip, looking me over. "Do you really want to spend such a glorious night with such tedious company?"

"My sister doesn't speak much," Raphael says. "She's not very bright. I'm afraid."

"Is that right?" The sergeant leans in closer to me, a smile spreading on his face. "That's fine with me. I like women who don't talk a lot. What do you say? Want to join me on a little night patrol, just the two of us?"

I keep smiling, letting just a little of my nervousness show. I try to emulate Tana's accent as I say, "That sounds wonderful, but I promised my brother I would stick with him. My father worries for me at night."

His eyes flash with a hungry look. For a few seconds, he doesn't respond, and I *know* that he spotted my accent. Panic crackles through my veins.

He sighs at last. "Your father is right. Such a pretty little thing should always have an escort. Bad people out here. Bad sort of men, so close to the border. Demi-Fey among them."

"That's why we have people like you," I say demurely. "To protect us."

"That's right."

"May his light shine brightly," I say.

He blinks and nods. "May his light shine brightly."

He rides off, and I let out a shaky breath. We ride on, trying to look casual.

Once they're far enough, Arzel exhales. "That was close."

"Too close," Raphael says. He looks at me strangely. "You did well. Your accent sounded much better."

I let out a long, shaky breath. "Thanks."

We ride into the grove of trees, and their gnarled branches arch over us, welcoming. In here, the moonlight flecks the mossy earth with silver.

Raphael turns to look at me, his eyes bright in the darkness. "No matter what, stay hidden until we return. If we're not back by sunrise, go back through the veil."

CHAPTER 15

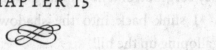

*T*ime crawls.

From the grove of trees, I keep checking the fields, looking for silhouettes on horseback. I glance at my pocketwatch to check the time. Not even midnight yet. The temperature has plummeted, and I wish I could start a fire. But that's out of the question. I hug myself, my breath steaming in the cool air.

My stomach rumbles. Nearby, Dickinson blinks at me, his eyes as black as his hair. Exhausted, I slide onto the mossy earth. The ground smells rich, a loamy scent that wraps around me. The moonlight streams through tree branches to dapple the earth with silver. The sound of chirping crickets is like a lullaby.

Reaching into my leather pack, I pull out some bread and cheese. I shove a chunk of cheese into the bread, and I bite into it. As I eat, I glimpse a firefly trailing through the air.

The rumble of incoming horses' hooves startles me. I shove my food back in the bag and cross to the edge of the grove. Fear spirals through me when I see who's thundering closer to me. It's not the other agents. It's the horny Fey sergeant, and he's aiming *right* for me.

I slink back into the shadows, but I can hear him galloping up the hill.

I run back to Dickinson, but just as I'm mounting, a deep voice stops me in my tracks. "You! You waited for me, didn't you, little minx?"

I freeze and turn slowly to face him. His coppery eyes gleam in the shadows, bright as a wolf's. He smiles at me, his canines flashing. "All alone now? I thought I smelled a lady's scent in the grove as I patrolled again."

I blink demurely. "My brother and the rest were chasing a large red stag. I was slowing them down. They should be back soon."

His smile is predatory and chilling.

"Not too soon, I hope." He dismounts from his horse and prowls close to me, the wind catching in his dark hair. "You are familiar, of course, with the rights of a Fey knight."

My mouth goes dry. No, I'm not familiar with the rights of a Fey knight, but I can guess it's something about taking whatever women they want.

In the hollows of my mind, my thoughts are screeching at me to run or to fight. I think of my knives, one in the boot, one on my belt, and a sharpened hair pin tucked in my locks. He won't expect me to attack him. I'm fast and—

I can almost hear Viviane. *You'll never be strong enough or fast enough to stab a large, trained man. Never.* Then what should I do?

Fight him with everything you have, Imaginary Viviane shouts at me.

And what do I have? I'm good at understanding what people want. What they need. Raphael pointed that out to me. I show people the version of me they want to see, but I need to work on making it convincing. Already, I've intuited that he likes innocence. Raphael told the sergeant my father wanted to keep me safe, and that sparked something in his eyes. He wants a pure, untouched woman. A shrinking violet.

In that case, I'll give him the opposite of what he wants.

"Of course I know the rights of a Fey knight." I smile at him. "I've been with many. And some squires."

He frowns. "What?"

"At least, I *think* they were knights and squires. It's not like I asked for the official paperwork." I shrug. "A man is a man." I move closer to him and touch my lips. "But I really should be more careful. One of them had something...I think it's called trench mouth?"

His nose wrinkles. "I see."

"I learned all sorts of tricks from a brothel in Ys." I touch the side of his face, grinning maniacally.

Triggered by my anxiety, the voice in my head start clamoring. *You're dirt, a disgrace. Diseased. Get back. Get back!*

I try to ignore the hallucinations, keeping my face still and the smile on my lips. The sergeant's face twists in disgust as I gently run the tips of my fingers down his cheek.

The voice keeps screeching. *You're disgusting. Just like that whore in Allevur. I slit her throat.*

I blink, the sentence disconcerting me, but it goes on. *Allevur will be a bloodbath again tonight after the ambush, if that traitor Varris can be believed.*

The sergeant's lip curls. "You're disgusting. Just like that whore in Allevur."

I yank my hand away, startled. He'd just said the words out loud that I'd heard in my mind.

Cold anger etches his face. He looks furious. Violent. My instincts are telling me to get the hell away from him as fast as possible—especially since he apparently slit the last "whore's" throat.

"Well, I suppose that's too bad," I blurt. "I'll have to find another man to satisfy my needs."

Panic tightens my chest as I take a quick step back and rush to mount Dickinson. I spur him on, and he lurches to a gallop through the grove. I cling to his reins as we race between the trees. I'm not exactly sure where I'm going, only that I need to get away from the sergeant. A low branch thrashes at my face as Dickinson thunders toward the road. His hooves pound on the dirt, kicking up dust around me. I focus on the earthen road as we gallop, the wind shrieking in my ears. I've never ridden a horse so fast, but I'm charging along the road that Raphael took earlier.

I glance back to where we came from, the border with unoccupied France. In the distance, the veil shimmers with pearly light. I can't return to the meeting point. Raphael told me I should get back through the veil and wait on the other side, but something stops me.

Allevur will be a bloodbath again tonight after the ambush if that traitor Varris can be believed.

I don't know anyone called Varris, and it's strange for my mind to conjure unknown names. But Allevur is where Raphael and the rest of the group are headed.

What if I'm not just hearing random voices?

An idea takes root in the hollows of my mind—I heard his words before he said them out loud. The exact phrase. *You're disgusting. Just like that whore in Allevur.*

The voice in my thoughts, then out of his mouth.

In the past, things the voices told me sometimes turned out to be true. Once, a voice whispered to me that the bookshop manager was having an affair with one of the other employees. Then I accidentally walked in on them in the office, his pants pulled down to his ankles, his pale butt thrusting back and forth. Another time, my mind conjured a voice about a customer in the shop, something about stealing books—two very expensive books, special editions signed by the author. Then I caught him stealing them, trying to run straight out the front door.

So what if what I've heard wasn't just nonsense conjured by a stressed mind?

What if it was magic that I shouldn't dismiss?

Because if my voices can predict the future, there might be a bloodbath scheduled tonight in Allevur.

It's a small Fey village, built on the ruins of a town after the invasion. Allevur is centered around a train station, some shops and farms, and the tavern where Raphael is supposed to meet the contact. But it's not a big city. Most of the French abandoned it during the war.

The ambush—was that planned for Raphael and the MI-13 agents?

I'm not sure how to get a message to Raphael. Even if I race after them on horseback the entire way, I'm *hours* behind. They'll get to Allevur within the hour, maybe less. There's no way I can catch up with them. All I can do is—

The train of Gobannos.

It goes through Allevur. That's the second stop in the occupied zone, arriving from the south. The Seneschal made us memorize the maps of this region, and also commit the whole train schedule to memory. There's a train leaving the border station at midnight, reaching Allevur at one in the morning.

I steer Dickinson west, heading for the train. As I ride, I pull out my pocket watch, and my pulse roars. I've got ten minutes to get there.

I spur on my horse, shouting words of encouragement as he gallops. Apparently, he's relieved to find that his timid rider has grown more daring, and he seems to relish the fast run across the road. Now his hooves hardly touch the ground. One thing is clear: the riding lessons at Avalon are paying off.

The wind tears at my hair, and I lean over Dickinson's neck, urging him to run faster. The dirt road carves through corn fields, and I race through a derelict village. Wooden shutters bang in the breeze, but in the distance, I see the flickering warmth of gas lamps. Balconies hang over the street, and the windows are barred to the night. A clocktower rises high above the town, and when I glance at it, my breath catches.

The bells chime twelve times. Midnight.

In the distance, I hear chugging and groaning along tracks. Steam billows, and my heart sinks.

I've missed it.

I'm gasping, trying to catch my breath. My chest tightens, but I urge Dickinson on, and we race to the station. The building is stone, painted white. Someone shouts at me from the platform, but my eyes are on the train. An open field runs alongside it. Gripping Dickinson's reins, we race to catch up.

The train of Gobannos is enormous, with a black and crimson engine. Billows of steam burst into the air above it, and the mist snakes around the train. I've never seen a train like this, one with shimmering cars that gleam with silver and gold, others so dark they seem to suck in all the light around them. How many train cars? Thirty? Forty? Impossible to count.

Dickinson gallops faster, and my chest thuds at the

sight of a boulder in our way. But the horse is already leaping high above it, and for a second, it almost seems like we're flying—and then we drop. I bite my tongue as we hit the ground and taste blood.

But we've reached the train, and I'm about five carriages from the rear. It's accelerating now, so I can't waste another moment.

All of this seems mad, an impossible feat the old Nia would never even dream of doing.

My heart is in my throat as I lean toward the rungs on the side of the train. I try to clutch at a ladder jutting out of a carriage, my fingers brushing it, but it's already gone.

The carriage moves ahead. I've got four more cars before I've lost it.

I manage to grip the next one, but my feet catch in the stirrups. I lurch free and nearly fall off the horse. I've almost lost my chance now, and Dickinson is spooked. He veers sideways, distancing us from the train.

"No, no, no, come on, Dickinson," I yell, pulling him toward the train again.

Two more carriages. But I don't reach out. I let the penultimate carriage go ahead as I free my right foot from the stirrup. Then the left. I'm gripping the saddle with one hand, wondering if I'm about to die.

Last carriage. I swing my hand and grab a rung. The force of the train yanks me off my mount.

My breath stops as for a few seconds, I dangle above the ground. Then I manage to grab the rung with my free hand and put my feet on the bottom rung. Clinging, shaking, I look back. Adrenaline courses through me.

Dickinson is already dozens of yards away, staring after me.

And I'm on the train of Gobannos, hurtling deep into Fey France.

Exactly as Raphael told me not to do.

CHAPTER 16

The wind shrieks in my ears and yanks at my hair. As I cling for dear life to the ladder, the train pistons chug beneath me.

I can't stay like this, hanging off the train. If the Fey spot me, I'll instantly be recognized as a spy. I glance down at the earth speeding beneath my feet. I need to force myself to climb up.

In the whipping wind, it's hard to convince myself to let go. My muscles agree and are locked rigid. Finally, I force myself to unclench my left fist. Almost instantly, I feel myself veering off to the right, buffeted by the wind and the train's rattling pace.

I grasp at the next rung on the ladder, and then, with a quick upward shift, move my right hand as well. Fear cascades through me as I climb one rung at a time. From above, a burst of hot steam washes over me, taking my breath away.

At the bookshop, I often climbed the ladder to reach shelves all the way at the top. But the ladder wasn't juddering in a windstorm like this, assailed by bursts of hot steam. And I didn't have to worry about certain death if I fell.

Fear rakes at my chest.

Another rung. And another. At last, I reach the top of the carriage, clinging to the metal bars to steady myself. Beneath me, the train rattles over the tracks, churning fast. Desperately, I search for a way *inside* the carriage. There's nothing—the carriage's roof is solidly shut—but then I notice a trapdoor.

Unfortunately, it's on the next car over.

I grip the rungs on the roof tightly as the train races through a darkened village.

With a hammering heart, I crawl across the carriage roof, flattening myself on the smooth surface. Then, on my hands and knees, I shift forward, grabbing for any handholds I can find—metal braces and brackets on the roof to stop me from falling.

The train tracks turns before I can grip a bracket, an almost insignificant bend, but for me, gravity shifts, and I tumble to the side, hands scraping desperately for purchase. I start to slide off the left side of the train, and then my fingertips brush something solid, a bar jutting from the roof. Grunting, I pull myself to the center of the carriage again, and the train chugs on.

Gritting my teeth, I crawl a few feet more to the edge of the carriage.

My stomach swoops at the sight of the gap between the cars and the ground racing by beneath the train. The chasm yawns before me. Between the carriages, the rails flash by with impossible speed. There's only one way across—I have to jump. And if I fall, I'll be crushed to a pulp beneath the train. My pulse thunders.

Steam billows around me. I gasp, inhaling it, and the acrid taste fills my mouth. The steam drenches my clothes, mingling with my sweat.

When it clears up, I force myself to crouch at the edge, and then I shuffle back a few steps. Before I can second-guess the wisdom of my decision, I take a running leap.

Time seems to slow as I hurtle through the air, the wind rushing over me. I'm certain I've made a terrible mistake, but I land with a jarring thump on the next carriage, my jaws snapping at the impact. The train whistle blows, the sound so loud that it rattles through my bones.

Reaching for one handhold at a time, I make my way to the trap door. When I get to it, I yank the handle. The trapdoor is metal, and ridiculously heavy. Groaning, I heave it open a crack and peer inside. Not a passenger carriage, thank the gods. Just cargo. Moonlight streams onto piles of crates around the edges of the carriage.

I let out a huff of frustration. There's no ladder. I'll have to jump, but the carriage floor looks far away. I open the hatch further and hang my feet over the edge. I inch inside and let go, then plummet to the floor of the cargo car, pain shooting through my ankle and up my leg.

"Shit," I hiss, stumbling to the side. I've twisted my ankle badly.

I roll onto my butt and grip my leg. If only Raphael were here to work his healing magic. I can almost picture him cradling my ankle in his hands, stroking his fingertips over exactly where it hurts, the heat from his magic pulsing over my skin. But when I stop imagining it, the pain races back through my leg.

My heart is a wild beast.

I let out a long, slow breath. I'm resting on the quiver and arrows, and they dig into my back. I'm dirty and wet, and I've torn my pants. My face burns and feels sticky, and when I wipe my forehead, my fingertips come out smeared maroon. Drying blood. I think I cut it when I was racing through the branches in the grove. Oh, and I bit my tongue.

I have the quiver, but I lost the bow on the way. Still, despite the injured ankle, this is overall a success. I'm alive, and on the way to Allevur.

Fuck. My elation dies when I realize that I've lost my bag, too—which had my forged papers in it. If anyone asks for them, I'm screwed. The disguise no longer makes any sense.

Once I get off in Allevur, my appearance will draw instant attention. I look around, searching for anything that might be a change of clothes, but all I see are crates nailed shut. On either side of the carriage, there's a door—but there's no way of knowing what's beyond it.

Wrythe taught us that the train of Gobannos is a

strange hybrid of human technology and Fey magic. Once inside, perceptions can become strange to those not used to magic. Carriages are glamoured or twisted into strange shapes as magic bends reality to its will.

It can be dangerous to venture into the unknown, especially now that I look more like a fugitive than an aristocratic Fey hunter.

I crouch down in the carriage and wait. Hopefully, I'll go unnoticed in here until I get to Allevur.

I unshoulder the quiver and stuff it behind a crate. As the train chugs along, I lean back and shut my eyes, trying to ignore the pain in my ankle. Have I made a terrible mistake? Rushing onto a Fey train because I heard a voice that *might* or might not predict the future?

It's certainly possible.

When the mission ends—assuming I get home safely— I could be kicked out of the academy and on the next boat back to the U.S.

The instant pang of sadness catches me by surprise. My life before Camelot was a different sort of chaos, one that made me feel tired instead of exhilarated. One where I spent lots of time alone.

No Tana, no Serana, no Darius.

No Raphael.

Not that I care about *him*.

I drop my head into my hands, trying to focus on the next step. I'm still in mortal danger. I'll deal with the fallout of my actions later.

The carriage door opens, and my head snaps up, pulse roaring.

A blond Fey steps inside, frowning. He's wearing a black uniform and holds a short sword, but even I can see that he's untrained, holding it as if he's holding a club.

I stumble to my feet, standing unsteadily.

He cocks his head at me, and his bronze eyes gleam in the dark, lupine and eerie. "Who are you?"

In the dim light, I can see the suspicion etched on his face. I can only imagine how I look to him. Dirty, bleeding, clothes ripped. I look *exactly* like a fugitive.

My heart speeds up. He'll take me into custody. In less than an hour, I'll be locked in a Fey jail, being tortured for answers.

My mind flashes to something I learned in one of my spy classes. Alleviating suspicion is a difficult task. But *shifting* it is much easier. You just need someone else to point a finger at. Unfortunately, there's no one here but me.

"Someone attacked me!" I say in Fey. "I…I think he was a demi-Fey. A stowaway."

He tenses, peering behind me. "Where?"

"I think he's hiding in the rear carriage."

"Stay here," he commands, and walks between the crates to a door behind me. He readies his sword, then opens it, stepping into the darkness of the last carriage. But from here, I can see it's also empty of people, which isn't ideal.

My breath shallows. I need to get out of here, *now*.

187

I run for the other door. Pushing through it, I burst into a passenger carriage. Fey dine at tables, sipping drinks and eating hors d'oeuvres. I've never seen so many Fey at once, and they're all looking at me, champagne flutes paused in midair.

My chances of blending in are now zero.

"There's a criminal on the train!" I shout, pointing back at the door. "A demi-Fey murderer. He's stabbed someone in the back carriage. Help barricade the door!"

Shouts echo off the carriage walls as I hobble across the carriage. With every step, pain screams from my twisted ankle up my calf.

When I glance behind me, I see two Fey men holding the door closed.

I take in the strange beauty of the place as I shuffle along. The Fey are draped in rich fabrics of burgundy and royal blue. In this carriage, vines grow over ornately carved wooden walls, and lights twinkle from the leaves. Music floats though the air.

But as I get closer to the end, a woman with a tiara and crimson hair points at me, shouting, "Stop her!"

No one is really listening to her. They're all focusing on the other end of the train, where the alleged murderer is pounding maniacally against the door.

Good. Chaos is my friend.

I limp along as quickly as my ankle allows me to. Just as I reach the carriage door, I look back. The barred door rattles, and the attendant shouts something from the other side. I slip through into the next carriage, slamming the door shut behind me. It's another passenger car, full of Fey sitting among the luxury of gilt-frame portraits and ivy-covered walls.

I play the same trick, with less satisfying results this time. I scream that a killer is after me, and yell at them to bar the door. While I hobble across the aisle, a single Fey man with silver hair makes a half-hearted attempt to question me, but I pretend not to hear him.

I burst through the next door, agony shrieking up my leg.

I'm prepared for the extraordinary, but the sight in front of me still stops me dead for a few precious seconds. The carriage is decorated like a ballroom, and I've wandered into an actual masquerade ball. There are no tables or benches, and Fey dance in long gowns and animal masks. Lights twinkle on the mahogany walls, and a harp thrums, a pulsing, sensual beat that throbs in my belly. Tiny jewels hang suspended in the air, glittering with light that reflects off a marble floor. The space appears to be cavernous, the dimensions all wrong for a train.

I limp inside, and some of the dancers glance my way, but almost no one stops dancing. Despite the pain in my leg, I feel the strange need to dance as well, and the music and the magic of the masquerade ball takes over my body.

This place is wildly disorienting.

Euphoria bubbles in my chest and slides through my veins, and I have to force myself to remember that I need to get to the other side of the carriage. I pirouette through the dancers. Giggling, I snatch a cat mask off a woman's face. She grins at me, her lips blood red. I don the mask and dance my way to the next door. My ankle throbs, but the pain is so dull now. I'm acting out the moves from my childhood, a few steps of the waltz, now an allemande, a chasse—

I land badly on my bad ankle and lose my balance. I hiss in pain and stumble into the carriage door. Snapping out of my haze, look back at the ballroom. Two black-clad guards are searching for me among the dancers. With my cat mask still on, I slip through the next door.

In the next carriage, violet smoke whirls around Fey in skimpy outfits. They recline on cushions, their limbs entwined. Some are smoking long cigarettes, others are kissing and groping one another. The smoke is cloying and sweet, and I hold my breath, but not quickly enough. Dream smoke, it's called, a Fey drug that has become very popular with the human elite for the past years. I glance at a man sucking on a woman's nipple.

I find myself staring, the dream smoke relaxing my muscles. My head spins, and I try to keep my balance, licking my lips as heat slides through my body.

My eyes close, and I sway, imagining Raphael's magic caressing me, that he's right behind me, his athletic body pressed against mine. For a moment, my mind blazes with a vision of me lying on that cushion, of Raphael kissing my naked skin—

Absolutely not.

I clench my fists and force myself through the carriage as quickly as I can.

I reach the next door and fling it open. It's dark in here, and I collapse on the floor, kicking it closed behind me.

I can't breathe. The rush wreaked havoc with my asthma. I search for my inhaler, except I no longer have my bag.

Shit.

A sudden growl draws my attention. The carriage is full of caged animals: great wolves with gleaming eyes, foxes, a giant bell jar of fluttering butterflies. Ravens perch in cages.

One of the wolves growls again, his eyes intent on me. I quickly glance at the cage door, relieved to see it's locked.

I've still got two agents after me, though. Perhaps the smoke has slowed them, but for how long? I have to keep moving.

Forcing myself upright, I hobble between the animal cages. My breath whistles, and my chest feels heavy. The Fey chasing me don't suffer the same affliction. I can go on for one more carriage, maybe two, and they'll be upon me.

Pain lacerates my ankle, but I make it to the other door. I glance at a caged wolf to my right, one with gray fur. His lip curls back, baring enormous teeth.

"Hey, there," I wheeze, leaning on my knees. "Hello."

He growls, his ears flicking back. I don't think I'm making a new friend here.

The lock seems simple. Obviously, there's no reason for a complicated lock on a feral wolf's cage because what sort of maniac would want to open it?

I recently learned in the academy that picking locks takes two tools: a bent lockpick and a strong metal prong for torc.

Gasping for breath, I remove the brooch from my corset and break the pin holding it. Then I yank the thin hairpin from my hair and stick it into the lock.

The wolf snarls at me, saliva dripping from his fangs. He snaps at my hand, and I quickly pull it back. I push the cat mask up on my head in case that placates him.

"Stop that," I order. "I need to concentrate."

His low growl sends a shiver up my spine.

I push the hairpin into the lock again and apply pressure as I start tinkering with the pin. I feel the slight click and twist the lock open. Behind me, the door opens, and a guard shouts something at me. I stand up and open the cage just a sliver. The wolf, recognizing the opportunity, lunges against the door of the pen as I yank the door open to the next carriage. I slide through, slamming it behind me.

I flatten myself against the door as something heavy— probably the wolf—smashes into it. Luckily, wolves aren't good with door handles. Then, from the other side of the door, I hear a deep male scream. A little tendril of guilt twists in my chest. My pursuers just met my lupine acquaintance.

Pressed against the door, I survey the new carriage. This seems to be a luggage carriage, lined with shelves of suitcases.

My mind kicks into action, and I snag a dusty-rose valise from one of the shelves. I pop it open and strip off my dirty, torn clothes. Panicked shouts echo from the other carriage. I pull on a long emerald dress with a plunging neckline and a slit up one side. I yank out a wide-brimmed hat and put it on. With shaking hands, I quickly secure the knife holster around my thigh.

I shove my clothes in the suitcase and slam it shut.

I hurry across to the next door and fling it open. Another passenger carriage, one with mahogany tables and flickering candelabras, where the occupants are drinking bubbly pink cocktails from champagne flutes.

I stroll in, masking the pain that races up my ankle. Wearing a serene smile, I drop into an empty seat at one of the tables, angling my hat to cast a shadow on my face. A woman with wavy silver hair sits across from me, and her eyes gleam with fiery shades.

"Good evening," she says to me in Fey.

"Good evening," I answer. "Do you know how long until we reach Allevur?"

"Not long." She frowns. "You have a bit of an unfamiliar accent, young one."

"I'm from Glenfark," I explain, hoping that it's faraway

enough to explain the foreign accent. It's a remote island in Brocéliande.

"Ah." She nods in satisfaction. "I should go there when I return from Fey France. I've heard it is quite beautiful."

"It's glorious," I say. "There's nothing like the sandy white shores of Glenfark."

The carriage door bursts open, and the large guard steps in.

There's only one of them now, and he has a nasty scratch on his face. This guard hasn't seen my face because I was wearing the cat mask. He's looking for a dirty woman with wet clothes.

"My son sailed to Glenfark once," the lady says. "He was there for four days. He said that he liked the fruit." She's wearing a golden gown with sheer sleeves.

"Yes, Glenfarkian fruit is delicious." I have no idea what fruit grows in Glenfark.

The attendant walks down the aisle, looking left and right. His eyes linger on me for just a second, then slide off. I do my best to look relaxed as possible.

He keeps going. As he gets further away, I start coughing.

"Are you all right, dear?" the woman asks.

"Yes," I rasp. "It's just the fumes of the train. They don't agree with me."

"Here." She rummages in her small black clutch, finding a tiny metal box. "Try one of those."

I open the lid to reveal pastel-colored sweet confections. Fey candy can be overwhelming, but refusing a gift in the Fey world is culturally unthinkable.

"Thanks." I cough and pop a pale blue sweet in my mouth.

Strong minty flavors erupt, curling into my throat and nose. I can practically feel my breath relaxing and my lungs opening up.

"It's good, isn't it?" She smiles at me. "Helps me on bad days."

"It's incredible," I manage. This is a million times better than my inhaler. Modern medicine has a lot to learn from the Fey.

The brakes screech, and the train slows.

A man's voice floats through the carriage. "Allevur! We have arrived at Allevur!"

My gaze flicks to the large guard. He's not paying attention to me, but he's standing by the door where I need to disembark. Through the opening, I see a stone platform. Gas lamps cast a warm glow over a few people as they bustle off the train.

"Didn't you want to get off on Allevur, young one?" the silver-haired woman asks.

"Yes." I smile at her, my heart beating hard, my eyes still on the guard. "Just catching my breath."

I wait for a few seconds, then stand up and walk over to the train door. As I reach it, the guard turns to look at me, his eyes widening.

"You!" he shouts.

The train is starting to move again. I open the door and leap off, just as the train chugs away. Pain shoots up my leg. The guard is hanging out the door, staring at me, baring his canines.

CHAPTER 17

$\mathcal{N}$o one seems to notice my awkward tumble out of the train.

I push myself up on the stone platform, putting my weight on my good leg, and dust myself off. The train station is made of glass, like a greenhouse, and lit with golden lamps. A clocktower rises from it, and I mark the time as five minutes past one. The large clock face is cracked, maybe from the war fifteen years ago. No wonder most humans abandoned this place.

Up ahead, a few people hurry through the station's open archway to carriages waiting on the other side. I hop on my good foot, one hand on the glass as I exit the station.

The town built up around the train station is small, with a cobbled road that passes between shops and shuttered homes on either side. The shops are closed for the night, the windows dark, but down the street, I see the lights of a tavern, the sign hanging above the door creaking forlornly in the wind.

A few soldiers linger by the station, and my spine stiffens at the sight of their blue coats. I try to disguise my limp as I walk. Clenching my teeth, I mask the pain racing up my ankle.

When I glance to my right, my breath catches. Between two shops is a view of dark, empty fields, and deep in the fields stands a gallows. Five silhouettes swing from ropes under the light of the moon. Fear settles into my bones. This is the true face of the Fey occupation, these bodies swaying above the grass.

For a moment, I wonder if one of them is Freya and dismiss the notion. These bodies have been there for a while. They look stiff, and the faint scent of death carries on the wind.

I shiver and hurry on. Based on the time, the others should be here soon, coming from the other side of the town square, not from the station.

Slowly, I make my way to the tavern, where warm lights beam from the windows. The outside is painted black with golden stars, and the creaking sign depicts a painting of a headless woman. This must be the meeting spot. I'd heard them saying the name of the location was a place called The Silent Woman.

As I get closer, I survey the layout. An agent should always have an escape route. The tavern has two arched wooden doors inset into a stone building. Oak trees grow around the side door, twining together above the entrance. I wonder if it's a kitchen door. Behind the tavern is a stable.

Passing by, I glance at the tavern's warmly lit window. A black cat sits on a stack of books, flicking her tail back and forth. I don't notice much else because I'm not stopping to linger. Mentally, I'm racking my brain for every detail of the map I memorized during the briefing.

I'm fairly certain they'll be coming from the southwest. Once I get past the town square, I take a left onto a dirt road with nothing but a few scattered homes and fields stretching into the darkness. I move slowly to avoid putting weight on my left foot. At last, I leave the houses and the village behind. Out here, stone walls surround patches of farmland, and wildflowers line the dirt road.

Fear crawls into my stomach, worries that I'm too late, that they already got here before I arrived. That they've been ambushed, taken. Desperate, I search for a sign of them in the darkness. Minutes crawl by.

Then I see them at last—a trio riding toward me. Relief washes over me as I recognize Freya's auburn hair, and as they ride closer, Raphael and Arzel's bright white shirts stand out from the shadows.

Raphael leads the way. In the shadows, his pale eyes pierce the dark. When he's only twenty feet away, his horse slows, and his jaw drops. He dismounts and strides toward me. "Pixie princess." A line forms between his eyebrows as he stares at me. "Nia, what are you doing here?"

"I had to warn you. I think you might be stepping into an ambush."

Freya and Arzel move their horses closer.

"How did you get here before us? And how did you end up in this dress?" Freya asks. "What the fuck is happening?"

"Did I hear the word *ambush*?" asks Arzel.

I look back at the main road but don't see anyone. "I heard someone talking about an ambush in Allevur. And since there's nothing else around here but The Silent Woman, I thought the ambush might be meant for you."

Raphael frowns at me. "What do you mean, you overheard someone? Who were you listening in on when you were waiting for us in the woods?"

I swallow hard. "It's tough to explain."

"Try."

"It's just something I overheard," I say firmly. "That's all you need to know, but if it's true, your life could be in danger."

The hilt of Raphael's sword gleams in the darkness. "Fine. We should at least check what we're walking into. Freya, can you slip ahead to check the tavern's stable? Arzel, circle around the building. Have a look in the windows, the roofs, the shadows. Search for anything that doesn't quite seem right, and make sure no one sees you."

Without another word, the pair ride off into the darkness.

Once we're alone, Raphael folds his arms, his penetrating silver gaze searing me. "What is it that you're not telling me?"

As the wind rushes over the grass, I breathe in the faint scent of woodsmoke and wild roses that grow along the field's edges. "Sometimes, I hear voices," I say at last. "I used to assume they were nonsense. But occasionally, the things the voices say come true."

He lets that sentence float between us for a few seconds, the silence broken only by the grass rustling in the breeze and a loud snort from his horse. At last, he says, "Okay. Tell me more."

"When I was waiting for you, the sergeant cornered me in the forest."

Raphael's expression hardens, and he shifts closer. "He *what*? What happened?"

I shake my head. "Nothing. He was easy enough to get rid of. But as it happened, I heard a voice in my mind, a voice that mentioned an ambush in Allevur. And I also heard a sentence just *before* the sergeant said it out loud, like I was hearing the future, maybe? I don't know that the bit about the ambush was accurate, but I didn't want to take the risk of ignoring it."

"A disembodied voice in your head warned you about an ambush in Allevur," he says levelly.

Frustration tightens my chest. "And he mentioned a traitor. Someone called Varris."

Raphael's eyes open wider. "How did you hear that name?"

"I literally just told you how I heard it."

He studies me. "His name is confidential. Only *I* know it. Not even Arzel and Freya know it. Varris is the person we're supposed to be meeting."

I *could* hear the future, then.

"The sergeant's thoughts said, 'Allevur will be a bloodbath again tonight after the ambush, if that traitor Varris can be believed,'" I tell him. "It doesn't seem like a good sign, does it?"

"No." His gaze slides down my body. "What happened to your leg? You were limping when I first saw you, and you're favoring your right leg."

"I sprained my ankle jumping into a train car from the roof."

"You did *what?*"

"That's how I got here," I say. "I took the Gobannos train. It was the only way I could make it here on time. But I didn't have a ticket, so I had to board the train through the roof."

"Why do I feel like you'll be the death of me?" he mutters, and kneels down.

"What are you doing?"

"Healing you. The left one, right?" He brushes the back of his knuckles over my ankle where it hurts the most. How does he know exactly where I need him to heal me?

The heat of his magic whispers over my skin, a glowing caress that makes my eyes flutter. He slides his hand around my ankle, but the sensation of his magic doesn't stop there. It's a faint kiss of velvet stroking up my thigh. As his magic sweeps over my skin, the pain dissolves, leaving only a throbbing heat in its wake. I lick my lips, my breath growing shallow.

"Are you nearly finished?" I ask sharply, trying not to think about how it would feel if his hand moved higher up my leg.

He pulls his hand away like he's been burned. "I'm helping you," he says, looking up at me in surprise.

"It's fine now, thank you," I say crisply, smoothing my dress to disguise my filthy thoughts.

He stands, and I breathe in his earthy, masculine scent. "Glad it's fine now," he says quietly. "You're rather tightly wound, you know that?"

Because I've been played by you before. "Well, we *are* on a dangerous mission."

His gaze moves past my shoulder, and I turn to see Freya galloping toward us, with Arzel close behind.

When Freya reaches us, she's still catching her breath. "Nothing in the stable..." She draws out the last word.

"But?" Raphael says.

"I mean *absolutely* nothing. No other horses. Doesn't that seem odd?"

"Something seems off," Arzel says quietly. "I peered in the tavern windows, and no one looked relaxed. It's the middle of the night, and they should be drunk off their arses on mead. Instead, they look stiff and tense. It looks like a funeral, not a party. And there are no musicians. Whenever I came here before, there was always music."

Raphael stares at me for several beats. "Okay. We're

not going in. It's a trap. Everyone on your horses. Nia, you're riding with me."

The hem of my dress hikes up to my hips as I climb into the saddle. I shift forward, gripping the horse's pommel, the cool night air sweeping over my bare thighs.

Raphael mounts behind me, pressing close against me, his body warm and firm. He reaches around me for the reins. I lean back against his chest. Heat radiates from his body, warming mine.

"Let's go," he says. "Back the way we came."

He whispers to the horse in Fey, and she takes off at a trot.

But we've hardly started when we hear the sound of pounding hooves behind us. Three riders are racing toward us.

"They've found us," I breathe.

Raphael swears under his breath. "Let's go!" He pulls the reins, and we take off at a gallop. "Hold on tightly."

I cling to the saddle's pommel, and he spurs the horse onto a dirt road carved between two fields. The horse pounds over the soil, its hooves splattering earth in all directions.

The twang of a bowstring rings out, and an arrow zooms by. I glance back. Freya and Arzel are keeping pace with us, but the three bowmen are closing in.

Our attackers loose another arrow, and Raphael hugs me closer, leaning to the left slightly just as the arrow zips past. Up ahead, something catches my eye—the glint of steel in the moonlight. A drumbeat of dread thumps in my chest. I can just about make out a group of Fey soldiers racing through the darkened fields, ready to block our path.

"Do you see them?" I shout into the wind.

"Yes." But Raphael isn't slowing.

In front of us, the Fey soldiers rush into the road, wielding spears and swords.

Raphael releases the reins with one hand and draws his sword. I want to pull out my knife, but it's taking all my strength to stay on the horse. A Fey soldier swings for us, and a spear hurtles through the air. I clamp my eyes shut, the sound of metal scraping against metal setting my teeth on edge.

When I open my eyes again, we're past the soldiers. A sharp throb on my arm alerts me that I've been cut, and blood drenches my shoulder.

"Are you all right?" Raphael shouts, his voice sharp.

"I'm fine."

"Raphael, company!" Freya shouts.

Glancing behind, I see more riders in uniform racing after us. The one in front has long white hair, and his teeth are bared in a bloodthirsty snarl.

Our horses are tired from a day of traveling, and Raphael's mount is carrying two riders. We can't outrun them.

Raphael yanks the reins, and our horse veers sharply off the dirt road. Across the field is an oak grove, silvered in the moonlight. We race toward it and leap over a fallen tree. I clench hard to the saddle. Another glance back tells me the riders have followed us. The one in the lead is a few yards away from Arzel, and the Fey soldier raises a sword.

Freya pulls her mount sideways to collide with the attacker. The soldier's horse rears, toppling over. To my relief, Freya manages to keep her balance and catches up with us. With his crossbow in hand, Arzel turns. He shoots a bolt toward the riders.

"Get down!" Raphael shouts.

We hurtle into the trees, the boughs arching above our path. I bend over the saddle, and Raphael leans closer. His body pressed to mine, we ride through the foliage, the earth and the gnarled roots beneath us dappled with moonlight. A shout rings out from behind until we break out of the grove and race into a field of berry bushes.

The breeze whips over me, and we straighten again. Two soldiers follow us now, but Arzel is lagging behind. There is an arrow lodged in his side.

"Arzel has been hit!" I shout.

Raphael slows his horse to turn back.

"I've got them!" Arzel shouts. Nocking an arrow, he aims at the Fey soldier with the crossbow. "Keep going. I'll hold them off!"

He looses the arrow as he rides, and it pierces a soldier's throat. Raphael curses in Fey and spurs his horse ahead. I turn, eyes wide, as the second rider catches up to Arzel. He's still trying to reload, and the soldier has closed the distance. Fear screams through my nerve endings.

"Arzel!" Freya shouts, as the Fey soldier swings his sword.

I shut my eyes and cling to the pommel. Behind me, I feel the solid wall of Raphael's chest. When I open my eyes at last, I see Freya fire at the final rider. Her arrow hits him in the eye, and he screams and falls off the horse.

But Arzel is no longer with us.

I can't see him where he fell—just the silhouette of his horse, riderless.

Freya rides at our side, her eyes glassy with tears.

Arzel is gone.

CHAPTER 18

The veil glows in the distance, ethereal, silver-violet radiance in the darkness, a pearl beaming from the shadows. It would be gorgeous if I didn't ache all over, if our horses weren't stumbling with exhaustion, and if the sadness of losing Arzel didn't weigh us down with the cold pall of grief.

As we draw closer, the veil's hum buzzes in my ears. I need to summon the reserves of my energy to get us across, but I feel nauseated and exhausted. I'm pretty sure I'm dehydrated.

I could almost fall asleep against Raphael with his arms wrapped around me. The way he shifts against me as he rides makes me want to close my eyes, and I lean back into the sensual heat and strength of his body. I feel his heartbeat through my back, and my eyes drift shut. After the horrors of the night, it's strangely comforting.

"Are you falling asleep on me, pixie?" For the first time,

the term almost sounds like an endearment. His voice is a quiet murmur, and his breath warms the shell of my ear.

"Of course not. I'm always fully alert."

"You might as well rest if you can."

"Riders!" The sharpness in Freya's voice has my eyes snapping open.

I turn to look, but I can't see a thing in the dark.

"Where?" asks Raphael.

"Following us on horse," she says. "I can't see them well in the dark, but I can hear the hooves getting closer."

Raphael tugs the reins, slowing his horse to a stop. "We need to dismount. My horse is at the end of her strength. She won't be able to go any faster."

"Same here," Freya says. "And we're more visible when mounted. Since I can hear their hooves, they might be able to hear ours."

Raphael slides off the horse, then helps me dismount. My leg muscles feel so cramped from the long ride that I nearly stumble to the ground.

"Silently now," he whispers, steadying me.

We creep forward, leading our horses through the grassy field and doing our best to make as little noise as possible. My heart jumps at every crackling leaf, every snapping twig. The two agents seem to be able to glide along the earth, silent as the air.

As we move, dawn starts to break, the sky blushing with coral, blending into indigo. As the sun rises, the pearly barrier reflects the dawn light—rust, violet, tangerine.

And then, all at once, Freya and Raphael halt. I take another step and freeze as well. A rumble grows louder, a faint vibration through the grasses. The sound of galloping horses.

"They're coming right for us," Raphael says. "Let's go."

He releases the reins and slaps his horse, who goes off in a mild canter. Freya does the same, her horse following Raphael's mount. Instinctively, the horses trot away from the veil.

"That'll buy us some time," Raphael says, his voice still low. "Let's run."

I race after his silhouette, desperately trying to keep pace. We run crouched, trying to stay in the shadows, but as we get closer to the veil, it becomes impossible. Now, the magical barrier is washing us in a shimmering glow. The only thing still keeping me moving is my adrenaline, which spikes as I hear the hooves thundering over the earth.

We make a mad dash through the grass, and the veil hums in my ears, prickling my skin like a thousand tiny needles.

Freya reaches it first and whirls to look at me. "Can we cross?"

"No," I whisper. "Wait!"

I try to concentrate on the magic, but I can feel the weight of their eyes on me.

"They're getting closer," Freya snaps. "Come on, Nia."

"Let her focus," Raphael says.

I can feel it, the mesh of energy, the thinness of the

weaker sections. If I channel my powers at one of them, the veil will crack and let us through. I summon all the energy I can muster, feeling for those vulnerable parts.

The veil keeps humming, the hooves pounding closer. If I don't figure this out *now*, we're going to die at the hands of the Fey.

"We'll have to go through," Freya shouts. "Either we live or we die. We can't afford to get caught, and they're almost here."

"Wait." I clench my teeth.

I concentrate, trying to forget about everything, the people whose lives depend on me, the mission, Arzel, whose death will be meaningless if I don't get us through. Only the veil matters.

And its noise seems to grow even louder in my ears.

"Nia, it's now or never," Freya says.

I turn to glance at the incoming riders. They're so frighteningly close, just a few yards away. The leader's eyes bore straight into me, a malicious golden gaze. With a snarl, he raises an enormous axe above his head, screaming a battle cry.

My fear nearly paralyzes me, but I use it instead to drown out my other thoughts. I hurl it at the veil, unfocused, directionless.

The entire veil flickers, its buzz dying. Raphael grips my arm and pulls me across.

I stumble, racing for a few steps through narrow fields crisscrossed by stone walls. An oak forest spreads across the landscape. Coppery light kisses the tree leaves.

My body feels frozen, shivering. Icy air stings my skin, and my teeth chatter. It looks like spring, but it feels like the dead of January.

The hum rises in my ears, and I can see the riders through the haze of the veil. They rear their horses to a halt on the other side, and one of them raises his bow.

Fuck. We might be through the magical barrier, but it won't stop arrows.

Something whizzes past me, but it's coming from behind. Freya's arrow finds a soldier's throat on the other side.

"Keep going!" Raphael shouts.

He and Freya are off again.

I follow after them, but my muscles feel frozen. I'm shivering violently, my body bitten by the cold. The glacial air pierces my body down to my marrow.

"Nia, let's go!" Raphael shouts.

My muscles are ice. An arrow from beyond the veil zooms by, inches from my face. "Go!" I shout through clattering teeth.

Raphael rushes back and scoops me up, pressing me against his firm chest. Enfolding me in his arms, he starts to run. Up ahead, Freya is covering him, unleashing one arrow after another into the misty veil.

As we reach the shelter of the forest, I'm shivering against Raphael's chest.

He slows once we get out of range. "You're freezing," he mutters.

"I used too much magic." And yet, my body feels

boiling now, flushed. "But I'm not cold anymore." I want to take my dress off. "I'm too hot."

"You're going into hypothermia." He raises his eyes, and the rising sunlight catches them as they spark gold. "Freya, wait. She lost too much heat. We need help. Now."

The world shimmers and fades for a moment. When I open my eyes again, it's just Raphael. Golden light dapples his high cheekbones. He's leaning against a tree, holding me close.

My eyes drift shut again, and I'm not sure if I'll manage to wake, but I don't mind either way. He's carrying me against his broad chest now, moving swiftly, like I don't weigh a thing.

What a strange thing to feel safe with Raphael.

It stirs a memory from long ago, something I'd tried to forget.

CHAPTER 19

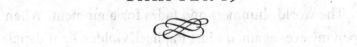

The world is rocking up and down, pitching like a ship. Violently.

I try to open my eyes, but it's too much effort. Ice slides through my bones, my blood. So cold. My body shudders, shaking like a dying leaf in the wind.

A voice rings in my thoughts, the sometimes violent sensualist. *I will taste you. Wrap your thighs around me. In a dark, consuming flame, we will burn, a comet in the sky.*

No violence tonight, then. I sink into oblivion.

* * *

I'M IN LOS ANGELES, in my childhood bed, surrounded by my stuffed animals. My head feels hot, my throat burns. I just woke from a terrible nightmare, one of a man with black hair and a spiked crown standing before me, a sword in his hand.

My room looks scarier than usual, with shadows climbing over the walls. I don't know if the man from my nightmare is hiding in one of them. A cough racks my chest. Panic crackles through me.

"Mom!" I scream.

Sometimes, she doesn't come when I call. Sometimes, she's not at home, especially when Dad goes away on work trips.

Now, I'm sure the evil king is lurking in my room, and I'm too sick to fight back. "Mom! Mom!"

Hot tears run down my cheeks. It's hard to breathe. Something is wrong with my chest, and I can't get enough air. When I cough, it's a low, strange noise that sounds very wrong. My throat is closing up, and I'm sure I need a doctor. I want to go into the bathroom for medicine, but if I step onto the ground, the murderous king will grab my feet. Is he the one stealing my breath?

"Mom!" My throat aches when I scream, and no one is coming to help. "Dad!"

Children need looking after.

* * *

SOMEONE'S TEARING at my clothes, and I want to keep them on.

Voices float through the air.

"She's not responding to my magic." Raphael's deep voice has a sharp edge to it. "I'm trying to heal her, but it's not working."

I open my eyes, but everything is blurry.

"I've taken most of her clothes off." Freya's voice pierces the air. "Warm her up, will you? I'm going to be sick again. But Raphael, I don't think you should get your hopes up. She hasn't practiced enough in moderating her magic use, and she unleashed all of it at once. No one can survive such a temperature drop."

I want to tell them I'm fine, but I can't seem to move. Maybe she's right. Am I dying?

"She'll be fine," Raphael says firmly.

"Well, warm her up, then, for fuck's sake."

"I will. She will be fine, Freya." His certainty is unwavering. "Throw more blankets on us before you get up again, will you?"

A warm body wraps around me, and powerful arms enfold me. The tension in the muscles beneath that smooth, warm skin belies his certainty. A tightness, tautness beneath the surface. Is he naked? Am I naked?

I'm trying to stay in the moment, but I float away again.

My mind slides back through the years.

* * *

I'M outside the library in the château. For three years, we visited, and for three years, I lingered near Raphael, standing where I could hear him and watch him from the shadows. He and his demi-Fey friends seemed like gods to me. All aristocrats—beautiful and untouchable. Princes of the château. So sure of themselves. I'd skulk in the corners of the library, pretending to read but listening in to try to understand what they said in Fey.

Raphael was only ever with them at night, his long limbs draped over the velvet chairs, sipping wine. He was only a year older than me, but he seemed so grown up. Sophisticated. I wondered how it would feel to be that relaxed and comfortable with myself, to let the ever-present knot in my stomach just melt. To smile with ease. Raphael was a little more serious than some of the others, sometimes contemplative, dreamy. But never nervous.

It felt like an ache in my chest to hear their camaraderie while I stood by myself. I wanted to be one of them more than anything—like the gorgeous demi-Fey girls who hung out with them, flirting and teasing them.

It wasn't until our third summer that Raphael spoke to me. I was seventeen, hanging around the library, hoping he'd show up.

One night, when he wandered in alone, I could hardly breathe. He smiled at me. It felt like I'd been raised in the dark, and for the first time, I had sunlight on my skin. He asked what I was reading, and I talked for far too long about my favorite poet, who'd died by drowning, then rambled on about how his wife had removed his heart, saving it before his body burned on the funeral pyre.

Raphael's eyebrows rose, and I remember my cheeks heating. Then he asked me if I wanted to meet him the next day. I was so unsure of myself around him, I almost said no. But I managed to nod, and the next day, I followed him through sun-drenched fields. He told me about the history of the château—that it was called Douloureuse Garde, a sorrowful fortress. During the Hundred Years' War, the English army had massacred everyone in the castle. Back then, they called those massacres the chevauchées, the harrowing, scorched-earth raids of the English. The kind that led to the capture of Joan of Arc.

And after the chevauchée, only one person was left here. The viscount had hidden in the dungeons while the rest of his people were slaughtered. He stumbled up the stairs to find the stones of his castle bathed in blood. So, it became the Douloureuse Garde.

Raphael told me about happier things, too—the château's alchemists and magicians from seven hundred years ago, who could predict the future by the stars. They foretold the rising and falling of empires.

He talked about the language of wine: how the vintners read messages in the leaves, how the roots and soil murmur secrets to the grapes. And under stress, when the earth whispers of famine, the grapes grow more flavorfully than ever. The vintners would purposefully try to stress their vines to make them thrive and burst with flavor.

In his beautiful Fey accent, he asked what I did for fun. All I could tell him about were the books, but he seemed to like hearing about them.

I remember the gold of his skin, and the cold silver of his eyes reminded me of the sun's rays breaking through storm clouds. I stole glances at his beautiful pointed ears and breathed in his masculine scent, faintly spiced like cedar wood and forest soil. That gorgeous scent is all around me now...

That day, he led me to the dungeon of Douloureuse Garde. He took me down beneath the earth where shadows swallowed us and told me the stone chambers were haunted by the viscount. The guilt had driven him mad.

When I was scared, I leaned into him, and he wrapped an arm around me.

His silver eyes shone even in the dark. Half-lidded, playful.

Beneath the earth, the air was freezing cold, but I felt the heat radiating off of him.

I'm still cold, the air piercing me, shaking me. Making my lungs freeze. Hard to breathe when everything stops moving, the air still as ice...

We wandered from the dungeons, back out to the sun-dappled grass under a yew tree, and lay flat on our backs. Our arms stretched toward each other. When our fingertips touched, I heard words in my mind: *Beautiful. Beautiful.* That time, I wasn't scared of the voices because they described what I saw before me.

But everything changed after the kiss. The kiss told me who he really was under that beautiful, golden-tongued exterior.

Warm arms pull me in close against a steely chest, and I gasp for breath.

* * *

EVERYTHING IS MOVING UP and down, a rocking motion. Normally, this would make me feel relentlessly queasy, but right now, I feel warm and safe. Magic thrums over my skin, making my pulse speed up. There's something particularly enjoyable wrapping around me.

My eyes flutter open. Bare skin on bare skin, Raphael's naked body pressed against mine. One of his arms is hooked around my waist, pulling me back into his abs. His arm is tight around my ribs, and my camisole is pulled up to just beneath my breasts. I'm not *totally* naked, I realize. I'm wearing underwear, but nothing else. I think it might be the same for Raphael behind me. My exposed lower back curves against his stomach, and his legs are wrapped around me. Blankets cover us.

I turn to look at him, and a tendril of my dark hair falls before my eyes. He looks back at me from under his long eyelashes.

"You're awake, pixie," he whispers. There it is again, a note of sweetness in the nickname. A half-smile flits over his lips.

"What's happening?" I croak.

He props his head on his fist to look down at me, but he's not pulling his arm away from my waist. Except now, his muscles grow more relaxed against me. "You had hypothermia. I had to warm you."

I frown up at him. "This never happened before when I used magic. At least, it wasn't this extreme."

"You'll need to learn to modulate it, and then it won't be as bad. You disabled the *entire* veil this time, for at least a few seconds. Hundreds of miles of a magical barrier. That was a tremendous surge of magic you unleashed. You nearly died, Nia. When we get back, you'll need a lot more training before I'm willing to let you risk your life again."

My gaze trails down his broad shoulder and his chiseled bicep, tattooed with dark lines that sweep over his collarbone. I have the strongest impulse to run my fingers over those inked vines, but I remember what happened the last time we kissed. "Is there any reason you still need to be in bed with me?" I ask. "I'm warm now."

His expression shutters. "I suppose not."

He rises from the bed, and I steal a glimpse at him. He's wearing only a small black pair of underwear, and my gaze trails over his powerful body. He pulls on his trousers, and I watch the sculpted muscles shift in his broad shoulders and back.

His gaze returns to me, and I jerk my head away to pretend I wasn't staring.

"Do you need some water?" he asks softly.

I lick my lips. "Yeah, I think so."

Still shirtless, he crosses to a table and pours me a cup of water. For the first time, I look around the room. Velvet-upholstered chairs stand against mahogany walls, their surfaces carved with nautical symbols. Light streams through round windows over a writing desk littered with papers and an inkwell. I lie in a lush bed with soft blankets.

Raphael hands me the cup of water. I take a few tentative sips and sink back into the pillows. "Thanks," I whisper.

"You saved our lives, you know. If you hadn't shown up in Allevur, we would have stepped into that ambush. Varris betrayed us. Either he double-crossed us, or they caught him, tortured him, and got the information out of him—how to summon us into their territory. Either way, he's compromised."

I let out a shaky breath. "Traitor Varris."

He pulls on a white shirt and starts to button it. "You heard a voice in your mind, and it spoke true."

"That's pretty much it."

"And this has happened before?"

I frown. "I always thought I was hallucinating. But now that I know I'm demi-Fey, I'm starting to wonder if there's some magic at play."

He pulls out a chair and sits in it. "Another power. You have two powers."

I swallow hard. "Wrythe says that when one person has several powers, they interfere with each other. Diametric powers. They're cursed and drive a person mad."

He cocks his head. "And you think the voices tell you about the future? Like Tana's ability to predict?"

My mind flicks back over some of the times I heard voices screaming in my head. Sometimes, they came true. Other times, it was lies or panicked thoughts, or just a litany of insecurities. Occasionally, pornographic thoughts boomed in my skull—about me, usually. Occasionally, they talked as if I was merely a passerby listening to a conversation of someone else.

With Tarquin, it was hostile. *You need to be put in your place. You should have been nice when you had the chance, and now look what you've done. Whore.*

When the sea serpent attacked us, it was a voice screaming that we were going to die.

All of them were raw emotions. All of them were triggered when others were near me.

"I think I might be telepathic," I said. "The voices reflect the thoughts of people around me. What they feel or think."

Raphael folds his arms, leaning back in the chair. "Well, you're right about powers interfering with each other. If you have two powers, it might explain your difficulty with controlling your magic."

I nod, thinking of what I've learned. Two powers intertwined weaken and destabilize each other. In some cases, over time, they cancel each other completely. And in other cases, the person possessing them is torn apart, either mentally or physically.

In less than a month, I've gone from being a bookseller with no powers to being a supernatural spy, to having one power too many.

A line forms between Raphael's eyebrows. "We will need to suppress your telepathy. If we're lucky, we can eliminate it altogether."

I've always wanted to get rid of the voices, but suddenly, I'm not so sure. "My telepathy saved your lives."

He flashes me a rueful smile. "And I am immensely grateful. But like I said, you almost died. We have several telepaths in MI-13. We have only two Sentinels. During this mission, you've demonstrated that you're on your way to becoming an amazing agent. But if we don't suppress your second power, you could die."

"Your bedside manner needs improvement." Nausea rises in my gut, climbing up my throat. I don't want to vomit in this bed, but I don't feel strong enough to get up yet. "Why am I getting seasick now? I was fine a minute ago."

He flashes me a sly smile. "Well, that was the effect of my magic. It didn't do much good to heal your magical affliction, but it helped with your seasickness."

I stare at him, suddenly wishing he'd climb back in bed.

"But you kicked me out," he adds.

"Perhaps that was a mistake," I say crisply.

I turn away from him, pulling the covers up over my shoulders.

I feel the bed compress as he slides in behind me, his body curving around mine. Already, his magic is working its way over my skin.

When I close my eyes, I conjure up the memory of being ghosted. After our kiss, I didn't see him for three days. And when I found him in the vineyards, he told me that he had lost all interest in me, that he had better things to do than to entertain a spoiled girl from America. Raphael, clearly, had better options, like the elegant and sophisticated women he spent time with at the château. Or women like Ginevra Pendragon. She's a Pendragon—no one would call her trash.

When I was seventeen, I spent the rest of the summer lying on the floor of my room, miserable.

His arm curls protectively around my waist. For just a moment, all my thoughts narrow to the feeling of his skin against mine.

Mentally, I jolt myself out of the pleasure. *Do not let yourself fall for him again, Nia.* I'd spent years building up my mental barriers against gorgeous men like him, and I would not let the walls crumble just because of his perfect body.

No more thinking of Raphael—not like that. He's going to end up with someone like Ginevra. I'd be an idiot to think of him as anything else.

CHAPTER 20

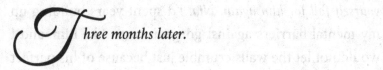 *hree months later.*

THERE'S ALWAYS a moment when I aim an arrow where everything but the target fades away. Here, in the combat hall, I forget the wooden beams inset into whitewashed walls and the charming crookedness of the hardwood floors. I forget the soaring timber-frame ceiling, the towering windows that cast bright sunlight onto a room full of cadets. I can no longer hear the swords clash as they practice, or the twanging of their bows. I block out the towering portrait of Merlin that hangs over the hall, watching over all of us.

I clear my mind of the graffiti people keep leaving on my door: the words *public bus* painted in bright reds and blues.

My thoughts go quiet, and the constant hum of worries dims, the fear that Mom has lit another sofa on fire or met another terrible man. I'm not thinking of Raphael or the way his muscular body felt wrapped around me all those months ago.

There's nothing but the bloodred circle in the center of the target like an apple of Avalon.

When I release the arrow, everything comes roaring back, all the sounds of the training hall, the chattering of thoughts in my skull.

It turns out I'm not a bad shot. I might even be quite good.

I raise the bow again and shoot one arrow after the next. Viviane paces around us, criticizing mistakes she sees. When she walks past me, she stops, watching.

My focus narrows again, and I forget she's there. The noise dims to a low hush. Sunlight streams onto the target.

I loose an arrow, and it thwacks into the red circle, the shaft quivering.

Viviane lets out a grunt—probably the closest she can come to complimenting me. Ever since we returned from that ambush in France three months ago, her attitude toward me has slightly shifted. She'll still point out every mistake I make, but she has at least stopped treating *me* as a mistake. And I suppose by now I've proven my loyalty.

Baby steps, I guess.

I glance sideways at Serana, who's training against a man with long brown hair named Loic. He wields an enormous sword, swinging it with both hands. Serana's dagger looks tiny in comparison, but she's holding her own. She darts in closer, her flame-red hair flying as she moves. Loic tries to strike, but he's got the angle wrong. She grips his wrist, twisting his entire arm behind his back. He drops his sword, and Serana turns to wink at me. She can't wait to get out in the field. I've been on three more missions in the past few months, and each time, she grills me afterwards, desperate for a chance of her own. She wants to know every single detail.

Not that I have much to say. Unlike the first mission, I usually just hang around the veil, waiting for the real agents to return. Since then, there's been no more leaping onto trains or lying half-naked in bed with Raphael.

I reach behind my back to draw another arrow from the quiver. The sounds of the hall dim to a quiet hum as I set the arrow to the bow string. With a practiced motion, I pull the string back, eying the target.

As I release the arrow, someone slams into my back, jarring my elbow. A voice screams in my mind, *Trying to act like a real agent, you grotesque whore? Nia Melisende— everyone gets a cheap ride.*

The arrow flies off target, lodging into the wall not far from Darius. He jumps sideways in alarm, holding up his hands, and stares at me with a shocked expression.

I grimace. "Sorry."

Someone tuts behind me, and I know who it is before I turn. Tarquin smirks at me, and Horatio, his cheeks red, is biting his lip like he's trying not to smile.

"Don't you have some serfs to harass or something?" I say. "I'm trying to work here."

There's still an echo in my mind from his thoughts, calling me a grotesque whore. My telepathy, like my other powers, is erratic, but it seems to happen only when I touch someone. Or, in Tarquin's case, when he touches *me*, since I would never do that on purpose.

"It was an accident, you lunatic," Tarquin says. "Anyway, if you can't shoot straight when someone gives you a little nudge, you won't be much good in the field, will you? Perhaps you would have been better suited to trying to sleep your way to the top back in America instead of here." His voice keeps growing louder, echoing off the hall.

The hall falls silent, and everyone turns to stare at us. I bite down on my tongue so I don't say anything that will get me kicked out.

"Or rather," he goes on at full volume, "Wasn't that your mother's plan? Passed along from one man to another until her allure faded, and she descended into destitution and coke-addled inebriety. I looked her up. So sad, really." He turns to the hall, grinning broadly. "Cocaine is expensive for someone like her, isn't it? Someone without a real job? I wonder how she funds her habit, living in her sad little rotten apartment. Have you seen the state of her teeth these days, though? Honestly, is it any wonder her daughter is desperately trying to shag her way up the ladder halfway across the world? Do you know what they called Nia back in LA? Slapper Melisende."

"That's not even American slang," I mutter. Nor was it alliterative.

Horatio guffaws. "I heard her nickname was Nia Shag."

"Lady Melisende the cock-hungry minx," Tarquin bellows.

The eyes of the other cadets burn into me.

Blood rushes to my face, and I'm about to lunge for him when a hand clamps around my bicep. Serana's grip is iron. "Calm yourself, Nia," she says. "Don't take his bait."

"You don't really want to come after a Pendragon, do you?" Tarquin asks in a mocking tone. "Wouldn't be very clever of you, considering we founded this place."

"Aw, poor Tarquin, so frustrated," I say, trying to keep my tone casual. "I've been on four missions at this point. And you...how many missions have you been on? Zero?" I wrinkle my nose in pretended sympathy. "It's zero, isn't it? The amount that you've contributed to the academy so far, just to be clear. Zero."

He snorts in disdain, but his fists clench as my barb hits home. "You're just the transportation. You don't really belong here."

"Tarquin," Serana says quietly, "if I see you get near Nia again, I'll sneak into your room in the middle of the night and cut off your bollocks with a rusty knife."

He narrows his eyes at her. "Are you threatening me?"

"Threatening?" Serana draws back in mock surprise.

"I'm just telling you what Tana saw in her cards. Isn't that right, Tana?"

Tana wanders over, her expression serene. "That's right." Her voice sounds dreamy. "Both balls, in the middle of the night. There's a lot of blood." She closes her eyes, inhaling with a faint smile. "I can see it even now. And the screaming…"

Tarquin's face grows pale. Everyone knows about the accuracy of Tana's predictions, and when her voice floats like that, it sounds downright eerie.

"Bloody witch," he snarls. "Let's get the fuck out of here, Horatio. We should have never let the mongrels in. It's like we willingly let the barbarians into Rome, you know?" He turns and stalks out the hall.

The training session is nearly over now, and a small crowd is staring at us. My mouth is dry. What sort of person would investigate someone's mother in another country just to insult them? Absolute asshole.

Serana is still gripping my bicep tightly.

"You can let go now," I say through clenched teeth.

"Right." She releases my arm.

Tana sighs. "It would have ended badly if Serana hadn't stopped you."

Shaking with anger, I turn to collect my arrows. I breathe slowly, deeply. I have no doubt that Tarquin will tell everyone about Mom. And as I've just received a rambling letter from her, I'm trying not to think of her at all. I'm already eaten up with guilt at the thought of abandoning her, and from her unhinged scrawl, it's clear she isn't doing well. She's furious with me for leaving her. In fact, she doesn't sound much kinder than Tarquin at this point.

I slide the bow and arrows back into the rack. When I turn, the hall has mostly emptied. Serana and Tana are waiting for me by the large, arched doorway.

My mind is roiling as I cross back to them.

"If I don't eat soon," says Serana, "I'm going to end up charging after Tarquin and rage-killing him myself."

We have twenty minutes until the next lesson. Serana is always famished between classes, so I've started making cheese and chutney sandwiches to keep her from getting cranky. "I've got you covered," I say.

I'm lost in a haze of worries as the three of us trudge down the stairs through the shadowy halls, but once we get outside, the bright midsummer sun warms my skin and calms my mood. Buttery summer light ignites the leaves of apple trees, and little baby apples hang from their branches.

The three of us cross the grass, which is dappled with forget-me-nots and primroses. I subtly scan our surroundings, trying to take in everything and everyone around me. It's a habit we're all supposed to develop. Something draws my attention, a strange tug, and I notice a tall woman with cherry red hair frowning at me. She turns and strides away, and I wonder who she is. Not one of the instructors or the regular staff, but she looked interested in me for some reason.

Tana sits beneath an apple tree, and we join her. I reach into my leather bag and pull out three sandwiches wrapped in wax paper.

Serana accepts my offering with a flutter of her eyelashes. "Thank you, darling. You are good at looking after me."

I smile at her. "Okay. Let's practice. How many people are behind you, and what are they wearing?"

She purses her lips as she concentrates. This is an exercise we've been working on for a while. Spies should always be aware of everything around them and take in every little detail, even when they look relaxed. A spy who doesn't notice they're being followed is a dead spy. Or caught—and everyone knows that being captured by the Fey is worse than death.

"Six people," she says. "Gisela and Oren by the statue. She's wearing a blue gossamer dress, and he's wearing those leather trousers that look far too tight, the same ones he wears every day. There are four demi-Fey women on the bench on the other side of the pond, all in dresses, two green, one purple, and one gold."

"Good, but it's not purple. It's more of a periwinkle gray," I say.

She glances over her shoulder. "Aw, right. But I was right about the rest."

"Those really are tight trousers."

"Who's behind you, and what are they doing?" Serana asks me in return.

I shut my eyes, trying to picture what I'd seen. "Gael,

Penelope, and Horace are standing by the old gravestones, the ones with the winged skulls. Gael is holding a mauve book and lecturing them about poetry." I open my eyes.

Serana raises an eyebrow. "You can't possibly hear what he's saying."

"But he's talking, and he's wearing that pretentious expression of his, and Penelope is looking at him all doe-eyed," I say. "That only happens when he's reading verse."

Tana laughs.

"All right," Serana says. "Now, which of them is carrying a weapon?"

I bite my lower lip, picturing it again. "Penelope is. Slight bulge in her boot. She has a shiv hidden there."

"Well done."

We both look at Tana.

She sighs. "Oh, please, don't."

"You need to master this for the Culling." I say this as gently as possible. I've come to learn that underneath Tana's serene exterior, she's a worrier. "You've got this. I know you can do it, Tana."

But the truth is, I'm not sure I believe what I'm saying. The Culling is only six weeks away. They'll test our endurance, our fighting abilities, our spycraft. And they'll test my magical abilities. A cadet who doesn't do well on the tests is removed from the academy. Occasionally, they leave grievously injured—or not at all.

The Culling is brutal. Avalon Tower can't risk sending out mediocre agents. If a spy gets caught during a mission, the consequences could be disastrous for all of MI-13. A captured spy could spill every secret we have.

Serana can barely pronounce Fey words. I can still barely control my powers. Meanwhile, Tana is having a serious problem with being aware of her surroundings. Even if she can easily see what's around her, she gets confused by *when* it's happening.

"Um..." She hesitates. "There's a...man behind me? He's wearing a blue tunic? He's smoking a pipe."

I look over her shoulder. A man is lying in the grass in a velvet waistcoat, reading a book. "Can you tell me more?"

"Well...he looks like the man from the painting in the dining hall. The famous bard, with the long beard...*oh*"— she deflates—"he *is* that poet."

"Taliesin?" Serana asks. "He's been dead for over a thousand years."

"Well, he was right behind me fifteen hundred years ago." Tana sighs. "This is hopeless."

"You'll get there." My chest clenches with guilt at the lie. I'm not sure Tana *will* get there.

"What about your telepathy?" Serana asks. "Have you been able to get rid of it?"

"It's going great!" I say brightly. "No worries at all."

Tana cocks her head. "She's doing the thing."

"Definitely doing the thing," Serana agrees.

I bristle defensively. "What thing?"

"Your voice gets higher and cracks a bit when you lie,"

Serana says. "When you're telling people whatever they want to hear."

Tana wrinkles her nose. "Which you do *a lot*."

My chest tightens. "So, not only am I vexed with diametric magic, but I'm also a terrible liar. Not the best qualities for a spy, are they?"

Serana grimaces. "You're still hearing thoughts, then?"

"Only when they're really loud, and I have to be touching someone."

"When are thoughts loud?" Serana arches an eyebrow.

"High-intensity emotions."

"Is it really that bad?" she asks. "Having two powers seems useful for an agent."

"Don't you remember what Wrythe said about them in class?" I ask.

Tana looks up at the sky and imitates Wrythe's pompous voice. "In the Fey realm, those with diametric magic are treated with contempt, as they usually are driven mad. They become dangerous and deranged, ravening idiots who will attempt to feast on humans and Fey alike. *Cannibals*."

I raise an eyebrow. "Exactly. And Mordred Kingslayer had diametric magic. He traveled across the lake from Avalon, broke into the castle, and slaughtered Arthur and everyone in Lothian Tower as they slept. I don't know if he ate people. He probably did."

Serana's eyes open wide. "In the very tower where we sleep? I had no idea it happened in Lothian."

Tana doesn't look surprised at all. She's probably seen all this in her visions.

"Yeah," I say. "I read about it in the cadets' library. After Mordred and the war with Morgan, they kicked *all* the Fey out of Avalon Tower for over fifteen centuries. At least, until they really needed us, but clearly, the Pendragons still aren't thrilled about it. And they're certainly not going to take any chances with another *mad mongrel*. I don't know if you've noticed, but I'm not popular with them at all. If they learn the truth about me, they'll call me the next Mordred."

Serana frowns. "But Raphael doesn't think it's a problem?"

"Only because he's desperate for a Sentinel." I bite my lip. "And maybe I've led him to believe I've suppressed my telepathy a bit more than I actually have."

"Bloody hell," says Serana. "Please don't devour me in my sleep."

Tana takes a deep breath and holds out her hand. "What am I thinking right now?"

I stare at her. "I'm not supposed to be using that power, Tana. I just explained that."

"Please," she whispers.

Surprised at the desperation in her voice, I take her palm.

As I hold her hand, I can feel her thoughts blooming in my mind. But Tana doesn't think in words, like most people. She thinks in images and feelings and emotions and—

"Darkness." My voice is hoarse, and a cold chill settles in my bones. "Death. It's coming...something is coming, and it's going to destroy everything in its path. There's a single drop of clear blue water, and it's being swallowed —" I yank my hand away, desperate to turn off the horror. "Gods." I somehow feel angry, though I'm not sure at what. "What was that? Is this what you feel all the time?"

I've never seen her with such a grim expression before. "Yes, for the past few days. The future is getting darker. Something terrible is coming for us all. And I think we're going to die."

A cold shudder traces up my spine. Overhead, the sky seems to cloud over.

"There was a little drop of water," I say. "Magical, somehow. Something that might hold off the death. Then a glassy clearness, like the surface of a lake. Moonlight glinting off it. But the shadows are trying to smother it, devour it."

Tana's stare is unwavering. "Oh, that's you. The glassy lake."

I blink at here. "I'm the *what*, now?"

"To stop the encroaching death, we need you."

"Because of my Sentinel powers?"

"We don't need a Sentinel. We need *you*. The Lady of the Lake. Do you know there hasn't been one in thousands of years? Not since Nimuë. And things didn't turn out well, did they, after what she did to Merlin." Tana smiles brightly. "But I think it's you. I keep seeing you in Nimuë's Tower." She grips my arm. "You must pass the

Culling. You need to stay in Camelot. And you absolutely cannot get kicked out or culled, or we are all *fucked*."

I've never heard her swear before, and she does it with a sharp vitriol that surprises me.

"What happens if she does get kicked out?" Serana asks.

Tana shrugs, and her dark gaze flicks up to the clouds. "The future isn't easy to understand. All I managed to glean from my visions and the cards is that Nia has to stay at Avalon Tower and join MI-13." Her gaze sharpens and lands on me again. "So you cannot fight with Tarquin. He's consciously trying to get you expelled. He's baiting you. If you lose your temper with him, his family will have you tossed out of Camelot. And then, I'm fairly certain we'll all die. Horrible, lonely deaths full of despair and regret."

I swallow. "Oh. Well, no pressure, then."

"And you cannot let anyone know about your diametric magic," Tana says emphatically. "Or the world ends. At least for us, but possibly for everyone."

"We can tell everyone about your vision," Serana said. "They'll listen to you. We'll go to Sir Launcelot or Viviane and—"

"No!" Tana snaps. "You can't tell *anyone*. If you tell them, they'll try to keep Nia in a bubble, hidden from the Fey king. They won't let the Lady of the Lake out of Camelot, and we need her out there. We need her to go on missions. Learning. Fighting for us. We need Nia."

My pulse starts to race. "Hang on. What do you mean,

keep me hidden from the Fey king? He has no idea who I am."

"Oh, he'll know." Tana glances at the gathering clouds again. "The Fey have psychics of their own. They will see what I see, eventually. The Lady of the Lake. And when they do, they'll try to destroy you. But Nia, you cannot tell anyone what I just said. Not even Raphael."

CHAPTER 21

I glance down at the handwritten note in my hand—a summons from Raphael. *Meet me in the Merlin Library. Sentinel training.*

My body glows with heat inside the tower. It's July, and there's not a hint of air conditioning in this place.

Tonight, instead of Raphael's office, we're meeting in one of Camelot's many ancient libraries. As I reach a stone landing, excitement flickers through me. I'm about to see inside the very place where Taliesin once penned his haunting poems. And some dirty ones, too— about fleshy orbs, rigid pillicocks, and pearly showers, and other phrases that people apparently found sexy way back in the Romano-British era.

I glance up at the carved mahogany doors. The metal knocker, shaped like a severed hand with long, clawlike fingers and an eye inset into the center of the hand, looks disturbingly real. If I were full-blooded Fey, I'd recoil from the iron, burned by the touch. But as I'm demi-Fey, I feel nothing as I reach for the knocker. It creaks as I raise it and bring the iron fingers down twice against the wood.

It's a moment before Raphael pulls open the door, wearing a white shirt with the sleeves rolled up. A tendril of his dark hair tumbles in his eyes, and he flashes me a half-smile.

His silver eyes pierce me. As always, his masculine beauty immediately makes my breath catch. *You're weak*, I tell myself. *Remember what he did.*

Walking past him, I survey the soaring ceilings. The sixty-foot walls are covered with faded, colorful, and leather-bound spines marked with gold letters and esoteric symbols. Ladders on wheels stretch up to the higher shelves. I breathe in the scent of leather and parchment and faintly recognize it as *him*. Raphael spends a lot of time here, I think.

I feel awestruck by this place and at one with the cozy, flickering lights of the many candelabra.

At the far end of the hall, a brass spiral staircase leads all the way up to the back side of the clock. The ticking of the second hand echoes off the ceilings—the beating heart of the library. I stare at the back of the clockface, an ancient mechanical marvel, its brass gears illuminated by the library's dancing torchlight. The hands move rhythmically, ticking and tocking. I can almost picture Taliesin in here, scribbling away.

But my task is different from Taliesin's. Unlike art, my task involves pain when I mess up. And there, in the center of the room on a carved oak table, is the veil box. In the little trunk, it shimmers and buzzes, making the hairs rise on the back of my neck.

Raphael pushes his hair out of his eyes. The warm firelight caresses his beautiful features. "Let's get to work, then. You still need to master your control over the veil."

"Why here?"

"I always do my best work here, and my clearest thinking. Maybe it will help you focus." He gestures to the desk, with the veil box glowing in the center.

I cross to it, my shoulders already tensing in anticipation at the pain that awaits me.

We've been training for the past three months, once a week. I've been getting slightly better, but about half the time, I lose focus and burn myself. Because of the diametric magic, my powers are erratic, crashing into each other unpredictably. No matter what I do, I can't smother my telepathy.

I pull out a chair, and Raphael takes a seat across from me. He folds his arms. "Let's start this time by channeling into the creative source."

"What does that mean, exactly?"

His silver eyes gleam. "Everything on earth comes from a divine, creative source—the force that drives nature, that created our world, our existence. It forged every drop of water and blade of grass. When we write poems and make art, we are conducting that power. It's nature expressing itself in the same way that it expresses itself as an apple tree growing from the earth, and the apples on its branches. That's where our magic comes from. That's the thing about magic, Nia. It doesn't really come from us. It's not ours, and we don't own it. It's a power we are allowed to use, a gift that doesn't belong to us. Do you understand?"

I stare at him, entranced. The firelight sparks in his eyes. "I think so."

"You need to let it flow through you. Get in touch with the force that created us."

"How, exactly?" I ask.

"One way to get in touch with the creative force is through free association. Or free writing. Just say or write whatever comes into your mind."

"What, *now*?" I ask, and he nods.

I'm already nervous. What does he want me to say? I'm usually so good at determining what people want from me, but I can't read Raphael. And moreover, I'm not supposed to be telling him what he wants to hear. I'm supposed to be tapping into that creative force, but I have no idea how, and I'm certain that I'll say something fucking weird.

"Nia," he says, "just say the first word that comes into your head. Then keep going."

"Rigid pillicock," I blurt.

He stares at me. Not a hint of a smile. Of course not, because even if he were having the absolute time of his fucking life, even if he were swilling champagne on the back of a glittering unicorn, the man would not crack a smile. He has no emotions.

My cheeks flame red. This is why I didn't want to do this. "Can we skip this, please?"

"Fine. Let's try it another way. Find the core of your Sentinel powers. Smother your other magic. Suppress your emotions to clear space."

I close my eyes. By now, I can do that. My mind shuts out the world. Mentally, I dive into the feel of the magic, ignoring all the distractions that surround me. I let go of my everyday anxieties, the tiredness of my legs, the stiffness of the wooden chair, the hollow pit in my stomach from missing dinner. I forget Raphael's gorgeous face and the way he smells.

Deep in my chest, I can sense my power. *Two* powers pulsing with energy, at odds with each other—wrestling like spirits of the light and dark. I feel twinges in my chest as each struggles to snuff the other out. As the magic battles inside me, goosebumps rise on my skin. A gust of wind skims over me, though from where, I have no idea.

The sound of whispers flitters around me—two voices, one angry and one sad. But the meaning eludes me.

I can imagine how people with two powers sometimes lose their minds. The opposing magic is powerful, pulling me in different directions, and I feel as if my mind might split.

In the hollows of my skull, red-streaked images flicker —the halls of Avalon Tower, splashed with blood. Mordred's work.

Screams echo off the stones.

I swallow hard, trying to pull out the thread of my

Sentinel powers, to untangle it, but that's impossible to do without awakening the telepathy powers, too.

Raphael has taught me to mentally see the magic inside me, to identify its color and sound. Right now, they're twined together. I *think* the Sentinel power is darker, a deep red, like the blood Mordred spilled in Lothian Tower. It also has a slower, deeper vibration. The telepathy powers are more violet, high-pitched and frantic.

Opening my eyes, I lean toward the tiny veil on the desk. I can see the magical net that created it. As I stare at it, I hone in on the spot that looks weakest. I channel my Sentinel powers, trying to make them swell. Red blooms in my thoughts. The quiet buzzing of the veil goes silent. I push my hand into the box, and the misty veil snakes around my fingers, up to my wrist—completely harmless.

Inside, threads of my magic twist and roil.

"Good," says Raphael. "But if you can, focus for a moment on your telepathic magic. Contain it in a bubble, then shrink that bubble until it's gone."

I breathe hard, envisioning the violet strands. But as soon as I give the telepathy my attention, it only seems to grow, hungry for more power. Now, the violet is devouring the crimson, a ravenous beast.

The veil bites at my wrist. "Ow!" I scream. Yanking my hand out, I massage my throbbing hand, and a chill racks my body. My teeth chatter, and I lean away from the box. "It was working until you told me to focus on my other power." Pain pierces my hand, and I feel irrationally annoyed with Raphael.

He holds out his hand. Glowering, I slide mine into his palm, and his healing magic immediately washes over my hand in a soothing pulse. I lick my lips. "I think it's better if I just focus on the dark red magic."

"We'll keep working on it, but I think you have to be able to completely smother your telepathy skills in order to master control of what we need."

"Yeah," I answer hollowly, my chest tight. I keep thinking about what I glimpsed in Tana's thoughts. The encroaching darkness, the tiny drop of water that gleamed in the shadows, the agonized screams that chilled me to the bone.

Everything depends on my ability to control this power.

A little part of me considers telling Raphael about the vision, but I keep my mouth shut. Tana seemed sure it was a secret I needed to keep.

"Do you really think I can pass the other tests in the Culling?" I ask. "Fighting, spycraft?"

Raphael shrugs slowly. "You don't have to be worried about the fighting test. Viviane told me you're pretty good with a bow, and as long as you demonstrate some rudimentary abilities with a knife and a sword, it will be good enough. Not all spies are fighters. And as for spycraft, you happen to be very skilled at delivering to people the story they want to hear. Back during our first mission, that sergeant wanted you to be a timid and naïve girl, and you sold him that story beautifully. It's the only reason your accent didn't matter at all. It was your instinct, Nia, to give him what he craved." He's looking down at the table, and I can see the shadow of his long eyelashes on his cheeks. "And that will be part of your test. You'll have to persuade someone to give you something they wouldn't normally want to give up." His gaze lifts, and my heart races at the intensity of those silver eyes.

"I *am* good at telling people what they want to hear. I never realized that living with a highly volatile addict would prepare me to be a good spy, but here we are."

He arches an eyebrow. "With *most* people, you tell them what they want to hear. You're not always quite so flattering with me."

"Well, Raphael, I worry that if your ego gets any bigger, it will need its own magical realm."

He leans closer to me. "But why is it, exactly, that I am the only one to whom you show your real self?"

My heart is beating faster. "Because there's no point pretending with you, is there? I heard what you thought of me. *Trash* was the word that got me, actually. You referred to my mother and me as trash. Yes, this was a long time ago, and no, I'm not over it. I overheard everything. And I don't blame you, not after one of my mother's spectacles, but I don't see why I had to be included."

After all this time, I can't quite believe I'm letting it all out.

He sits back. "I never said that. I wouldn't have."

My chest tightens. "But I remember it. Right after

mother got drunk again. She was falling down the stairs, and you had to help carry her back to our room. You had already stopped speaking to me…" I'm dangerously close to mentioning our kiss, and I really don't want to betray how much I'd thought about that single kiss over the past ten years, and we already know I'm terrible at lying. "Anyway, you'd stopped speaking to me. But Mom was drunk, and you and your rich friend helped carry her to our room at the château. And the next day, I overheard you talking to your posh friend about how we were trash."

"I wouldn't have said that."

Anger flickers through me. "Not in English, but in French. 'Des ordures.' One of you said, 'People like us don't spend time with people like that,' and the other one said, 'Yes, isn't she trash? She and her mother.'"

He nods, frowning. "Ah, guilty as charged, in part. I *did* say, 'People like us don't spend time around people like them.'"

I stare at him. "I'm not sure I see how that's much better. What do you mean, 'people like them'? You've been making digs at me like that since I first saw you on the dock in the south of France. You said I should be getting drunk on champagne at the beach, or that you don't expect much from people like me. It's not really much better than saying *trash*, is it? What's the fucking difference?"

My pulse is racing out of control. No one in the world makes me feel unhinged quite like Raphael does, and it really doesn't help that he never displays a single freaking flicker of emotion. That I'm yelling at a robot.

He breathes in sharply, then swallows. "I'm sorry. I didn't mean it how you seem to think I did."

"Then how, exactly, did you mean it?"

"What I meant, Nia, was, 'We don't spend time with rich people.' You still seem to think I was rich. I never was. Some of the demi-Fey at that château were, but I was a fugitive with no money. I came from Brocéliande to the south of France with nothing, fleeing Auberon. I was literally barefoot when I arrived. And at the château? I was employed there to pick grapes. I wasn't a guest like you. I worked in the vineyards, and you were a guest. When I said *people like us*, I meant poor fugitives. And when I said *people like them*, I meant rich Americans. We were from two different worlds, that's all. And I'm assuming that you didn't stick around to hear my reply because I wouldn't have accepted anyone calling you trash, nor did I believe it."

I swallow hard. "Oh." I bite my lip, my cheeks burning. "I'm not rich, either, as it happens. That vacation you interrupted? I saved up for five years. I live in a dingy apartment with my mom. Walter was rich—the man I thought was my dad. But they never married. She used to find rich boyfriends, but the money was never ours. And once she got older, and her looks faded—well, it's harder to find a rich boyfriend. I work in a *bookstore*, Raphael. Mom and I eat bargain-brand cereal for dinner most nights."

"I see." His pale eyes gleam, and it's the closest I've ever seen him come to showing real emotion. "Perhaps we've misjudged one another. And you're not what I used to think at all. I thought you were…"

"Spoiled." It comes out a bit sharp. "Is that where the *princess* thing came from? Pixie princess?"

"I really did say that, didn't I? I know it's not the truth now." A line forms between his eyebrows. "So, when you saw my room, and you said, 'It's not the sort of room meant for trash,' you were referring to yourself? I was sure you were calling *me* trash."

My jaw drops at this. "Oh, gods. You thought that I was calling you poor trash?"

A faint smile curls his lips. "Listen, let's forget all that." He leans forward. "Can I show you something? It's my favorite part of Camelot, and hardly anyone else knows about it."

I was shocked to realize that yes, I really did want to see whatever it was he had to show me. Just like when I was seventeen and he'd invited me to see something at the château, and I'd jumped at the chance. Last time, such an invitation was followed by a month of me crying on the floorboards. After all, even though he didn't call me trash, the man had still ghosted me.

Still, I wasn't a teenager anymore, was I?

This time, I wouldn't let my defenses down.

"What do you want to show me?" I ask.

I see a dimple in his cheek as he almost smiles. "You'll see."

CHAPTER 22

*R*aphael pulls a torch off one of the stone walls and leads me to a large painting. I frown at the image—another one of Mordred Kingslayer, wearing his spiked crown over dark curls and a long black cape. In this image, he's beheading a blonde woman who kneels at his feet. It's about ten feet tall and gilt framed.

"Is it true that he had diametric magic, and that's why he murdered everyone?" I ask.

He sighs. "Maybe, but I don't think that's why the massacre happened. It's the prophecy. The one about the House of Morgan."

A chill skitters up my spine. "Auberon is descended from Queen Morgan. And the Dream Stalker, too."

"And that's why they need to die. They were born with the same violence running through their veins. The moment they get the chance, they'll break in here and slaughter everyone."

He reaches for a book on the shelf to the left of the portrait. As he pulls it out, the portrait pops open like a door, creaking. He turns back to me with an arched eyebrow. "You're not going to tell your friends about this passageway, are you?"

"Your secret is safe with me."

Holding the torch, he leads me into a dark corridor. Light and shadow dance over the stone walls, and the narrow hall stretches on.

"Where are you taking me?" I ask.

"To the Tower of Nimuë."

I breathe in sharply. Tana had mentioned her name. The Lady of the Lake, like me, apparently. Tana had seen me in her tower. "Where is it?"

"It stands in the lake, with a bridge leading out to it. Nimuë was a powerful water Fey, back in the days of primal magic. As Lady of the Lake, she was an envoy between the Fey and humans. From her tower, Nimuë gave Arthur his sword, forged from Avalon Steel. And she gave Merlin and Arthur their torcs, too, from the same sacred metal."

"So, her tower was a meeting point at one time?" I ask. "Between humans and Fey?"

"Exactly. Arthur met with the Court of Merlin at dawn and twilight. In the early days, Arthur and Merlin worshiped the gods together—gods of the rivers and oaks, and the earth itself. But the other Fey court plotted against that unity."

"Queen Morgan," I add. "But what happened to

Merlin? Did Queen Morgan kill him?"

"No, but they say she persuaded Nimuë to do it. Merlin was in love with the Lady of the Lake. Some said they even had a child. But over time, Nimuë started to think Merlin was becoming too human, too English. Arthur's court stopped worshiping the old gods, and Merlin went along with it. He abandoned the gods of the rivers and lake and the forest groves. Nimuë accused Merlin of giving away secrets of Fey magic to the humans who wanted their land. So, she used her magic to seal him in an oak tree, and he was never seen again. They say his ghost haunts the oak groves nearby."

"It doesn't seem like it helped the Fey of Avalon." A shudder prickles over my skin. "They're gone now. What happened to them?"

"After what Mordred Kingslayer did, the humans retaliated with a vengeance. The Fey lost the war. Utterly defeated. Queen Morgan was killed on the battlefield. Auberon was only a baby, so Mordred took him to France, and Mordred's mages burned up their magic creating Brocéliande, the realm where the broken Fey empire could live in defeat. We think Mordred went mad after the loss and eventually ended his own life. He was already insane, of course, but it only got worse. That was all a long time ago. I imagine Auberon has probably been stewing on his revenge for ages. And the prophecy still lives."

An old, mossy stone ceiling arches over us. Words are carved in the stones, though they are too faded for me to read. I'm enraptured by this place, my curiosity sparked.

The hair rises on the back of my neck. I feel like I'm walking into the past, and part of me never wants to go back.

"Does the prophecy worry you?"

"Not if we destroy the House of Morgan. I couldn't keep my parents safe, but I can keep this place safe." He glances at me, his eyes gleaming in the dark. "One day, I plan to end her bloodline."

I want to ask him more, but we're already at the end of the passage. He slides the torch into a wall bracket, and the light wavers over a small red door. It's tiny, almost like it's made for children. Raphael bends down and pushes through. The fresh air sweeps over me as he leads me out and onto a mossy stone bridge. We're not far from the lake's edge, and the bridge stretches out far above the water with low stone walls on either side. The air is thick with the scent of oaks and apple trees.

I glance back at the castle, and my breath catches as I stare at the sprawling walls. The dark, glassy lake spreads out into the night, a mirror to the stars. Lake Avalon always seems smooth and calm, and the moonlight gleams off its still surface. Tonight, everything is washed in silver. The hot summer air is sultry, fragrant with the scent of apple blossoms.

As my eyes adjust to the dark, I can see old runes carved in the stone of the bridge, worn by time. Camelot is a vast and beautiful place, thousands of years old. I can't quite believe I'm living on the bones of so much history.

Raphael pushes himself up to sit on the bridge's wide

stone railing and pulls a silver flask out of his pocket. With a sly half-smile, he hands it to me. "It's very strong," he warns.

"Is this part of our training?"

"It is."

I take the flask and sit down next to him, stretching out my feet toward the ledge. I'm wearing the usual Fey attire, a sheer dress and almost nothing else. I've generally stopped feeling self-conscious in it—except for right now. Because sitting next to Raphael in the hot summer air, I feel acutely aware of my legs and cleavage on display.

A cascade of stars spreads out above us, and the night air kisses my skin. "So, this *is* part of training?"

"In a way. You need to get in touch with the creative force, and it helps to be in awe of nature, where you see its work etched in the sky and on the land. And from here, you can tune in to the history of the place. The mead is to help you relax."

I take a sip of it. It's drier than the mead in the dining hall, and the sting of alcohol burns my throat. "This *is* strong."

"Don't have too much, or you'll lose your inhibitions. And I know how Americans get when you lose control."

"We're not as bad as the English," I mutter. Already the drink is warming my chest. I take another sip. "You think my problem is that I have too many inhibitions?"

He nods. "You are a bit tightly wound."

My jaw tightens. "Maybe I'm a bit disoriented. My life has been moving too fast for the past four months. One minute, I'm on vacation. The next, I'm on a boat, getting attacked by a sea monster. And—"

I stop myself short. I don't want to talk about the deranged, scrawled letter I got from my mother today. She told me that if I didn't return home, she would die. My mother is a master of the guilt trip. It's not clear from the letter how she would die, but there are allusions to walking into the sea.

"What is it that you're not saying?" He leans forward, his eyes gleaming with curiosity.

"What happened to your family?" I ask, deflecting.

He winces nearly imperceptibly. "My mother raised me. My father was never in the picture. Auberon considered my human mother an enemy of the crown, even though she hardly had any money. I don't understand what he had against her, except that he blamed all his failures on humans. And she was human." He leans back against the wall and stares out at the river.

Sensing he needs a drink, I hand him the flask.

He takes a sip. "We didn't realize how far he was going to go. This was before the invasion of France, when our world was still secret. And we never imagined...my mom thought if she just kept quiet, he'd leave her alone. So, we kept to ourselves. But one day, Auberon's soldiers raided our home. There was no trial, no jury, no chance to repent. Dawn broke, and they slaughtered my mom in the garden."

His jaw clenches, but he keeps talking, as if he's forgotten I'm there. "We'd all been in bed, then someone knocked on the door." He takes another sip. "They wanted to kill everyone in the house. My sister screamed at me to run to the forest, that Mom was gone, and they were after us. I ran. I thought she was behind me." A line forms between his eyebrows. "She wasn't, and I ran back to find her, but I couldn't find her anywhere."

My chest aches. "How old were you?"

"Nine. My sister was sixteen."

I swallow hard. "And you never found her?"

He hands me the mead. "I kept searching the forest, living off berries and water from the stream. She never came. I think I was half-dead when a demi-Fey family found me and took me with them to France. It was really amazing luck, I suppose. I was heartbroken, but they brought me to the château with them, and I started working, picking grapes." He glances at me. "You know the rest. And now this is my home, and I will defend it with my life."

This is a different side to Raphael, a softer side I've never seen. I don't think he lets many people see the real Raphael. The thought sends warmth spilling through my chest.

"Now you," he says softly.

I take another sip of the mead and lick my lips. "I'm not sure my mother is going to make it without me."

"Why?"

"Because she needs me to look after her."

"She's convinced you of that."

There's a lump in my throat. "It's also, unfortunately, true."

"You get your own life. Demi-Fey live for a long time, but even we die someday. You have to die when it's your time, and no one else can do it for you. That means you need to live for yourself, too."

"So, is that who you're living for? Just yourself?"

The wind toys with his hair. "No."

"Ah, you don't take your own advice."

"We have different situations."

I stare out across Lake Avalon. In the late summer night, the air is humid, and steam seems to rise off the lake. The air smells of earth and oaks.

The mead is supposed to loosen my inhibitions, but instead, it's making me feel sad. Maybe it's the old, bony claws of guilt clinging to my heart. A memory rises in my mind. After my disastrous birthday, when Walter kicked us out of the mansion. She wouldn't get off the floor for weeks, wouldn't eat or bathe. I remember washing her with soaked cloths.

Sadness carves through me. Sometimes, she said I was the only thing she did right, the only thing she could be proud of.

Raphael's hand presses flat against my back. I glance at him and feel his magic spreading along my spine, heating my skin. His magic is like warm water spilling over me, making my pulse race. Something about it makes my breath catch.

My gaze slides to him. "Why are you using your healing magic on me? I'm not broken."

Lips parted, he leans in closer. "I can feel your sadness."

His gaze is intense, almost as if he means it. Of course, the truth is, he's a heartbreaker.

"So, you're not only a magical healer, but you're also a magical antidepressant, too," I say, trying to sound flippant.

He pulls his hand from me. "You can't tune into the creative force if you're too sad."

"Oh."

"Let your mind go blank," he says softly. "Don't think about what I want you to say. Don't think about what *anyone* wants from you. You need to clear your mind."

I stare at him, entranced by his full lips and sharp jawline. The wind toys with his black hair. I stare at the rings of blue at the edges of his silver eyes.

"Say the first thing that comes to your mind," he murmurs.

"You're beautiful."

The silver in his eyes grows brighter. "So are you." The faintest hint of a smile curls his lips, and the rich scent of apples floats on the wind. "I dare you to jump in."

"To the *lake?*"

"No, jump into the bridge." He rolls his eyes. "Yes, the lake." He stands and kicks off his shoes.

"Is it deep enough?"

I stare at him as he unbuttons his white shirt, devouring the sight of him, the tattoos that sensuously coil around his muscles, the masculine power of his body.

He turns back to me with a wicked smile. "Are you coming, American?"

He climbs onto the low stone railing and jumps. I hear the splash and rush over to peer down. From far below, he grins up at me. "It's lovely."

It's *far*. Twenty feet, maybe. Is this safe? Oh, fuck it. I slip my shoes off and climb onto the railing. My heart races. I told him he was beautiful, and he literally leapt off the bridge to get away from me. Am I surprised?

As I crouch on the bridge's edge, the wind kisses my skin.

Fuck. It.

I push off, my gut tightening as I plummet through the night air. There's a shock as I plunge into the cool, clear water. I drift down for a moment, then kick my legs, swimming higher again. Raphael is waiting for me at the surface. He smiles at me. His dark hair is slicked back, and droplets of water bead on his skin. My pulse is racing, my breath shallow. That was fucking exhilarating. When was the last time I actually felt this alive?

We're swimming close together, and his limbs brush against mine under the water.

Heartbreaker.

I'm already growing breathless, and I start to swim toward the shore. I hear him swimming behind me. When I reach the part of the lake shallow enough to stand, I turn to look at him. He stands up in the water, his gaze searing me. Water spills down his bare skin in rivulets. The cool night air sweeps over my soaked dress.

Raphael's gaze moves over me, and I glance down. My already thin dress has gone transparent, and my hard nipples are standing at attention. His fist clenches, and I see his jaw tighten. His heated gaze meets mine, and I think—for the first time—I'm seeing the real Raphael. The unguarded Raphael who forgot to manage his expression. My chest flushes.

"What made you decide to jump in?" I ask. "You're not usually fun."

He's so close to me now, studying me intently. His expression looks almost desperate. "Because I wanted to kiss you, and I'm not supposed to. And you make it hard for me to stay in control of myself. You destroy my self-control, Nia." His eyes flick down to my lips.

My breath quickens. My heart is still pounding from the wild thrill of the jump, and his heated gaze makes my soul light on fire.

"I can look, but you know, I'm not allowed anymore," he murmurs. But his lips are hovering over mine anyway. Nearly touching.

I lick my lower lip, and his eyes flash at the movement. Our breath mingles in the air. My heart thumps rhythmically.

He'll break my heart again.

I'm about to force myself away from him when his lips press against mine. Liquid heat cascades through me. He slips his fingers into my hair, gently at first, then tightening. His tongue slides against mine, languid and sensual.

I want more of him. Here in the lake, his enormous, strong body presses against me. His tongue sweeps in, tasting me. I moan against his mouth, and his kiss grows deeper. I'm back in those sun-drenched fields with the summer heat gilding my skin.

Slowly, he nips at my lower lip. With an agonized sigh, he reaches for my hips and lifts me until my legs are wrapped around his waist and the hem of my dress hikes up to the top of my thighs.

I kiss him back, and he groans softly. Heat radiates from his body, and I slide my hands into his hair. His fingers flex on my ass. I roll my hips against him, and his kiss grows more desperate, hungry. Heat flows into me, trailing from my chest into my core. I want to rip our wet clothes off and pull him down on top of me, into me.

With excruciating slowness, he withdraws from the kiss. He stares into my eyes, the silver in his pupils almost glowing. He lets out a long, slow sigh, and his expression looks agonized. "I'm sorry, Nia."

My heart twists. He's about to ditch me again, isn't he?

"I was trying to not kiss you, pixie," he says softly.

I take a deep, aching breath and unhook my legs from his waist, standing on my own in the lake. Of *course*.

"Same. Well, it was the mead," I say, my voice cracking a little.

He turns away from me with his hand on his forehead. "There are rules at Avalon Tower about relationships." His voice sounds husky. "It's strictly forbidden, and of course it is, because it can risk the success of our missions. I can't risk either of us getting kicked out. Especially not you, when I know how important you are." He runs his hand through his hair and casts me one last look. "Next time, we meet in the daylight. I can't let this happen again."

He walks into the shadows, and I turn to stare out at the moonlit lake. I wonder which of these oaks was the one where Nimuë sealed up a heartbroken Merlin, trapping him in isolation for all time.

I brush my fingers over my lips. Was it just the mead that made him kiss me?

Heartbreaker. There's the old Raphael again. I did warn myself, didn't I?

I run my fingers over the clear, still lake water. I do truly feel at home here. *Lady of the Lake.* Could it be true?

Maybe Raphael should be careful, or he'll find his tormented ghost haunting these apple groves.

CHAPTER 23

*I*t's a moonless night, and the only light cast on the dark waves is the faint glow from the veil. My breath catches as I stare at the shimmering fog rising from the sea. Mist spills over the waves as we bob in our tiny rowboat. We left the sailboat behind, climbing into this little thing so we could sneak up on the Fey barrier unnoticed.

Saltwater mists my face, and the buzz of the veil's magic thrums and prickles over my skin.

It's my fifth mission, but it's the first time we're entering by water. I'm not sure I feel ready for this.

Shadows cloak us, which makes Raphael, Viviane, and Freya happy. But for me, it's making me more seasick to have no horizon. And I keep wondering if a sea serpent could be looming beneath the inky water.

The mystical fog floats over the waves, and as we move closer, I can see some tendrils of the veil beneath the surface. It plunges into the depths, all the way to the bottom of the sea floor.

Seasickness rises in my chest, and I swallow the nausea. I pull my gaze up, trying to look for something approximating a horizon. My gaze settles on Raphael's large back as he pulls at the oars. Freya guides him and Viviane from the bow as they row.

Raphael turns to look back at me. "Are you ready, Nia?" I can hardly hear his voice over the buzz of the veil.

"Yeah," I lie.

Ignoring the nausea, I focus, blocking out every one of my fears, the memory of Raphael's lips on mine, and the discomfort of the wooden seat I've been perched on for hours. Inhaling the marine air, I look inward. For those few seconds, I almost feel like I'm back in Raphael's study, focusing on the practice veil.

My two powers mingle together, bloodred and pale violet. I focus on the scarlet, the slow and deep magic that can take us through the veil. With a long exhale, I envision the red magic as a ravenous beast consuming the violet. The mist's buzz around me goes quiet.

"Now," I say hoarsely.

Raphael and Viviane pull hard at the oars. Usually, as soon as I stop the veil, everyone just rides as fast as they can through it before I lose focus. In this instance, we can't race that quickly. Despite their swift rowing, we seem to move at a snail's pace, the waves and currents pulling us left and right. I clench my teeth, forcing myself to block out everything except the slow, pulsing magic that whorls inside my chest.

The bow of the boat plunges into the misty veil, and the fog envelops us. I can't even see them anymore, only the sound of the oars as they strike the water. Every time they plunge into the sea, bioluminescent light flickers around them and spirals off in shimmering undercurrents.

Finally, we cut through the mist and reach the other side. Once we're through, I can relax a little, and the hum of the magic returns. The chill instantly bites at my skin. It feels much colder out here at night in the damp boat than it does in Raphael's study. My teeth chatter, and the air stings my face. I'm wrapped in a fur coat, but the frost is underneath, carving down to my bones. Like a devouring winter wind, the cold consumes every last bit of my heat. I hunch in my coat miserably and shiver. Closing my eyes, I imagine the fireplace in the Taliesin Library and the golden light wavering over cozy reading nooks.

Freya lets out a long breath, and I realize she'd been holding it the entire time. It must be difficult knowing that your life is in the hands of a mostly clueless rookie.

In the distance, we can see lights off the castle on Jersey. The island has a long and bloody history. First, it was ruled by a druid class until the Roman invasion. Then came the Norman invasion, the Hundred Years' War, a siege during the English Civil War, occupation by the Nazis—and finally, conquered by the Fey empire. After being independent for decades, it's now a playground for a terrifying prince from the House of Morgan.

Today, Prince Talan—the Dream Stalker—rules Jersey. He took an ancient castle and remade it into his own, renaming it Château des Rêves—the Dream Castle. A hedonistic palace by the sea, where rich and powerful Fey can find anything their hearts desire, as long as they pay tribute to him. Under his command, the Château des Rêves has become a vast, towering castle for pleasure-seekers and romantics.

"Okay," Raphael says. "Let's go over everything one more time."

We don't need to, not really. Like every mission, we've pored over our cover stories, obsessively memorized plans, and scrutinized the maps for hours on end. But this is Raphael's method, his way of reminding us that we're in this mission together, that each of us has a role to play. And this time, I'm included. Since I can't wait for them by the veil in the middle of the ocean, the best course of action is for me to join them on the mission, despite Raphael's reservations.

"I'm Mabel de la Rue," Freya says. "A human chamber-maid in the Château des Rêves. I was hired after three chambermaids were overcome with a sudden stomach flu this evening."

This alleged sickness was a contribution by an insider, a demi-Fey who lived in Jersey and worked with Camelot.

"As soon as I get the go-ahead," Freya continues. "I'll

waltz in to clean the prince's room and search for the maps."

According to our intel, King Auberon recently decided that he wants his son to become more involved in the Fey army's leadership. He sent maps to the prince, marking the up-to-date locations of the Fey military bases in the occupied territories. This is a priceless opportunity for us. Once we get our hands on those maps, our agents can act —infiltrating and sabotaging Fey bases, crippling the king's army in a way that would take them years, even decades, to recover from.

But Raphael also has a personal reason for this mission. He's been digging for hints about his sister for years, collecting scraps of rumors, tidbits of information. With the knowledge he's pieced together, he's now convinced that his sister is still alive, and that her prison could be marked on one of the maps.

"I'm Elizabeth Fallaise," Viviane says. "A new Fey performer in the cabaret of the Palace of Pleasure, with a scintillating display that includes two winged snakes and a crystal orb, which I can do very uncomfortable acts with. Unfortunately, because I'm new, I mistakenly go to the bottom floor in search of my dressing room, which is how I end up at the vault. If the maps aren't in the prince's room, that's where we find them."

Raphael raises an eyebrow. "I'm Lord Agravain Lyoners, a bored Fey aristocrat on holiday from Brocéliande. I'll be the go-between. Anything out of the ordinary during the operation goes through me."

I swallow, trying to suppress the urge to puke, wishing we could be on land already. At least the heat is returning to my body. "And I'm Lady Igraine Lyoners, Agravain's equally bored wife, hoping for a view of the castle's orgies. My husband has a wandering eye and has failed to satisfy my needs. I'll be at the cabaret, where I'll be delighted to get a glimpse of the crown prince with his renowned sexual appetites. In reality, I'll be watching his retinue to make sure they don't go anywhere during the search in his room."

"Hush," Viviane murmurs. "We're getting closer."

The oars pound rhythmically in the waves. I turn to see the castle on a rocky hill, looming over rows of tall wooden houses that line the shore. Around us, sailboats bob in the sea.

My gaze is drawn to the palace. A castle existed here for eight centuries, but I'm sure the original was nothing like this new, enchanted creation. It *glows* like a star in the night sky. Silver light gleams from the towering walls, streaking the waves with white. Pearly spires stretch high toward the moon, and vines climb the pale stone.

From the castle, faint music floats on the sea air. I lick the salt off my lips as we drift closer to an empty dock. My stomach twists. This mission is immensely, insanely dangerous. Raphael promised to stick close to me—hence, his cover story as my husband.

Hopefully, we all make it out of here with our sanity intact. Our professors don't even allow us to speak the prince's name. We're trained to avoid thinking about him because if you think of him, you can dream of him. Then, the wicked prince can invade your nightmares and ruin your life. Apparently, in dreams and real life, he's an expert in torture. An artist of pain.

We glide up to a wooden dock that juts out into the sea.

I pull my fur coat tighter around me.

I can feel all the what-ifs popping in my mind. What if our source is wrong? What if the Fey soldiers noticed our little boat and are waiting in ambush right now? What if—

"Let's go," Raphael says, hopping off the boat. He ties it to the dock. Freya climbs out, then Viviane. I step out last.

Beneath my fur coat, I'm wearing basically nothing—a silver silk chiffon bit and a G-string. Apparently, it's what an aristocratic Fey housewife would wear to the Château des Rêves. I want to keep the fur coat on, but I know that's not in the cards because Lady Igraine Lyoners does not give a single Fey fuck if people stare at her exposed nipples or ass.

With regret, I drop the fur coat in the boat and fold my arms over my chest.

I turn to the agents. Raphael is dressed in a crisp shirt and a waistcoat, clothing that can at least somewhat protect him from the sea air and allow him to hide a few weapons. Male spies have a real advantage in that regard. Freya is wearing the black and white uniform of a chambermaid from the Château des Rêves, which apparently means a short skirt, a clingy black top, and not much else. And Viviane, in her cabaret dress? A fishnet would be less revealing. Let's just say that despite what she declared in class, there are quite obviously no knives in her knickers this evening.

Raphael carries what looks like a white laundry bag full of gear and weapons. He hands it off to Freya. "Ready?" he whispers.

The four of us can't be seen walking together, so Freya takes off first, heading for a long stone stairwell that zigzags up the rocky hill. Partway up the stairs is a landing with dark archways—the servants' entrance. Freya and Viviane will be let in by our contact down there.

Viviane turns back to us and nods once, then takes off up the stairs after Freya. My nerves flutter as I stare at the castle. The shimmering stone and sharply peaked spires gleam like silver-blue blades against the night sky.

Raphael glances back at me as I walk, and I know he's trying to assess how I'm feeling. He was nervous about me coming on the mission and worried that I'm going to fuck this up. If we're caught in the castle, we'll be tortured slowly and sadistically until we betray every last crucial piece of information that will leave MI-13 in ruins. And it will all happen under the wicked and watchful eye of Prince Talan.

I'm dead silent as we start to walk up the stairs, climbing the rocky slope that overlooks the sea. At the weathered stone landings, torches light the way. The light and shadows twist in a ghostly dance on the stairs.

Music from the castle hums in the air, mingling with the sound of crashing waves.

We pass by the dark arches inset into the rocks, where Freya and Viviane have already slipped inside. We keep going up, heading for the guests' main entrance.

As we walk higher up the stairs, the sea wind whips over me, stinging my skin. I feel pretty much naked in this dress.

"Are you all right with this?" Raphael asks quietly.

"If I weren't," I whisper, "it would be a bit late for you to find out."

"You look tense."

I focus on relaxing my jaw. That's where my anxiety shows up, according to Raphael.

The stairs have led us up the hill, where a wrought silver gate is inset into towering stone walls. Through the gate, a garden spreads out—moonflowers, black roses, bloodflowers, and hellebores bloom, bathed in the faint glow of the palace itself. The pale stone towers and turrets rise high above us, pocked with narrow, warmly lit windows.

Staring up at it, I let out a long, slow breath. If everything has gone according to plan, our contact already has our names on the guest list.

Raphael rings a bell next to the gate. A few moments later, a guard in ceremonial armor walks up to the entrance. "Yes? How can I help you?"

"We're Lord Agravain Lyoners and Lady Igraine Lyoners of Brocéliande. We're expected," Raphael says, his voice laced with boredom at the mundane conversation he's forced to partake in. He slips his hand into his pockets and pulls out two cream-colored invitations with silver writing. "Here."

We wait for a moment as the guard inspects the invitations, the brisk wind biting my exposed skin. The sweet fragrance of the moonflowers mingles with the scent of brine. Finally, the guard swings the gate open, and we step inside.

My heart pounds as we cross into the garden, feet crunching on the gravel path to the castle doors. Wrythe has thoroughly drilled the many Fey torture methods into our heads—some of which literally involve drilling—and by this point, I wonder if he's done us all a disservice. It's hard to think clearly through the raw fear vibrating through my bones, and fear can lead to terrible decisions.

We cross through the garden to a steeply peaked oak door to the palace, which must stand twenty feet high. Before we left on this mission, we'd memorized every inch of the layout of this place, but I didn't quite have a sense of exactly how massive it would be. The door swings open before us, and a Fey butler stands in the entryway, his dark hair slicked back. He's wearing a black velvet doublet and a sword at his waist. He shoots me a disdainful look. "Your invitations?"

Raphael hands them over again. The butler motions for us to enter, and I don't thank him as I walk past. Lord and Lady Lyoners would not debase themselves by talking to the help.

Arm in arm, we walk slowly through a chandelier-lit stone corridor, following the sound of music. Raphael's powerful, calm presence is reassuring, his arm warm and sturdy against mine. Lady Igraine Lyoners might be frustrated by her husband, but all I feel is a powerful magnetic pull toward Raphael.

In here, the air is heavy with the scent of night-blooming jasmine. At last, we reach the large hall.

My pulse races as I take in the resplendent scene before us: the Fey cabaret.

CHAPTER 24

*a*rm in arm, we enter a hall with soaring ceilings and walls made of what looks like twisted, bone-white tree boughs. The branches soar two hundred feet high, meeting above us in a Gothic-style rib-vaulted ceiling. Lights float in the air and glitter from the arboreal walls. Ivory white columns flank a stage with diaphanous curtains on either side.

Around the hall, some of the guests sit in chairs, drinking cocktails. Others stand on the marble floors, arms draped lazily over each other, watching the stage. A balcony sweeps above us, where people drink and dance.

I glance at Raphael and find his expression, as ever, difficult to read. He's watching the stage, towering over me. Slowly, he glances down at me, and I wonder if he's noticed that I'm still not relaxed. The trick here is to observe absolutely everything while looking like you're half-drunk, swaying to the music and lost in the moment.

The job requires me to be a placid lake on the surface with roiling undercurrents beneath.

Raphael gives me a lazy half-smile. Taking me by the hand, he leads me to a chair facing the stage, sits, and pulls me into his lap. Leaning against his broad chest, I breathe in his intoxicating scent—the rich, woodsy smell of him tinged with the leather of bound books. The feel of his sculpted body against me helps me relax, which was probably his plan. He slides his arm around my waist, breathing out with a soft, wistful sigh.

I try to focus on the show and discreetly keep an eye out for the prince. The show itself is enchanting. Twenty Fey dancers dressed in shimmering, translucent robes swirl on the platform, their movements smooth as liquid, their skirts flashing, showing a leg, a thigh, a glimpse of curves. Four of them hang from crimson ribbons that dangle from the ceiling, performing complex somersaults above the crowd. All is expertly accompanied by the orchestra, the music brimming with joy and ferocity. This place feels like a cathedral of lust.

Raphael rests his hand casually on my hip, and I am acutely aware of the heat radiating from his palm through the thin material of my dress. My mind slides back to our kiss in the lake. Was that the mead at work that night and the sultry summer air? The enchantment of the lake?

When I glance at him, for just a moment, his eyes dip down. His fingers flex on my hips, his jaw tightening with tension. He drags his gaze away, back to the stage.

Right. We're here to be on the lookout, to search for

those subtle signs of alarm among the Fey. A lapse of attention could mean death.

He shifts me slightly, then lowers his face near mine. "Do you see the guards?"

His whisper warms the shell of my ear.

I scan the hall and spot eight guards, dressed inconspicuously as staff but hiding short swords within their suits. Movement in the upper balconies makes me suspect that there are at least two more bowmen, their eyes trained on the crowds. A lot more security than our sources reported. And there's an obvious reason for it.

My blood runs cold as Royal Prince Talan, the Dream Stalker, prowls into the hall.

Raphael's fingers twitch against my skin.

With an insouciant swagger, the prince towers over the rest, looking like a god. He has black hair, with a few strands at the front that almost reach his chiseled jawline. His full lips curl in a faint smile. The entire room is staring at him, and a hush fills the hall. I feel the power of him whisper over my half-naked skin. Rumor says he might be one of the only people in existence with real, primal magic.

Two gorgeous women are draped over his elegant suit of deep blue and green, the colors of the sea. The many rings that gleam from his fingers probably cost hundreds of millions.

My heart races. His eyes are so dark, they're nearly black, framed by black eyelashes and thick eyebrows. Tan skin, high cheekbones, tattoos that climb his neck—his striking beauty is hard to look away from.

I force myself to glance at the stage again, but I keep watching him from the corner of my eye. In the periphery of my vision, I see him drop into a chair at the head of a long table. A blonde woman falls into his lap. I steal a quick look and see him lazily stroking his fingers over her ribs, watching the stage. He oozes seduction. Is that how he gets into people's dreams? They dream of sex, and there he is. Except when he arrives, he's not there to deliver pleasure, but pain.

Someone hands him a crystal glass of wine, and he leans back, taking a sip. Around him, a group of Fey are laughing and talking with each other. But it's easy to see that although they try to act naturally, they're all watching him. Trying to get his approval with a joke or a comment. Women dance in his line of vision—writhing, sexual movements. The prince is the obvious apex of the group. And not just the group. Everyone in the hall seems to focus their attention on him. As much as the show is wonderful, the Dream Stalker is the real star. And all he has to do is lounge rakishly in a chair with a woman in his lap and soak up the attention like a black hole.

"Madam? Sir?" A woman in a black uniform leans down. "Would you like a champagne cocktail?"

I nod curtly, like Lady Lyoners would.

From my position on Raphael's lap, I scan the rest of the room. Raphael leans into my throat, his lips against it. In a low voice, he murmurs against my neck. "Exit strategies?" Heat from his breath warms my skin. He pulls me in a little closer.

I see three exits—the door we came in, the door used by the servants to bring drinks, and the door by the stage that probably leads backstage. Surveying the hall, I notice a few more armed Fey and make a mental note of their position. I yearn for my own knives, which were impossible to hide in this outfit.

A Fey man stumbles, his velvet trousers brushing against me for a moment. In a rush, his thoughts instantly invade my mind, desire and excitement in equal measure. He turns to look down at me, pupils dilated with lust. I break eye contact, my face already flushed from the stranger's emotions. In this place, people's thoughts would be unusually loud. Strangely, I can't hear a single thought from Raphael, even though his arm is wrapped around me.

Like his emotions, he must keep his thoughts concealed from me.

Right now, I'm still enveloped by his arms, leaning against his broad, iron-hard chest. He's so big that my head nestles in the crook of his neck.

The waitress saunters over with a tray, carrying two champagne flutes. She hands one to me and one to Raphael. "I hope this is real champagne," I say, because Lady Lyoners is an absolute bitch.

She blanches. "It's sparkling wine from Bryn Yr Ellyllon, in Brocéliande."

I let out a shudder. "Fine." I flick her away.

Raphael's silver eyes dance with amusement, and a faint smile curls his full lips. He glances over my shoulder at the prince, and I follow his gaze. All eyes are on the beautiful prince, so no one notices us gawking. There are three men and five women in the group circling the Dream Stalker. One of them has an insignia we memorized in Wrythe's class, marking him as the major general in charge of the northern army. His name is Shaelan, and according to our intel, he's a close confidant of the prince. He leans back against a column, taking a sip of wine. His silver hair hangs down to his chin. The châtelain of the castle stands nearby, recognizable by the sigil on his jacket, embroidered with golden skeleton keys. He's responsible for managing the grounds of the castle and all its defenses.

As the song on stage ends, the dancers bow. The prince drains his glass, his expression bored. The light in the theater dims, and six muscular Fey push an enormous glass tank onto the stage for the next act.

Water Fey swim inside, their breasts bare, hair floating around them seductively. They spiral in the tank as the music starts again, a stranger, slower tune that tugs at my soul. One of them swims to the center of the tank, where a large rock protrudes out of the water. She climbs onto the rock and smiles at the crowd, which has gone silent.

And she starts to sing.

I've heard of sirens, and in my Avalon Tower classes,

I've studied them a bit. But the accounts about them use words like "beautiful singing" and "almost hypnotic."

Now I realize that there's no way to actually describe a siren's song. Not with words, anyway.

The music skims over my body like warm water, and I feel like she's singing to me, and to me alone. Although she doesn't speak in a language I understand—something older than Fey—the song's story is instantly obvious to me. This siren is singing about the day when I was seventeen, and Raphael took me to explore the fields.

I nestle into Raphael's neck, feeling lost in the memory. It was a perfect day. The thrill of exploring the dungeons, then lying in the long grass in the humid summer air. Breathing in the rich scent of the earth and the heady scent of lush grapes. He handed me some, and the flavor burst in my mouth. A smile had curled his perfect lips as he looked at me, and the grass tickled my skin. Our fingertips brushed, and the next thing I knew, his body was pressed against mine. The kiss ignited me, warming me like sunlight through a ripe grape—

The only reason I can't fully lose myself to the siren's song is the constant murmuring of someone talking nearby. He's speaking incessantly throughout the song, driving me insane. True, the siren's song about my day with Raphael probably doesn't really speak to everyone, but can't he just appreciate the music in silence? I wrench my attention away from the song just to look at the rude bastard that's interfering with the show.

"Nia," Raphael says quietly in my ear. "Stay alert. Don't get mesmerized by her song."

As my attention snaps away from the siren, I realize the obvious truth. The siren is not singing about my day with Raphael long ago. It's the magic in her song, the music intertwining with my own memories. Even now, back to my senses, part of me wants to sink into the beauty of that memory. But I need to block out the effect of her voice. I look around me and see the mesmerized crowd. Some have tears running down their cheeks. Others are trying to get on stage, expressions of pure lust etched on their faces, while guards are holding them at bay. The guards, I realize, are wearing earplugs. They're immune to this magic.

Raphael pulls my face close to his and whispers, "I want to follow one of the guards, but I need you to stay alert here. Keep your attention on the prince. Don't listen to the siren song."

I slip out of his lap, and he stalks away. I can only thank the gods that he couldn't hear *my* thoughts. I grip the champagne flute, doing my best to block out the intoxicating effect of the music. Dropping down into the chair, I glance at the prince. Unlike everyone else in the crowd, his beautiful face is inscrutable. He doesn't seem quite as entranced with the siren song as the others do. As he sips his wine, I realize I can see Mordred's dark beauty in his features—the sharp cheekbones, the sensual lips. The dark, almond-shaped eyes. All he needs is a spiked crown, and I'd be looking right at the image of one of those gruesome portraits. *The House of Morgan...*

I glance at the Dream Stalker and see his dark eyes searching in the crowd. He's not looking at me, and yet I feel the full intensity of his attention like an electrical charge.

He cocks his head, staring at the stage again. A lock of his black hair rests on one of his sharp cheekbones. A chill ripples over my body.

A deep, murmuring voice floats through my thoughts, and my heart skips a beat. It's the phantom, sensual voice I often hear. He's speaking in Fey about a party he threw, and the heat of desire that made bodies shimmer with the otherworldly colors of twilight. And the flame-haired woman so obsessed with the pleasure of his tongue that she stripped naked the moment they were alone together. He delighted in the poses she struck for him that night, baring herself in every way. She likes it when he tugs her hair. And yet, he feels something is missing...

My pulse starts to race. It's him, isn't it?

The voice I've been hearing all these years when I'm alone and tired. The sometimes violent, sometimes sensual voluptuary who speaks to me when I'm in that liminal space between waking and dreaming, murmuring in a velvety voice.

Of course it would be him—the Dream Stalker. It makes sense. Dreams are woven from our worst fears and greatest desires. And that's what his voice has always been in my mind.

My heart is beating wildly out of control. I've been hearing his poetic, dark, and often absolutely filthy thoughts since I was about eighteen. Oh, gods, sometimes I actually *liked* hearing his voice. Sometimes, it turned me on.

How can it be? My telepathy only works by touch. How could I have heard his thoughts all these years, even when we were thousands of miles apart?

He suddenly seems to tighten, his thoughts more aware. They seem to be searching for something. For *me*.

We're close enough for him to sense me.

A small crowd of dancers gets between us, blocking me from his view. From what I know of Prince Talan, he can weave dreams and nightmares, harvest the fears and fantasies from the darkest recesses of our minds. I don't want him noticing me at all, and apparently, he's already been in my head. Right now, I fear his consciousness is brushing against mine, exploring my secrets.

Who's in my mind? His seductive voice murmurs in my thoughts. *Who are you, telepath?*

I can feel his magic searching for me, seeping into my subconscious like ink in water, exploring all the feelings in my psyche.

And as he delves into my emotions, a rush of confusing images floods my skull.

Mom hurling a glass at me, and it hits my forehead...

I'm reading a book in the bookstore, desperate to be somewhere far, far away...

I overhear Raphael, talking to his friend, and the word *trash* echoes off the walls...

I pull my mind away, visibly flinching.

From what I understand, he's not a telepath, but he's drawn to emotions. And as he tunes into them, he brings up memories I've tried to bury.

I glimpse him through the crowd, twirling his wineglass and looking utterly bored. Shadows carve his cheekbones. His cold expression is impossible to read, but his dark eyes turn my blood to ice.

I don't think it's Auberon who's destined to destroy Avalon Tower. I think it's this beautiful Dream Stalker elegantly lounging in a chair. With his glittering rings and relaxed posture, he looks decadent, libertine, someone who could seduce you to your own death. I can feel his malign presence from here, coiling over my skin like smoke. Searching for signs of the person who invaded his thoughts.

With a racing heart, I slip further into the crowd, blending in, keeping my expression slack as I gaze at the siren. From the corner of my eye, I see the prince whisper something to the woman in his lap. She gets off him, and he stands, turning to the door. *Shit.* I have a feeling he's heading back to his room to fuck that woman.

I need to warn Freya.

One of the women in his group catches his sleeve, smiling at him, imploring him to stay, buying me precious time. I keep my gait slow and unhurried so as not to attract attention, but I'm on my way to the corridor. The further I get from the siren's music, the easier it is to focus. It's mercifully empty out here.

Beneath vaulted ivory arches, I hurry toward the stairwell. The prince's chambers are on the third floor, and that's where I'll find Freya. I just want to make sure I get there before Talan does.

Lifting the hem of my dress, I bound up the stairs two at a time. On the third floor, I push through a door on a landing. Mullioned windows stretch up to a high ceiling, and vines grow over the stones. I stumble, pretending to be drunk. There are guards standing outside Talan's door, and I need a good cover. His door is twenty feet tall and painted green, with two enormous guards standing out front. With a dazed smile, I stumble closer to them in a zigzag.

"Excuse me? I seem to be a bit lost. Can you direct me to my room?" I slur my words, my face slack, talking just loudly enough for Freya inside to hear.

He smirks at me, amused by my drunkenness. "Which room is yours?"

I frown. "I don't recall, exactly," I say in a loud and drunken voice. "It's the one with the tapestry of the diving hawk."

Diving hawk was our code word to indicate that the prince is coming.

"I'm not sure where that is," the guard says. "But if you want to wait for me down at the main hall, I can help you look when my shift is over."

The door opens, and Freya steps out, a bulk of sheets in her hands. She looks at me. "Can I help you?"

"She's lost," the guard says. "Can't find her room."

Freya grunts, as if annoyed at the hassle. "Come with me, madam." She rolls her eyes at the guard, and he grins at her.

She grabs my arm, tugging me close to the stairs.

"The prince left the cabaret," I whisper. "I didn't know if he was coming up here."

"Fine," Freya says. "The map isn't there. I looked through every inch of his room."

In the spiral stairwell, she pulls me aside. I'm still catching my breath.

"I think I saw him," she whispers. "Earlier. The Dream Stalker. He scares the shit out of me."

I swallow. "Yeah." At some point, I'd have to tell her what happened, but there isn't time now.

As we get closer to the lowest floor, she goes ahead. There's no reason for a chambermaid to be hanging out with a lady.

When a minute has passed, I make my way outside to a balcony overlooking the sea. Below us, the waves pound on the black rocks. The salty wind whips at me as I cross the terrace. The three of them are already waiting. The door closes behind me.

"It's not in his room," Freya whispers.

Raphael curses quietly under his breath. "Not in the vault, either. And we checked the logbook. The prince hasn't deposited anything lately."

Under the moonlight, he looks out over the dark ocean. With his dark expression, it doesn't take telepathic powers to figure out what he's thinking. This map was his one hope of finding his sister.

For Raphael, these maps weren't just an MI-13 mission. Finding the prisons in those maps might help him recover the only family he has left.

CHAPTER 25

"We need to leave," Freya says.

"Wait." Raphael whispers. "Maybe the map is in the châtelain's chambers. That would make sense, wouldn't it?"

Freya glances back through the doors. "Raphael, there are a thousand places the map could be." Her voice is sharp. "We can't bumble around here. If we stay much longer, the scheduled coast patrol will block our escape. And at some point, someone might wonder why Viviane isn't getting on stage—"

"Go down to the boat. If I'm not there in ten minutes, leave without me." Desperation laces his tone.

Freya scowls. "Absolutely not," she says. "We're not leaving without you."

"That was an order," Raphael snaps. "I'm going to check the châtelain's chamber, and you're going to wait for me outside. If any guards see you, leave. If I take longer than ten minutes, leave."

He pushes through the glass doors into the hall and is gone.

Viviane folds her arms. "Fuck that. I'll stay as lookout down the hall from the office to see if anyone's coming."

"I saw the châtelain in the cabaret," I say. "I'll go back and make sure he doesn't leave."

Freya blinks and shakes her head. "This is stupid, but fine. I'll keep an eye on the palace's security."

I take off first, heading back to the cabaret. As I stride there, I resume the character of Lady Lyoners, only slightly more drunk now.

Deep inside, I know Freya is probably right. Raphael has no idea where the map is, and he's acting out of pure desperation. Maybe Prince Talan isn't even keeping it in his castle. Wildly searching for a single parchment in this enormous place is a doomed endeavor.

But I can't get Raphael's devastated expression out of my mind.

In the cabaret, I'm relieved to see the aquarium with the siren is gone. Instead, three Fey women are whirling around the stage dressed in little more than thin golden chains. The prince's entourage is watching, but Talan is gone. Now that the Dream Stalker isn't present, a few of the other guests have approached the group, trying to sweet-talk their way into his inner circle.

The châtelain is still there, swilling a red cocktail. At

the very least, he won't be barging in on Raphael ransacking his chambers.

A sudden, dangerous idea pops into my mind.

What if someone in that group knows where the map is? If they do, maybe I can find out.

Feigning a drunken sway, I saunter closer to their table. I breathe deeply, concentrating. Drawing out the frantic, violet-tinged magic, I let it spread through my body.

As the magic billows through me, I sense the feelings of people around me. I can't read their thoughts without physical contact, but I can *feel* them, thousands of emotions and ideas and desires waiting to be found. Waiting to be *seen*.

Dancing by their table, I try to appear like just another hedonistic Fey. I sweep past them, letting my fingers drift very delicately over a man's shoulders.

Maybe Aenor would agree to invite one of those dancers to our bed tonight. Perhaps if I suggest it, like something that I'm doing as a favor for her...

I peer a little deeper into his mind but don't sense anything about the map. I sashay along, pretending to be mesmerized by the show, and brush against a woman in a green dress.

I shouldn't have drunk so much mead. This is the fifth day in a row I've had too many bottles...

Nothing there, either. A few more steps, and I touch another man's shoulder in passing.

I can't get that tune out of my mind. It's driving me insane...

These invasive thoughts sweep around the inside of my skull, deafening. Each one carries with it unfamiliar emotions, strange images from people's pasts. It's like having a loud conversation that I'm not a part of in my head. I can barely focus, but I have to keep going.

The tip of my finger touches another man.

That bastard Orhan, I'll throw him to the wolves. He thinks he can do that to me?

And another woman.

I miss Alarice so much...

And another woman.

Mother, why did you leave us?

The flickering of your funeral pyre still lingers in my vision, interfering with my sight. It's been two months, but I can't seem to move on. I still remember our last talk. Well, our last fight. It feels like we were always fighting, and about the most trivial things. Like our final conversation, about the skirt I was wearing, of all things. If I had known it would be the last time I would hear your voice, I would have changed the skirt. I would have burned that skirt, just to see you smile.

I want to recall our happier times.

I remember how hurt you were that summer dance when I refused to dance with you. Back then, I was so worried about what my friends would say. And now, I would give anything for one last dance...

I wrench myself away from the woman, heart thudding. She's talking to someone across the table, saying something inane about the primrose and violet salad, and her turbulent thoughts still whirl in my mind, intermingling with those of the rest of the people I touched. Almost automatically, I move forward and touch someone else.

I wish I were dead. I will never forget the humiliation and embarrassment. Why?

Why have I done it? That waitress told me, "Enjoy your meal," and I told her, "You, too."

You, too.

As if she were also eating a meal.

That smile she gave me, that damnable, pitying smile. And now I see her across the room, talking to another waitress. I know what she's doing. She's telling her about me. How I said, "You, too," like an imbecile. Now they're laughing! As they should. I wish I were dead. Did anyone else hear me say it? I can never show myself in public again. I should walk off the cliff into the ocean before I do something even more mortifying. Oh, gods, now I've spilled wine on my trousers. Why me? What have I done to deserve this?

And I stumble away as the anxieties churn and roil in my mind like a storm. The woman's grief twines with other emotions of desire and irritation and anger. They're drowning my own thoughts, but Raphael needs me to do this.

I don't remember why, but I touch someone else.

He calls me a friend, a cousin. But how much does he really respect me? "Lumos, take this to my room." Or "Lumos, go get us some food." Or "Lumos, make sure my horse is ready." I'm third in line to the throne. Why order me around and not the others in his retinue? If he were no longer alive, I'd be second in line to the throne. And he's never managed to have children, which surely is a sign from the gods.

Well, I won't take his disrespect much longer. Next time he tells me to do something, I'll tell him to do it himself. Ha! He should be serving me. That would be a shock for him. "Talan, why don't you find us a couple of girls for company?" "You know what, Talan, why don't you carry my satchel, you dog?"

Of course, he's the prince. But I'm his cousin. And father used to tell me that a man has to have a backbone, or people will tread all over him. And he was right. It's time for me to grow a backbone.

I totter away, not sure who I am, just knowing this is what I do. I touch people and take their thoughts as my own. I am all of them. I reach out to take another one.

I just can't stop thinking about her, no matter how much I try. Even right now, with the dancers on stage, all I can do is watch her. Those turquoise eyes, that sweet smile. The way she tilts her head when she's amused...like she's doing right now.

How do I tell Elora how I feel?

Do I show her the poems I wrote about her? Oh, gods, even the mere idea makes me shudder. Those terrible poems. If anyone ever found them, I would die of shame. I should burn them, except that would be burning my own love.

Perhaps I should send Elora flowers. From a mysterious admirer. A dozen forget-me-nots every evening, so she always remembers me. And then, one night, after she's been showered with hundreds of blooms, I will tap on her door with a bouquet of a dozen more—vibrant violet-blue petals. And then she will know...

Oh, gods. She'll know that I am a creepy and deeply obsessed man. That's all she'll know.

Oh, Elora. For years, we have been friends. How can I stretch my hand across to meet yours beyond friendship, reaching for something more?

My body is gone, and I don't know who I am anymore other than a fog of thoughts. Am I eating a strawberry right now? Or drinking mead? Am I even here, or is this a dream? I had a purpose once, and a name, but I can't remember either. It's Lumos, right? The prince's cousin and third in line to the throne.

I need to get back to my body, but I can't find it, and there are so many thoughts sweeping through my skull. I'm lost in a labyrinth of emotions. I am not Lumos, that's absurd. I don't even *like* Lumos. Once, he grabbed my ass in the hall to impress Talan.

No, wait, he didn't grab my ass. He grabbed someone else's. Who am I? I search for myself, but I'm too far gone.

All I can do is add more and more minds to the din in my head.

This salmon is overcooked. I should get the waiter, but then everyone will say that I'm being a killjoy again. Is it my fault that I have a sophisticated palate? Surely—

I know I forgot to buy something. Let's see. I bought a dress for Callice, and the goblets. And of course I remembered the necklace for Astrid. And...

"Nia." A voice is calling me, familiar and so far away.

The dueling sword for Marcus. Oh, I know! I forgot the—

I can learn to dance like this. One step forward, two steps back, then sweep the hands. I can practice in my room later...

"Nia, snap out of it." That voice again, calling me, so sweet and alluring, but it's getting in the way. I need to concentrate so I can get the dance steps right.

How do they twist their hips like that, though? Can I do that? I'll try in front of the mirror—

"Nia!"

A beautiful man shakes me, and I blink at him in confusion through the cacophony in my head, a million people talking at once. Who is this man? I don't really want to pay attention to him, but he's gorgeous, and he looks worried. The chorus of voices in my skull is deafening, but I want to reassure him that I'm fine.

Except that I don't feel fine. I don't even feel like I can talk right now, like my lips aren't mine. Or maybe that I have too many mouths. If I open my mouth, twenty people will talk all at once.

"Nia, what happened?" he whispers. There is alarm in his alluring silver eyes and worry. He's worried about me, and it touches something in me.

Raphael. I sigh. I like Raphael, though I shouldn't. I might not know who I am yet, but I'm sure of that. The man with the silver eyes is Raphael, and whenever I look at his gorgeous face, I go weak.

"I'm...I'm..." I attempt to explain. "So many...thoughts."

He frowns, then his eyes widen. "You read someone's thoughts? Here?"

"Not someone..." I try to recall. "Everyone's."

"Oh, gods, *why?*" His hand is on my waist, holding me up.

I lean into him. He smells amazing. "I wanted...to find the map. For your sister. And I thought..." I rest my head rest against his broad chest for a moment, not entirely sure what I'm doing. Am I supposed to be avoiding this gorgeous, strong man?

At last, a clear thought pierces the chaos. "I know where it is!"

"Where?"

"It's in my leather satchel."

"Nia, you don't have a satchel."

"Talan is always trying to get me to carry his stuff," I whisper. "He's ordering me around. *Lumos, do this. Lumos, take that. Lumos, watch my documents—*"

"Who the fuck is Lumos? Do you mean Comte Lumos de Morlune?"

"Yes, that's my title, you fool!" I snarl. Then, I shake my head. "No, wait. I'm not Lumos. He's an ass-grabbing twat. But he has the map."

I whirl to look for the comte. All those people around the table, talking and laughing. They have no idea I've invaded their minds. Unbelievable that they can sit there, as if nothing's the matter, when I've glimpsed the raging chaos in their heads. And there. Lumos, with his bright red hair streaming over his broad shoulders and his satchel by his side. Resentment pours off him.

I lean in closer to Raphael. "See that guy with the

bright red hair?" I whisper. "That's Lumos, and that's his satchel. The map is in there."

"Are you sure?" Raphael whispers.

"Yeah, Talan made me carry—" I clear my throat. "*Told* him to carry it." It's hard to concentrate, to formulate the words. "It's there. The map's there."

"Okay, lower your voice," Raphael says softly. "I'll get the satchel, and then we get the fuck out of here."

"Yeah," I mutter. He's probably right. We should leave, though I don't remember why. I stare at the chandeliers.

He lets go, and I almost collapse. It takes all of my concentration to control my limbs. It feels like I have thirty arms. Thirty legs. I half expect the people around the table to lose their balance as I stumble, because we're all linked, aren't we?

I pull my gaze back down just in time to see Raphael walking idly past Lumos. In a swift, casual move, he grabs the satchel from the marble floor. He's by my side in the next few breaths.

He grabs my wrist. "Okay. Let's go. Nia? Let's go. What are you looking at?"

His dark hair frames a perfect face.

"Elora," I mutter. "Isn't she wonderful? Do you think she would ever love me back?"

Gripping my wrist, Raphael pulls me toward a stairwell. He doesn't understand my heartbreak over Elora. How could he? Who could understand a friendship like this?

"Nia," he whispers in my ear, "do you think you can

run down the stairs? We're going out through the servants' entrance."

"I think so," I say softly. "But I don't even know who I am."

He tugs my wrist, and we're bounding down the stairs. But I can't tell where my body is, and it's only a few steps before I stumble and fall. Raphael sweeps me up in his strong arms, and I melt against him.

CHAPTER 26

I'm sitting in a chair with my eyes shut, holding my head in my hands, hoping to anchor it and keep it in place.

"Raphael, we have to go." I hear Viviane's voice through the cacophony. Her words intermingle with the voices in my mind.

Raphael sits next to me, stroking my back. "Just give Nia a moment."

I listen to them talk from a distance, wondering who Nia is. It takes me a few deep breaths to remember. Ah! Nia might be me.

"What's wrong with her?" Viviane snaps. "What has she done?"

"She'll be fine," says Raphael.

"Why don't you tell me the fucking truth?" the woman says sharply. "She's overdosing on some kind of magic, isn't she? I can feel it emanating from her. Except it isn't

301

Sentinel magic because there was no veil in there. So what, exactly, is happening?"

Raphael lets out a sigh. "Telepathy. She used it on too many people at once. But you cannot tell anyone she has diametric magic. We need her." He sounds short, impatient. "They will kick out anyone with two powers. They'll say she's going to be another Mordred. She's not trained in telepathy, so she didn't know the dangers. We've been trying to suppress that magic, but I guess she thought it might be useful. Viviane, we need her."

Freya swears. "How many minds did she read, three? Four? If it's four, she might already be lost to us. She's strong, but I don't know if she can hold the thoughts of that many people at once."

"I don't know," says Raphael. "It might be more than four."

"I think it's twelve," I mumble. "Or thirteen. It's hard to count because they keep jumbling together."

Silence follows my words, and I wonder for a minute if they're even here, or more voices in my mind.

I open my eyes to find Raphael, Viviane, and Freya all staring at me, stunned.

"What?" I ask faintly.

"Please tell me you didn't." Raphael's fingers flex on my back. "Telepaths aren't supposed to read more than one or two minds close together because they can lose themselves in the sea of consciousness."

"The sea of consciousness," I repeat, staring at a flagstone floor. It sounds nice. And appropriate. That's what

I have in my mind right now. A nauseating, churning sea.

"It can't have been twelve," Raphael says firmly.

For a moment, I almost believe him. "At least twelve," I repeat.

"That's impossible," Freya blurts.

"There was Lumos, and Gaia, and Belrior." I count them on my fingers. "And Calixto, and Nia—"

"*You're* Nia!" Viviane snarls.

"Oh, right. *I'm* Nia. Anyway, there were at least twelve. Thirteen including Nia, but I guess she doesn't count? I mean me. Me doesn't count. I doesn't count."

I frown. That doesn't sound right, either, but the words are confusing. So many of them. Nia knows a lot of languages, but Calixto knows different languages, and so does Gaia, and the grammar and words keep getting muddled in my mind.

"Gods," Freya says.

"We need a different getaway plan," Viviane says. "She won't be able to control the veil like this."

This room is all shadows and stone arches, like a crypt beneath a cathedral.

"Why?" I ask, trying to focus on the conversation. It keeps me grounded, reminds me who I really am, Calixto.

No, hang on. Nia. I. Am. Nia.

"Because we need to go through the veil," Viviane says. She sounds furious.

"Okay. We did that once, we can do it again," I point out.

Raphael looks at me. "I agree."

"Raphael." Viviane's voice is steely. "She can't get us through. If what she says is true, she's gone. It's a marvel she can still talk, but we don't know who she even *is* anymore. And there's no way in hell she can focus enough to use her Sentinel powers."

"Yes, I can." I know it's true. I feel both my powers pulsating inside me, awake.

"She can," Raphael repeats after me. "She'll get us through. There's no other way, in any case. The royal prince has probably already found out that his map is gone. We have to get out of here *tonight*."

"The map!" I suddenly recall. "We have the map?"

He flashes me a dazzling smile. "We have, thanks to you."

"Okay. Good."

Raphael slides his arm around my waist and helps me stand. I stare at the torchlight flickering on the walls. "Where are we?"

"In an empty room in the lower level of the Château des Rêves," says Freya.

She's a chambermaid. I narrow my eyes at her. No, she's *pretending* to be a chambermaid. She's a human agent! I should tell Talan at once, and then I'll finally have his respect.

No, hang on. I'm Nia. I shut my eyes and take a deep breath, trying to pry apart the pieces of my mind that belong to me.

We step out to one of the hallways in the château. I'm

completely disoriented, don't even recall how we got here, but Raphael leads us confidently. He sets a brisk pace, fast enough to get out quickly, but slow enough to avoid making too much noise and draw unwanted attention from the servants down here.

We pass a small kitchen and a threadbare woven rug. The ceilings are lower than the ones upstairs. We walk past numerous rooms identical to the empty crypt we just left. A coat of arms hangs on one wall. I try to keep pace with them, but my head is still shrieking. I see the world through a haze, but Raphael's arm around my waist steadies me.

Raphael stops short. "Hang on. We missed a turn."

"Are you sure?" Viviane asks.

"Yeah. We need to go back." He turns around. "Come on."

I follow him, past the threadbare rug, the coat of arms, and twenty or more other rooms. So many rooms.

"What the hell?" Raphael mutters, looking around.

"I think we missed a turn again," Viviane says.

"There were no turns, Viviane," I say.

"What are you talking about?" she snaps. "There were a dozen turns. Where's Freya?"

My heart thuds. Freya is not with us anymore.

"Something's wrong," Raphael says.

"She probably went outside and didn't notice that we weren't with her," Viviane offers, but I can hear the uncertainty in her voice. "Come on, I'll lead. Through there, see?"

She points at a fork in the corridor that we somehow missed before. Now Viviane takes the lead, marching confidently on. We walk past the coat of arms again.

"We were here just a second ago," I say.

"No." She shoots daggers at me. "And you're the last person we should be listening to."

"No, see?" I point at the coat of arms. "It's the same antlers. And that same threadbare rug. We keep walking back and forth."

Raphael's fingers tighten on my waist. "We're disoriented somehow. Have we been drugged? All we need to do is get outside."

"Well, we came from the left passage," I say. "So we should probably take the right."

I start walking, but everything seems to be moving slowly, much too slowly. I'm walking as fast as I can, but I can hardly budge. I look down and realize that my feet are stuck in the threadbare rug, and with each step, I'm getting pulled back. The rug has become a strange, muddy goo.

"I'm sinking in the rug!" I shout in alarm.

"Don't shout," Raphael says. "Hang on. Where's Viviane?"

It's just the two of us now, and I'm knee-deep in the rug and sinking faster.

"We must have been drugged." Raphael's grip around my waist is solid, but somehow, I'm sinking and he's not.

"No." My stomach swoops. "The Castle of Dreams has

become the castle of nightmares. This is the Dream Stalker's work."

It's obvious now. Prince Talan must have realized his map is missing, and now, he's trapped us.

"No way," Raphael says. "He doesn't even know who we are."

"He doesn't need to." I've visited a dozen minds, minds belonging to the prince's confidants, enough to learn things about him. "He can sense people's subconscious when they're nearby. We're trying to get out, and we're scared of being caught. That makes us different from everyone else in this place. He's honed in on our minds and wrapped us up in this dream."

Raphael's grip tightens around my waist. "And he knows where we are?"

I shake my head. "I don't think so. Not yet. But if we don't get out, they'll find us eventually." I'm up to my thighs now in the liquidized rug. "Raphael, I'm drowning in this."

"It's in our minds," Raphael says slowly. "Nia, even dreams can be controlled if you know it's a dream."

"I can't get out of this!" I panic as his grip on my waist slips, and I sink deeper.

Raphael shifts his hold on me, taking my arm in a vise-like grip. "Don't move." His muscles flex, and he slowly pulls me free. The viscous rug gives way with a disturbing sucking sound.

I tumble into Raphael and cling to his steely chest, breathing hard. "We have to get out of here. Now."

"Hang on." He shuts his eyes, and his black eyelashes cast shadows on his cheeks. "Concentrate. This is in our mind, right? So try to picture us finding the way out. Picture us finding Viviane and Freya on the way."

I do as he says, closing my eyes. It's hard to concentrate, but I do my best to imagine us reunited with Viviane and Freya, grabbing them by the hands and fleeing the castle.

"Okay," I whisper.

"Come on."

He's holding my hand as we walk, and there, at the far end of the hall, is the door that leads to the stairs and the sea. I can even see the glittering waves through the window.

"It's working," I say softly.

Raphael nods.

We rush for the door and hear a shout for help. Turning, we see Viviane and Freya running toward us, a wall of flames roaring down the hall behind them. Smoke billows, stinging my lungs and eyes. A fit of coughing racks my body, and though I know it's just a dream, I can't make the flames go away. The heat sears my skin. We're going to burn.

Someone grabs me by the wrist, and I'm running, my eyes streaming from the smoke. Is the door gone again? We're trapped in a waking nightmare. Over my coughing, I hear Raphael shouting instructions to Viviane and Freya, telling them it's not real, that they have to imagine us getting out.

We're lost again. We can't find the door. Soon, I fear, we'll be back at the beginning, back to the threadbare rug and the coat of arms. The Dream Stalker is toying with us. We're his puppets, and he is pulling the strings.

"No, not there," Raphael says. "Over here!"

Gripping my wrist, he pulls me to a random kitchen door. He yanks it open—

And salt air washes over me, and a spray of stars twinkles in the night sky. Stone stairs zigzag down to the sea. We're free.

I inhale, the wind whipping at me. The night air is incredibly clear, and I can fill my lungs at last. Raphael has led us out of the nightmare.

"Come on, we don't have much time," he says.

We run down the stairwell, back to the dock where we left the boat. When we reach it, I almost sob in relief. We made it. I can't believe we got out. As I step into the boat, Viviane cuts the mooring rope with a knife. We push off into the sea, and oars plunge into the waves as Viviane and Raphael row.

The sea spray drenches me, and I hold on to the edges of the boat. Up ahead, the shimmering veil waits. Strangely, the misty magical barrier feels like safety.

"Nia, will you be able to get us through?" Raphael asks.

"Yes, just get us closer."

"The current is a real bastard," Viviane grunts as she pulls at her oar. "It's hard to row in this thing."

"Yeah." Raphael grimaces as seawater dampens his shirt.

I listen to the oars striking the water, staring at the veil. It doesn't seem to be getting closer.

I glance back. "We haven't left the dock!"

"It's the bloody current." Raphael shouts over the waves.

"Aren't we in a bay?" Freya is heaving for breath. "There shouldn't be a current."

I stare at the murky water. Even in the dark, I can see the water churning as they struggle with the oars. Storm clouds gather overhead, blocking out the moon and the stars. Shadows gather around us.

Now we're actually moving. The powerful current pulls us along with it, but not toward the shore. We're spinning in a circle.

"We're trapped in a whirlpool," Raphael says, alarmed.

Fear grips my heart as I cling to the boat. The whirlpool is enormous, a yawning void. The boat whirls faster and faster, around and around, as Viviane and Raphael try to row us out.

"No," I whisper. "We're not trapped in the whirlpool. We're trapped in the waking nightmare. We never left the Château des Rêves."

CHAPTER 27

*R*ain pours from the sky, and the water churns, our tiny boat rocking in the speeding torrent. Raphael shouts instructions that are impossible to hear as he tries to free the boat from the deadly current. Viviane's oar is wrenched out of her hands. I make the mistake of glancing at the center of the enormous whirlpool, an abyss waiting to swallow us. A void. Nothingness. The end.

With seawater spattering me and my heart thudding with terror, it's hard to convince myself that none of this is real. But it's not. I'm sure of it. Whirlpools such as this simply don't exist in the normal world—that's a nightmare thing.

Raphael was wrong. Although the dream is in our minds, we have no control over it. Our fantasy of escape is just that—a fantasy. The Dream Stalker let us *think* we were escaping, like a cat toying with a mouse, but we're still there. Our bodies are still in the Château des Rêves, enfolded in a terrible nightmare. Sooner or later, the dark prince and his guards will find us. Fear crackles through my nerves.

If I know I'm dreaming, can I force myself to wake? I pinch myself, but that doesn't help. Pain is real in this nightmare, and it's not a way out. If we drown here, I feel disturbingly certain that would mean the end for us.

What does the Dream Stalker want? I've heard his thoughts for years. He craves pleasure and beauty, but he always feels alone. If I'm in the château right now, as I suspect, could I slip into his mind as I accidentally did before? Maybe—only then—we can find a way out of this nightmare.

The thought of going anywhere near him, much less his thoughts, scares the shit out of me. I've already come close to losing my sanity by invading too many people's thoughts. It would be dumb to risk drowning in a sea of consciousness again, but do I have a choice? Not if I wish to escape this nightmare.

Gripping the slippery wooden edge of the boat, I close my eyes and focus on the magic inside me, the frenetic, high-pitched, violet magic that allows me to hear another person's thoughts.

As I summon it, I recall the way the prince's mind felt as it touched mine. Dark, brooding. Obsessed with sex.

I channel my telepathic powers at that mind and feel something brush my thoughts, a shadow of another entity.

Dark. Alluring. Seductive. But right now—above all —furious.

But it's hard to concentrate with the boat heaving up and down, threatening to spit me into the void. My fingers tighten on the wet wood. With racing breath, I grasp at that other mind, fumbling with my powers, stretching them toward his dark temptation like I've never done before.

And then, from far away, a voice.

Where are you, little dreamers? Where are you hiding?

His voice is velvety smooth, but a sharp fury slides beneath it. I can feel his wrath as he holds us captive.

I will drown you, and you'll wish you were dead, but you'll keep drowning, unable to breathe, water filling your lungs. In dreams, death cannot save you.

I cling to his thoughts, ignoring the terror filling my heart at the thought of that eternal hell. There must be a way out.

Ah, it's you again, isn't it? The little telepath in my thoughts. I can feel you. I may not have seen you, but I felt you. I can let you out of this. You only need to tell me where you are.

Fear vibrates through me. I clench my teeth and try to calm my mind. He can't read my thoughts, but he can feel my subconscious. And my subconscious is terrified.

Now, where are you and your friends hiding, little telepath? If you show me, I'll let you wake up. It'll save us all time...and you a lot of pain. Trust me, you don't want to be in this night-mare much longer. I can make it exquisitely painful for you.

The boat groans and shudders, and then splits at the

center. I plunge into the sea and sink beneath the water. I kick my legs to rise to the surface, floundering wildly as a wave crashes on top of me. Frantic, I fight my way to the surface again, gasping for air. It's nearly impossible to focus on the prince's thoughts. The water is icy, and my muscles are seizing up.

There's no way out, little telepath. I am in complete control of you—your body and your mind. I have the power to kill you or let you live. Submit to me.

Another hard wave pushes me under. I know the truth. If Talan finds us, the only thing next on my schedule is being slowly tortured to death.

I try to hold my breath, but I'm too late. My mouth fills with water. Water in my throat, in my lungs. I can't breathe, darkness is all around me, and the bone-penetrating cold. And I know that the prince is speaking the truth. Only he can free me from this nightmare, and he won't. Not until he finds where we're hiding.

In my terror and desperation, I draw on my powers again, trying to read deeper into his thoughts. But I can't focus. Instead of summoning the violet magic, I accidentally draw on my Sentinel powers, too.

My lungs burn as red and violet magic entwine, a tangle I can't unwind. A twisted magical hybrid that shouldn't exist, telepathy that shatters and *breaks* things. I aim that raw energy at the prince's mind and let it erupt.

I can feel his surprise as the surge of power hits him. I manage to snap something inside his mind, and he reels back in pain, breaking contact. The darkness around me flickers, and I gasp and open my eyes.

I'm in the room in the Château des Rêves, lying on the floor. Raphael, Viviane, and Freya are all lying on the stones. Their eyes fly open, Freya gasps as if still searching for air, and Viviane's hands jerk as though she's still trying to swim. And then they all freeze.

Viviane is the first to lift herself up. She looks around, her face as pale as milk. "We're back?"

My teeth are chattering, and the cold stings my skin. My fingers are numb.

"We never left," I say. "It was *all* a nightmare, including the moment we thought we got away and the boat."

"And now?" Raphael asks grimly.

I clear my throat. "I think I got us out of the nightmare."

His eyebrows flick up. "You got us out? How—"

Shivering wildly, I force myself to stand. "I'll explain later. We don't have much time. They're searching for us. The Dream Stalker knows we're still here. It's only a matter of time before he recovers and traps us again."

Freya glances at the door. "Won't he send his guards after us?"

I think about the flash of pain and surprise I felt when I let my powers explode in the prince's psyche and cracked something in his mind. "I bought us some time. But we have to leave. Now."

Two months ago, they would have argued. Viviane would have asked who the fuck I thought I was. Freya would have subtly rolled her eyes. But they follow my suggestion without discussion. In the past few months at Avalon Tower, I've managed to earn their trust.

When we leave the room this time, we head straight for the door. This time, the rug doesn't suck me in.

At last, we're outside, and the night air stings my skin. I know it's not arctic, but it feels that way.

Does anyone else know yet that the prince was hit with a magical attack? Is he sending people after us? I hope to gods not. I can't imagine what the prince's vengeance might be like.

I glance back at the castle but don't see any signs of alarm. I breathe in the cool, salty air and long for the comfort of the fur coat.

Raphael sees me shivering and wraps his arm around me as we hurry down the stairs.

"Did he see you?" asks Raphael. "Does he know what you look like, if he sends guards searching for the telepath?"

I shake my head. "No, he never looked at me. He saw inside my memories, but that's it."

Keeping to the shadows, we hurry down the zigzagging stairs overlooking the rocky beach. Despite the lacerating cold, I feel a wild euphoria. It was a near miss, but we escaped.

I glance up at the stars. Is it really possible that dawn hasn't arrived yet? The past few hours felt like days, stretched out through the nightmare. When we reach the dock, I half expect the boat to be in pieces, shattered by the enormous whirlpool. But it's still intact, waiting for us. My fur coat sits dry on a bench. The four of us hop in, and I pull the coat around me, trying to warm myself. In no time, Viviane and Raphael are churning their oars into the sea.

This time, we're off without a hitch. The marine wind whips at me, and I hug myself tightly, trying to feel my blood flowing again, my muscles softening after the glacial post-magic chill. Still, my teeth hammer against each other.

"Ship," Freya says, her voice low.

I look back and see a large ship, moving fast and piercing the water. The misty, pearly veil glows behind it, and I see it in silhouette. It's aimed unerringly straight at us.

"Another one there." Viviane nods to the north, where a large shadow is looming closer.

My stomach drops. The ships are moving between us and the veil. Our anchored sailboat waits for us on the other side.

"How did they find us?" asks Raphael sharply.

"The prince." I swallow. "He knew we were heading for the boat. He saw it in the nightmare and read our intentions. He must have given the order to search for us on the water."

"They're catching up," Freya mutters.

Cannons thunder in the distance. Then, a terrible shriek, becoming louder and louder.

"Grapeshot!" Raphael shouts. "Everyone down!"

I flatten myself on the bottom of the rowboat, and a second later, something screams past me. Splashes echo all around us as the deadly shots hit the water, tiny cannon rounds aimed to wound and kill people. Grapeshot scatters and doesn't need to be accurate. Our pursuers don't need to sink our boat. They only have to hurt us and slow us down so they can catch up.

"Faster," Viviane grunts, sitting up.

She and Raphael row as quickly as they can toward the shimmering mist. The hum of the veil buzzes over my frigid skin.

"They're getting closer," Freya shouts.

"Viviane's hurt," Raphael says.

"I'm fine," she says, though blood pours down her arm.

After a few seconds, she drops the oar into the water and groans. I lunge and grab it before it's lost.

"Can you row, Nia?" Raphael asks. "Can you row and lift the veil at the same time?"

It would have been better if I switched seats with Freya, but there's no time. "I can do it." My muscles are frigid with the cold, but if I can't row, we're as good as dead.

I lock my sights on the veil and start to row. I've only done this a few times, on short boat trips on a lake or a pond. Rowing in the ocean isn't the same. I know that I need to paddle in rhythm with Raphael, and I do my best to adjust to his pace.

The veil thrums loudly against my skin as we pull at the oars. The cannons boom again. I hunch in my seat and pray but keep rowing. One of the rounds hits the boat, and Freya lets out a shriek of pain. I don't know if she's hurt or dead, and I can't afford to look. We're nearly at the veil—way closer than I thought. The ships are almost on top of us. No time to stop or focus my powers.

Raphael and I keep rowing as I mentally focus inward, grasping at the blooming crimson magic. I let it swell, then fling it desperately at the veil.

The hum goes silent as our boat plunges into the mist. We drift through to the other side, and I heave out a slow, shuddering breath and look back. Freya is still alive. The ships in pursuit are maneuvering. The cannons boom again, but in the dark night, with the veil hiding us, the shot goes wide.

Shivering, I let myself relax. Not only did we make it out, but we've got the map with us.

CHAPTER 28

I blink slowly, trying to focus on Wrythe, who is standing at the lectern, stroking his blond beard. Light streams in the tall, mullioned windows over the rows of students. The Seneschal drones on. I think he's talking about the veil.

It's been four days since we returned from our mission on Jersey, but my head still feels foggy. Even now, the residual thoughts of a dozen other people fill my mind like static, and I get terrible, debilitating headaches. My only respite is the constant supply of herbal tea from Tana. It's nearly impossible to concentrate, which is unfortunate. The Culling is coming up fast, and I'm struggling to learn anything, despite staying up till two a.m. every night studying.

"No wall in history has ever been as effective as the veil," Wrythe says. "MI-13 agents can't swim or tunnel underneath, or even fly over the veil. There are some rare magical items, orbs and crystals and such, that provide some protection from veil magic, but they're unstable, and many die trying to use them. Auberon's mages keep the veil raised, stopping humans from invading their territory. Unfortunately, our *only* way of reliably going through the veil is with our Sentinels. At the moment, we have only one qualified Sentinel. As my brilliant niece Ginevra and I were just discussing, our command has been forced to resort to using untrained, subpar alternatives." He cuts me a sharp look, and the rest of the class turns to stare at me, as though I've done something terrible.

"Even though we all know," he goes on, "that until a cadet passes the Culling, he or she hasn't proven what it takes to function as an agent of Camelot. But these are desperate times, indeed. Desperate times."

I meet his eyes calmly. *Untrained, subpar alternatives?* That's me, and yet, without me, the last mission would not have happened at all.

On the benches across from me, I see Tarquin and Horatio smirk. Tarquin mouths, *Subpar.* Serana, sitting by my side, tightens her fist, and her pencil snaps in half. I smile at her and hand her a spare.

"Every agent needs to be intimately familiar with the veil," Wrythe continues. "We cannot have undercover agents gawking at it like fools, drawing attention to themselves. This is the reason for the field training mission that leaves this evening."

A murmur of excitement runs through the hall. This

field training mission has been almost all anyone has talked about for the past few days. All the cadets and the majority of instructors are leaving on a ship. The plan is to take them on a brief three-day tour along the veiled border.

Everyone except me.

Raphael already let me know that since I'm very familiar with the veil, there's no point in me going. Instead, he wants to use this time to work on my Sentinel magic, preparing me for the Culling. And given how foggy my brain has been, having the extra time to prepare isn't the worst thing in the world.

We've all been forgoing sleep, cramming maps and information and Fey grammar rules into our skulls. I've been helping Serana with her Fey language while practicing my lock-picking skills for one of the tests. Serana does her best to help Tana and me with our fighting abilities.

I rub my eyes, fighting off the exhaustion. When Wrythe lists the cities that the veil borders, Serana nods off. As her head bobs, I elbow her. She snores and startles awake.

"Ms. O'Rourke." Wrythe's sharp tone pierces the hall as he addresses Serana.

She blinks blearily. "Yes, sir?"

"Since you've been so attentive, perhaps you could list four cities in France that the veil's southern border cuts through."

"Um…"

"Incorrect."

"That wasn't…I was just thinking out loud—"

"I assume thinking out loud is the only way you'd get any thinking done." He snorts.

More laughter from the Pendragons. My spare pencil snaps in Serana's grip.

Wrythe's lips curl. "By the time we leave tonight, I want you to submit to me a paper listing four of those cities, with the names of our contacts there and how best to get in touch with them. You, too, Ms. Melisende, since we all know that ignorance can be quite infectious. That will be all."

The room fills with the sound of rustling paper and murmuring as everyone stands up to go to dinner.

"That utter wanker," Serana mutters as she crumples her notes into her bag.

"Watch it," Darius says in a whisper. "He might hear you."

As we head for the dining hall, Serana touches my arm. "Sorry, Nia. I didn't mean to get you in trouble."

"Don't worry about it." I adjust the bag on my shoulder. "The veil is sort of an inverted U. I'd choose Bordeaux, Poitiers, Bourges, and Marseille or Avignon. And I already know the contact names and everything. We'll do the essay in no time at all."

"You're incredible," Serana says, relieved. "I was sure it would take hours, and I still need to pack for the training mission."

"How do you manage to keep so bloody calm?" Darius

asks me. "Wrythe is constantly making snide remarks about you. The Pendragons hate all demi-Fey, but they're clearly targeting you."

I shrug. The truth is, compared to the Dream Stalker's torments, Wrythe's barbed remarks don't trouble me at all. "I don't care what he thinks."

We cross into the majestic chamber, where the sunlight pours through towering windows onto lavishly set tables. The portraits of Queen Guinevere and King Arthur loom over us all.

I walk to the cadets' table, doing my best to avoid contact with other people. The last thing I need is more telepathic voices ricocheting in my skull.

"I can't wait to see the veil," Darius says. "I've never seen it before."

"I'm excited just to leave Camelot," Serana says. "I haven't stepped out of these walls in a year."

I sigh. "I think I'm going to miss you guys when I'm all alone in my room."

Serana drops down at a table with empty chairs. "Sure you will. I bet you can't wait to have it all to yourself without my snoring and Tana hogging the bathroom."

I smile at her. She doesn't realize how much I've come to love having friends in my life.

"Hi, Nia!" A woman across the hall shouts my name, and I turn to see her smiling at me. She's next to a man with platinum blond hair. Both of them grin and wave.

Flustered, I wave back.

"Fans of yours." Serana says. "Word got around about

the mission. Everyone knows that you took down the Dream Stalker."

"I don't have fans." I laugh. "And unfortunately, I did not take him down. The man is still alive and well."

But maybe I feel a little flicker of pride as I scoop some wildflower salad onto my plate. It's an Avalon Tower classic of pansies, violets, dandelion leaves and an elderflower vinaigrette. The main course is wild mushrooms with rice, seasoned with butter and thyme. The rich scent of it makes my stomach rumble. Already, my mouth is watering, and my mood brightens.

At first, when I went on missions, I was treated with suspicion and jealousy. Tarquin and the Pendragons spread around the term *public bus*, then *Naughty Nia* and a whole host of other names. For months, others in the academy followed the Pendragons' lead, whispering Tarquin's nicknames, sometimes painting them on my door.

That changed after the last mission. Now, a different sort of rumor has spread. I don't know how because everything that happened was supposedly classified. But people know enough to realize that I played an important role in the mission.

I take a bite of the buttery mushrooms and rice, savoring the faint taste of truffle oil.

Serana has already shared some of the wild gossip she heard about the mission. That I single-handedly fought the Dream Stalker, straddled him, and snapped his neck. Others say that I saved everyone by galloping on a stolen horse across the island of Jersey. But the story she found most outrageous was one where the agents had all been trapped in an endless nightmare by the Dream Stalker, and that somehow, I broke us out using only my mind.

I sip my mead. In any case, the general opinion of me has definitely shifted for the better. And while Tarquin tries to keep the mockery alive, everyone else seems to be losing interest.

Tana plucks a fluffy berry pavlova and drops it onto her plate. "And how was Wrythe today?"

"An arsehole," Darius answers. "Wouldn't expect anything else of him."

"Are you ready for the big trip, Tana?" I ask.

Tana isn't going to see the veil. Like me, she's seen it often enough, but they need her with them to sound the warning in case of danger. The academy doesn't want to lose their entire year of cadets because they failed to take proper precautions.

"Yes, all packed." Tana gently nudges Serana. "You'll forget to pack your socks, so I already packed some for you."

"Well, now that you told me that I'll forget, I'll definitely remember," Serana says, her mouth full. "I like to do the opposite of what people expect."

"No, you will not. The cards do not lie." Her gaze slides to me. "And speaking of which, I'm still wondering about that lovers card. Remember? A lover from the past? It wouldn't be Raphael, would it?"

My stomach drops. Sometimes, it's deeply inconvenient having a psychic friend. "He's taken, isn't he?" I say, flustered. "Serana, when you first brought me to Raphael's room, Ginevra was in there." I try to look casual as I drum my fingertips on the wooden table. "And Raphael wasn't wearing a shirt. Aren't romantic relationships strictly forbidden here? Guess we shouldn't tell anyone about it or ever bring it up again."

The words all come out in a frantic tumble, and Serana arches an eyebrow. "Now, what is going on here, exactly? You and Raphael?"

I shrug, trying to look casual. "Don't be ridiculous. He hates me, remember?"

Tana narrows her eyes at me. "But you knew him in the past, didn't you? And it wasn't just a friendship."

My stomach swoops again. "*Me*? We were just talking about Ginevra. Ginevra," I repeat.

"You didn't answer my question."

"She *really* doesn't want you to get kicked out for something dumb, like shagging an instructor," says Serana. "You'd better not lick or otherwise touch him while we're away and you two are alone."

"The lover from the past..." Tana prompts again.

My cheeks flush. "Fine. I knew him, yes. Ages ago. It was in Bordeaux, and he kissed me once, and then said I was a spoiled American and never spoke to me again until I saw him in the south of France. The day I met you, Tana. He fully ghosted me, and I've never shagged him."

"Dickhead. Did you see his knob?" asks Serana. "I'm just very curious, because I imagine it—"

"I have not."

Darius rests his chin in his hands. "I'd risk getting kicked out for someone who looks like him, honestly."

Tana's stare is penetrating. "The cards suggested that a love from the past is also in your future."

I take a long sip of mead. "Well, anyway. Good news, everyone! My headaches are gone. I'm right as rain."

Serana nods. "You're doing that thing again."

Tana's grips her glass of mead so hard, she's at risk of breaking it. "Okay, you need to be absolutely ready when the tests come, and focused. You cannot fail. You and I have to pass, Nia. And you cannot get kicked out."

"I get it." My voice comes out a little sharp. "I am studying as hard as I can. No pressure, right?"

"Why are you so intense about Nia passing?" Darius asks. "I mean, we all really need to pass, right? Why are you harassing the poor girl?"

Tana, Serana, and I exchange quick glances.

"Yeah," Serana says. "Tana is just really worried that Nia will fail the fighting part. But I keep telling her she doesn't need to worry. Nia can kick anyone's arse these days. Even the Dream Stalker. At this point, she could thrash a demon of the abyss in a one-on-one fight."

"Some demons are actually pacifists and refuse to fight, even when cornered," Tana says, staring at the window.

Serana's forehead scrunches up. "I was just speaking metaphorically, I guess. There are no demons in the world, Tana." Her face has gone pale. "Right?"

"Right." Tana sips from her mead and smiles faintly. "It's better to think that."

"Well, that's a thought that's gonna fester," Darius mutters.

"Anyway, you don't need to worry." I spear a strawberry with my fork, though I've lost my appetite. Tana's prophecy is stressful enough without her constantly reminding me of it, then adding in a whole bunch of other stressful predictions.

The sad truth is, I'm not at the top of my game, and my diametric magic is still wildly unpredictable and out of my control. At least, for the upcoming month, I will be out of danger. The only thing I have to do is master every spy skill that exists and memorize the entire Fey history.

Darius loses interest in our discussion, his eyes following Nolan, a tall cadet who goes with me to Amon's advanced class for Fey language. Serana rolls her eyes at me. Darius has been obsessing about Nolan for weeks.

"I'll catch up with you girls later," Darius mutters, getting up, and walks after Nolan.

"I don't get Darius's taste in men," Serana tells me. "That Nolan guy is nothing special."

"I don't know. He looks nice. And he's wicked smart."

"Eh. I prefer more shoulders on my men."

"More than two?" I ask, bemused, fishing the last bits of my salad from my plate. When I look up again, Tana is staring at me, her eyes wide. A feeling of dread sinks into my stomach.

"What?" I ask.

"The shadows are closing in. Death hunts you. During the trials, the darkness will start to envelop you. If you don't survive, we all die. England is lost. Scotland and Wales, too. The rot will creep from the Cliffs of Dover all the way to the highlands. It starts during the trials."

She takes an enormous bite of her berry pavlova without breaking eye contact as she chews. I'm not sure what's more unnerving, her disturbing prophecy or the way she stares at me as she eats.

A cold fear settles over me.

CHAPTER 29

*D*ear Mom,

          I chew on the end of my pen.

The only sounds at Lothian Tower tonight are the rain hammering the windows and the occasional clap of thunder. It feels eerie here. Abandoned. For three days, I've been mostly alone in my room, cramming for my tests and practicing my Sentinel powers.

Lightning flashes outside. A few seconds later, thunder booms, vibrating the stone walls and making the candles gutter in the candelabrum.

I stare at the blank page. I hadn't realized how much noise I'm surrounded by at all times. Serana loudly knocking things around or swearing under her breath, sometimes randomly breaking into song. Tana, reading the cards yet again for Darius, checking if love is on the horizon. And through the door, I can usually hear the sounds of cadets talking loudly, their voices echoing in the cavernous halls. Now, the silence is eerie. Every now and then, I convince myself I can hear the faint screams of everyone being murdered by Mordred Kingslayer, the echoes of centuries ago floating over the stone.

It's a good time to write to Mom.

Yet, as I stare at the page, I don't feel like I have anything to say. I want to calm her, to reason with her. But her latest scathing letter lies on my desk, practically radiating anger and dysfunction. And it's not like I can tell her I'll be back soon. Or hell, even tell her where I am.

I sigh and try again.

This trip has been eye-opening. The beaches and the coast towns of—

My pen blurts a glob of ink, staining the paper and blurring my words. I try to blot the mistake, but the letters smudge, and now the word "beaches" looks like "bitch."

I take a fresh piece of paper and start again.

Dear Mother,

I hope you forgive me—

Another ink blot. Now "forgive" looks like "forget."

I grab another pen and a third piece of paper.

Dear Mother,

Finally, I am out of your grasp, you pathetic hag. I don't need to listen to your constant complaints and narcissistic chaos, and I don't need to clean your puke off the—

I stare at the parchment, horrified. I don't know what made me write that. My hands are shaking now.

I stand up, and my chair tips over and clutters against the wood floor. I bend to pick it up and accidentally hit a pile of Serana's books. The books topple, papers scattering everywhere. Fucking hell. What's wrong with me? I just wanted to get in touch with my mom, and I'm losing it.

While I'm stacking up the books, the framed portrait of Merlin falls off the wall and tumbles onto Tana's bedside table. I leap to grab it, but I'm too late. It drops atop the candle and catches on fire. Flames rise from the bedside table, and the acrid scent of smoke coils into the air.

Heart racing, I snatch a blanket to put out the flames. What the hell is happening?

As I try to smother the fire, the room seems to be coming apart around me. Vines snake off the walls, writhing in the air. The diamond panes in the windows shatter, spraying glass over the room. The wood in the wardrobe and desks turns dark and soft, becoming rotten and weak. The desk crumbles into decaying pieces before me.

I struggle to catch my breath, blood roaring in my ears.

Cracks form in the stone walls, and pieces of mortar start to crumble. Across the room, a heavy wooden ceiling beam crashes to the floor. The room is rumbling as if an earthquake is shaking Camelot. An enormous slab of plaster falls from the ceiling, missing me by a hair. I scream in panic and try to rush for the door, but it won't open. The wood is warped and decaying. Holes form in the wall, and then entire sections collapse above the windows, exposing a starry sky with a drift of clouds in the distance.

Outside, the shadows are shifting, an enormous silhouette that blots out the moon and stars. A gargantuan figure of darkness, a void shaped like a monstrous warrior. As tall as the tower itself, maybe even taller. The vast silhouette lifts a huge arm and points at me, and I feel another presence inside my mind, amused and delighted by my horror.

There you are, little telepath. I found you. I hear you crying, and no one is coming to help.

I can feel his ice-cold wrath, but also his fascination. He doesn't know what I look like yet, but he can sneak into my mind and sense my fear of him, like a cat who's found a particularly lively mouse.

And now, he wants to play.

You can't escape me, little telepath. As long as you go to sleep at night, I will always find you. This is my realm. My domain— one of fear and desire. And here, you are completely under my control.

The shadow clenches a fist, and the floor around me is suddenly swarming with snakes, crawling over my feet, slithering, hissing. I'm frozen with fear, can't even breathe.

You shouldn't have stolen from me. You have no idea what powers you're toying with. Where are you, telepath?

The silhouette has deep blue eyes. The prince's eyes...

The snakes writhe up my body, and I open my mouth to scream.

I bolt upright in my chair with a shout of fear. My heart is pounding wildly, hammering against my chest. I'd fallen asleep at my desk, and the candles went out. Darkness cloaks the room, but everything seems solid again. My unfinished letter to my mother lies in front of me. Rain is still hammering against the windows.

With a shaking breath, I search for the Dream Stalker's thoughts. But no, he's gone. I'm awake, alone.

And then the shadows move, and I realize that I'm not as alone as I'd thought.

CHAPTER 30

*shadowy figure stands by Serana's bed. For one hopeful moment, I think it's Serana, returned already. But no, that doesn't make sense.

For one thing, he's well over six feet tall and wrapped in a black cloth from head to toe. Only his eyes are visible, golden and malevolent. And there's something else about him, a strange vibration emanating from his body. My heart skips a beat. I just barely have time to register the curved scimitar in each hand before he lunges at me. Behind him, lightning flashes, and thunder rumbles through the stone walls.

Reflexes take over as my daily training with Viviane starts to pay off. I grab the thing closest to me—my tea mug—and hurl it at him. He tries to dodge, but I caught him by surprise, and the cup smashes into the side of his head. He stumbles, giving me enough time to jump out of range of the scimitars.

He lets out a strange hiss, and it takes me a second to realize that he's laughing. My heart thuds violently in my chest, my breath coming in short bursts. I try to assess his body language the way Raphael has been teaching me. Based on his casual stance and the way he looks at me, the careless way he holds his blades, he doesn't see me as a threat. I can hardly blame him. I'm a tiny, unarmed girl in pajamas he found sleeping at her desk. And there he is, towering over me, a warrior with a weapon in each hand. But as long as he underestimates me, I have an advantage.

I pretend to stumble, kneeling by my bed, letting out a shriek of fear, raising my left hand to protect my face. He takes a step forward, lifting one of his scimitars to slash at me. Blood roars in my ears as I grab for the dagger I keep hidden under my pillow. With its smooth, obsidian hilt in my palm, I strike, aiming for his stomach.

He blocks me with his other scimitar. Still, I manage to cut his fingers, and he lets out a hoarse curse, dropping one of his blades. I'm already rolling away, his other blade barely missing me. I jump to my feet.

For a sliver of a second, we stare at each other.

He's not underestimating me anymore, which is deeply unfortunate. His wounded hand is curled into a fist, dripping with blood, but he still holds a scimitar in his other hand.

I'm by Serana's bed now, and it's a mess like always. And, like always, she's got weapons scattered on and around it. I quickly grab a sword, holding it in front of me. I can't let him see how heavy it feels in my hand. I have only the most rudimentary training with swords, but he doesn't need to know that. I let my lips quirk a bit, showing confidence that I don't have. Masking my real emotions.

He doesn't lunge forward. Instead, he eyes me cautiously, taking his time. And then he whispers something that sounds Fey, though I can hardly make out what he's saying.

Around us, the air begins to hum, and a charge brushes over my skin. A shimmering mist rises from the floor, tendrils curling towards me.

My stomach drops. It's veil mist. This is a veil mage. That vibration I noticed before is the veil's hum, coming from within his body. He doesn't need to cut me down. He can kill me with magic.

Or so he thinks.

I summon my Sentinel powers. I don't need to conjure up powerful emotions because this asshole coming into my room at night and trying to kill me has done the job already.

Concentrating, I focus my magic at the mist, disrupting it as the tendrils touch me. The hum in my ears disappears, and the mist curls harmlessly around me. The mage stumbles, disoriented by my response, and I lunge forward and stab at him. He parries my sword, nearly tearing it from my fingers. I jump away as he swings clumsily at me.

All this time, he's made sure to stay between me and the door, blocking my escape. But now, it doesn't matter because I finally hear what I've been waiting for since I let out that scream: footsteps pounding through the hall, over the flagstones. Distant still, but I can feel the vibrations. And through the walls, I hear Raphael's muffled voice calling my name.

The intruder doesn't even turn around. Does he not hear Raphael? But then I hear him whispering again. And the mist rises around the door.

He lets out his eerie laugh as I stare in horror, realizing what's about to happen.

Raphael will barge through that door, straight into the mist. It will kill him in seconds.

I let my fury course through me and summon my magic to disable the mist, except this time, the mage is ready for it. Before I can snuff out the power of the mist, he slices at me, forcing me to jump back, breaking my focus. The mist rises all around the door, shimmering in its unearthly colors.

"Nia!" Raphael cries, closer now.

I gather my powers, and the mage lunges again. I dodge, his blade whispering inches away from my throat, my concentration disrupted.

"Nia, I'm coming!" Raphael calls outside the door.

I tug at my power for the third time. The mage strikes once more. This time, I ignore his attack, flinging my magic at the mist.

The hum stops, the veil mist flickering.

The mage's scimitar sinks into my stomach, and searing agony spreads through my body as the blade plunges in. I try to scream, but I can't. I make a strangled sound as the mage rips his scimitar from my gut. The door bursts open, and Raphael charges in.

Blinded with pain, I fall to my knees. The mage whirls, and my thoughts become hazy, drowned by the horror of my lacerated stomach. I try to speak and taste blood on my lips.

Raphael slashes the mage's throat. My vision blurs as he kneels by my side and curls his powerful arms around me. "I've got you, love. Don't worry, I've got you."

I try to answer, but I can't breathe. I can't move. And I can feel my life fading away.

CHAPTER 31

*A*s the pain ebbs, heat spreads through my body. I'm in Raphael's lap, folded in his arms. His hand is pressed on my belly, and his healing magic spills over me. My heart races, and my breath speeds up. His warm magic kisses my skin, such an intense feeling that I almost forget the horror of what just happened.

I hardly feel the pain anymore. Raphael is pale, and there's something in his expression that I never expected to see.

Fear.

So, the man does feel emotions.

"Are you okay?" His voice cracks. "Does it still hurt?"

I shake my head. Right now, the pain is just a horrible memory, replaced by the warmth pouring from his fingertips over the flat of my stomach and the hollows of my hips. His muscular arms wrap protectively around me. I feel completely safe in his embrace.

"How does it look?" I ask.

He looks down at my stomach and pulls his hand aside. "Better. Almost healed."

I feel the rumble of his deep voice through his chest, and I relax into him. His magic is intoxicating. I wonder if it feels this sensual to everyone he heals, or just the women who know he's bad news and can't resist him anyway.

He gazes at me intensely, his expression twisted with worry. Maybe it's the sight of the blood soaking my pajama shirt and shorts.

"I'm okay," I say again. I never thought I'd have to reassure Raphael.

He nods, but I'm still curled in his lap, his hand pressed on my skin. Heat pulses beneath his palm, making my breath hitch. "You're okay." Is he reassuring himself?

"Maybe I should clean the blood off."

He nods once, then scoops me up against his enormous chest.

"I can walk now," I protest.

He's not listening. Cradling me in his arms, he manages to get the bathroom door open with one hand. Moonlight streams in the windows over the room.

Gently, he lays me in the porcelain tub. "I...um..." He clears his throat. "It's dark, but I'll turn around. I could leave you, but I need to know you've healed."

For once, Raphael's ice-cold composure has abandoned him, and he is rattled. While I sit in the bath, he lights some of the candles on the shelves. They cast a cozy glow over the bathroom, the warm light wavering over the walls.

He sits with his back to me. I feel a twinge of pain as I shift and twist in the tub, stripping out of my blood-soaked pajamas and underwear. I drop them on the floor next to the bath, horrified at the mess. Blood runs from the pajamas onto the stone floor.

I turn on the tap, and hot water fills the tub. Steam curls into the air, and rain still patters against the windowpanes. It's comfortable in here.

"Raphael, you powers are truly miraculous. That would have been fatal."

"They're not my powers," he murmurs. "I'm just the conduit."

"Well, if you weren't such a good conduit, I'd be dead."

"I know," he says quietly to the wall.

I glance at his broad shoulders, hating how much I wish he were in the water with me.

As the bath fills, I splash water over my body, cleaning myself off. My fingers run over the place where I'd been stabbed. My skin is healed, smooth. Maybe a tiny ridge, but not much else.

"He was a veil mage," I say.

"We'll talk about it later. Just forget him for now, Nia. I'm going to make sure you stay safe. That was fucking…" His voice trails off.

"I've never seen you flustered before."

"*Flustered* isn't exactly the word for it."

It's so odd, but right now, I can't remember what the pain felt like, even though it happened a few minutes ago. Blood swirls around the bath water, and I take a deep breath. I don't want to stay in the murky bath much longer. I stand, letting the water drip down my body in warm rivulets. "Can you hand me a washcloth?" I ask.

He stands and pulls a folded washcloth and towel from a chair, keeping his gaze averted as he hands them to me. At this moment, I almost wish he were slightly *less* of a gentleman. I want to feel his hands on me again. I want him to wrap me in those muscular arms.

But there are *rules*, apparently.

With the cloth and soap, I wash my body completely. Fully cleaned, I let the bath drain and towel myself off. I step out of the tub and wrap the towel around me.

Raphael stands and rubs his forehead, still facing the other direction. "May I see where you were stabbed? I want to make sure it has healed."

"Sure." I drop the towel to my hips, wrapping it around my waist. He turns around, then drops into the chair like he's been struck, staring at me. Still damp from the bath, my nipples peak in the cool castle air. Slowly, his eyes rake down my body from my bare breasts to my stomach. He's sitting, and I'm standing, but he's so much larger than me that we're hardly at different heights.

Gently, he touches my waist and traces his fingers down my belly. I feel as if he's still healing me, his warm magic licking at my skin.

"Perfect," he murmurs, and his eyes flick up to mine. "You are perfect."

As he looks up at me, his pupils dilate. My heart hammers. *Don't forget what he is, Nia. Deep down, he's a heartbreaker who can't deal with his own emotions.*

All it takes is his penetrating silver eyes on me to send molten heat sliding through my veins. And now, I'm forgetting all about the fact that he ghosted me long ago because his touch dissolves any thought of caution. He tugs me closer—just a little. The next thing I know, I'm sitting in his lap again. His hand slides around the back of my neck, the sensation electrifying. At this point, I've pretty much forgotten about the dead mage in my room and all the years I spent hating this gorgeous man. I only know that the power radiating from his rugged body is making my breath catch. It's not just how he looks, it's *him*, too, and the way he seemed so completely undone by my injury. It's the way he's finally dropped his guard.

I curl against him, the towel still slung loosely around my hips. He leans down, his lips hovering close to mine. His magic strokes my body, a hot rush of power that skims over every inch of my bare skin. He slides his fingers into my hair, tugging my head back. With an agonized sigh, he presses his warm lips against mine, and I come alive with light and warmth. My breasts brush against his powerful chest, and a deep ache fills my core. As his tongue sweeps against mine, I run a hand down his hard abs toward the waistband of his trousers. He moans.

He kisses me deeply, with sensual strokes of his

tongue, until I want to rip his clothes off him. One hand is fisted into my hair, the other gently wrapped around my waist, like he's still afraid of breaking me. Until that hand shifts and traces slowly up my spine.

He nips at my lower lip, then pulls away for a moment, his expression searing. He kisses my throat, and my head falls back, my thighs clenching.

Lightning flashes in the stone bathroom, and a deafening crack of thunder rumbles through the walls. Raphael pulls his lips from my throat and searches my eyes. When we kissed, I tasted whiskey on his tongue.

A little tendril of uncertainty coils through me.

He presses his forehead against mine, his fingers still tangled in my hair, and lets out another agonized sigh. "Nia." My name is a whisper. His throat bobs. "I should not be doing this. Avalon Tower cannot lose you." When he meets my gaze again, his silver eyes pierce me. "But I need to keep you safe. You'll stay in my room tonight. You can have the bed." His gaze sweeps down my body. "I need you to get dressed, though. *Now*. Before I forget what the fuck I'm doing."

My heart twists as I pull up the towel around myself. There it is again. The retreat.

But he's also right. Tana told me that if I get kicked out, everyone will die. Avalon Tower has no tolerance for romantic relationships, and I don't want to ruin things for Raphael, either. The stakes are too high to risk it. I can't erase the image of the encroaching darkness from my mind, that little drop of water being swallowed by shadows.

I twist the towel *very* tightly around myself. "Just give me a minute."

He nods. "Of course. The assassin clearly went after you because you're a Sentinel. I'm going to make sure our other Sentinel is safe." He looks dazed. "I'm just going to get rid of the body first."

* * *

I LIE THERE, wrapped in Raphael's blankets while he lights the candles around his room. They glow with warmth over neatly stacked bookshelves, the light gleaming off gold-lettered spines. His bedsheets smell clean and faintly of soap. Everything in his room is in its place. His desk is tidy, his bookshelves organized, the flagstone floor completely clean.

Rain still patters down his tower windows, sliding down the glass panes in little rivers. I shrug off the blanket and stand. I cross to the window, and I peer outside. Lights glow in the distant timber houses of Camelot. Far below his tower room, a stone bridge spans a cobbled street, bathed amber in the glow of gas lamps. I watch as a cloaked woman crosses the bridge in the rain. Two large men with swords flank her.

When she glances up at me, I see her bright red hair, the color of cherries. I've seen her before, looking at me.

She blinks up at the tower, and something about her tugs at me, as if there's a thin thread connecting us.

"Who's that?" I ask.

Raphael peers through the rain-slicked window. "Ah. You felt it, didn't you? *That's* the other Sentinel. Her name is Nivene. Auberon wouldn't have sent a veil mage as an assassin for just anyone. He must have gone for our Sentinels. That's why I assigned her these guards."

I wince. I'm not sure the assassin went for me because I'm a Sentinel. But I'm not supposed to tell him about Tana's prophecy. That they're probably not after Nivene at all. They're after me because I'm what Tana calls the "Lady of the Lake."

"After tonight," he goes on, "I'll make sure your door has guards. You'll be well protected."

I stare at him as he unbuttons his white shirt. Gods, his body is perfect, and the candlelight sculpts every one of his chiseled muscles. He grabs a blanket off his bed and carries it over to a red velvet chaise longue beneath a window. He curls up, his pale eyes flicking to me.

We're not touching. We're across the room from each other. I didn't really know if this is a whiskey-induced mistake, but I feel comfortable with him.

He flashes me a smile, a full, genuine smile that I've never seen on him before. I won't be getting over that smile, ever. "Good night, pixie."

My eyes drift closed to the sound of the rain.

But just as I'm relaxing, a horrible thought comes to

me. The moment I fall asleep, the Dream Stalker could turn up again.

"Raphael?" I ask. "Do you know any way to protect yourself against the Dream Stalker's magic?"

He shakes his head. "As far as I know, the only way is to never attract his attention."

Well, *fuck*.

CHAPTER 32

*I*t's been nearly a month since the assassination attempt, and I've been haunted by something other than the Dream Stalker. In fact, I haven't heard from him at all. Viviane is certain that he's been called back to the Fey realm and can't reach me from there, at least for now.

So instead of the prince's torments, I'm plagued by anxiety about the Culling.

And right now, it all begins.

Two weeks of trials, tests, and sleeplessness. Success and failure. Life and death. All options are on the table.

Even though I'm just a spectator today, my body is tense.

Summer clouds slide over the sun, and the humid breeze kisses my skin. The stone benches of Camelot's ancient arena, Knight Riding Court, are packed. Once, this was the site of deadly jousting matches. Bashed skulls, pierced helmets, severed limbs—let's hope the first round of the trial by combat isn't quite so violent as it was in Arthur's day.

Out of all four trials I will face, the only one I'm not worried about is the written test tomorrow—I've got that nailed. But the other three scare the shit out of me. In just a few days, I have to pass something called the "shadow trial," which is a total mystery that changes year to year. Then, my own combat trial here in the arena, one week from today. And finally, the magic trial, where I have to prove my Sentinel abilities. The ones I still haven't fully mastered.

But it's not just me who's worried. I sense the tension in the air concerning what's about to unfold.

I take a deep breath. Lightning spears the sky, and a few people around me jump. I pull my jacket snugly around me. Thunder rumbles, and a light rain spatters against my face.

As much as I hate it, the rainy weather reminds me of sleeping in Raphael's bed with the rain pattering on the window. Hugging myself tightly, I glance back at him sitting behind me. His pale eyes are focused straight ahead, and I'm not sure he even realizes I'm here. Since the night of the assassin attack, he's been nothing but formal and guarded. His old emotional restraint has returned. Perhaps he only lets down his guard when the alcohol is flowing.

I turn to the arena, my skin prickling with the appre-hension thickening the air. Are any of us really prepared for this? Across the sandy tiltyard, the three trial judges wait in an elevated, covered pavilion. They sit in large wooden chairs that might as well be thrones—Viviane, Wrythe, and Amon, garbed in long, embroidered robes of blue and silver that remind me of Merlin. Wrythe sits in the middle, his golden torc flashing as another bolt lights the sky.

In just a few minutes, two cadets will battle one another, and their performance will help determine the torc they earn in the end. Will they become knights with gold or silver torcs? Squires with brass or copper? Or will they fail so miserably they'll get tin—meaning they're culled?

"Gods, I can hardly breathe," Serana mutters by my side.

The rain starts to pick up, dampening my hair and jacket.

"I've given up on breathing altogether," Darius says. He may be having a panic attack, but the man's silver eyeliner is impeccable. "My trial by combat is tomorrow. Have you heard that sometimes people die?"

My stomach clenches. "I'm sure not very often," I say. "They're not going to want to kill their graduating class."

Right?

We stare ahead at the arena. Slowly, the first two cadets march in. There's Horatio—Tarquin's pink-cheeked lapdog—and Nolan, Darius's crush. Both of them are ridiculously tall, their shirts wet with rain. Horatio carries an enormous sword, its blade dulled. Nolan has a rapier in one hand, a stiletto in the other. His long brown hair drapes down his broad back.

"Smash him, Horatio," Tarquin yells from the crowd.

"Go on, Nolan!" Darius shouts. "You've got this!" He turns to us, muttering, "Gods, he's hot."

Cheers erupt through the crowd until Wrythe stands and raises his hand. "Wait for the command to begin!"

Silence settles. My heart is thudding, almost as if I'm standing in the trial ring myself.

Wrythe seems to be drawing out the waiting, and a nervous hush settles over the arena. The long, silent wait feels excruciating, and my chest muscles tighten.

I can almost imagine myself out there on the dirt, facing off against one of the better-trained cadets. Waiting for the moment when a sword might pierce my gut, an experience I have no desire to repeat.

As I hug myself in the rain, Tana's warning about the trials still rings in my mind. *Death hunts you. During the trials, the darkness will start to envelop you. If you don't survive, we all die.*

The rain is pounding down now, turning the arena into mud. Without waiting for the command to start, Nolan lunges, his rapier poking Horatio's shoulder. The crowd starts roaring, and I realize I'm screaming as well, cheering for Nolan. His attack was sharp, seizing the element of surprise. Horatio wasn't expecting that.

I have a good feeling about Nolan today.

"Begin!" Viviane shouts, even though they've already started.

MI-13 spies aren't honorable. We fight dirty, and we take pride in it. Better to be cunning and alive. I suspect Nolan will actually *earn* a point for attacking before the trial formally began.

Horatio swings, and Nolan barely dodges, rolling aside in the mud. I expected Horatio to take a second to recover, since his sword is huge and cumbersome. But when Nolan thrusts again, Horatio easily parries him with his blade, then swings and hits Nolan's foot. With a sinking feeling, I realize that Horatio is much stronger and faster than he appears. He can easily handle that enormous hunk of metal, swinging it as if it weighs nothing. God*damn* it.

Nolan now seems more cautious, eyeing Horatio carefully. He jumps back as Horatio swings again, then rolls to avoid another swing. He's buying time. Trying to exhaust his opponent.

"Come on, Nolan!" Darius cheers.

I glance across the yard at the judges. Their faces are impassive and show nothing. The only sign of emotion is the tightness in Viviane's lips. I recognize that expression from the hours upon hours I've spent with her in training. And I already know what she's thinking. Nolan won't be able to exhaust Horatio. She's frustrated with his decisions.

Horatio looks like a lumbering idiot, but he's tireless. He can spar for hours. I've seen him do it. Nolan should know that. He should have paid attention. When possible, we're expected to know everything we can about an opponent, and in this case, that includes the other cadets.

Sure enough, Horatio keeps swinging, not even breaking a sweat. His swings seem clumsy, but I can see his footwork, his poise. He's trying to fool Nolan, make him think that he's a mindless brute. Horatio, I think, is much cleverer than he lets on.

Nolan finally parries one of Horatio's swings, then, with an elegant twist, thrusts forward with his stiletto. Horatio stumbles back.

"Yes! Go Nolan!" Serana screams.

"No..." I mutter. "Don't fall for it—"

But he does. Emboldened by Horatio's stumble, he moves forward, thrusting directly at Horatio's unprotected chest. Horatio's sword blocks it. Quick as lightning, Horatio tears Nolan's rapier from his hand, sending it flying. Another swing smashes into Nolan's arm.

The blade is dull, but it's still heavy, and Nolan screams in pain, an agonized, animal screech, and I wonder how badly that arm is broken.

Tarquin and his friends are now the ones cheering, wild with victory.

Darius, Tana, and I can only watch in silence. I glance at the judges, wondering when they'll call an end to it. Quite clearly, Nolan can no longer fight.

From what I can tell, Viviane and Amon seem to be arguing with Wrythe. From here, I have no clue what they're saying.

Nolan's arm is hanging limply by his side. All he has is his stiletto, held in his left hand. His non-dominant hand.

If he could, this would be the time to surrender, but surrendering in a trial of combat means failure. The worst thing an undercover agent can do is surrender because if the Fey take us prisoner, they will torture us until they've extracted every last bit of damaging information from our minds. An agent is expected to fight to the death. Or in this case, until the judges call it.

Which they aren't. They *could*, but they don't seem to want to.

Wrythe stands with his arms folded, shaking his head. Viviane is screaming at him, red-faced. Maybe she wants to call it.

And then Horatio goes for Nolan. Not just one swing, but a series of punishing lashes, swiftly and expertly delivered. Hitting his chest, his leg, his broken arm. Nolan stumbles back and collapses.

Wrythe finally nods, and Viviane turns toward the combatants.

And Horatio smashes his heavy blade into Nolan's head.

Viviane stares, stone-faced.

Darius leaps up and runs through the crowd, trying to get to his friend. The tower's doctor is already there, kneeling by Nolan, trying to heal him.

But there's too much blood, and Nolan's eyes are gazing sightlessly at the sky. Horatio stares down at him, his face expressionless.

"Oh, gods," Serana mumbles.

And now the doctor shakes his head, and Darius stands over his friend's body, crying.

"He just killed him," I say. "Nolan was done. It was obvious. There was no reason to do it. He quite clearly could have won the trial without the final blow."

Serana stares straight ahead. "They should have stopped the fight."

"Viviane and Amon wanted to," I say. "Wrythe didn't agree. What's the point of allowing cadets to die?"

"There's no point," Serana says. "But it happens. It's brutal, but Horatio demonstrated that he fights well. He'll get high marks for this trial."

Wrythe slaps Horatio on the shoulder, and Horatio has a tiny smile on his ruddy face.

When Tana told me the darkness was coming for me during the trials, I had imagined another assassination attempt.

I hadn't really pictured dying at the hands of a fellow cadet.

CHAPTER 33

$\mathcal{O}$n the night of the shadow trial, I stand with the other cadets in a ruined church not far from the Tower of London. The written test a couple of days ago was easy enough, but I have no clue what's in store for tonight, only that it's taking place outside.

With no roof above, moonlight washes over us. Vines with greenish-white flowers cling to half-broken stone arches.

The last time I went to London, I was ten years old, before the Fey invasion. Mom and I stayed for a week in a house Walter owned. I didn't see much of the city then. There were lots of parties at the mansion, and I remember adults sleeping all over the house—on floors and sofas— with empty alcohol bottles and smoldering cigarettes all around. I only saw a few glimpses of London, on the way to and from the airport.

Now, finally, I get to see some of the ancient city—the

Tower of London, the River Thames, and a pub called the Hung Drawn and Quartered, named after a nearby execution spot.

From one of the stone arches, Wrythe paces out onto the grass.

"Tonight," he bellows, "your task is to steal a replica of Excalibur, hidden somewhere in this part of London. Perhaps by the Tower. Perhaps by the river. Maybe *in* the river. Like a true mission, the details are sparse, but there are a few contacts spread throughout the city with information. There might also be unknowing participants who have their own knowledge to share. The usual rules of the city apply, and no one may carry weapons. This isn't about brute force. This is about cunning." He turns and paces. "And of course, only one of you will find the hidden Excalibur. Whoever does will have a strong shot at a gold or silver torc. Perhaps none of you will find it. In any case, we will score you according to your individual achievements, as poor as they might be." He shoots me a sharp look.

"Could he be any more patronizing?" Serana whispers.

I'm about to answer when I notice someone in the shadows—the cherry-haired woman I've seen before in Avalon Tower. The other Sentinel, Nivene. What's she doing here?

"The trial will begin in fifteen minutes," Wrythe says. "Those of you who are capable of independent thought best use this time to plan."

Almost instantly, we form into small groups. Serana,

Tana, Darius, and I walk into the shadows of the vestry, one with stone walls, Gothic windows, and no roof. Here, we have a little privacy. Vines climb the walls, and moonlight streams down over us.

I peer through one of the glassless windows to see Tarquin, Horatio, and three of their closest hangers-on huddling together in the grassy nave. Wisps of fog waft through the air.

Wrythe walks by the Pendragon crowd and whispers to Tarquin. In response, Tarquin smiles and nods.

My mouth drops open. "I think Wrythe just tipped off Tarquin."

"Of course," Serana mutters. "The Pendragons don't get gold torcs through skill. But *we* need to actually come up with a plan."

"Yeah." Darius sounds listless. Ever since Nolan's death, he's hardly talked. He doesn't seem to care about the trials or anything else anymore.

"Tana," I say, "have you foreseen anything? Any thoughts?"

Tana shakes her head. "There's something misty about the trial. Foggy. I can't really see it, but I can feel it. I can't say if it's real or magically created."

"Okay. London's often foggy, isn't it?"

"And there's a big fucking steam fair nearby," says Serana. "There are rides and weird arcades all around Tower Green. I'm sure Wrythe planned this with as much chaos in mind as possible."

A flash of red catches my eye, and I turn to see Nivene

staring at me from an arched doorway. She jerks her head, motioning for me to join her, then slinks back into the shadows on the other side of the nave.

"Give me a second," I say. "I'll be right back."

"What?" Serana grabs my arm. "Nia, the trial is about to start. We need a plan."

"Just a few minutes." I give her an apologetic look. "Start without me."

I slip away, weaving between the groups of cadets gathered under the moonlight. I spot her scarlet hair and follow her into a leafy, derelict tower.

My heart pounds. This is insane. My first trial is about to start, and everything depends on me passing it. I can't waste my time on whatever this is. What am I doing here?

She turns to face me, her jade eyes piercing in the dark. "Hello, Nia."

She leans back against a wall, arms folded, scrutinizing me. Her gaze is impenetrable and unblinking. Up close, I can see that a long, faded scar runs down her left cheek. A teardrop pendant hangs around her throat.

"Hi," I say. Standing close to her, I feel the tug between us grow even stronger. "You're Nivene, right? The other Sentinel."

"That's right." Her voice is soft and sad. "The other Sentinel."

"It's nice to finally meet you, but this isn't a good time," I say. "The shadow trial is about to start, and if I fail this—"

"I need your help *now*. The lives of all the people here are at stake."

I blink. "What are you talking about?"

"All this time, you've been training to be an Agent of Camelot," she says. "To go beyond the veil into Fey France. To spy on Auberon's forces. But surely you realize there's a second side to that coin."

It takes me a second to catch up. "Yeah." My voice cracks, just a bit. "While we're spying on Auberon's Fey, they're spying on us."

"Precisely." She nods. "Fey spies, saboteurs, and assassins. There's a war going on, and it takes place on both sides of the veil. You were the target of such an operative, right?"

"A veil mage broke into my room," I say. "He tried to kill me."

She uncrosses her arms and steps forward. "And now, another of Auberon's veil mages is here. Right now. I've felt him…somewhere nearby, just ten minutes ago. Auberon's spies must have found out about this trial. Really, it's a priceless opportunity for the Fey. All of Avalon Tower's cadets in one place, and many of the knights, too. And what's worse, they're about to split up. A skilled assassin would be able to take them out one by one."

"If that's true, we have to stop the trial," I say. "We need to tell them—"

She lets out a short, bitter laugh. "If only. Do you think I haven't tried that?"

"Then why is the trial continuing?"

"Avalon Tower is weighed down by protocol and politics. I know you've noticed that." Nivene looks at the huddled cadets. "I've never been very good at convincing anyone of anything. That was my sister's skill."

I notice the past tense. "Was she at Avalon Tower, too?"

"Her name was Alix, and she had just fallen in love for the first time. And now, she's gone."

The name sparks a memory. "She was the other Sentinel. The one who died."

"Yeah." Nivene's voice turns to a whisper. "I never realized how good she was at what we did until she was gone."

"Disrupting the veil?"

"Being a Sentinel is about more than disrupting the veil, Nia. MI-13 Sentinels were always in charge of watching. Keeping everyone safe. Disrupting the veil is just a tiny aspect of that. And when we needed to raise the alarm, it was Alix's job to persuade the knights. I'm not good with politics, and Wrythe bloody hates me. When I tried to warn him about this, he didn't listen."

"Raphael would listen."

"Raphael isn't here right now, and he doesn't always listen, either. Anyway, Wrythe is a stubborn arsehole." Nivene purses her lips. "The time for convincing is over. You and I are Sentinels, and we need to act. I can't stop this on my own. In a few minutes, the trial will start, and all these cadets will spread out, becoming targets. The veil mage will begin to strike."

I swallow. "What do you need me to do?"

"Our powers will help us track him down."

I recall the hum when the previous veil mage struck at me and nod.

"We should split up and find him. You check out the steam fair. I'll cover as much ground as possible north of here. If you spot him, *do not engage.* If he's cornered, he'll summon the veil to cause a diversion. In the middle of London, that would be a disaster. Hundreds of deaths. Take this." She hands me a tiny conch shell.

"What's that?"

"Do you remember microphones and earbuds before the war? This is the Fey equivalent. It'll let us communicate. Put it in your ear."

I remember Bluetooth earbuds. They were quite comfortable. This is the exact opposite. It scratches my ear when I put it in, and I have to shove it hard for it to stay. "Argh. Couldn't the Fey put rubber around it? Seriously."

"It'll do," she says, and as she speaks, I hear her voice from the conch as well, a strange echo in my ear. "Go. Start the trial. Look for the veil mage as you go. And if you spot him, let me know. We'll figure it out from there."

"Okay."

She pivots and strides through the peaked tower doorway and into the shadows. Her voice whispers through the magical conch shell in my ear. "Good luck, Nia."

CHAPTER 34

No matter what Nivene said, I must try to stop the trial from taking place. If Avalon Tower postpones the trial by even one day, Auberon's operation will fail tonight.

As I march straight to Wrythe, the night breeze rushes over me. Wrythe is staring at his pocket watch, standing alone on the dark grass. His bored expression quickly changes to annoyance when he notices me.

"You have three more minutes, Ms. Melisende. I realize that your chances of passing are minimal, but surely you want to appear to be making an effort."

I lean in close. "Nivene, the other Sentinel, believes there might be an enemy assassin here," I tell him. "Auberon's forces know that the trial is taking place, and they're using the opportunity to pick off the cadets."

He stares at me, and a line forms between his eyebrows.

"You must know that one of their veil mages already tried to take me out in Avalon Tower," I continue. "They're on the attack. Surely the word of an experienced Sentinel is worth checking out?"

"*Something* is worth checking out," he finally says.

I exhale in relief. "Good."

"It's worth checking how you've come so far, seeing that you're so desperate to avoid this trial that you're willing to invent a ridiculous threat. Do you realize how dangerous it is to spread disinformation like this?"

Irritation flares. "I just spoke to Nivene—"

"Nonsense!" he barks. "I am the Seneschal, and I should fail you right now for this attempt to disrupt the trial. I will give you one more chance, but don't come to me with this codswallop again."

"I know I'm just a cadet, but Nivene isn't. Are you really going to risk the lives of all these cadets just because you're too arrogant to listen?" I blurt.

A second later, I realize how loudly I've spoken. Silence settles around us. Serana and Tana both look at me, mouth ajar in horror.

"Oh, Ms. Melisende," Wrythe whispers. "You'll regret saying that. You are done. Participate or not, it's all the same to me. Tonight, after this trial, I will see to it that you're expelled."

My jaw drops, and I back away. I can hardly breathe.

Wrythe turns to the rest of the cadets. "What are you staring at?" he snaps. "The trial has begun. Get going."

The cadets rush out of the church ruins, slipping into

the city streets. Tana, Serana and Darius stay behind. And Wrythe, of course, who retreats to a stone wall to fold his arms and scowl.

My lungs feel tight as I walk toward my friends in the vestry. I pull out my inhaler and take two puffs.

"Did he just expel you?" Serana asks me.

"He certainly threatened it." I feel sick. "But believe it or not, there are more important things happening right now."

If Nivene is right, the rest of the cadets are still in mortal danger—including my friends. On top of that, this attack would virtually destroy the future of MI-13.

I force myself to focus. "Forget Wrythe. I need your help, and I need you to trust me. Nivene just told me there's another veil mage here, like the one who tried to kill me. And he's here to take us all down."

I quickly explain the rest, and my friends listen in shocked silence.

Just as I'm finishing, there's a whisper from the conch shell, and I lift a finger to my ear. "Nia," Nivene says, "I'm heading to Whitechapel. What's the fair looking like?"

I clear my throat, touching the conch. "I'm still at the church."

"Why are you still there? The veil mage wasn't there. I'm not trying to be rude, but are you thick?" Nivene asks.

Her tone is sharp and judgmental, and I'm quickly catching on to what she meant when she said she's "not good with politics."

"Hang on a second, Nivene." I look at my friends. "I

have to go, but I need your help. Can you get Raphael or someone else from Avalon Tower over here? He was on the boat with us when we came to London. I know this is a lot to ask when we have a trial going on, but if the other Sentinel is right, we're in deep trouble."

"How are we supposed to find him?" Serana asks. "I have no idea where he is."

I think about it quickly. "Most of the knights will be at St Katharine Docks, where the boat came in. Possibly Westminster or Downing Street." My mind whirls. "Or that secret weapon store where MI-13 gets its supplies on Artillery Lane." I look at Tana. "Okay, there are several possibilities, but try to find them, however you can. Tea, tarot, whatever works. Maybe split up to cover more ground. Just, please, go as quickly as possible."

"What are you going to do?" Serana asks.

"Nivene and I can sense veil mages," I say. "I'm going to help her find him. Hurry." I start walking, glancing back at them as I do. "We don't have much time."

I speed out of the derelict churchyard and head along a curving road that leads to the Tower. Wisps of fog coil past me. I pass a pub with warm lights, steamed windows, and the chatter of people drinking inside. I break into a jog over a flagstone pavement until the steam fair comes into view.

Fog hangs over the brightly colored rides. Since modern technology stopped working, we've gone back to some of the more old-fashioned pleasures—steam fairs, carriage rides with horses, steam ships. In fact, if Wrythe expels me, I'll be heading back to the U.S. on one of those pretty soon.

A group of men are walking past a merry-go-round, drinking beer from plastic cups. As I pass, one of them stumbles into me.

He says something to me, something about giving him a smile. But I can hardly hear over his screaming thoughts.

I WANT TO RUB MY FACE IN HER TITS.

I glower at him. "Fuck off."

"What did I do?" Nivene asks in my ear.

"Not you."

It's crowded here, and I can smell the beer coming off everyone. My telepathic powers flare, and I worry it will make it hard to hear the veil magic.

I walk past a ride made to look like swinging ships, trying to smother my telepathy as people brush past me, and summon the threads of my Sentinel powers, listening for the quiet hum of the veil mage. Stopping at a stall, I buy a pint of beer. If I'm going to blend in here, it seems necessary.

With my beer in hand, I slip into the crowd. "I'm at the steam fair by the Tower," I tell Nivene. "Nothing yet."

Lights flash around me, and shouts pierce the air.

"Okay," she says, her voice vibrating strangely in my ear. "I'm nearly at Brick Lane. Nothing here yet."

"From how far away do you think we can sense him?"

"Depends how trained you are. I can probably sense him from a few hundred yards. But you? Twenty, thirty yards, tops."

There's that "bad at politics" thing again.

But I think she's also right. Even when I'm near the veil itself, I don't hear the buzz until I'm a few dozen yards away. And with everyone drunkenly shouting around me, I can hardly think straight.

An enormous pipe organ is shrieking to my left, while on my right, a loud machine is emitting a stream of pink steam with an ear-shattering hiss. On top of that, Nivene is whispering in my ear, demanding that I walk faster, concentrate, tell her as soon as I sense anything, wanting to know why I haven't found him yet, and—

It's there and gone. Just a hiss, a murmur, so weak that I sense it more than I hear it. But it's familiar and resonates with my magic. The hum of a veil, somewhere to my right, already dissipating.

I push my way in the direction I think it came from and move through the fair, closer to the river. As I nudge against a large man, I get a glimpse into his thoughts, something about a cuckoo clock he wishes he hadn't bought. I push his voice away, trying to suppress my telepathy while letting my Sentinel power grow. Tuning out the distractions feels impossible, like trying to thread a needle while jumping rope, but *there*! That hum again, just a hint, but this time, it's more constant. I can follow it through the crowd.

"Cheer up, love!" a man shouts at me. "Might never 'appen."

I'm already past him, by the river walk now. There are

no more rides here, but stalls of people sell fish and chips and pies.

I know he's somewhere down here by the dark, glittering Thames.

Now, the hum is getting louder in my ears.

"Nia, I'm in Whitechapel," Nivene says. "I think I'm going to turn around and—"

"I have him," I say breathlessly.

"What? Where?"

I catch my breath. It takes me a second to remember what this entrance to the Tower is called. "I'm at Traitor's Gate by the Tower. I can't see him yet, but I can definitely feel him. He's on the move, heading for Tower Bridge."

"Bloody hell, I'm way too far north," Nivene says. "Don't lose him. And no matter what, don't engage him. Wait for me, okay?"

"Got it."

There are a ton of people on the riverside walk, and I scan them as I move, assessing each person for risks, details, pieces of information. A policeman saunters over the cobblestones, looking unconcerned. A couple is making out against a tree, and a man is trying to jog but somehow going the same pace as everyone walking.

Then I see him.

He stands out because of his clothes and his height. He wears a hoodie that shadows his face and black pants. All black, just like the other veil mage I encountered. Not different enough from other bystanders to draw attention...unless someone's looking.

Now that I've spotted him, the hum grows louder. Just as he glances over his shoulder, I slip behind the slow jogger, sticking to the shadows. As I do, I realize the veil mage has doubled back and is heading into the thick of the fair.

It's hard following someone alone. Usually, when tracking a person, you do it with a team. Then, you can break away as someone else switches with you. Have enough people working together, and your target never realizes he's being followed at all. But when doing it alone, I have to improvise. Let the target get out of sight constantly. Do my best to camouflage myself in the crowd, sipping my beer like I'm just another drunk person. My one advantage is that even though I can't see him, I can still hear him humming in my ear, the buzz over my skin.

I whisper updates to Nivene, telling her each ride and stall that I pass.

She's on her way, trying to get a taxi to get here faster. She keeps telling me not to engage him, repeating the admonition so many times that I wish the conch shell had a mute button.

But I can still hear him. He's moving to the outskirts of the fair, heading north. He hurries past the rides, but he's still close. I think the humming is coming from a stone and brick church. A blue sign on the marks it as ALL HALLOWS BY THE TOWER—FOUNDED 675.

I think the hum is coming from there, but Nivene isn't here yet.

I'm standing at the edge of the fair, just before a stall with a horseshoes game and prizes of creepy eyeless dolls.

While I pretend to be interested in the stall, I keep my focus on the hum behind me, making sure that it doesn't shift. It's a tricky thing to do, like trying to taste music or listen to the sunlight. Sentinel magic isn't supposed to be used to track a person. But as far as I can tell, he's still there, inside the ancient church.

I smile at the stall keeper, a balding man in a tracksuit, and pay for a single ticket.

"There you are, love." He hands me three iron horseshoes.

When I touch them, if I focus very hard, I can feel a faint tingle on my fingertips. But since I'm not fully Fey, it's barely noticeable.

"I'm totally gonna win this thing," I say.

"I have no doubts."

My first horseshoe goes way off mark. "Damn it! I was so close!"

"All in the wrist, darling."

"Hey, do you think that old church is open? Do they have bathrooms?"

"Bathrooms," he repeats.

"Toilets. The loo. I have to pee, and I hate the portaloos." I toss the second horseshoe. A bit closer but still way off.

"No idea, really. Not sure I've ever been in a church. Not my thing. Pretty sure they close at night."

"Have you seen anyone going in there?" I ask.

"Nah, looks dark," he says skeptically. "Not recently, anyway."

I still hear the buzz coming from that church.

I toss the third horseshoe, and it's so off the mark that it nearly hits one of the eyeless dolls. "Ugh! I really want to win one. Give me another try." I pay for another ticket.

He hands me three more horseshoes. "I'm sure this time you'll get it. You're definitely getting the hang of it, darling."

"I know, right?" I toss the first one, nearly taking his head off.

"Church was open earlier, though. I saw people going in. Not being funny or nothing, and I'm not prejudiced. Nothing against demi-Fey. But they're just not right, you know? They just didn't look right. It's the eyes." The large man grimaces. "Feel like they're gonna steal my soul. Creepy fuckers."

"Wow, demi-Fey? I've never seen one. What did they look like?"

"Fucking weird, pardon my language. The man had pointy ears, obviously. Dark hair. Tattoos on his arms, eerie silver eyes like metal. Beautiful blonde woman with him. You know, I don't mind the women demi-Fey quite as much. I'd give her one," he says thoughtfully. "Pardon the expression."

I toss a horseshoe, and it clatters to the floor of his stall. A thought starts to blossom in my mind. "Did they have anything with them?"

He shrugs. "I don't know. Why do you ask?"

I open my eyes wide. "Well, like you said, they're dangerous. And you know the saying, if you see something, say something."

He holds up a finger. "Do you know what, love? The fella *was* carrying something. It was in a box, like a musical instrument or something. They never brought it out again." His eyes widen. "Do you think they could be planning something? You don't think it was a bomb, do you?" He scrubs a hand over his mouth. "With all these people here? Should I call the police?"

I toss both horseshoes one after the other, so off the mark that one nearly hits one of the prize dolls. "It's probably nothing. I doubt demi-Fey even know how to make a bomb. We don't want the police shutting the whole fair down over an empty box."

What I know at this point is that Raphael and Vivian came in earlier and left a package here, then left.

The Excalibur replica.

The veil mage's plan starts to crystallize in my mind. This is where the trial ends—the veil mage figured that out. Why chase people through the street when they're all going to come to the same place?

I casually lean on the side of the stall and glance back at the darkened church.

Then my heart sinks. Across the street, I see Tarquin and Horatio peering in the entrance to a building. Wrythe must have tipped them off to the general location, but they don't know the exact building yet.

A teeny, tiny part of me thinks it would be tempting to

let them blunder into the trap, but as much as I hate them, I'm not going to let Avalon Tower cadets die at the hands of our enemies.

"Nivene, where are you?" I whisper.

"The bloody cab driver went the wrong way!" she shouts. "Will you fucking turn around, you absolute muppet? Not you, Nia. The cabbie. No, I will not pipe down—"

"I can't wait, Nivene."

"What? Wait, Nia—"

I pull the conch shell from my ear and pocket it.

"Third time lucky?" The stall owner hands me the horseshoes.

"Sure, why not?" I take them and quickly toss them again. Two land right on target, cluttering as they clunk together.

"Blood hell, how did you do that?"

"I must have got the hang of it."

He goes over to pick them up, then looks around for the third one.

"Listen, mate," I say, leaning in to whisper. "Can you do me a favor? See those two guys over there?" I point at Tarquin and his friend. "They're students I know, and I want to prank them." I pull two twenty-pound notes out of my pocket and slide them onto the counter. "I'm gonna hide. Can you call them over? Act as if you have something important to tell them."

He pockets the cash. "What do you want me to say?"

"Tell them you've got King Arthur's sword. You know, Excalibur?"

He raises an eyebrow. "I don't get it."

"It's an inside joke. Ask them to guess a password, and if they get the password right, they get Excalibur." I slide another twenty-pound note onto the counter. "It'll be hilarious, trust me. Give them the doll I just won, tell them it's a clue. All I need is five minutes, okay? Just buy me five minutes."

He shrugs and stuffs the third twenty into his pocket. Tana had insisted we all bring cash for bribing, and she was—as usual—correct. "Happy to oblige."

I race around the church to the entrance at the other side, my feet pounding over the flagstones. As I run, I hear the stall owner calling Tarquin and Horatio.

I find the arched stone doorway and push inside. The veil mage left it unlocked. He didn't want any cadets to get lost, of course.

It's dark as I enter, but the hum of his magic fills the air around me.

CHAPTER 35

*M*y heart batters my ribs as my eyes slowly adjust to the pale moonlight streaming in through stained-glass windows.

"Did I win?" My voice echoes off the high stone ceiling. "Did I get here first?"

He steps into the aisle, his golden eyes glowing. As my eyes adjust, I can see the smile on his lips. He thinks I'm his first prey of the day, a dumb cadet jumping headfirst into the trap. I take two steps toward him.

"Do you have the sword?" I ask eagerly. "Do I need to, like, give you a password or something?"

He's holding the Excalibur replica but not handing it to me. Instead, he raises his hand and whispers an incantation. The hum intensifies as tendrils of veil shimmer into existence around me.

But I've been expecting it.

Unleashing my banked powers, I lash out at the newly formed veil, shattering it. The hum goes silent, and the veil mage stumbles, shocked. He drops the sword, and it clatters to the stone floor.

I lunge for him, gripping the horseshoe that I'd palmed a few minutes ago, and smash him in the nose, hearing the crunch of bone. He shrieks, the sound echoing off the towering vaults, and stumbles back, still screaming. The air smells of burned flesh.

I am *so* glad I don't have that reaction to iron.

Without wasting another breath, I rush for him and press the horseshoe onto his cheek. He screeches, trying to pull my hand away in panic, but I only press harder. With the metal on his skin, he's growing weaker.

He falls into the aisle. I leap on top of him, shoving the iron against his face. A disturbing sizzling sound rises from his skin, and I ignore the growing nausea in my gut.

We keep struggling. He never stops screaming, scratching ineffectively at my face and hands. My jaws are clenched in fury, my arm trembling with effort.

And then he goes still. His arms drop, and the screaming stops.

Is he faking it? If I release him, will he leap up and stab me? Wheezing, I keep the iron pressed against him, grinding that horseshoe into his face. Is he breathing?

The wood door slams open behind me, and powerful hands lift me off the mage. I whirl, ready to strike with the horseshoe again, and see Raphael's beautiful face staring down at me. He grabs my horseshoe-wielding arm, stopping me from battering him with it.

"Take it easy," he says. "I don't think he's getting up again, and I'd rather not get smashed with that."

I let out a shuddering breath, suddenly dizzy. Raphael slips his arm around my waist to steady me.

Nivene rushes in at last, her scarlet hair damp with sweat. Chest heaving, she runs down the aisle and crouches by the veil mage. "Definitely dead," she says after a moment.

I feel sick to my stomach. Somewhere, in the back of my mind, I realize that I've taken a life for the very first time. I had to do it, of course, but it feels as if I've taken a step over a threshold I never imagined myself crossing.

Wrythe steps into the nave. "What is this?" His voice echoes off of the stone arches.

"You...should...have...listened to me," Nivene pants, still catching her breath. She must have jumped out of the cab at some point and just sprinted here.

Tarquin appears in the church doorway. "She bribed someone to distract us. That's not allowed, is it? Bloody *bribery?*"

Raphael turns to face him. "Piss off, Tarquin. You're not needed here."

"I want credit for getting here first!" Tarquin shouts.

Nivene turns around and slams the door in Tarquin's face, a muffled yelp accompanying the loud thud.

Raphael abruptly pulls his arm from me and rakes a hand through his hair. The moonlight casts a silver glow over his perfect features, sparking in his eyes. "Report, Melisende."

It's been six months since he'd first demanded my report back on the ship with the refugees. I still remember the muddled report I gave him back then. And he still makes me feel a surge of confusing emotions, especially since he's gone into *knight* mode, calling me "Melisende."

Of course, I knew he was like this, didn't I?

I manage to recount the events that led to this moment with all the relevant details. As I go through it, Nivene, Wrythe, and Raphael listen without saying a word.

When I'm finally done, Raphael turns to Wrythe. "Well?"

Wrythe looks at him with disdain. "Well, what?"

"Nia and Nivene warned you that the trial was a trap. Why didn't you postpone it?"

"They gave no evidence. I can't entertain every hysterical worry that goes through someone's head just because they *sense* something. My wife *senses* impending doom ten times a day. She *sensed* that she was having a heart attack yesterday. And do you know what it was? Nerves. That's all. Ten hours in the emergency room for her nerves. And do you know what else? It was completely outrageous for Ms. Melisende to take him on without a knight. As soon as she saw the veil mage, she should have turned back and found someone more experienced. *Then*, with actual proof, with *data*, I would have canceled the trial. We could have captured this assassin and interrogated him instead of just killing him. But she went after him alone, risking the lives of everyone involved, in the desperate hope that I would revoke her expulsion. And now, a valuable source of intel is dead."

"You gibbering wank stain," mutters Nivene, low enough that I can just barely hear it.

"Her *expulsion?*" Raphael repeats in a low, incredulous voice.

Wrythe narrows his eyes at me. "I intended to kick her out of Avalon Tower for insubordination, and I'm still fairly certain it's the right call. But I suspect the other knights of the Round Table will be difficult about it. And given the circumstances, I'm willing to give her one final chance."

I reach down and pluck the replica sword from the stone floor. If I had Nivene's knack for politics, I would tell Wrythe what I really thought of him.

Instead, I give him a curt nod. "Cheers, then."

"We will obviously need to reschedule the shadow trial." Wrythe sighs. "Ms. Melisende can do it properly with the rest of the cadets."

"No," Raphael says.

Wrythe frowns at him. "Right. You think she should be expelled after all?"

"*She* won't do the shadow trial again. She's shown her leadership by sending cadets to call for backup," Raphael says. "She followed an enemy agent through the fair without being noticed. Then she managed to delay two Pendragon cadets and arm herself with an improvised weapon. She finally ambushed a powerful enemy agent and took him down. Not to mention that she got her hands on the Excalibur replica, which was the trial's goal, one that's supposed to guarantee the highest marks. She not only passed the trial, she deserves the highest score for it, according to the rules we set out."

Wrythe lifts his chin. "I recognize that you are a knight of the Round Table, but this is obvious favoritism. What, exactly, is the source of this favoritism, I wonder?"

"I'm sure you will agree," Raphael adds smoothly, "that when we report this to the rest of the knights at the Round Table, we can leave out the part where *both* Sentinels tried to warn you about the assassin, and you dismissed them as hysterical women because you were annoyed with your wife."

Wrythe clenches his jaw in fury. Finally, he says, "If she hadn't maliciously bribed someone to waylay Tarquin, he would have arrived here first. At the very least, he deserves the highest score as well. A tie."

Raphael lets out an exasperated sigh. "Fine."

"Tana, Darius, and Serana should be given a high score, too," I say. "They managed to get the backup we needed."

Wrythe frowns at me. "I'm willing to give them a passing grade, but this isn't a free-for-all, Ms. Melisende. We have protocols and procedures in Avalon Tower. Protocols decided at the sacred Round Table."

"Bunch of bollocks," Nivene says. "Bollocks, bollocks, bollocks."

"Passing scores will be *fine*," Raphael intervenes, giving us both a warning glare. "I'll see if they want to retake the trial or if they're fine with a passing grade. And that's it. We're done here."

"We *are* done here, Mr. Launcelot," Wrythe says, "but we're not done with the trials. In time, no doubt, we will see who truly belongs here and who does not."

CHAPTER 36

I walk down a stone tunnel toward the Knight
Riding Court, Tana by my side. Her mouth is
set in a grim line, and she seems on edge.

"Neither of us can get culled, you know," she says,
glancing at me. "I'm certain now that we both have an
important role to play."

I swallow hard. "I don't doubt it. We'll be fine. Let's just
get through this trial."

The tunnel runs below the spectator stands. Once, the
knights of the Round Table would have ridden their
horses through this tunnel on their way to strike each
other with lances. Arthur himself probably traveled
through this exact passage. But Arthur, I'm sure, felt much
more confident than I do now.

For the past several days, we've been watching combat
trials, and they all seemed so skilled. So brutal.

We're both in hard leather armor, reinforced with

chainmail beneath it, and it weighs me down as I walk, pressing on my shoulders and chest.

Today, it's me against Tana. The only thing making this bearable is that she was matched with me, probably because we're both small, unskilled, mediocre fighters compared to the rest.

We step out of the tunnel into the sandy arena, and the bright sun hits my face. It's September, but it still feels a million degrees in this leather and armor, and I'm already sweating.

I glance at Tana, and she smiles at me. Hopefully, after watching our duel for ten or twenty minutes, the judges will be so bored, they'll end it out of sheer tedium.

The wind whips at my hair, and my nerves spark. The spectators in the stands are watching us intently. Since I got the replica Excalibur, they're all paying *very* close attention to me.

I don't like being the center of attention, and my pulse races.

Raphael is in the stands. He's watching me, too, his jaw clenched tightly.

"We'll do fine," I tell Tana, more to reassure myself.

"Yeah, sure." Her voice wavers, and I can hear the worry laden in her voice. "Let's just get through..." She trails off, her gaze going unfocused. "What? You can't do this at the last minute."

"Do what?" I look around, trying to see what has upset her, but everything seems normal—the judges on their platform, the spectators in the stands.

She blinks, frowning in confusion. "I thought...never mind."

I'm about to ask her what she thought she saw, but Amon calls for everyone's attention from the platform.

"Today's trial by combat will be between Nia Melisende and Tana Campbell. We will start in—"

Wrythe suddenly leans in and whispers something in his ear. Amon turns to him and shakes his head. Viviane stands, looking furious. Amon mostly seems confused.

"What's going on?" I ask Tana.

"Nothing good," Tana says.

Now Amon is nodding, his face dejected. Wrythe folds his hands at his waist, looking pleased with himself.

"There's been a change in today's trial," Amon calls out. "Apparently, Tana Campbell's psychic abilities are urgently required on a mission. So, today's trial by combat will be between Nia Melisende and Tarquin Pendragon."

My stomach plummets.

"What? You can't do this at the last minute," Tana calls out.

"Tana Campbell," Wrythe bellows. "That is an order."

My heart races. When I turn to look behind me, I see Tarquin already moving through the crowd, prepared with his sword. He *knew* this was happening, and Wrythe still waited until the last minute to announce the change.

"This is bullshit," I mutter. The last time Tarquin and I fought, he had me pinned within moments. He's bigger than me, stronger than me, faster than me, and he's been training since he could walk. He's also wielding a long, heavy sword, which I can't parry properly with my flimsy rapier. I am utterly fucked.

Tana grips my arm hard. "Nia, remember. You *have* to pass."

"How?"

"Use everything you've got," she says. Her suggestion echoes Viviane's instruction so similarly that a chill runs up the back of my neck.

She pivots and stalks out of the arena, back into the tunnel. Off on a bullshit mission that I'm sure Wrythe made up to fuck with me.

I'm left standing by myself in the old tiltyard, sweating into my clothes. My breath feels short and sharp, and I wonder how much blood Arthur spilled on this sand.

Slowly, with a thin smile, Tarquin stalks in front of me. He closes the distance between us and leans down to whisper, "Ah, the public bus." His voice is low so only I can hear. "Remember what Horatio did in his trials? I'm going to do so much worse. A sacrifice to Arthur. Nia, you were never meant to be here."

My thoughts go quiet, and I keep my face inscrutable as I glance at his sword. Sure, the blade is dulled for the trial. But like Horatio's weapon from that first trial, it's heavy enough to kill. And I have no doubt that is Tarquin's plan.

This is no longer about just passing the test. This is about survival. And I can't pull any punches.

"Begin!" Amon shouts.

I leap forward and thrust my rapier at his face, aiming

for his eyes. He stumbles back but manages to parry my thrust, nearly pulling the rapier from my hand. Quickly, he pushes with a swing at my body that I barely dodge.

Both of us take a step back and scrutinize each other. I can see the tiniest hint of surprise in his eyes.

He goes at me with half a dozen swings and thrusts. I dodge them, jumping back each time. But he's hardly making any effort, and I'm already out of breath. I used my inhaler before starting, but it isn't enough to get me through the immense effort of this trial. I can't go on leaping around like this without getting completely winded. When he thrusts again, I parry with my knife. But as I do, my knife is torn from my hand, spiraling out of reach.

Fuck.

He swings, and I manage to duck.

From below, I strike upward, aiming for his face. But now he's ready and smashes his sword's pommel into my shoulder. I grunt and stumble back, barely dodging his next swing.

He's already figured out how to predict my moves.

Fear pierces my chest, and I realize that I need to incapacitate him quickly. Take his eye out, tear his nose in half. With my thin, dull blade, his face is my only option. And he's not going to let me get close to it.

I need to use everything I have—but all I have is this shitty rapier. Sure, I'm faster and stronger than I used to be, but so is he. I can feel my face going red, my body overheating. I'm drenched with sweat.

And my lungs are whistling, constricting...

One last, desperate idea takes root in my mind. As he swings at me again, I dodge to the side and feint with my rapier, driving him to parry. His hand nears mine, and I press the back of my hand against his, letting my telepathy powers unfurl.

I will put you in your place, demi-Fey. His voice rings in my head. *Get your hand off me.*

I can sense what he's thinking—that I'm trying to grab his wrist. And I know what he has planned. He's going to pull his arm away, up and to the left.

Swinging, I strike with my rapier down and to the right. It's a move that makes no sense in my current position. But as he reacts, he exposes his midriff. I thrust my blade at his stomach.

"Ugh," he grunts.

I leap back and grin. He reacts like I assumed he would —furiously. Now, he's coming for me twice as hard. I dodge once, twice, three times, then pivot. With a quick twist, I manage to touch his exposed neck with my fingertips. His thoughts pour into mine, a river of calculating rage.

I sense his next strike, move to avoid it before he even starts, and suddenly, I'm behind him. I get another thrust in.

Tarquin is an asshole, but he's not stupid. He seems to realize he's being manipulated. He whirls, but he doesn't go for me again. Instead, he studies me warily. He's breathing hard, and a lock of his slick brown hair dangles before his eyes. He presses his thin lips into a line, breathing through his flared nostrils.

As he tries to figure out what's going on, his pale features look pinched.

I need to come up with a plan that's more than just reacting to his strikes. When I touch him, I can feel his thoughts. And when I stop touching him, they dissipate, but not instantly. I can almost feel the link between us stretching before it snaps away.

Can I use my powers to maintain that link? To keep our minds connected even when I'm not in contact with him? I have to use every advantage I can get.

He darts forward and swings at me, using the length of his sword to keep me from touching him. He doesn't know I'm telepathic, but he seems to have figured out that I'm trying to touch him for a reason.

My breathing is already labored. I have to finish this fight soon.

So, when he swings again, I let the dull blade hit my armored side. The strike knocks the wind out of me, and I know it will leave a brutal bruise under the armor. I nearly fall down, but instead, I grab at his hand, faintly brushing his fingers.

I'm about to end you, bitch.

I already sense his next move and barely manage to duck as the sword goes for my head. Then I leap back and focus on the connection between us. I'm not touching him, but it's still there.

The telepathic strand stretches between us, and I

enforce it with everything I have, pushing my powers as far as they will go. And it doesn't snap. Tarquin's thoughts keep pouring in, disturbing and extremely useful.

Amid his hatred of me and downright insanity, I can glimpse his moves before he makes them. I can dodge them more easily, even make a few attacks of my own. But it's not enough to turn the tide of our duel. For one thing, part of my concentration is constantly on using my magic, and I'm also fighting with the distraction of his insipid thoughts in my mind.

My breathing is getting harder. Since his strike hit me, I feel like I can't fill my lungs, and it's taking a toll. I'm getting dizzy. I have maybe one or two minutes before he manages to take me down. And I doubt the judges will stop the trial in time since they didn't give a fuck before.

Gritting my teeth, I draw even more telepathic power and pour my concentration into our connection. I sift through his surface thoughts, his hatred, his anger, his intentions. I drill down, down, down, deeper into his psyche, looking for the source. Something I can use.

A memory.

A family dinner. Tarquin is a little boy at a long dining table set with candles. His parents leave to go into the drawing room, and he sits with his cousins. Tarquin is ecstatic, left to talk to the big boys. He wants to show them his collection of Fey coins. He reaches into his pocket and pulls one out. The moment he does, one of his cousins slaps his hands, and the coins tumble away. Tarquin yelps with surprise.

"Listen to the little mummy's boy cry," his cousin says in a plummy accent. "Poor thing dropped his pennies."

"Mummy's boy? More like mummy's little baby," another cousin pipes up.

Tarquin sniffles and bends down to pick up one of the coins. The oldest cousin kicks him in the bum, and he falls over, burning with anger. He's flat on the embroidered rug, wanting to call for his mum. But they'll only tease him more.

"Aw, poor mummy's baby fell down," says his cousin.

"You know what I think? I think the little mummy's boy stinks. Did he soil himself?"

"Is that right, baby?" the other one jeers. "Have you not been house-trained yet?"

"Shall we put the stinking puppy in the dog kennel with the other animals?" The cousins are closing in on him as he scuttles back, cornered. The looks on their faces are cruel. Vindictive. Predatory. "But you'd better be quiet. The rottweilers will kill you if you cry."

A sword swings inches from my face, and I tumble back, gasping. For a few seconds, I've been lost in Tarquin's horrible memory. He nearly finished me. Thank the gods I snapped out of it in time.

I suppose I know what turned him into such an asshole. Viciousness begets more viciousness. For the first time, I almost feel sorry for him.

But I can't afford to. Whatever happened to him in the past, this Tarquin is literally trying to kill me. And I need to take him down.

"What happened, mummy's boy?" I say, imitating his cousin's accent. "Do you belong in the kennel with the other animals?"

His eyes widen. "What did you just say?" he snarls.

"Poor mummy's boy. You know, the rottweilers will kill you if you cry."

I have to move quickly as he screeches in fury and tries to bludgeon me in the head. The power of his rage is so intense that it flays our telepathic connection. His thoughts vanish from my mind, and he goes after me.

But no longer am I fighting the careful, cunning Tarquin. This guy is mindless, a raging, furious child throwing a tantrum. All his years of training are forgotten. He uses his sword like a battle-axe, swinging carelessly, trying to annihilate me. The judges, noticing the change, are shouting that the trial is over, but Tarquin can't hear them. Perhaps he doesn't even know where he is anymore. He's no longer fighting me. He's a little boy raging at his bully cousins.

I jump to the left as he swings, his sword lodging itself deeply in the ground. As he tries to pull it out, I bash his face with the pommel of my rapier. I feel his nose crunching. As hard as I can, I kick his wrist, and a bone snaps.

He screams in agony as I jump back. His hand dangles at his side uselessly, his sword stuck in the ground.

At last, Wrythe shouts that the trial is over. The cadets are roaring, screaming,

I can hardly catch my breath as I glance at the judges. Wrythe and Amon both look horrified.

But Viviane meets my eyes, and her lips twist in a tiny smile.

* * *

THERE'S a small grin on my lips as I watch Tana and Serana battling each other in the tiltyard. For them, it's the last trial. They've aced everything else, and I can tell by the distinctly coordinated whirling and swinging that they've choreographed this. Serana's ginger hair flows around her as she pivots gracefully.

Today, the summer sun beams down on us. It's been a few days since my tournament against Tarquin, and my muscles still ache.

But today's competition is a dance, not a battle. Serana has even allowed Tana to draw a little blood to make it look real, but I already know that neither of them will end up hurt.

Darius leans in to me and whispers, "If Serana were actually fighting Tana, she'd possibly be dead by now. Let's hope Tana doesn't face any real threats in the field."

"We'll all keep her safe." I clear my throat. "Assuming I pass."

"You'll pass," he says. "Can you believe I got copper? I didn't even think I'd pass at all. I was certain I'd be culled."

Darius has a habit of fishing for compliments, and I have a habit of indulging him. "Don't be ridiculous. Of course you passed. You're brilliant. We all know this."

"Thank you, love. Are you nervous for your magic trial tomorrow?"

My stomach clenches, and I feel like I want to throw up. "Nope."

"Liar."

"Hold your arms!" Amon shouts. "The trial is concluded. By a small margin, Serana O'Rourke is the winner."

My breath catches. They're about to announce the torcs.

I watch as the trio of judges confer for a few minutes in a tense huddle. Viviane is pulling out papers, pointing to them.

I swallow hard.

At last, Viviane turns to the arena, and the wind whips at her blonde hair. "Tana Campbell," she bellows. "Silver!"

Darius grabs my arm in a death grip, grinning. "She's a knight! She's a fucking knight."

"Serana O'Rourke," Viviane calls out. "Silver!"

I feel the grin splitting my face from ear to ear. "Holy shit. This almost makes up for the fact that Tarquin and Horatio got gold."

"They're going to be insufferable. Well, they didn't earn theirs, did they? Tarquin lost to you. But these torcs actually make sense." Darius is bouncing in his seat, and he reaches down to pick up a blue paper bag. "I knew it. I fucking knew it. I mean, I didn't realize it would be silver, but I knew they'd pass. Obviously."

He pulls out a bottle of champagne and with a whoop,

uncorks it. Champagne fizz bursts over the people in front of us, and they yelp with irritation.

Suppressing a laugh, I say, "Don't you want to wait for the two knights?"

"No, I'm drinking this now. I've got twilight cake, too. It's time to bloody celebrate. Also, they're knights now, so who knows if they'll even hang out with us anymore? They'll be at the knights' dining hall from now on." He lifts the bottle to my lips. "And you, Miss Nia, are going to do fine tomorrow. Absolutely fine."

I take a sip of bubbly, and he pulls it away, admonishing, "Not too much, love. You need to be clearheaded tomorrow. Wrythe will try to mess you up, you know?" He raises the bottle to his lips and pours the champagne down his throat.

What, exactly, might Wrythe have planned for tomorrow?

CHAPTER 37

$\mathcal{I}$ stand on a balcony overlooking the smooth, misty lake. Oak and apple trees line the calm shore. In the fall air, I can smell the apples growing.

I've come out here to clear my thoughts before my final trial—one that I'll be undertaking in front of every instructor and cadet at Avalon Tower. I don't need any more dire warnings about how if I fail, everyone dies. Just the thought of being stared at by so many people has made me too nervous to eat. My lungs feel tight as I breathe in the foggy air.

It's cloudy today by the lake, and the chill crawls down my collar, settling on my skin. Mist roils and twists over the glassy surface.

I still have no idea what it means that I'm the Lady of the Lake—if that's true—but I feel drawn to this calm pool of water. I'm at home here. Did Queen Morgan rule from across this lake? I've never seen what's on the other side.

As I think about her, the prince's dark voice whispers in my thoughts. *The shadows play in the quiet, stony solitude of my chamber. The cold night speaks to me, whispering of my final kiss. The goddess of death, her wicked tongue blessing mine...*

"Fuck off, Talan." I shiver, feeling like the quiet, cold air of the lake is freezing me to the bone. It worked, though. My thoughts are clearer now.

Turning, I head back through the balcony door, hugging myself as I walk through the towering gothic halls.

By now, the Culling has ended for most cadets.

But I have one more trial, the Sentinel trial, and I'm on my way right now, my nerves buzzing like the hum of the veil.

I can hear it as I approach the combat hall.

The magical mist thrums through the corridor. In about ten minutes, I'm going to be tested on my skill with the veil. There's a lump in my throat, and I swallow hard. If I manage it, I'll become an official Agent of Camelot. If I fail, beyond the terrible physical pain that the practice veil tends to unleash, I'll be culled, and everyone will die.

All eyes are on me as I walk through the vaulted corridor, but I don't look at anyone. I shouldn't be worried. I've done it with the *real* veil a bunch of times before, but I always get more nervous in front of a crowd.

This final trial has become one of the most talked about —the final test of the Culling. Serana told me people are placing bets on me, and that the odds aren't in my favor. I'm not *entirely* sure why everyone thinks I'm doomed to fuck up. It's not like I've messed up any of the missions so far.

As I approach the combat hall, I see Raphael standing before a set of towering carved oak double doors. Nivene stands by his side, her cherry red hair tied up in a bun.

"Nia," he says.

"Hey," I answer weakly.

"You're all messed up," Nivene blurts. "Diametric. Cursed."

I raise an eyebrow. "You know, you really have a way with people."

"I mean, you're a Sentinel *and* a telepath. It weakens your powers and turns you mad."

I press a finger to my lips and cut a sharp look at Raphael. "I thought you said to tell no one. And why are you bringing this up now when I'm supposed to be focusing?"

"Nivene can help," Raphael says. "We have a few minutes before the trial starts."

I'm thrown off by this change in the plan. I'd been trying to clear my head, not learn new things at the last moment.

"It's fine," I say. "I've handled the veil before. The real veil, not this fake one. You have nothing to worry about." I know what he needs to hear. "This will be easy."

"You don't understand," Raphael says, and for the first time since the assassin's attack, I see him almost...afraid. "This is not the veil-in-a-box we used during training.

There's a veil mage working with MI-13. He's the one creating the veil for this trial. And he's in the pocket of the Pendragons. Wrythe is furious that you beat Tarquin. It makes their gold torcs look like a fraud, so he's primed this mage. The man is extremely skilled, and he's going to make this nearly impossible for you to pass."

Ah...so *that's* why everyone's betting against me.

Nivene looks pale. "I've just been in there. This veil barrier he's creating? It's the real thing. And it will kill you if you don't disrupt it completely." She grips my bicep tightly, her fingernails digging in. "Kill you."

Fear cuts me down to the bone, but I force myself to shrug and give them a placid smile. "Fine. But how hard can it be compared to the real veil? It's thousands of miles long and rises above the clouds and sinks under the sea. This can't be more powerful than that. It's all contained in the combat hall."

Nivene turns to Raphael, scowling. "I thought she's supposed to be intelligent."

Raphael sighs. "Nivene, that's not the way—"

"The entire problem *is* that it's a smaller veil!" Nivene barks. Her words echo off the high ceiling. "The border veil is large, so it's stretched thin. You've seen it yourself, I'm sure. When you look at how the veil is built, you can actually see the holes and weaknesses in its structure because it's spread out so far."

Tension weaves through the air, sharpening the atmosphere. She's right. That's exactly what I see every time.

"*This* one is condensed into a single room," she hisses. "A force so powerful, it'll *disintegrate* you if you step in it without your magic. Evaporate. We'll send your remains back to your mother in a matchbox. Just dust."

I feel the blood draining from my face. "Are you trying to scare me until I can't think straight?"

"I'm trying to say," she goes on, "you'll need all your focus to disrupt it, okay? And right now, your powers are unstable because they're *powers*. Plural. Fucked up."

"Okay." I still don't know what she wants from me, but I now feel like puking.

Raphael is studying me closely, and his eyes seem to have more contrast than ever—the pale silver ringed with bright blue. His dark eyelashes lower. With the way he's staring at me, I feel as if he's reading all my secrets. Like *he's* telepathic. Sometimes, I get the sense he knows exactly how much I think about him, and about every time we kissed. And about the way I felt wrapped in his strong arms as he healed me, his hand on my stomach.

Then, I'd felt safe around him.

Right now, I have absolutely no idea what he's thinking, but the intense look in his eyes has my nerves fluttering. His unreadable expression often has the power to unnerve me.

"It's fine, you two," I say. "I know I need to suppress the telepathy."

"But that doesn't work, does it?" says Raphael coolly.

"That's why I'm here," Nivene says. "Sentinels don't

just disrupt veils. We disrupt magic in general. If you cooperate, I can sever your telepathic powers. For good."

My stomach drops, and I take a step back. "Hang on."

Nivene steps in closer. "Sentinels are surgeons. Professor Throckmorton discovered this technique a few years ago to remove power from Fey prisoners. Now, obviously, I don't want to remove your Sentinel powers. But what if I can remove your telepathy? Granted, I've never tried it before, but I think it's possible. I can already feel it inside you. Violet, isn't it? It has a wild, frenetic energy. Give me your hand." She holds out her palm. "I'll see what I can do."

My blood roars in my ears. I hadn't realized until now exactly how attached I feel to the voices I hear, to this power. Or that my instinct tells me I need to keep it.

Nivene frowns at me. "I'll guide you through it. Come on, we don't have much time." She shakes her palm. "Nia, take my hand."

"I'll be fine without your help." I need to tell them what they want to hear, or they'll rip part of me away. "I've actually managed to control my telepathy at this point. I don't even sense it at all now. It's suppressed."

"You're lying," says Nivene.

"Nia," Raphael says, "you must do this. Avalon Tower needs another Sentinel. This isn't just for you. Lives depend on your Sentinel powers."

My heart pounds against my ribs. My telepathy is a part of me. I'm not going to let them take it away. It was the power that saved me during that combat trial. And that mission? We never would have found the map without this skill. But that's not what Raphael needs to hear, is it?

And I don't really know how to explain it to him because it's mostly just instinct.

I plaster a smile on my face. "Why bother with this when I've got it under control?"

"You told me that you don't even like hearing those voices," Raphael says. "Nia, I know this is not ideal." He reaches out and touches my arm. His eyes are pleading. Warmth from his fingertips pours into me. "But if you don't do this, I'm afraid you will die."

I wonder how much that would bother him on a personal level versus just robbing MI-13 of another desperately needed Sentinel.

"Even *I* can't disrupt the veil he's conjuring there," Nivene says. "Well...I probably can. I'm really good at this. But I'm not plagued with diametric magic, and I'm much better trained—"

"Nivene, stop," Raphael says sharply.

Her nostrils flare. "Fine. Talk some sense into her. But better be quick because they're about to start. And I can sense that her magic is more conflicted and erratic than ever."

She pivots and stalks into the hall.

"You're not telling the truth, are you?" Raphael's eyes search mine like he's trying to read me. He's sifting through each one of my secrets. I can feel it, and it sends a shiver up my spine. Does he know that every night before

I go to sleep, I think of him, of being curled up in his arms and breathing his scent?

A bell rings inside the hall, signaling that I'm about to start.

I swallow hard. *Tell people the things they need to hear to calm them down.* My ever-faithful strategy. "I'm going to go in now," I say in a dulcet tone I always used to placate Mom and give him a sweet smile. "It will be fine, Raphael. You taught me everything I need to know. You're a brilliant teacher."

I clean up messes. It's what I do. I keep people calm, happy, and safe. I'm a balm to soothe panic and rage and bare feet pierced with broken glass. I'm a blanket of fog to cool a sofa burning from a lit cigarette. I smile at the police when they come to the door, and I get them to leave happy. "Everything will be fine," I say again, touching his shoulder.

His ice-cold gaze doesn't soften.

The heavy wooden doors to the main hall are shut, and I push them open with all my strength. They slam against the walls, announcing me with a loud crash. The room falls still, and everyone turns to look at me.

Cadets and teachers pack the chamber, seated on rows of bleachers that surround the combat hall. Just for me. There are even some faces I haven't seen in Avalon Tower before, members of MI-13 who've come to watch me, including some with gold torcs. In the center of the room, the veil writhes before the mage.

Its power is immense, the humming in my ears

drowning out everything else. A roiling cloud of magical mist shimmering with colors, thick and impossible to look through it. It's not very big. Ten feet high, maybe, and six feet wide, a gleaming wall of magic towering over me.

A few feet away from the veil stands Wrythe and a figure draped in black robes—the veil mage.

"Nia." Raphael's deep voice stops me in my tracks, and I look back at him. "I gave you an order, Nia. I ordered you to tell me the truth."

I stare at him, aghast. Why is he so determined to fuck up my focus right before the trial that means everything? Right here, in front of everyone.

"Not now," I whisper.

I can feel everyone staring at us.

"Not now?" His voice is cold and quiet. It's like I don't quite know him anymore. "I'm a knight. I'm not your friend, Nia. I brought you to this academy for a reason, and it wasn't because I liked you. I need you to be a Sentinel. I don't know what foolish notions you've got in your head, but you should have done as I told you. I see now that I was right about you before, wasn't I? You're a spoiled, selfish girl who grew up in dissolute chaos, and as a consequence, you know nothing of the real world, or of war, or of what it means to make sacrifices for other people. As far as you're concerned, this is all a game."

I stare at him, stunned. My cheeks flame red, and my stomach twists with nausea. "What happened to you?"

His face is an expressionless mask. "What happened to me? I don't think you understand." He leans closer. "I don't think I like you very much, and I never have." He seems to hesitate for a moment, and his fingers tighten into fists. "From what I can tell now, *trash* is a perfectly accurate description."

There it is. The blow I've been waiting for all along. The heartbreak I knew he'd deliver. My eyes sting, and a lump forms in my throat. He's the same fucking Raphael he always was. The one who ruined my life all those years ago.

A bolt of rage thuds in my head, making it hard to think. I turn away from him, stepping deeper into the room. The veil's humming is muffled now because all I hear is the rhythmic beating of my own heart. My chest is aching and hollow.

My gaze flicks to the enormous portrait of Merlin hanging on the wall. He wears a deep blue robe flecked with silver stars. I think of him, imprisoned in that oak tree by the woman he loved. Sealed up, abandoned, with roots growing into his chest.

I am the cold mist coiling over the lake, I tell myself.

I pause, fury igniting my blood.

I turn back to Raphael. A woman with white-blonde hair stands beside him, and it takes me a minute to remember her name. Ginevra, I think—the Pendragon agent with a gold torc. She's tall and elegant, her hair neatly swept up into something like a tiara. And she's whispering to him, her eyes sliding to me.

I'm now utterly distracted from the *extremely* important task I'm about to undertake.

But right now, I'm not the calming, soothing Nia who wants to make everyone feel better. Right now, I'm a raging tempest churning the lake waters. I'm the sword forged in fire beneath its surface.

I narrow my eyes at Raphael. "Do you know what, Launcelot?" My voice echoes off the hall.

His attention cuts to me, and Ginevra stares at me with raised brows.

Heat ebbs from my veins, and I feel as if I'm turning to ice. "You've proven yourself to be the same self-obsessed twat you always were. You don't have to be wealthy to think you're better than everyone else, do you? To some people, arrogance comes just as naturally as breathing. And in reality, Raphael, I saved your ass more than once, you egomaniacal, solipsistic, stuck-up *prick*. Do not speak to me again unless it's an order. Unless it's life or death. You're not good enough to speak to me, and you never were."

My words have a growl in them that echoes off the combat hall. Raphael visibly flinches. *Good.*

The hum and buzz of the veil returns, and wrath floods my veins. I turn back to the veil mage. I know everyone is staring, stunned. I know they'll be talking about this for weeks.

But right now, I don't give a fuck what they think.

CHAPTER 38

*M*y cheeks are flushed with anger, and molten rage flows through my blood.

Amon is telling me something, perhaps explaining the terms of the trial, but I can't hear him over the ringing in my ears.

And in any case, I don't need instructions.

Wrythe interrupts Amon, bellowing an introduction. Something about how he's the Seneschal, and it's his job to protect us from getting our hopes up. That this test separates the chaff from the wheat, and clearly, I'm the chaff.

But all I'm really listening to is the screaming hiss of my own fury. *I don't think I like you very much, and I never have.*

"The trial of the veil is about to begin," Wrythe calls out. "Within the veil, we have placed a replica of Merlin's wand. Ms. Melisende will have to—"

I move toward the veil before he even finishes and summon my magic, letting the red bloom, a furious cloud. Red, the color of wrath. As I move closer, I immediately see what Nivene was talking about. The shimmering energy strands that make up the veil are enmeshed so densely that I can't see any points of weakness in the magic. Nothing thin or fragile. No place to channel my magic. This veil is a wall of death.

Raphael's words are still echoing in my skull. *This is all a game to you. From what I can tell now,* trash *is a perfectly accurate description.*

My heart hammers, a war drum.

Burning with rage, I pull at my magic, and it fuels the hot crimson inside me. I don't bother searching for a weak spot. I hurl my magic at the veil, my teeth grinding together. To my right, the veil mage stumbles, then falls flat on his back. The buzz of the veil sputters and dies, and silence fills the hall. I hear only my own pounding pulse.

When the mist is completely silent and no longer buzzing over my skin, I stride inside.

Pearly white fog wraps around me. My foot kicks something, and I hear it spinning across the floor. I reach down for the wand and grip its gnarled wood.

I march out of the veil and toss it at Wrythe's feet. It clatters noisily.

"There you go," I say. "Your wand, *sir.*"

The veil mist slowly dissipates, and the mage seems to be unconscious.

A buzz of whispers fills the combat hall.

I hear little snatches of what they're saying. "Did you see—"

"Didn't even slow her down—"

"That veil mage just *dropped*—"

Wrythe stands, arms folded, glaring. His blond mustache twitches.

"I'm so, so disappointed to have to say this." His voice booms across the hall. "But as Seneschal of this institution, I must protect you all. It is my job to shield you all from cheaters and liars. Clearly, Ms. Melisende has found a way to cheat. No one can simply step into a powerful veil like that without preparation. A veil this powerful takes time to dismantle. We *all* know that. Of course, this is the risk we take when letting anyone in, regardless of background."

"Sorry to disappoint." I raise my own voice. "But maybe your veil mage sucks. Everyone connected to you is here by virtue of nepotism."

His fingers twitch. "Do you really think I'd let a cadet get away with speaking to the Seneschal like that? And after what you just said to another knight?" he roars, looking for agreement around him. "We have protocols and procedures here. We have deference for those in superior positions. And at Avalon Tower, we do not cheat. So why don't you tell me who you had helping you? Is it the other Sentinel? Nivene?"

Fury still burns through me from Raphael's words.

"I'm not a cadet anymore," I say. "I just passed, and I'm an Agent of Camelot. This is not just a game to me, and despite what some of the knights might think, I belong here."

He lunges forward. "As Seneschal, I'm saying you did *not*."

He grabs my arm in fury. As I'm already thrumming with power, my telepathy engages at the sudden touch, connecting me to Wrythe's mind. Tendrils of violet spiral out from me, slipping into his thoughts. I get my first glimpse into Wrythe's psyche.

What shocks me is how empty it is. Like a void.

Even when I read Tarquin's mind, I could feel his belief and fear. He believed he was better than me, and under that, he was afraid he couldn't prove it. He believed in his family and the importance of being a Pendragon, and needed to prove himself to them. And even though he's a twat, he believed in taking down Auberon, that it's important, and that without it, humanity will fall.

But Wrythe has none of that. He has no beliefs beyond his own desperation to climb up the rungs of power in MI-13. He wants to lead Avalon Tower simply because he craves power. He doesn't care for the lives of the agents or the humans he's supposed to protect. To my shock, he doesn't even care about Tarquin or the rest of the Pendragons. The only reason he treats them differently is because of how they reflect on him, being his kin. He values their loyalty to him because it secures his position.

But there is only one real person in Wrythe's mind: Wrythe.

In his twisted mind, I'm an obstacle on his way up. He has to prove I don't belong here simply because that was his opinion when I first arrived, and he needs people to believe he's infallible. That he's the only one who can lead. That only through unrelenting loyalty to him will Avalon Tower prevail because he is the only one with answers.

I never wanted the demi-Fey here.

Is that why Raphael had made a public spectacle of telling me I don't belong here? So he can prove himself to Wrythe?

Get on board with referring to Nia as a useless waste of space if you want to keep your position...

I'm already burning with rage, and Wrythe's narcissistic thoughts are like pouring oil on a flame.

Molten fury erupts inside me, and my red and violet magic fuse together, my telepathy and Sentinel powers intertwining to create that hybrid, chaotic force. I slam it into Wrythe's mind and pour myself into his skull. Such a simple mind, focused on one pathetic motivation. A simple mind to prod and push. And I do, demolishing the weak walls he has within, taking his thoughts for my own.

I will bind my enemies in the oak trees to feed the hungry earth. I will spill your blood into the lake.

Wrythe stumbles back and blinks, dazed. Then he opens his mouth.

"Nia Melisende is incredible!" he shouts for everyone

to hear. "She has surpassed my estimations in all the trials, proving she is a worthy Agent of Camelot, and she has without question passed this trial. Furthermore, I want to add that I am a twat, caring for no one but myself. Having me as a Seneschal is an insult to the great history of this academy and...and..."

The connection between us snaps, and his mind vanishes from my own.

Silence settles in the hall, and I feel as if the whole academy is holding its breath.

I'm shivering, the result of an explosion of my magic. I hug myself, clenching my teeth to avoid them from chattering.

Wrythe points at me with one trembling finger. "She was in my mind!" he bellows. "She forced me to say that. This is an *attack* on the Seneschal! A psychic attack. And an attack on a knight of the Round Table is an attack on Avalon Tower itself. *This* is the very reason we did not allow demi-Fey here."

Amon looks utterly confused. "Wrythe, what *are* you talking about? How would her Sentinel powers allow her to control you?"

Wrythe eyes widen as he realizes the implication. "You've got diametric powers!" he snarls. "You have two types of magic, just like the monster Mordred Kingslayer. Of course. I knew something was corrupted about her. And *this* is why she doesn't belong. Don't you see how dangerous this is?"

Amon stares at me, frowning. "Surely that cannot be. If

Nia had diametric magic, it would be unstable and weak. It would destroy her. But we've seen her in the trials. And like you just said, she surpassed our estimations in the trials, including this one. That's simply not how diametric powers work."

"She did *not* pass the trial!" Wrythe shouts. "She *made* me say that she did. I felt her in my thoughts. I felt her malignant presence, as rotten and corrupted as Mordred himself."

Another silence follows his condemnation. And then, excited murmurs throughout the hall.

Amon's silver torc gleams under the light of the chandeliers. "Are you saying...are you saying she's capable...of *mind control*? Of compulsion?"

Even *I* am caught unaware. Mind control? No, of course not. I just...Wrythe's mind was so simple. So one-sided. Even a child could manipulate it.

Right?

Wrythe himself had taught us about the five primal powers: weather manipulation, amoromancy, polymorphism, compulsion, and conjuration. The five primal powers. The powers that don't exist anymore in Brocéliande or beyond it. Obviously, I can't do that if it no longer exists.

Wrythe blinks. "As I said, she is an enemy of Avalon Tower. She should be imprisoned at once. This is treason."

Raphael stalks closer. I avoid looking at him, feeling the rage seething within me at his presence. He looks just as furious as he did before. He turns to the crowd, his icy

C.N. CRAWFORD & ALEX RIVERS

eyes surveying them. "Everybody out!" His voice carries over the hall. "This is a matter for the knights of the Round Table. No one else."

His voice has a quiet command that immediately has them leaping up and shuffling for the doors. I turn to join them when Raphael says, "Not you, Nia. You stay."

I fold my arms, trying not to glare at him because that would be petulant. There are bigger things at stake right now.

I catch the worried eyes of my friends as they leave, and someone helps the dazed veil mage up off the floor. Finally, the door shuts. The only people in the room are Viviane, Raphael, Wrythe, Amon, and me. Just a few knights of the Round Table and me.

"You knew about this," Wrythe hisses at Raphael.

"About what?" Raphael quirks an eyebrow.

So *now* he has my back? Dickhead.

Wrythe's eyes narrow at Raphael. "Is there something going on between you two? Something that would get you kicked out of Avalon Tower?"

"Don't be ridiculous," I say sharply.

"As you may have heard me say," Raphael adds in a glacial tone, "I don't like her very much, and I find her personality irritating. But like it or not, her magical powers will be an asset to MI-13."

I stare at him, anger still coursing through my veins.

"The girl has diametric powers," says Wrythe. "Did you know? Did you cover that up?"

"Yes, I knew," Raphael says quietly.

My heart sinks. Why is he *telling* them?

"And you didn't think to share it with us?" says Wrythe. "With the Seneschal?"

He loves referring to himself in the third person.

"I shared it with the people who needed to know," Raphael says. "*You* didn't need to know."

"I technically outrank you. You've brought a mongrel into Avalon Tower, one with diametric magic. Do I need to remind you about Mordred? You let her participate in critical missions, risking the other agents—"

"I'll remind you that I was at each of those missions, Wrythe," Raphael says. "If anyone's life was at risk, it was mine."

"And mine," adds Viviane.

Raphael cuts her a sharp look. "And Nia's powers and skills saved us. Several times."

"Whatever Raphael should or should not have told us," Viviane says, "I am clear on one thing. She passed the last trial. She's now an agent. These are our rules. Our protocols and procedures." On the last two words, I'm pretty sure she's mimicking Wrythe's plummy accent.

Wrythe shakes his head in disgust. "She clearly cheated her way through. A random person from off the streets?"

"I didn't cheat," I say.

"Quiet, girl. I don't even know why you're here," Wrythe snaps at me. "Fine. We can use her as a Sentinel like you first suggested when she came here, Raphael. She can open the way for abler crews. She's the transportation. If you all *insist*, I don't even mind giving her a brass torc. But I'll be damned if she—"

"I'm sorry, a *brass* torc?" Viviane says. "Didn't we agree she passed the shadow trial with the highest score?"

"She passed the written trial with the highest score as well," Amon says.

Raphael nods. "And during the combat trial, she beat Tarquin Pendragon, and if I'm not mistaken, *he* got a full score for that trial, so obviously she does as well."

"And this trial..." Viviane raises her eyebrow. "Well...I don't know *what* you'd call what she demonstrated here."

"I can't believe this." Wrythe seethes. "Do you *really* want to give this wretch something above a brass?"

"A gold torc matches her results," Viviane says.

I can only stare at them with my mouth ajar. A *gold* torc? Like *Raphael's*? My heart flutters.

"No," Amon says.

We all look at him.

"Finally, someone with some sense," Wrythe blurts.

Amon nods gravely. "I am Avalon's historian. And I know all of our laws and ceremonies. There's only one precedent for this. Only one Fey from Avalon Tower's history had one of the primal powers." Amon looks up at the wall. My eyes follow his to the painting that hangs above the combat hall. Merlin.

"The founders were clear," Amon says. "There are individuals that carry a different torc. Those are the founders of Avalon Tower. King Arthur. Sir Galahad. And Camelot's primal sorcerers, like Merlin."

"Not *like* Merlin," Wrythe sputters. "*Just* Merlin. He was Camelot's *only* primal sorcerer."

"Merlin passed the Tower's trials, which were then conducted by the Lady of the Lake," Amon says. "He would have received a gold torc, but because he could manipulate the weather—and that is a primal power—she gave him a torc of Avalon Steel, forged by dragon fire."

"You want to give her Avalon Steel? Are you mad?" Wrythe splutters.

Amon shrugs and looks at the ground. "I don't *want* to. I have to. We have protocols."

"Protocols and procedures, Wrythe," Viviane says, again in his accent.

"Because you think she has mind control powers?" Wrythe's voice becomes unhinged. "Compulsion?"

"You just told us that she did." Amon frowns. "That she made you say what you did."

"Or did you really mean what you said when you called yourself a twat?" Viviane asks.

"What is the point of being Seneschal when I have two *demi-Fey* working against me?" Wrythe snarls, and cuts a sharp look to Amon. "And a bearded idiot from the common classes. This place is going to hell, do you know that? It's all falling apart."

He pivots and storms off, slamming the doors behind him.

"Now, then," Amon beams. "Nia Melisende, welcome to Avalon Tower. We will grant you the torc the moment we can get our hands on Avalon Steel. There's not much of it left because it has to be forged on a stone in the lake using dragon fire, but rules are rules."

Viviane turns to cross out of the hall. She throws open the door. The entire academy is out there, waiting. She stares at them for a moment, then lifts her chin and shouts, "Avalon Steel."

And at her words, all hell breaks loose.

CHAPTER 39

I knock three times on an imposing set of dark oak doors, the thick wood reinforced with nails.

I glance back at Tana and Serana. They're staring at the door, their shoulders hunched, expressions tense. Serana has a coffee stain on her shirt, but it's too late for her to change.

We're on the top floor of Merlin's Tower, the one no one is allowed to visit unless summoned.

None of us know why we've been called, only that the knights of the Round Table are waiting for us on the other side of the door.

"Do you have any sense of what they want?" I ask Tana desperately.

She shakes her head and crosses her arms in front of her chest. She's been quiet and withdrawn the past few days, and I keep hearing her moaning in her sleep. I'm well aware that there's something she's not telling me.

"I hope they're not changing their minds about us becoming knights," Serana mutters, fingering her silver torc nervously. "They can't do that, right? At this point?"

Torchlight burns from columns on either side of the door, wavering over the carvings that rise up twenty feet. On one side of the wood are engravings of swords, crowns, and a scepter—symbols of royalty. On the other are twisting nature symbols, a man's face formed with leaves, and plants with three leaves. My gaze slides to the top of the door. Etched in the stone is the cycle of the moon.

Shadows from the burning torches dance over the stone walls and floor.

At last, the door groans open. Slowly, the three of us cross inside.

I stare in awe at the hall, the size of a particularly large cathedral. Pale blue light flows in through an ornate window a hundred feet high. The pearly rays gleam off a round table of polished wood so large that it seats about fifty chairs. Only about ten of them are empty, and the rest of the knights are staring at us. Nivene is among them, her scarlet hair like a flame in the streaming sunlight.

Flanked by Tana and Serana, I slowly walk across the flagstone floor. I try not to look at Ráphael. Instead, I keep my eyes on the tall portraits on the far side of the hall. They span from the floor to twenty feet above: Arthur,

Merlin, and Guinevere—each of them wearing a metal torc, pale with a hint of rose. Avalon Steel.

Mine isn't ready yet. And that means I'm the only one here without a torc.

I glance at the round table again. I didn't realize there were quite this many Round Table knights. And as much as I try to avoid looking at Raphael, I can't help it. My gaze always goes to him, whether I want it or not. His beauty is like a command I can't ignore.

The pale light glints from his eyes, making them spark like metal. These are the most important MI-13 agents in the world, and I only want to look at him.

With a sinking heart, I realize Ginevra Pendragon is sitting by his side. She wears her hair long, with a few braids threaded with jewels. In the pale light, she looks more beautiful than ever. When I glance at the portrait of Guinevere on the wall, I can see the clear resemblance. It occurs to me that she must have been named after her ancestor.

She leans in, whispering to Raphael. Her eyes are on me again, a smile on her lips. I feel my face flush.

This is exactly why romance is forbidden here because my mind is very much not on task, and I have to stop myself from walking out the door.

It's been a week since I last spoke to him, when we screamed at each other. Soon after the trial, part of me wondered if his outburst was calculated. Did he know that making me angry would bring out my power? But when he failed to show up at any point to explain himself, I realized that might be false hope. If his insults were fake, the man had *plenty of time* in the past week to let me know. It wasn't like he'd been away on a mission. I'd seen him around. And when I did, he simply looked the other way.

I breathe in deeply, scanning the rest of the table. Of the forty or so around the table, Raphael and Ginevra are the only ones wearing gold. The rest are silver. So where are the other Pendragons?

Viviane gestures at the empty chairs. "Sit, please."

The three of us walk over to the empty chairs. We sit down just as the doors groan closed behind us. I feel the power of the table hum over my skin.

On the other side of the hall, the portrait of Merlin clicks, and the entire thing creaks open. A man steps through it, looking like a warrior who traveled through time. He has a long gray beard, and his face is lined with age. Unlike the rest of the people in the room, he's dressed in actual chain mail armor with a silvery breastplate. And emblazoned on the breastplate is the Merlin Court coat of arms I've seen around this tower—one with an owl, stars, and the cycle of the moon. His armor groans as he crosses the large hall.

For a moment, I wonder if the rumors are true, if Merlin never died, and maybe he's returned to us through his own portrait. But this man looks nothing like Merlin, and he wears a silver torc.

"Who is that?" I whisper to Serana.

"Sir Kay," she whispers. "He is the leader of MI-13."

He crosses to an empty chair set at the round table and takes a seat.

"Thank you all for coming on such short notice." His deep, commanding voice resonates around the room. "What we're discussing today is of the utmost secrecy. There will be no sharing of any of this with anyone at the academy. Or, obviously, outside it."

I exchange looks with Tana and Serana. What are the three of us even doing here?

"As you all know, MI-13's efforts are held back by the veil," he continues. "We make do with our Sentinels opening the way to small task forces, but it has limited our options."

Nivene raises her eyebrow at me and nods.

"The veil is maintained by the Fey's magicians," adds Sir Kay. "Up until two months ago, there were ten. However, one of them was sent to assassinate one of our Sentinels and was killed." He glances for the briefest second in my direction. "And *another* veil mage was sent to take out our entire cadet force, and was also, luckily, stopped and killed." He clears his throat and takes another glance at me. "There are now eight remaining, which is better than ten."

Ten minus two equals eight. My first grade teacher, Mrs. Mermenstein, would be proud of us all.

"Eight veil mages are still enough to maintain the veil around Fey France," he continues. "However, according to our scholars, seven are not."

Around the table, others start to murmur as well. Then Sir Kay thumps the table, and silence falls over the hall.

"The two attacks by veil mages have demonstrated that the Fey are scaling up their aggressive operations," he says. "This is already enough to indicate their plans for something even bigger in the future. But if that wasn't enough, one of MI-13's most powerful psychics is with us in the room—now a knight herself. Ms. Campbell, would you share with the room what you told me yesterday?"

All eyes turn to Tana.

I can see the tension around her mouth, but she lifts her chin. "I've seen a terrible force coming from the Fey realm in the near future. Avalon Tower falls, taken apart stone by stone, and the blood of our agents feeds the earth. I've seen the deaths of each and every one of the courageous knights and agents in this room. The bodies lying unburied, picked at by scavengers. And soon after, humanity will follow."

A terrible silence follows her words. I stare at my friend, and her dark eyes gleam. I have no doubt she's actually seen those images. I've heard her crying in her sleep. Now I know why.

"Is it definite?" Nivene asks. "Or something that can be stopped?"

Tana shakes her head. "It's not written in stone, but we don't have long to stop it," she says. "A few weeks."

"Fuck that," Nivene says.

"Yes," Sir Kay says. "As our eloquent Sentinel points out, this is not ideal."

"We need to bolster our defenses," a knight with white hair calls out.

"The time for being on the defensive has passed," Sir Kay says. "Thanks to the efforts of our agents, we've procured a map of critical military locations in the Fey realm. We've been researching these locations, collecting information. Six of them, along the border, house Fey veil mages. As I've explained, once one of them dies, the veil becomes unstable. It is then that we can move large forces and strike, hitting other critical locations and stopping the upcoming Fey attack that Dame Campbell has seen in her visions."

This is a mission briefing—the largest and most important I've ever been in. And it's already clear what he wants us to do.

"The people in this room are the best agents among MI-13," Sir Kay says, his gaze circling the room, meeting each one's eyes. "And we're sending you on the riskiest mission we've taken since the Fey invasion. We will send two groups to two locations along the border. Once there, our Sentinels will open the way to move inside Fey France. Each group will split into three small task forces and move toward the locations of the magicians. There will be six task forces altogether. We need you to kill the magicians. One is enough, but six is even better. Once that happens, the veil will fall, and I will lead a large surprise attack into Fey France."

"What about the Pendragons?" Nivene asks. "I can't help but notice that almost *none* of them are here. But of course, you did say the *best* agents are all here, didn't you? So, I suppose that's no mystery at all."

Ginevra looks furious at this, which gives me a tiny shiver of pleasure.

Sir Kay sighs dramatically, and I get the sense that this is a long-repeated argument. Perhaps one of those arguments that made Nivene "bad at politics." If they weren't so desperate for Sentinels, I'm pretty sure she'd be long gone.

"Apart from Ginevra, the Pendragons will remain in Avalon Tower, monitoring our progress," Sir Kay finally says.

Nivene snorts. "Right, sitting on their incompetent arses while we risk our lives, and they reap—"

"*Thank you*, Nivene," Sir Kay snaps. "Your contribution, as always, is very much appreciated. The task forces have already been established, and I will now read them out. Group one, Freya and Serana. Group two, Nivene, Meliahad and Tana. Group three, Viviane and Antoreau. Group four, Nia, Ginevra, and Raphael. Group five..."

He goes on, but I don't follow as he lists the rest of the groups. My task force includes me, Raphael, and a woman who might be his lover.

I catch his eye, and my chest cracks open.

CHAPTER 40

J crouch behind a rock, the crisp September air
rushing over my skin through the thin fabric
of my dress. There's enough of a chill today that the
dewdrops have nearly turned to frost, and my elegant Fey
disguise doesn't offer much protection against the cold
wind.

From a hillside, Ginevra and I are watching a small
town nestled between fiery, autumn-touched hills, just
inside the border of Fey France. From where we hide, a
little dirt path wends down the hill to a cluster of stone
houses and shops, and a church steeple gleams in the
sunlight.

I peer through a metal spyglass at an ivory mansion
at the edge of the town and the enormous ivy-covered
walls that surround it. The veil mage's mansion wasn't
hard to find. At three stories high, it towers over most
of the other buildings in town, and the front gate

looks fit for a king. It's a gorgeous place—creamy stone with pale blue shutters that match the double front door.

And somewhere in there is the Fey we need to kill.

I peer through the lens again. The mansion is about three hundred yards away, but with the spyglass, I can easily see who goes in and out, making a mental note of each one.

We've been here for over an hour, searching for signs of an ambush, and my muscles ache as I crouch. Somewhere in that town, Raphael is scoping things out up close. Soon after we got through the veil, he rode ahead of us to scout, leaving us in the company of each other for the majority of the journey. Neither of us was grateful for that.

The golden light shines off Ginevra's sun-kissed skin. "Well, American, I don't care what anyone says about you. You are truly a scintillating conversationalist."

I glance at her and raise an eyebrow, saying nothing.

"Sorry, you know what?" she continues. "What I actually meant to say is that I'm about to die of boredom after traveling for two days in your bloody tedious company. Do they not teach you how to speak in America, or do they just sit you in front of a TV when you're a baby and hope for the best?"

Ginevra refuses to call me by my name, and at this point, I'm all out of patience with the Pendragon attitude. So, I've hardly spoken a word to her.

I let silence fill the air again and turn my attention to

the tavern in town. It's going to be our first stop on our mission.

"It's a shame I wasn't sent alone with Raph," she adds. "He and I get along very well *indeed*. I know he's demi-Fey, but he's different to the others, isn't he? He's intelligent. Instead, I've got you for company."

I clench my jaw. "I don't see anything of concern yet," I say sharply, ignoring her bullshit. "No hidden weapons that I could spot on anyone going in or out."

"One of the men had a knife in his boot," she says, her own glass held to her eye. "Perhaps that's the kind of thing you'd notice with more experience. But I don't think it's a major concern."

"Good."

She turns to me, narrowing her sapphire eyes. "Did they really give you Avalon Steel on the basis of one trial?"

I plaster a smile on my face. "I received top scores in all other trials as well. I've earned it."

"Ridiculous," she mutters. "I doubt you actually have a primal power. It should have been tested more thoroughly. How does anyone know you didn't bribe someone else to attack Wrythe?"

"Someone else with primal powers? And who would that be?"

She shrugs. "Or you might have drugged him, for all I know, until he believed he was mind controlled. All I'm saying is that it obviously needed testing before such a rash decision was made. Bloody outrageous."

The sound of footfalls on leaves turns my head, and I

turn to see Raphael striding through the grass behind us. My heart speeds up at the sight of him, looking divine in his crisp white shirt and navy trousers. He's gazing right at me, the golden sunlight glinting in his pale eyes. He carries a small valise that will be part of our disguise.

"There you are," he says quietly.

Ginevra stands and flashes him a charming smile. "Thank the gods you're here. I've missed your company, Raph! You're always terribly amusing."

"Is he really?" I murmur.

"We didn't see anything of concern at the tavern," she goes on. "Four men and two women went in during the past hour. Three men stepped out. I'd estimate that's normal traffic on a day like this. No sign of an ambush."

"Good." Raphael's jaw clenches. "Ginevra, I need you to stay here on the lookout, at least until Nia and I get into the cottage. If you see anything that looks like an ambush or attack, run for backup."

She crosses her arms. "Are you sure you don't want a more experienced agent to go with you? Someone who knows you better?"

"We discussed this. Nia's magic might come in handy. And you're the fastest rider among us. We need you to deliver messages to and from command. For now, stay hidden and keep a lookout for anyone suspicious approaching town." He turns and starts walking down the hill. The autumn landscape is bathed in flaming shades, gilded by the sun.

I follow him, carefully avoiding the thorny branches.

I'm wearing a pale blue dress as part of my disguise, and I don't want my costume to be accidentally ripped.

Raphael cuts me a sharp glare. "So, we're back to where we started, are we?"

"Your friend Ginevra is fucking lovely, by the way," I mutter. I have a million questions I want to ask him about what he said to me, but this isn't the time. We're about to go into a very dangerous situation, and we both need to be focused. I didn't need any emotional turmoil turning me into the next Alix.

As we near the town, Raphael glances at me. "Our cover story is that we just got married," he says. "We'll walk around a bit first and observe, then head to the tavern to meet the contact. Try to act as if you don't hate me."

"I can *act*."

"Oh, believe me, I know you can act." An edge undercuts his velvety tone, and he's giving me an expression I cannot interpret.

We're already at the cobbled road that rings the town. Raphael grabs my hand and gives me what looks like a loving smile.

We walk through town, just a couple of newlyweds, hand in hand. And that's all people around us see—the two of us looking in shop windows, at bakeries. When we stop to peer in the window of a cake shop, Raphael slides his arm around my waist. I do my best to ignore how amazing he smells and how good it feels to lean against his muscled body. I try not to think about him. I need to keep my eyes on those around me, taking in the looks people give us, trying to assess threats.

Using the window's reflections, I keep an eye out for anyone who might be following us. Of the people who pass us by, I note two I find suspicious: a woman who makes a point to avoid looking at us, and a man who follows us briefly before breaking away.

We stop to look at a flower shop with gorgeous wildflower blooms and crowns in the windows. I stand on my tiptoes, and Raphael leans down. "Two possible informants," I whisper in his ear. "A woman and a man."

"I saw," he murmurs. "The man followed us because he enjoyed staring at your arse, for which I can't blame him. The woman avoided looking at us because she had a recent breakup and seeing a loving couple makes her want to scream."

"How can you tell that the woman had a breakup?"

"Because I know how heartbreak looks," he says darkly.

I sigh. "If only she knew the truth about us."

Another inscrutable expression. "Maybe we should focus, like you said. Let's go to the tavern."

He takes my hand and leads me to the tavern, a stone building with blue shutters open to the light and candlelit tables set up on a wide stone terrace. Lanterns cast a wavering glow over the walls.

Although we've been monitoring it for more than an hour, part of me is still scared of a trap. My muscles tense as I casually look to my left and right, making sure there are no armed guards waiting for us. My gaze sweeps over an ivy-covered wall that curves to the left and the Fey ambling along the sidewalk to the right.

We walk up to the tavern's blue door, and Raphael pulls it open. Inside, sunlight pours through the windows onto wooden tables and tile floors. Rough-hewn beams span the ceiling.

As we make our way to the polished oak bar, I check the back door, planning the best route in case we need to make a run for it.

"Good afternoon," the barman says in French, wiping the bar with a cloth. He's human but nearly as tall as a Fey, with braided ginger hair that flows over his shoulders. "New in town?"

"We're here on our honeymoon," Raphael says in French, tinged with a Fey accent that he's dialed up. "We recently got married."

"Congratulations."

"It was a marvelous wedding," I say, sliding my arm around Raphael's waist. I feel his muscles tense a little under his shirt. "On the beach, with the sand through our toes."

The barman's hand pauses as he recognizes the agreed upon phrase. "Sounds marvelous. Maybe when I get hitched, I'll do it on the beach as well," he says, giving me the second part of the phrase.

Raphael casually leans on the bar. "We rented a small place nearby," he says.

The barman nods. "It's a good place for a honeymoon. Lots of nice picnic locations and such."

"I don't know how much we're going to leave the house," Raphael says with a smile.

I look up at him, my gaze trailing over his strong jawline. "Or the bedroom," I add.

A man at the bar snorts into his wine glass. He turns to Raphael and waggles his eyebrows.

Good. By the end of the day, every human and Fey in town will have heard about the horny couple in the cottage. It's a perfect cover for why we won't be leaving it.

"What can I get you?" asks the bartender.

"Some mead would be wonderful," I say.

"And a baguette and cheese," Raphael adds. "We'll take it with us."

The barman pours two glasses of mead, then goes to the back and returns a couple of minutes later with a paper bag and a baguette sticking out the top. We both finish our mead, take the bread with us, and leave.

Outside, I break the bread in two. As we expected, there's a little pouch baked inside, and inside the pouch are a key and a tiny map. I scrutinize the map, then scan the street until I find a small cottage with a garden outside —directly across from the veil mage's mansion. The cottage is narrow, and the second story has a steeply peaked roof. Blue shutters are wide open on two large windows on the top and bottom floor. Even in September, lavender still blooms out front, and ivy climbs the stone walls.

"That one," I say, then rip off a chunk of bread and bite into it. I'm starving.

We enter the garden, and the air smells heavy with wildflowers and a hint of marjoram. I slide the key into the front door and turn it. The lock seems old and rusty, and the door creaks on its hinges.

Through the open shutters, light streams into a tiny room with white walls, a threadbare embroidered rug, and walls lined with bookshelves. Dust motes float in the air, catching the light. There's hardly any furniture in here —just a few wooden chairs and an aged harpsichord.

On the other side of the hall is a tiny kitchen with a pale green cabinet, a wooden table, and a fireplace-style stove. Copper pots and pans hang from wooden ceiling beams. It's not even roomy enough for Raphael to stand upright.

"We need to get the horses," I say.

"I'll go tonight," Raphael answers. "The barman will let me keep them in the tavern's stable."

I turn to a stairwell with aged wooden steps. When I climb to the top, I find a single bedroom. It's a cozy attic with an A-frame sloped wooden ceiling. Of course, there's only one bed.

I hear the stairs creak behind me, and Raphael's deep voice ripples over my skin. "I'll sleep on the floor."

"No need to be a martyr," I say. "We can just alternate."

I walk to the window and peer through the old, warped glass. Iron gray clouds slide over the sun, casting shadows on the street.

Across the road stands the large mansion with towering columns out front and the stone wall surrounding it. Two enormous Fey guards stand before the gate, armed with halberds. I survey the mansion itself. Large, three stories high, with vines creeping up the stony walls. Through one of the windows, I glimpse a figure, someone sitting by a fireplace, reading a book. I slip the spyglass from my pack and hold it to my eye. My heart skips a beat as I take him in—pumpkin-orange hair that runs past his shoulders and a glint of metallic eyes. He wears the dark robe of a veil mage. I already know his name from the intel MI-13 has on him.

"It's him," I tell Raphael. "Caradoc."

Even from here, I can hear the faint humming that emanates from him.

That's the man I'm going to kill.

CHAPTER 41

The skies opened up a few hours ago, and they haven't let up since. I wonder if Raphael is out there getting soaked on his scouting mission. In fact, I think it might actually be hailing right now.

On the top floor of the attic, there's no fireplace, and a draft whistles through the cracks in the window. It's now ten p.m., and I'm keeping the lights off so no one can see me staring outside.

The autumn chill envelops me, and I shiver, gazing at the warm glow of the mansion across the way. Firelight wavers over Caradoc. He's back in his library with mead and a stack of books. Lucky man.

Outside, the Fey soldiers are drenched from the storm, and I watch them change guards. Two more show up dressed in cloaks. The sodden guards stalk away, looking relieved. It's been fourteen hours of surveilling the house, and I already recognize all four of them, even with the cowls over their faces. They are, as I've nicknamed them, the Silver Fox, Redbeard, Rosy Cheeks, and Ball Scratch. All named for their physical qualities, except for Ball Scratch, named after his favorite activity. Silver Fox and Rosy Cheeks are the ones arriving now. I check the time and mark it in the log.

10 pm: Guard shift change.

Raphael and I have been swapping shifts at the window throughout the day, hardly speaking.

One thing is already clear: killing Caradoc—or even just getting close to him—will be extremely difficult. He's only left the mansion twice, surrounded by a retinue of six large, armed bodyguards. The mansion itself is fortified, not just by walls and guards, but by magical wards, too. From here, I've been able to spot the enchanted inscriptions and rune marks on the windows and doors. I might be able to disrupt them with my Sentinel powers, but I'm not entirely sure. I've never done that before.

For now, all we can do is keep watch and wait for an opportunity.

The stairs creak, and I reach for one of my daggers. I turn, relaxing a little when I see that it's Raphael. His white shirt is soaked through, and his hair is drenched with rain. "It's started to bloody hail."

"Ginevra's gone?" I ask shortly.

"On her way."

Ginevra went out with our fastest horse to inform command of our progress and to check for updates about the rest of the teams. I will miss her company.

Ha. No, I won't.

"What did you learn?" I ask.

"The servants are all people Caradoc knows personally," he says. "When one of them is sick or missing, they have Fey from the town fill in. Never someone they don't know."

"And what if they all fell sick at the same time?" I ask. "They'd have to get someone else then." My mind is already sifting through the ethics of giving food poisoning to an entire town.

He considers that. "Maybe. But it'll also draw suspicion. Fey don't get sick as easily as humans do."

He's holding a white box wrapped with string, and he slides it onto the windowsill. The surface is slightly damp. "What's this?" I ask.

"I remember you saying you liked lavender cake, and I saw some in the bakery." He takes the spyglass from me and starts staring out the window.

I take the box and sit on the bed, scooting back cross-legged. I pull the string on the box, unwrapping it. "You got me cake?" I'm still confused. This doesn't square with his rant about not liking me. "Why?"

"Because you said you liked it. You told me you ordered the lavender cake, but you got blackberry."

I stare at his large back, stunned. "That was six months ago."

"Right."

Silver moonlight filters through the window, and I notice that his shirt has gone transparent from the rain.

I glance down at the cake again—white frosting, little lavender blossoms. "You told me that you don't even like me. So that's why I'm confused about the cake."

He whirls away from the window to stare at me, his silver eyes piercing the dark.

"You said that you didn't know what 'foolish notions' got into my head," I continue. "You said that you never liked me, that I'm a spoiled girl who grew up in chaos and knew nothing of the real world. That all of this was a game to me. So, explain the cake, Raphael. Because if it was all a ploy to bring out my power, why did you never explain that to me?" I know he was at Avalon Tower this past week, just like I was.

He leans down, palms pressed flat on the mattress on either side of my thighs. The light from the window sparkles on the droplets of rain on his eyelashes and his high cheekbones. "You never replied to any of the letters I left in your room."

My breath goes shallow. "*What* letters?"

"The letters that I have been writing to you every day since your final trial," he says slowly. "Wrythe was always watching us, and I couldn't speak to you privately. He kept saying that you were my favorite. Wrythe implied we were fucking, which would have got us both kicked out." His gaze sweeps down me, and a droplet of rain falls from his wet hair onto my lap. "I explained all this in the letter after your final trial." He straightens, folding his arms. "Serana said she'd pass them on."

I stare at him. "Well, she didn't." My heart thuds, and

the pieces start to slide together in my mind. She and Tana were very worried I'd get kicked out. Tana saw something in her cards, and she knew it was about Raphael.

He straightens and starts unbuttoning his wet shirt. "I can't say I'm surprised. Wrythe was spreading rumors that you and I were falling in love. He was going to use it as a pretext to get rid of both of us. Viviane tried to convince him that you had notions about me but that it wasn't reciprocated."

I arch an eyebrow. "She couldn't have done it the other way around?"

Raphael grabs a towel and starts to dry himself off. I'm staring at his chest, my pulse racing. The moonlight tinges his muscles with silver and shadow. He towels off his hair. "I was trying to put the rumors to rest. Also, I needed you to be angry. That was in the letters I wrote, too."

"So you *did* want me to be angry?" I try to reassemble everything I know. "After all that time telling me to ignore my emotions."

"Anger wasn't my first choice." He freezes, and his silver eyes cut to me. "You refused to let Nivene remove your telepathy, and that meant you needed your anger to pass. It was a risk, but it worked."

He starts to unbutton his trousers, and I'm tempted to stare. But *one* of us should be watching the mansion. I stand and cross to the window, picking up the spyglass.

I stare through the lens, trying to focus on Caradoc, but I'm partially thinking about the fact that Raphael is peeling off his wet clothes in the same room with me, and also trying to understand what he's saying. "Explain yourself. Because it doesn't matter how clear you made it in the letters if I never read them."

"I tried to teach you to master your emotions, like I do. To let the creative force take control instead of expending energy on emotions. Anger can burn up magical force. But that's not how you operate, is it? You spend so much energy telling everyone what you think they want to hear, trying to soothe people and placate them. Analyzing what people want, giving it to them so they stay calm. That's how you grew up, isn't it?"

My throat tightens. "Maybe."

I steal a glance in the glass's reflection. Raphael is turned away from me, pulling on a dry pair of trousers. My gaze sweeps over his half-naked body.

"When you finally screamed at me and told me what you thought, you let go of worrying about what other people felt, what they needed. You finally stopped wasting energy trying to manage other people's feelings. Then you had more power for yourself." He buttons his trousers and turns. "And what a power it was." In the reflection, I watch him come up behind me. "Were you watching me just now, Nia?" he murmurs.

My pulse races. "No." I clear my throat. "Fine, yes."

He presses a hand against the window frame and stares through the window over my shoulder. I can feel the heat radiating off his body. "Getting to know you, I learned we don't all use magic the same way. You channel the creative force through your emotions, not by blocking them. I remembered reading something Merlin had written about magic, and it didn't make sense to me. Merlin said he *used* his emotions, his heartbreak and love and anger, and that made his magic stronger. On our first mission, I saw you disable the *entire* veil, fueling your power with fear. And your anger at me gave you that explosive magic we saw on your final trial. It's what let you access a primal power for the first time in over a thousand years, Nia. You're like the grapes at Douloureuse Garde."

"I'm like the grapes?"

The corner of his lips curl. "Remember? The vintners would stress them to make them grow. They'd starve them of nutrients or water, and the grapes would grow stronger and enhance the flavor. For you, stress can make your magic thrive."

I shoot him a sly look. "So, the fact that I thought you were an asshole—that's what turned me into the next Merlin?"

A wry smile. "I didn't say 'next Merlin.'"

"Have I mentioned the Avalon Steel, though?"

"I wonder if Nimuë trapped Merlin in the oak because he wouldn't stop banging on about his Avalon Steel," he muses. "But yes. The fact you thought I was, as you say, an asshole, helped you pass the Sentinel test. I must admit, I didn't anticipate just *how* angry it would make you."

"You were very convincing."

Across the street, the lights flick off in Caradoc's library.

In the dark, all I can see is the glow of Raphael's silver eyes.

"Might as well get some sleep while he does," he says. "You take the bed."

CHAPTER 42

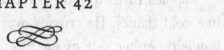

$\mathcal{I}$ take a bite of the lavender cake, and its sweetness melts on my tongue, with a hint of floral flavor. "Do you want some cake?"

"It's all yours." He's already lying on the floor.

While I eat, I glance out the window again, and my heart skips a beat. Silver Fox is staring right up at me, peering through a spyglass. "Raphael," I say quietly, "why are Caradoc's guards spying on us?"

"*What?*" He leaps to his feet and joins me at the window. "Step back a bit."

"They can't see us in the dark, can they?"

Raphael shakes his head slowly. "No, but maybe that's the problem. They know honeymooners are staying here. We've had the lights off the entire night, which might be a bit weird. Look like you're getting ready for bed. We're going to need to add a bit of realism."

I drop the spyglass, and Raphael lights the candle. I

turn away from the window and pull off the dress I've been wearing all day. I'm wearing a silky camisole and underwear beneath it. The air is absolutely frozen in here, and goosebumps rise on my arms.

Raphael turns to look at me, and his silver eyes burn like cold flames. He crosses over to me and presses his hands on either side of my head, against the glass. Heat from his body warms my skin, and his gaze lowers to stare at my lips. "I'm going to need to kiss you."

"For realism," I whisper.

He brushes his thumb over my lower lip. "For the mission."

"For England."

He presses his lips against mine, claiming my mouth. There's hunger in his kiss, and molten desire slides through my belly. He reaches under my ass, lifting me up to rest on the windowsill, and his kiss deepens. I run my hands down his abs, even though I don't think Silver Fox can see the movement. Raphael threads his fingers into my hair, and I wrap my legs around him.

As his fingers tighten in my hair, he pulls my head back, kissing me more deeply. He presses between my thighs, and I feel him growing harder. My hips roll against him. He smells like rainwater and musk, and I can no longer remember exactly what we're doing here, only that I ache for him, and I have since the first time he kissed me. A thrill shakes me to my core.

He pulls away from the kiss, his eyes heated, breath

heavy. One of his hands is still on my ass, the other in my hair. "I've wanted to kiss you for a long time."

"But it's not allowed," I whisper.

He looks half in a trance and shakes his head.

"And Ginevra?" I ask casually. "She was coming out of your room, and you weren't wearing a shirt."

His eyebrows rise. "When was that?"

"When you got me my new wardrobe."

He hasn't released me from the windowsill yet, and his fingers flex slightly on my ass. "That was six months ago."

I shrug. "You remembered the cake from six months ago."

The candlelight gilds his perfect features. "Ginevra has no boundaries," he says quietly. "That day, she was delivering a report from the field and burst in when I wasn't ready for her. I suspect she did it intentionally. She's shallow and irritating."

I nod. "Oh, you noticed that, too."

He lets out an agonized sigh. "I think that was a persuasive enough show for the guard, don't you?"

"Yeah."

He lets go of me, and I slide off the windowsill, already missing the warmth of his strong body. I blow out the candle, and when I turn to look outside, I see Silver Fox lowering his spyglass with a disappointed expression. He wanted more of a show. Honestly, so did I.

In my camisole and underwear, I crawl under the covers and pull them around me. Rain hammers against the window.

There's a thin blanket on top of the bed. With a little stab of guilt, I watch as he pulls it over himself on the hardwood floor.

"There's no heat in here," I say.

"I've certainly slept in worse conditions."

I sit up in bed, and my gaze slides down over his broad shoulders, his powerful biceps.

"I can't sleep in the same bed as you." His voice sounds husky. "Perhaps your friends were on to something when they destroyed my letters. After all, Tana does see the future, and after what happened to Alix..." His gaze rakes down my body, lingering at my breasts, peaked beneath the silk. "Fuck." A line forms between his eyebrows, his pale eyes burning with the heat of stars.

"What's wrong?" I let the strap of my camisole fall down.

"You look fucking perfect." He drags his hand over his mouth, then pulls his thin blanket over himself and turns to face the other way. "I'm going to sleep."

Outside, the cold rain and hail are thundering down.

"That blanket won't be warm enough," I say. "There's plenty of room in the bed, you know." It's not entirely true. It's just a double bed, and I know we'd be pressed against each other. "I'm perfectly good at keeping to my side."

"Good night, pixie." The wooden floor creaks as he rolls flat onto his back.

Without a fireplace, the room is only about fifty degrees, and his blanket is more fit for summer.

I'm fairly certain I won't be able to sleep. Won't be able to stop thinking about how it felt just then when he kissed me, the way he pressed himself against me, the way his tongue brushed against mine and I wanted to moan. I imagine myself lying in this bed with him, my face nestled into his throat. My thighs clench, and every inch of my skin has become sensitive and desperate for his touch.

"You're still awake," I say.

"How do you know?"

"Because I've slept in a room with you before, and you snore horribly."

"Bollocks, I do."

I smirk. "Did you really not know that?"

"I don't have many nighttime guests."

Good.

My throat tightens.

He said he'd slept in worse conditions. Now, I'm thinking of what he would have looked like as a traumatized little boy at the edge of the Brocéliande forest, waiting for a sister who never showed up. Starving. Sleeping on dirt and moss.

I can't bear the thought of him lying cold on the floor anymore. He deserves the bed. "Will you just sleep in the bed, Raphael? You're being an idiot."

A loud sigh. "Well, how could I resist that charming invitation? Have you been taking etiquette lessons from Nivene?" The floor creaks as he gets up.

My pulse races, and I turn away from him, facing the window. The rain slides down the glass, and I feel the bed sink a little as he climbs in. His body feels warm near mine.

I lie completely still. If I move, I'll scare him, and he'll run away to the floor again, and I'll have to think of him as a little boy sleeping on the dirt. He spreads the thin blanket over the two of us, tucking us in.

The air is heavy with his seductive scent. And in fact, as long as he's in the bed, I'm very much *not* thinking of him as a little boy. I'm thinking of how fucking perfect he looks as a man. The way the warm light of the candle caressed his muscles with shadows. I think of his hips moving between my thighs.

He's not quite touching me, but he's close.

I don't even do it on purpose—at least, I think I don't—but my hips shift back *ever* so slightly until my ass brushes against his hip.

"Are you trying to tempt me?" he asks in a low murmur.

"Hmm? No."

I peer at him over my shoulder. His jaw is set with tension, and he's gripping the blanket so tightly, it looks like he's going to rip it.

"I wouldn't dream of it," I say. "It's just cold in here, is all." And yet, all my senses have narrowed to this one point, exactly where my ass is brushing against his hip, and I can't bring myself to move.

You're tormenting me on purpose, and I absolutely cannot stop thinking about the perfect shape of your breasts through that camisole, or what your nipples would feel like in my mouth.

I realize, with a thrill of shock, that I'm hearing his thoughts for the first time.

He lets out an agonized sigh and turns to me, curving his body around mine. Oh, gods, his thickly corded body feels amazing against my back. His arms slide around me, his chest like steel.

My hips shift back into him *just* a little more, and I feel the enormous length of him against my ass.

Oh, gods, Nia. I want to explore every inch of your perfect body.

He's rock-hard behind me, and an ache starts to build between my thighs. And suddenly, that's all I can think about, because apparently, demi-Fey men are blessed in every way.

I wonder what he'd do if I reached back, slid my hand into his trousers, and stroked him over his underwear— just lightly up and down over that glorious length. And now I can think of absolutely nothing else.

I swear I'm not doing it on purpose, but my hips shift back again. His muscles tense. His hand slides around my waist in a protective embrace. His fingers tighten on me, right above my hip bone. "Nia." His voice sounds deep and husky.

"Yes, Raphael?"

"This is a terrible idea." His breath warms my throat. "Especially since you screamed that I've never been good enough for you, and I never would be."

My cheeks flush. "Did I scream that?"

"Yes, and it sounded like you meant it."

"Ten years ago, you kissed me, then entirely stopped speaking to me. It seemed very much like it was happening again."

He leans closer, murmuring, "You don't know why I stopped speaking to you back then, do you?"

"Because you thought I was a spoiled American."

"No, I started to fall for you the moment I saw you. I thought you were perfect. I still do. But your mother explained to me that you were mistaken. She said you thought I was rich, and she knew I wasn't. She told me that you were looking for someone wealthy. She said the moment you realized I was a grape picker, you'd be gone. She was very persuasive at the time. I believed her then, but I don't anymore."

My jaw drops. "Oh, gods. She really said that to you?" I *wish* I could say that sort of thing wasn't in her character. "You know what, I'm not as shocked by this as I should be."

My body presses into his.

You're what I've been missing all these years. His thoughts echo in my mind.

Was this the first time I was hearing his thoughts? My mind flashes back to the vineyards all those years ago, when our fingers touched, and I heard the words *beautiful, beautiful, beautiful...*

"I hear your thoughts," I whisper.

A quiet chuckle. "Stop listening. They're about to become wildly inappropriate." *I want to hear you moan my name.*

His hand slides into one corner of my underwear. Now his thumb is brushing slowly up and down over my hip bone. With his free hand, he pulls the hair back from my neck. "This is a terrible idea," he repeats.

Because if I can't strip you naked and fuck you hard, I will lose my mind.

I turn to face him, and his mouth is so close to mine. "Why is it such a terrible idea?" I whisper. The moonlight washes over him. I find myself tracing the sinuous curves of the tattoos that coil over his shoulder and chest. "We're just cold. They can't blame us for being cold. Do they want us to freeze to death?"

I'm desperate for you. Desperate the way a starving man craves fruit. I've dreamt of this for years, and I want to taste every inch of your skin.

"Right," he says. "Of course, we're just getting warm. For the mission."

"For England."

He pulls me in even closer against his hot, steely body.

I sigh, closing my eyes. I'm thinking of him ripping off my underwear, parting my thighs, and filling me with his enormous cock. I'm also glad that he can't hear *my* thoughts because his sounded significantly more romantic than mine. Really, I'm mostly thinking about his dick.

His fingers stroke slowly up and down the hollow of my hips, and heat flows through me. My nipples push against my silky camisole. I'm trying to play it cool, but the sexual ache has my thighs clenching, and all I can think about is how desperately I want him to fuck me.

His hand is too high, and yet, with each slow stroke of his fingers over my skin, my core tightens. His fingertips glide over the top of my underwear, warmth over silk, a light touch. My breath hitches.

Take my time with you...

I imagine his mouth between my thighs, kissing me. I turn back to him and tangle my fingers in his hair. My hip presses against his erection.

I need your mouth wrapped around my cock.

My heartbeat races, and desire flushes my chest.

I want all the silk off my body. I want the heat, the glow, the delicious stroke of his bare skin against mine.

I turn, looking up at him, and lick my lips. He stares at my mouth. "My camisole is making me cold," I say.

"Take it off, then."

I reach down to the hem and pull it away. I lie on my back, staring up at him. My breasts peak in the cold air, and Raphael's burning gaze rakes down my body.

Bloody hell. You're going to be the sweet, blissful death of me.

"You're beautiful," I say.

"You're not so bad yourself." *You're the most gorgeous person I've ever seen.*

He leans down, and his mouth closes around one of my nipples. He licks, his tongue swirling. My breath goes shallow. I need him inside me.

Do you have any idea how long I've wanted you, Nia?

His mouth is on my breast, and one of his hands is curved around my ribs. *And after I took you to the lake, I couldn't stop thinking about how you looked with your dress clinging. The droplets of lake water on your eyelashes. You looked like you were born from that lake. Sexiest thing I'd ever seen.* He pulls his mouth from me again, staring at my breasts. *At least, until now.*

He traces my lower lip with his tongue. Desire courses through me, and I open my mouth to him. He's kissing me tentatively—teasing, shallow. Tantalizing. He's holding back, and yet my body lights up for him like a lantern. He kisses me deeper, his tongue sliding in. As our tongues meet, erotic currents of magic skim over our bodies, filling us. He tastes like perfection.

As he kisses me, he caresses my breasts. I moan lightly into his mouth. I don't want any of this to stop—ever.

And this is why his kiss had the power to ruin my life all those years ago, because already, my body is desperate for him, and I can hardly remember the mission. His kiss grows insistent, desperate. His hand slides between my thighs, finding my wetness, and I groan into his mouth. My hips shift at the contact.

As he touches me, his thoughts echo in my mind. *I've wanted this for so long, and right now, I literally don't give a fuck about anything but you.*

I move against his hand, my body swelling with pleasure. He's teasing me with agonizing sweetness, stoking my body into a fevered flame.

He pulls away with a little bite to my lower lip. My core pulses, and he stares into my eyes. Even in the dark, I can see the silver and dark blue.

"Can you still hear my thoughts?" he whispers.

How about I fuck you now?

"Right to the point."

He gets up to his knees, and I don't even wait for him to take off his trousers. I reach for them, freeing his erection, and my jaw drops in awe.

I run my finger down his shaft.

Godsdamn it, she will ruin me.

He reaches for my panties, gripping them hard. But he's not taking off my underwear yet. *Take my time...*

Instead, he slides between my thighs and leans down to kiss my throat. His tongue sweeps over my skin in lazy, languorous strokes. My body is electrified, my heart pounding and my chest flushing with desire. I tilt my head back as he kisses me.

Gently, he palms my breast, his tongue flicking over my nipple. Liquid heat pulses through me. I want him *inside* me.

Need to take my time with you...need restraint...want to bury myself in you...

I don't want him to take his time. As I wrap my legs around his hips, I ache for him. I reach out and stroke his cock again.

He pulls his mouth from my throat. "Nia." His voice is husky, and he says my name with a certain reverence. He sits up, his gaze stroking my body.

His jaw clenches, and then he reaches for my underwear and pulls it down slowly to my thighs, then to my knees, my ankles, and off. He moves between my thighs, and his silver eyes gleam in the dark as he takes in the sight of my naked body. He looks almost awestruck.

I let my legs fall open wider in invitation and start touching myself while he watches.

Have you thought of me before while you pleasured yourself?

"Often," I say out loud.

I want to hear you moan.

He grabs me by the waist, pulling me closer to him. I can still hear his thoughts, but they're basically incoherent at this point, and the only fragment I get is *want you.*

Slowly, carefully, he slides into me. I gasp at the size of him as he sheathes himself in me, one inch at a time. "Raphael."

My desire for you will burn me alive.

His metallic eyes pierce me, searching me. A pleasure that is painfully intense grips my body as he fills me completely.

"Nia." He says my name like a prayer.

I will lose myself in your heat.

He moves slowly, and I twist my fingers in his hair, breathing hard. My desire feels incendiary, dangerous.

You'll be the end of me.

When he leans down to claim my mouth, I feel perfectly connected with him. With the way he's kissing me, fucking me slowly and carefully, I know exactly how he feels. I am filled with a sense of being cared for, as if his healing magic were pouring into me, stroking and caressing me. The erotic caress of his magic slips around me.

"I've thought of this for so long," he whispers. "Of you."

Rocking with pleasure, I move my hips against him, seeking release. His fingers curl into my hair, tugging it a little bit, He moves faster now, thrusting into me, and his eyes meet mine.

"Nia." My name is a whisper on his tongue.

I wrap myself around him, hands dancing over the hard muscles of his back. His lips meet mine again, kissing me as I seek my pleasure.

My body clenches around him, thighs tightening, fingernails raking down his back as he reaches his pleasure at the same time as I find mine. My back arches, and stars dance in my vision. As my orgasm crashes through me, my mind goes blank. I wrap my legs around his hips, never wanting to let him go.

"Raphael," I gasp.

His eyes search mine, and he brushes a damp lock of hair from my face.

"Who could blame us?" he whispers. "We had to stay warm."

* * *

ONE WEEK LATER.

I stand, staring through the spyglass. This time, Silver Fox and Rosy Cheeks are on guard.

We've spent the entire week giving them a bit of a show, every now and then making out in front of the window, just a couple of newlyweds. And I actually felt like a newlywed at this point because the moment Caradoc's lights go off, Raphael pulls me into bed and starts stripping away my clothes.

Not that I'm complaining.

The door creaks open, and I turn to see Raphael standing in the doorway. His expression is grim.

My heart kicks up a notch. "What's wrong?"

"I'm afraid our honeymoon is over. I've just met with Ginevra. She brought an update from MI-13. They say that one of the task forces was discovered."

My stomach swoops. "Which?" I think of Serana and Tana, my heart clenching with fear.

"The sixth. A new agent named Benedict and a knight named Aldous. The only good news is that they didn't allow themselves to be taken alive. They slit their own throats before the Fey could torture them for intel."

I knew Benedict. He was sweet, shy, with a surreal sense of humor. I cannot in my wildest dreams imagine him slitting his own throat. Did Aldous have to do it for him?

Suddenly, I feel as if someone had poured cold water over me. We've been in here for a full week—watching Caradoc, yes, but also very much enjoying every night when Raphael made it his mission to give me as much pleasure as possible. Strangely, this had started to feel like a real vacation, a trip for pleasure. But that's not reality, and all the warmth drains out of me.

What would happen if we had to slit our throats? Would he do it for me?

This is why love is not allowed: neither of us would want the other to die. And sometimes, agents have to.

This also has me wondering if I should have stayed at home in the bookstore, where I was safe. But I suppose a life suffocated by boredom and isolation isn't much of a life at all.

"Anything else?" I ask.

"The other task forces are stumped as well. All the veil mages are very closely protected in mansions warded with magic. They rarely leave unless they're surrounded by guards. Freya and Serana managed to sneak to the inner perimeter of their target's mansion but couldn't get through the wards."

"Maybe a Sentinel can."

He nods. "There's one more thing. Tana reported that our time is growing short. If we don't act soon, we will all die."

Tana and her dire proclamations. Blood roars in my ears. "Time to act, then."

"Tonight. We'll use the darkness to our advantage." His jaw clenches. "And yet, I just want to keep you in here, where you're safe, and not let you get anywhere near the Fey. But that's not why we're here, is it?"

I let out a long, slow breath. "Raphael, this is what I've trained for."

CHAPTER 43

*N*ightfall has wrapped the town in darkness. I stand inside our cottage, peering through a window into the street. Raphael is out there, and I'm mentally willing him not to get caught.

My heart speeds up, and I check my knives again—one in my boot, one hidden in a secret sheath within my sleeve, one strapped to my back. I sharpened all of them before we left, even though they were already sharp enough. Still, the ritual helped calm me. Apparently, I've become the sort of person who soothes herself by sharpening blades. The Nia of six months ago—the one who worked in a bookstore—would be alarmed by this transformation.

Caradoc's mansion and its enormous walls dwarf a little neighboring cottage, one very much like this one. One that could easily go unnoticed next to such a palatial home.

Except unlike this one, the little cottage across the street is now on fire. Flames climb the walls—Raphael's skillful work, a dancing scarlet and orange blaze against the shadows.

In front of the mansion gates, Silver Fox finally notices the smoke coiling into the air. "Fire! Fire!" he shouts in Fey, running back toward the mansion.

I stare at the smoke outside, which is thickening into a heavy black cloud. Even inside and at this distance, my eyes are starting to tear up. This small town has no fire station and not a fire hydrant in sight. Pandemonium is about to erupt on this street.

More shouts ring through the air. This is my moment.

I step outside, blinking the smoke out of my eyes. A breeze ripples over my skin, thick with ash.

Just as we planned, the street fills up with people running for buckets of water to douse the flames. Silver Fox runs out from the front gate, carrying a fire extinguisher that looks comically small, given both the size of his body and the ferocity of the blaze. I'm genuinely impressed that Raphael was able to stoke such an intense fire so quickly.

Someone has dragged a stack of large tin fire buckets into the road. I grab one and carry it inside to fill it with water at the cottage sink. Once it's full, I drag it outside again. The weight of it tugs on my arm, and I heave it across the street toward Rosy Cheeks, screaming at him in Fey to help before the whole neighborhood burns down.

He glowers at me, unwilling to leave his post. I lift the

bucket toward him, then falter, the bucket nearly tumbling from my hands. I gasp at the guard. "At least help me carry it," I shout. "It's too heavy."

"Fine." He takes a step closer, gripping the bucket in one hand, and we shuffle along. From the corner of my eye, I see Raphael move behind us, a shadow in the night. I let go of the heavy bucket, and the weight of it makes Rosy Cheeks stumble. From behind us, Raphael hits the guard's head with the pommel of his sword, and the guard crumples. Raphael sheathes his weapon, and we grab the unconscious guard, dragging him through the gate. In the chaotic night, no one notices a thing.

Once inside, we drag the guard between the rose bushes and the towering stone wall. The shadows envelop him.

"What if he wakes up?" I whisper.

"We're not going to be here that long," Raphael says.

We hurry to the front door. As soon as I get closer, I can sense the unseen ward, pushing us away. But this magic feels very different from the veil. I hear no hum, and when I focus, I can't sense the same tangled weave of energy. Faintly, I can feel its power thrum over my skin, raising goosebumps on my body.

"Can you disrupt it?" Raphael asks.

Adrenaline courses through my veins. "I can try." I concentrate, summoning my Sentinel powers. Focusing, I search for an image of the ward in my mind, but it's hard to get a feel for its dimensions. There's nothing to channel my powers *at*. I try sending them out, as if I'm feeling my way in a dark room. Searching for something, anything. But as far as my magic is concerned, there's nothing there.

I shake my head. "I can't. I don't have a sense of it, the shape or the color, the sound. It's blank."

Raphael frowns at me, and I see the flicker of worry in his expression. If *I* can't get through the wards, the other agents won't fare any better. The veil mages are too protected, and our time is running out.

"Nia," Raphael whispers sharply. He grabs my hand and pulls me behind a stone column. From the shadows, I peer out. Silver Fox stands before the gate, frowning in confusion. He's noticed his missing friend.

"Wait here," Raphael says softly in my ear. "I'll handle him."

I grab his arm and drag him back.

"What?" he whispers.

"Maybe he knows how to unlock the wards," I say. "Let me check."

He hesitates, then nods. I wait until the guard turns the other way, searching the street. Then I move through the shadows. With the thick smoke in the air and the chaos outside the gate, the guard doesn't see or hear me as I draw closer.

I concentrate, tugging at my telepathy, letting the powers stretch through my body. I hide behind the wall, then carefully stretch out my arm. From the other side of the gate, I brush my fingertips over his back as lightly as I can, then dive into his mind.

His concern for his friend, Atel, is foremost in his

thoughts. *Did Atel go to help with the fire as well? But he said he would wait at the gate. What if the fire gets to the mansion? We might need to evacuate Caradoc. But where is Atel?*

Gritting my teeth, I delve deeper, searching for anything I can find about the wards. How can we get through the wards?

The answer lies there, just under the surface of his worried thoughts. The wards are easy to get through as long as you're permitted to enter the mansion. Then, you just touch the door and chant the incantation, and the door opens.

Which doesn't help us at all. Raphael and I aren't permitted.

He feels my finger on his back and starts to turn around. I yank my arm away, quickly retreating into the shadows. He opens the gate and takes a step inside. Time moves at a snail's pace. If he peers to the right, he'll see me.

A desperate idea blooms in my mind. Stepping forth, I touch him once again. But as I do, I summon both my powers, violet and red. They fuse together, Sentinel and telepathy twining and blending into a raspberry-hued, pulsing power. I force it into the guard's mind, breaking down his mental defenses. He senses the intrusion, and while his body freezes, his psyche is trying to break free.

But I am everywhere. In his thoughts, his emotions, his memories.

His overwhelming emotion is fear because of the fire and the chaos, and his missing friend. I whisper a treacherous thought. *Just open the mansion's front door. Then you will be safe.*

His eyes scan the garden, searching for the person who's touching him, hurting his mind.

No. Don't look around. Death will follow.

I can feel the thud of his terrified heart. Can sense his erratic breathing.

Walk up to the door of the mansion. Get inside, and then everything will be all right.

He totters forward. I keep close behind him, still touching, as he lumbers up to the front door. I never let him pull away, maintaining the telepathic channel between us. I whisper encouragement in his mind. *Yes. Just a few more steps. Open the door, and then everything will be fine.*

He touches the door and whispers an incantation. The thrum of the ward disappears.

Exhaling, I pull back from him. Before he can recover, Raphael smashes the pommel of his sword into Silver Fox's skull.

I shiver with the Sentinel's chill, feeling nauseous. My sight goes double with the effort I exerted. Raphael grips me by the waist, and I let him lead me inside to find Caradoc.

CHAPTER 44

The air outside is thick with acrid smoke, but inside, the mansion is somehow worse. Toxic, sickly. Out of nowhere, I think of Mom.

Now that the noises of the chaos in the street are muffled, I can hear the hum of Caradoc's veil magic much more clearly.

We walk softly over an ornate rug in the foyer, and it mutes our steps. After a week of spying on him, we know that Caradoc spends the majority of his time on the second floor, in his library.

Raphael glances at me and raises his eyebrows, trying to ascertain that I'm okay.

My mind is still chaotic, bits and pieces of it cluttered with the guard's thoughts. But I give him the thumbs-up and pull the knife from my boot. Raphael unsheathes his sword, and we both creep deeper into the front hall toward a heavy set of double doors. By now, we've already mapped the house as best as we could by watching it through the windows.

We chose our moment carefully—ten at night. At this time, there's a changeover in the staff between the evening crew and the late-night shift. There's still a cook in the kitchen, and Caradoc's personal maid, who is hopefully in her quarters.

As I think about her, I get a flash of memory—kissing her passionately, hidden together in the pantry. She's human, and I'm Fey...not my memory, but one that belongs to Silver Fox. It makes me dizzy, and I have to stop, just for a moment. Raphael glances back at me, and I motion for him to go on.

The door opens smoothly, and the stairs beyond are thankfully stone, not creaking wood. No sign of the cook or the maid, but I still can't shake the feeling that someone is watching and hearing us. That the mansion itself *knows* someone has intruded.

As we climb the stairs, the humming grows louder, and the veil mage's magic buzzes over my skin. On the second floor, Raphael turns toward the door of the library. But I grab his arm and shake my head. I can hear the humming coming from the mage's bedroom.

Raphael turns, and I follow behind him. As he touches the door handle, he glances at me. My mind roars with fear.

I nod to him, and he flings the door open. He storms inside, and I rush in behind him.

The walls of the bedroom are painted a deep maroon

flecked with black, like a rotting rose. Caradoc stands by the window with his back to us. From here, he's watching the fire.

Something's wrong. I should have noticed it earlier. The humming, just a little too loud. And it surrounds us now.

I glance up.

The entire ceiling shimmers—a misty veil arching over us. A trap. As Caradoc turns toward us, he lets the veil drop.

Cold fear crashes over me, and I summon my Sentinel powers. I hurl them into the deadly mist around us, but it's a fraction too late for Raphael. Tendrils of the mist reach him, and he stumbles and falls, his sword clattering on the floor.

Cold panic rakes its claws through me.

My magic dissolves most of the veil, but it's still clinging to Raphael, wrapping around his chest. I kneel by his side, using all of my mental energy to pull the magic away from him, one strand at a time. If any of it pierces his heart or his skull, he's gone.

I hear Caradoc's footsteps behind me, and as I glance back at him, he clamps his hands around my throat. His fingers tighten, and he knocks me over, pressing his knees against my chest. I struggle, desperately trying to breathe.

Frantically, I try to keep my mind on Raphael, feeling for the magic that surrounds him. All my focus is intent on the wisps of pearly death snaking around his body. My vision goes dark, starry. I rip the last strands of veil magic off him.

Time slows down.

My head spins as Caradoc's iron fingers squeeze, crushing my throat. I strike at his arms as hard as I can, and his fingers loosen. I take a deep, ragged breath, but he's still on top of me, reaching again for my neck.

I use my magic to creep into his thoughts. I will take over his mind, make him hurl himself out the window. But as soon as I enter his thoughts, I realize how impossible that is. Caradoc's mind isn't simple like Wrythe's or Silver Fox's. In fact, I can hardly make sense of his mind at all. He is hundreds of years old, maybe a thousand. He's seen empires rise and fall, had seventeen wives and innumerable lovers. He doesn't care for love or money or power. His thoughts are mazelike, a tangle. Trying to control him is like trying to swim up a waterfall.

Instead, I find myself getting lost. Swallowed. Panicking, I try to pull away, but I can't find my way back to being Nia. I am becoming a part of Caradoc, and I can't feel the pain of my own suffocation anymore.

Because now, I'm seeing what he knows.

About the invasion.

Images and memories flit through my brain too quickly for me to process properly. There's a training academy. Fey herbalists walking between Fey soldiers lying on beds. A dragon being injected with something and roaring with pain. A large Fey army marching with dragon banners. A tincture created by Fey alchemists. A brew of strange herbs mixed with…iron.

That's what Auberon has been working on. Iron weapons stopped their army all those years ago, but the tincture will make them immune. He's creating a Fey army impervious to its effects.

Iron is the only way humans have held the Fey back. Without it, they'll burn through humanity like wildfire, destroying everything in their way. We knew the Fey were planning something, that we needed to stop them, but we didn't realize we were already too late.

We wanted to destroy the veil, but it doesn't matter. The Fey were about to drop it themselves. They're going to send their army over the border.

Caradoc was at the meetings when they planned the invasion; he's seen the map spread out on a table, marked where the forces will enter. I hear the plan for the fake assault on southern France—the one everyone would expect.

But that's not the real attack.

Auberon is headed for England.

If only I could warn them, but he's choking me again. Now, I can see myself through Caradoc's eyes, lying on the floor, mouth opening and shutting, desperate for breath, eyes bulging. I'm seconds away from death. There's nothing I can do. We failed.

A sudden sharp pain rips through me as my chest is pierced.

No. Not my chest. Caradoc's. He gapes down, the

blade of a sword protruding from his rib cage. His fingers go slack, and his jaw drops. A scarlet drop of blood falls from his lips as he slides off me.

I slam back into my own body, gasping for breath. Caradoc topples onto the floor, dead. Above me, Raphael stands, deathly white. Blood drips off his blade, and he kneels down. "Nia, are you alright?"

"Yeah." My voice cracks, and it hurts to talk.

"We did it. Caradoc is dead." Raphael slides his arm around my waist and helps me stand.

"No." I lean into him, touching my bruised throat. "It doesn't matter. I saw Caradoc's mind. The Fey are launching an assault. They have an army of...of iron-impervious Fey."

He falls silent for a moment. "That's impossible."

I rest against his powerful chest, my head spinning. "It's not. Fey herbalists learned from human medicine, like immunotherapy. They developed a way to do it by exposing their soldiers to microscopic amounts of iron, then slowly increasing it. Thousands of Fey died in the process. That doesn't matter to Auberon. He just wanted his army. And now he has it."

I can hear Raphael's heart racing.

"When are they attacking?"

I try to think back to what I'd heard in Caradoc's mind, sifting through that wild flood of knowledge. "I think...in a week or two. But we just killed Caradoc, which means the veil will drop in a few hours. Auberon won't hesitate.

He'll launch the invasion as soon as the veil is down. All we did was make it happen sooner. We need to inform Sir Kay. We need to prepare all our forces."

Raphael's fingers tighten on me. "MI-13's invasion force is waiting in southeast France for the veil to fall. They'll storm Fey France as soon as it happens."

"That's not where they need to be! We need to get our forces where the Fey are actually planning to attack." I think back to the invasion plans, the maps. "They plan to land near Dover."

"Are you sure?" Raphael curses under his breath. "It's going to be hard to get them there in time. If what you say is true, the Fey army will already be on the northern coast of France. MI-13's force is at the southern border, nowhere *near* Dover."

"We need to alert the British military right now. They have to be ready and inform Dover. They need to evacuate the city for the battle that's about to happen. Do you remember what happened in Brittany? Once the Fey arrived and the war started raging, they left nothing behind but ash. The streets were full of the dead."

He scrubs a hand over his jaw. "We can send Ginevra with a message to MI-13's invasion force, get them to change their course."

I nod. "And *we* should ride as fast as we can back across the veil. We need to get to a working phone."

* * *

I STARE INTENTLY as Raphael argues on the phone. "Because I'm telling you," he shouts, "she saw into his mind. She's a telepath...no, she's not just a new recruit. She has Avalon Steel. Captain? Captain?"

I hear the drone of a dial tone on the other side. They weren't listening to us.

Both of us are grimy and exhausted. We rode all night. By the time we reached the veil, it was long gone.

Raphael's first phone call was to MI-13's command, to inform them of what we'd found. But all of MI-13's agents were out in the field—some on the assassination task forces, the rest with Sir Kay's invasion force.

His second phone call was to his contact in the British military.

"He wouldn't listen," he says, his expression grim. "Auberon's plan worked spectacularly. As soon as the veil dropped, Auberon launched a fake assault on southern France. French and British military responded in force. The majority of the British army and navy are there now."

"But that's not where the iron-impervious Fey are going to strike," I say, sickened.

"MI-13 are sending everyone to Dover, but the majority are too far off," Raphael says. "We're among the closest."

I swallow. "We need to collect as many agents as we can and get to Dover as soon as possible."

He nods. "Exactly what I was thinking."

My stomach drops. There are tens of thousands of

people in Dover, and they have no idea what is about to hit them.

CHAPTER 45

Two days later.

With my bow and quiver of arrows strapped over my back, I stare at the horizon, the salty wind whipping at my face, eyes squinting with effort. Morning is breaking over the Strait of Dover. In the dawn light, the famous white cliffs are a rosy-gold streak across a periwinkle horizon.

Our little ship is racing toward England's shoreline. I keep searching for the smoke and debris that would signal death, or Fey ships clustered around the Port of Dover, but there are no signs of battle yet, just the honeyed sunlight dancing over the sea.

A calm, tranquil morning, which is ironic considering what's about to happen.

"How's your stomach?" Tana asks, joining me at the ship's rail.

I grip the rail hard. "I've been worse." It's been a long

two days. Before we got on the boat, we managed to gather a few other members of the task forces that had been sent to assassinate the veil mages. Freya, Serana, Nivene, and Tana got on board with us. There aren't nearly enough of us, but it's better than nothing.

The cold breeze whips at my hair, and dread settles in my stomach.

"Can you see anything new?" I ask. "Any future glimpses into what's going to happen to Dover?"

She shakes her head. "It's always hard to see through battle fog. The future is now as unknowable to me as it is to you."

"Do you hate that?"

"Not as much as you'd think."

I take a long breath and try to calm my roiling stomach.

"We're almost there," Tana says softly.

I see houses in the distance, the breakwater jutting out into the sea. I squint, searching for smoke, for wreckage. "Are we too late?"

"I don't think so," she whispers, handing me a pair of binoculars. "We might be just in time."

I peer through the glass. Things look still, and the cranes aren't moving. No vessels coming or going, and I don't see any sign of Fey ships.

British troops are deployed around the port, carrying rifles.

Maybe MI-13 were able to get through to them, even if we weren't. I let out a long, slow breath.

The sun is rising higher, bathing the coast in gold as we race to the port, a network of piers and docks that jut out into the sea, dwarfed by the towering, dawn-kissed cliffs. Seagulls swoop overhead, shrieking into the autumn wind. As the ship starts to slow, we maneuver into berth, the engine purring. An old stone castle looms over the cliffs, bathed in a golden hue. The Union Jack and the Port of Dover flags fly from its turrets, snapping in the wind.

Nausea is making my stomach churn and my mouth water, and I'm desperate to get off the boat onto steady land. The moment it docks, I rush onto the pier and lean over, bracing my hands on my knees.

Here I am, the great Avalon Steel agent, trying not to hurl on the pavement because I can't handle a few waves.

When my nausea subsides, I straighten and see an army officer with a fully gray beard striding up to Raphael. The officer is flanked by four armed men. "Who the hell are you?" he barks. "The port is closed."

"I'm Agent Launcelot, Secret Service," Raphael says, and flips an ID card at the man. "I need to talk to the person in charge."

"You can talk to me," the man answers impatiently. "I'm Captain Atkinson. I'm in charge here. Secret Service, you said? Which section?"

"Atkinson, the veil is down," Raphael says, ignoring his question. "And the Fey are about to invade England. We need to—"

"I've been told all this, but it's no longer a concern," the man snaps. "We've been getting ready for the past two days, but the threat is controlled now. Yesterday, there was a battle between British forces and the Fey in the south of France. A platoon of tanks with iron ammunition wiped half of them out in an hour. They're not going to make it here."

My stomach drops. "No, that assault is a feint," I interrupt. "The real force is coming this way. They're going to land here. Soon."

He raises an eyebrow at me. "I've been told they will not make it out of France."

"Did you evacuate the city?" I ask.

"I'm not going to panic people for no reason. Like I said, they're not going to make it here. It's being handled in France."

"Then where is everyone?" Raphael asks.

"Safe. Perfectly safe. We had an alert of a dragon flying a few miles southeast, so we told everyone to get in the shelters, just in case. And we have anti-dragon guns ready if the monster swoops near."

"Anti-dragon guns?" I ask.

He rolls his eyes. "Look, love, don't worry about it. The military has been preparing for this. These anti-dragon guns shoot a volley of iron-cased ammunition with deadly precision. We can handle a dragon, even two if they show up. Which I don't think they will."

"These dragons are immune to iron." I grit my teeth. "And there'll be more than two. You need to evacuate the city."

"Absolutely not! That's what the shelters are for. An

evacuation would be utter chaos. Utter chaos," he repeats for emphasis. "And for what reason? The threat is in *France.*"

"Captain!" one of his men calls.

Atkinson's face has gone red. "Look, I've dealt with some of you 'intelligence people' before, and if you ask me, it's a misnomer. Intelligence for you lot." He wags his finger at our small group. "*Always* thinking you know best, don't you, spooks? You hate that the army is in charge here, that we've got things under control. We're wiping the Fey clean off the map in southern France, and even if a few stragglers get here—"

"Captain!"

"—we can handle them. This is Dover. We've been thirty miles from the border with Fey for the past fifteen years. You think we've been sitting on our arses? We've been preparing for this. There's so much iron in this city, we can take down every Fey soldier on earth, and there'll still be enough for—"

"CAPTAIN!"

Atkinson whirls around. "*What?*"

"We just got word from command. There are dragons and ships incoming."

The captain's fingers curl into fists. "How many?"

"They're not sure, exactly, but it's a very large force."

I point to the horizon. "Why don't you count them yourself, Captain?"

They appear in the distance amid the clouds, at least a dozen red, green, and black dots. Dragons. And below them, a glinting mass of clipper ships with billowing sails that are roseate in the morning light. Mist whispers along their keels, and dragons swoop above them, washed in gold.

My breath catches.

"Fuck." Atkinson stares at the enormous Fey force, then mutters, "Let the little fairy boys come. We'll blow them back to fairy hell."

"Captain, listen to me," I say, feeling my patience coming to an end. "This Fey army can't be stopped with iron. They outnumber you at least ten to one, and they'll be here in less than an hour. You have to evacuate Dover, or they will massacre everyone here. Remember what happened in Brittany?"

"Love, I don't think you know as much as I do about Fey and iron. Our castle is well stocked with cannons. And I'm not evacuating anything unless the Chief of the General Staff or the Prime Minister orders me to."

"Then get them on the phone," Raphael snarls.

Atkinson glares at Raphael. The men stare at each other for a few seconds, but then Atkinson looks away. "Get off the streets, agents," he says gruffly. "It's going to get messy here, and you lot are not cut out for what's about to happen. I'm going to the castle, and you can fuck off."

He walks away, barking orders at his men.

"What an arsehole," Serana says from behind me.

I turn around to face the others. "We'll have to get as many people out as we can."

A line forms between Raphael's brows. "Tana, do you think you can figure out where the shelters are that he mentioned?"

"Definitely," she says.

He nods. "Good. Take Serana and find them. Nivene and Freya, we'll need to figure out the fastest route to get all the civilians out. There will be chaos, and we've got to make sure that the way is clear and open."

"On it," she says.

"What about Nia?" Serana asks.

I clear my throat. "Raphael and I will buy you time." I raise Tana's binoculars. "Mind if I borrow these?"

"Take them," she says.

The dragons are looming closer, and I can make out the foremost ships and the glint of weapons on their decks. Immediately, my quiver of arrows feels wildly inadequate. "I know we're spies and not soldiers, but this really would be a great time to have some gun training," I say.

Raphael slides me a worried look. "Today, we are soldiers, it seems. We're heading to battle, whether we're prepared or not. I want you to stay close to me the whole time, do you understand? I can't have anything happen to you."

Fear flickers in his eyes, and I remember a time when I thought the man didn't feel emotions at all.

CHAPTER 46

*R*aphael and I charge up the narrow stone stairs at Dover Castle behind a line of British troops. I've hardly slept in the past few days, and my breath is wheezing, but adrenaline is spurring me on.

As I run, my steps echo to the beat of my pounding heart.

At the top of the stairs, the door opens onto sun-washed battlements. The autumn breeze whips at my hair, and I stare out at the gold-dappled sea. The sight of the incoming fleet steals my breath. So many clipper ships, each with three masts and at least twenty sails. They're racing closer, a legion of them, each one packed with armored Fey soldiers. Dragons fill the skies, their scales gleaming with ruddy light. Their wingspan is the width of a house. Fear trembles along my ribs.

Through the binoculars, I see one of the dragons

unleash a gout of fire into the pearlescent sky, and the sight makes my stomach clench. Three of these dragons could raze Dover in an hour. I count fifteen.

Between the clipper ships, sea serpents undulate rhythmically, monsters from another world. Feyhorns blare on the ships. Their war trumpets are six feet high, rising into the air above the soldiers' heads, with bells at the end shaped like wild beasts. Their haunting, sonorous call floats along the marine wind, and a chill seeps under my skin.

We're not ready for them. England isn't ready for them.

Atkinson is standing by one of the cannons, barking orders at his men.

"Wait until they're close enough," he shouts. "I want each of the ADGs aimed at a different one. Coordinate with the other towers. We have six guns. That should be enough to take those beasts out of the sky before they reach us."

ADGs. Anti-Dragon Guns. I remember Tana's words from months ago. *Spy boys and their acronyms.* That was the day I met the spies, and it feels like years ago. It's hard to even imagine myself as the person I was at the start of that day, a chick on vacation who just wanted birthday cake and a teensy bit of champagne on the beach.

And now I'm watching a fleet of Fey warships and a squadron of fire-breathing dragons race toward the Cliffs of Dover, hellbent on destruction.

But there's no going back.

I turn to Atkinson. "Those dragon scales are thicker than tank armor. All you'll do is irritate them."

"I swear I told you to fuck off," he spits at me.

"You need to listen to her." Raphael's voice is pure steel. "She knows more about this invasion force than anyone else."

"Both of you, get off the battlements!"

I consider arguing, but there's no time. The dragons are getting closer.

"I'm sorry," I say in a low voice.

The captain's eyebrows rise. "For being a pain in my arse?"

"No, for this." I reach out and touch his cheek, already channeling my powers at him.

I see it all. A boy growing up on stories of heroics during the Fey invasion. He joined the army for adventure, but by the time he was ready to fight, they'd already reached a ceasefire. And then constant disappointment. His career stalled because he never knew the right guy, was never good enough. Finally, he ended up commanding the defense force in Dover—a force that never did anything.

This was his big chance, at last. *The damn Fey don't know what they're in for. I've been waiting for the chance to become a hero my entire life.*

He's thrilled at the size of the fleet, by the soaring dragons. He'll be known as the commander who stopped the Fey, even when he was vastly outnumbered.

I clench my jaw. One man's ego will lay waste to every civilian in the area.

Not if I can help it.

Pushing further into his mind, I force my will against his. Unlike Caradoc, he's easy to manipulate. Years in the army taught him that someone always outranks him. In this case, it's me.

I lean forward, acting as if I'm talking softly to him for the sake of anyone watching. And then I give him one final mental push.

He clears his throat, looking stunned, then says in a loud voice. "This woman's name is Nia Melisende. She's a Fey military expert from secret services. She will be taking command."

The soldiers around us stare at me, uncertain. They've been training with Atkinson for more than a year. Nothing prepared them for a random woman taking control, which means I can't give them time to think it through.

"You won't be able to harm the dragons," I tell them, my voice steady and authoritative. "Their scales are too thick. And they're immune to iron, so even if a missile gets through, it won't kill them."

"So, what do we do?" a soldier asks.

I squint at the line of incoming dragons, reaching for Caradoc's memories. There—a possible weak point. "That dragon, the silver one with a red sheen." I point at the huge beast. "He's older, weaker, and his scales are thinner. He didn't get the full iron immunity treatment because it was making him too sick. If you concentrate your fire on him, you might be able to take him down."

"What about the rest?" another soldier asks.

"The Fey don't have many dragons, and they're planning for a long campaign. They don't want to lose *any* dragons in this attack. If we take one down, the rest might pull back to avoid further casualties and let the troops do the work."

I have no idea if it will work, but I pray that it does.

"The dragons will be in range in twenty seconds," someone shouts.

"Coordinate with the rest of the ADG teams," I say urgently. "All cannons on that dragon. Do it. Now."

"Wait," Atkinson mutters.

Damn it. He's recovered. I turn to him, opening my mouth, but Raphael is already by his side. His hand is on the man's neck, applying pressure, using the size of his big body to block the soldiers' view.

Atkinson's eyelids flutter, and he collapses into Raphael's arms. "He's sick," Raphael mutters. "I'll take care of him.

The soldiers aren't paying attention to Raphael at this point. All eyes are on the incoming dragons.

"Ready," a large sergeant booms. Shouting orders into an old-fashioned radio, he instructs the artillery to aim for the silver-red dragon.

The soldiers shift the cannons, heavy, primitive weapons that work with cranks and pulleys. None of the fancy targeting tech we had before the Fey invaded work anymore.

I focus on that one sickly dragon flying behind the rest of the squadron.

"Fire!" the sergeant roars.

I cover my ears, but the blasts are still deafening. One shot goes wide. The second one, aimed much better, hits the dragon's body…and ricochets off. I groan in despair.

But now other guns across the castle battlements are firing, and more from the stone sentry points that line the cliffs.

I lift the binoculars and see a spray of blood from the silver-red dragon. He rears his head back and shrieks, plummeting toward the sea. I watch through the glass, expecting the beast to crash into the water, but he starts beating his wings again and levels off. Not dead, but obviously badly hurt.

The other dragons veer away and then circle back. Even from here, I can see the fury in their predatory eyes. For a few seconds, our lives hang in the balance. If they swoop down upon the city and unleash their wrath, we're doomed to burn.

To my relief, they spread their wings, and the squadron falls back. No need to risk dragon lives when the Fey troops are almost upon us, and they will do the job.

"Well done." Raphael touches my lower back. "I've got something to show you."

He leads me to the other side of the tower, where we

can see the streets of Dover. People line the roads. The evacuation has started, but it's not fast enough.

There are people milling together in long columns. Raising the binoculars, I see Serana leading one of the columns through the streets.

I look at Raphael. "We need to buy them time."

"Um...excuse me?" a male voice calls out. "Commander Melisende?"

Commander? I like the sound of my new title. Commander Melisende it is. I turn to the man. "Yes?"

"What's that?" He points out to sea.

I turn to look, and my heart sinks.

Shimmering fog rolls ahead of the Fey battleships, a presence that buzzes loudly in my ears. The veil.

Why hadn't I thought of this possibility? The veil isn't a wall anymore. It's a weapon.

"They don't need to risk their lives to conquer England," I mutter. "They intend to kill everyone with the veil."

"Can you disable it?" Raphael asks, an edge to his voice.

My legs feel weak, and my thoughts are so panicked, I can hardly think straight. "For a few seconds. A minute, maybe, but eventually, I'll have to stop. All they have to do is blanket the city with it and wait."

Raphael has gone completely still, the autumn breeze toying with his dark curls. "I thought killing Caradoc meant the veil was disabled."

"Just the border veil," I say. "Which was hundreds of

miles long. This thing is much smaller, but still large enough to roll through a city. All they need is one veil mage to..."

I trail off, searching the approaching ships through the binoculars and listening to the sounds of the veil, focusing on where the humming is strongest.

"What is it?" Raphael asks.

"There!" I point to a ship where a figure stands at the bow, draped in black. "That's the veil mage. Sergeant, do you have marksmen?"

He frowns. "Yes. But...didn't you say the Fey are impervious to iron now?"

"Some of them. But bullets will still stop them, even if the iron isn't poisonous. Shoot them enough times, and they die, just like a human. Can you take that Fey magician out?"

The sergeant barks his commands into the radio, and the rifles start firing.

The air shimmers. More firing fills the air and clouds of gun smoke. The figure still stands, and the sergeant curses.

"What's going on?" I ask.

"Some sort of magical shield," he says.

The veil is almost upon the city now. Focusing, I summon my Sentinel power, letting it bloom inside me. I can see the mist clearly as it moves forward and the magical energy woven around it. And beyond the veil, a different barrier. Unfamiliar. That's the one I need to disable.

"I might be able to take it down for a few seconds," I say. "Sergeant, fire on my mark."

"Yes, Commander."

I clench my jaw and channel my powers at the barrier. It isn't like the veil, a web I can untangle. It's more like a fixed wall of energy, and my powers just bounce off it.

"Nia," Raphael mutters.

I grit my teeth. There's a point in the barrier where the magic seems thinner. I lash at it with all my strength.

It shatters.

"Now," I shout.

I hear the sound of guns firing. The freezing cold of exhaustion slides down to my bones, and I start shivering. Raphael wraps his arm around my waist, enveloping me with his warmth.

"We need you to stay with us, Commander," he whispers in my ear.

I tremble and lean into him, staring out at the fleet, the ships' sails billowing in the wind.

I let out a long, slow breath. The veil has disappeared. The veil mage lies slumped on the ship's bow. Dead, maybe. I pray that he was the only one. I don't have the strength to do that again.

As I scan the horizon, I don't see another veil rising from the sea.

I pull away from Raphael and move to the other side of the battlements, looking out at the city.

There are still *far* too many people clogging the Dover streets.

"They'll take the city with their troops," Raphael says grimly.

"Okay," I whisper. "Then we have to slow them down, give the rest of the civilians time to evacuate. Otherwise, Dover will become a bloodbath."

"Let's get down to the docks. We'll need a barricade."

CHAPTER 47

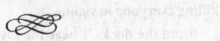

I crouch behind a makeshift barricade formed of cars and military vehicles near the docks. A line of British soldiers waits alongside me, guns aimed forward. We're clearly no match for this army, but we can at least try to slow them.

I peer over the hood of a car to see the clipper ships sailing for the shore. We managed to sink one of them with our cannons and damaged another severely, but the rest are still coming.

Volleys of arrows fly overhead, darkening the sky for a few horrifying moments. We can't return fire. The Fey are mostly protected from our guns with their magical barriers. There's only one of me to disable them, and I'm at the brink of exhaustion.

Cannons and guns thunder around us, and I survey the scene—arrows jutting from the dead on our side of the barricade, blood spilled over the streets. Acrid smoke floats through the air.

I hunch lower behind the car. Arrows litter the pavement near me, and the sound of screaming punctuates the battle. Soon, the Fey will be charging through Dover, killing everyone in sight.

From the docks, I hear the low, rhythmic beating of a Fey war drum, the booms loud as the cannons. The Fey blow their Feyhorns, a low and terrifying din that pierces my chest with primal fear.

Another volley of arrows shadows the sky above us, and I press close against the car door. More arrows clatter to the ground, inches from me.

I peer over the hood and see the first three ships glide onto shore. My heart thunders as the Fey warriors jump onto the dock, their armor limned by the morning sun. Surrounded by their shimmering magical barrier, they charge, their ragged battle cries floating on the marine wind, a sound as horrifying as a banshee scream.

The sergeant glances at me.

"Not yet," I say.

"Steady!" he shouts at the soldiers.

More and more Fey storm ashore and swarm the cramped docks. The first Fey warriors are only twenty yards from us.

I summon my powers—a bloom of scarlet in my mind —and smash through their magical barrier. Their shield shatters. The heat bleeds from my body, leaving me cold.

"Fire!" Raphael yells, wrapping his arms around me.

Dozens of semi-automatic guns fire around me, the sound deafening.

Iron is not poisonous to this Fey army, and their bodies are stronger than the bodies of humans, but if you shoot them enough times, they *will* die.

Shivering, I see many of the first attackers fall to the ground, dead or wounded. We may not have many soldiers, but the guns are effective.

Raphael pulls me closer. He's trying to keep the chill away, but he also wants to protect me, wrap me up in cotton to keep me safe, but that's not why we're here, is it?

The Fey keep coming, line after line of them, shrieking war cries against the hail of bullets.

Even with our guns, the attackers are upon us. Chaos breaks loose as they scale the makeshift barricade and the soldiers fire their guns.

Raphael bounds onto the hood of a car and unsheathes his sword. A Fey leaps after him, and Raphael cuts his throat, then immediately disarms another. He kicks a third attacker off the hood, then stabs him in the back. He is a whirlwind of violence, cutting down anything that comes close.

But the barricades near us have already been breached, and Fey warriors storm into the streets of Dover.

I unshoulder my bow and let an arrow loose, hitting a warrior's side as he's about to batter a human soldier to death. Another arrow flies over the mark.

More guns fire—marksmen we deployed in surrounding buildings. Anarchy reigns around us, and the smell of blood mingles with gunpowder. At least the barrier protecting the Fey is gone now.

And yet, some of them seem nearly impervious to bullets. A Fey warrior gets shot in the chest, but it barely slows him as he storms into a building with one of the snipers. A few seconds later, a dead human soldier crashes out of a window on the top floor.

As I nock another arrow, a Fey leaps in front of me. He's six feet tall with silver hair, and his mouth is open in a feral roar. He swings his battle-axe at me.

I roll away, and he bounds after me. As he tries to strike again, he stumbles, a shocked look in his eyes. He falls to his knees, blood pouring from his chest. Raphael stands behind him, his blade dripping scarlet. "Nia, we need to go."

I nod and get to my feet. "Sergeant, sound the retreat."

Raphael wipes his sword clean. "The sergeant is dead."

I follow his gaze and see the sergeant lying a few feet away from me in a puddle of blood. His eyes stare emptily at the sky.

"Retreat!" Raphael shouts at the soldiers. "Go, go!"

The soldiers obey, firing the occasional volley as they fall back. Atkinson has trained them well. The marksmen cover for each other, managing to get further away while slowing pursuit.

Raphael takes my hand and drags me out of the line of fire. I'm practically tripping over my own feet to keep up with him. We run toward the docks, the sounds of guns and screams filling the air. I'm already running out of breath.

"We need to get up the cliffs and out of the city!" I shout at Raphael.

"We won't make it," he says. "Too many Fey are already here."

"Do you have a better plan?"

"Back to the boat."

He's right. Miraculously, the boat we arrived in is still intact and docked at the far end of the pier. Although the Fey came with an entire fleet, they've mostly landed on the other side of the port.

"What about the sea serpents?"

"They won't go after one small boat. They're here to protect the fleet from the British navy. I hope."

"You *hope*?"

"We don't have a ton of options."

We reach the long pier and start running down it, waves crashing to each side of us. The boat is just a couple of hundred yards away. In five minutes, we'll reach it and get out of—

Oh, fuck.

Some warriors are still debarking, and five of them are marching toward us on the dock, blocking our way to our boat.

"Raphael!" I cry out.

We skid to a halt. Two of the Fey warriors at the rear of the group are among the most terrifying I've ever seen, a man and a woman, each nearly seven feet tall, clad in black armor. Their matching red cloaks flutter behind them like battle standards. The woman holds two battle-axes, one in each hand, and the man wields an enormous sword, the blade glinting in the sunlight. Compared to these two, the Fey in front of them seem like toy soldiers.

"The twins," Raphael says grimly.

"Who?"

"Maertisa and Vidal. Two of the fiercest captains in Auberon's army. They must be in command of this force."

I swallow. "Oh." I turn to retreat and find our way blocked by three more soldiers. They're advancing on us. "We're trapped."

"Nia, stay close to me," Raphael says, raising his sword.

I stand with my back to Raphael, facing the three Fey coming from the direction of the city. My mind screams as they rush at us. I loose my arrow, and it pierces the throat of one of them, but the twins and their lackeys are bearing down on us from the other side. Raphael moves in a blur of speed, his blade whooshing through the air. He cuts down one Fey soldier, then kills the next with a sweep of his blade. He locks swords with the third.

Two Fey soldiers charge at me, and I unsheathe my knife. I can hear Viviane berating me in my mind, *Who brings a knife to a sword fight?*

I duck as the first swings his sword, then pivot and touch his hand. Channeling my powers, I use the absolute terror I feel as fuel, pushing my fear into his mind. There is no time to process the strange thoughts that assail me.

Instead, I crash against his senses, confusing him, making him mistake friend for foe. He turns and runs his blade through his Fey ally. I jerk my mind free as the Fey stares at the soldier he just killed.

"Einion!" he cries in anguish.

His confusion gives me an opening, and I lunge at him, thrusting my knife into his throat. His mouth gapes in shock and pain, and then he topples off the pier and into the foamy sea, disappearing beneath the waves.

Breathing hard, I turn around. Three dead Fey lay at Raphael's feet. He's fighting with Vidal, their swords clanging loudly as they duel. The woman, Maertisa, is gone, probably swallowed by the waves like the last Fey soldier I killed. I crouch in a battle stance, gauging the distance to Raphael and his opponent. The huge Fey is maybe a dozen yards from me. As I prepare to attack, someone grips my hand and twists it.

I yell in pain and drop my knife. A blade is pressed against my throat, and I reach for the knife hidden in my boot.

"I wouldn't," Maertisa whispers in my ear, pain flaring in my neck as she digs the blade deeper into my skin.

On the dock in front of me, I watch as Raphael parries a powerful stroke by Vidal, then twists his sword, sending his opponent's blade spinning into the sea. Vidal grapples for Raphael's sword, but Raphael smashes the pommel into the man's face. Vidal falls to his knees, and Raphael raises his blade to finish him off.

"Raphael Launcelot!" Maertisa shouts, her blade tightening against my skin. "Your reputation precedes you."

Raphael glances back. Seeing my predicament, he grabs her brother and places his bloody sword against Vidal's neck. "Harm her, and you will be a single twin," he says coldly.

We stand frozen on the dock, the sea wind shrieking around us. Blood drips down my neck and into my collar. I dare not even swallow.

"Well, this is interesting," Maertisa says, almost as if she's enjoying herself.

"Finish her, Maertisa," Vidal snarls.

Raphael presses the sword closer to the other man's neck. "Quiet," he says, "or you lose an ear."

"Now, then, none of that," Maertisa says silkily. "We're not human barbarians, after all. Let's talk."

"We have nothing to talk about," Raphael says. "You let go of the woman, and we go to my boat. When we reach the boat, I will release your brother, and we will leave."

"I don't think so." Maertisa laughs coldly. "Release my brother first, and then I'll let my new friend go."

"Not happening."

"Then we stand here until my soldiers arrive to see what's keeping their captains," Maertisa says.

"If they even come close," Raphael snarls, "I'll kill your brother."

"Ugh. What's with all the killing, Launcelot?" Maertisa sighs. "I've heard tales, but I had no idea you were so bloodthirsty. Fine. I'll tell you what. We go to the boat *together*. Once there, we release our hostages at the same time and call it a draw."

Raphael considers this. "Okay."

I channel my telepathic powers through the fingers tightened around my arm. Almost instantly, I'm in Maertisa's mind. It's like reading the mind of an ancient, cunning spider. Her past is littered with dead Fey who've crossed her path, and she's planning to do the same to us.

"Raphael, it's a trap," I blurt. "As soon as we sail away, she'll send a sea serpent after us. They obey her commands."

"Well," Maertisa laughs, amused. "She's a telepath. That's so much fun! I have to admit she's right. But who knows? You might manage to outrun a sea serpent in that boat."

I've had enough. I tug at both my powers and pour myself into her mind. I will make her drop her knife and—

None of that, now, she thinks, and slaps my mind away.

I gasp, the connection broken.

"You will *not* fish inside my mind again," Maertisa says aloud. "Try that one more time, and *you'll* be the one to lose an ear."

"Don't touch her," Raphael says, clenching his jaw.

"I'm growing bored," Maertisa snaps. "If we wait here long enough, you two will die, but so will my brother. He's an oaf, but I like him, so that's not going to happen. I'm also obviously not going to let you both go. That would be ridiculous. Auberon would flay us alive. *But* I actually have a reasonable offer. Let us take you alive."

"That's not going to happen," Raphael growls.

"You misunderstand. I'm not talking about both of you —just *you*, Launcelot. I'll let the girl go."

"Don't!" Vidal shouts. "You can take them both—"

Raphael squeezes the man's neck, and Vidal sags, unconscious. "Now," he says, his voice steely. "You were saying?"

Maertisa seems unperturbed by her brother's treatment. "I was saying, all I want is you. I'm willing to let the girl sail away."

Raphael snorts. "You'll send a sea serpent after her as soon as you have your brother back."

"I won't. You can keep that sword to my brother's thick neck until this young telepath is well on her way."

"No, you can't," I cry. "She's lying. She just wants you alive. She wants to torture you so they can learn all you know. We can't be taken alive."

Raphael clenches his jaw. "Why do you even want me?" he asks.

Maertisa shrugs. "I could not care less about you. But Auberon's psychics have been shrieking about the one person who might be able to stop him—the Guardian of the Lake. They say that's you. And Auberon wants a chat, to figure out how one man could thwart all his plans."

I gasp. *The Lady of the Lake.* That's not Raphael. That's

me. Auberon's psychics must have homed in on the general vicinity, but they got the wrong person.

"It's me Auberon wants," I blurt. "Tana told me. I'm the Lady of the Lake. The *Guardian* of the Lake. She's been telling me this for months. You can't let them take you. Listen, take Vidal on board the boat. Maertisa won't send a sea serpent after you if you take her brother hostage. You can get away—"

Raphael holds up one finger. "How do I know you're not lying?" he asks Maertisa.

She sighs. "Ask your telepathic friend. I'll allow her a peek. She'll tell you that I speak the truth."

Raphael looks at me. "Do it."

I nod, but not because I intend to play her little game. Once I'm in her mind again, I'll make her let me go.

I connect with her again, using my power, and instantly see that she's being honest. She will let me go and allow Raphael to hold her brother hostage until I sail away. It's a risk. She knows it's a risk, but she suspects Raphael wouldn't kill her brother until I'm out of the sea serpent's range. And by then, she reasons, there'll be so many soldiers on the pier that she could disarm Raphael, even if he decides to cut her brother's throat.

I won't give her that chance. I go for her mind, channeling all my powers into her head, feeding it with the flaming roar of the fierce protectiveness I feel for Raphael. I will take control and make her drop the knife—

This time, she pushes me out even more violently.

"My patience is wearing thin, telepath," Maertisa says.

"I told you not to do that. Now, tell your commanding knight the truth of my thoughts, that I will let you go and you can sail away, as far as your heart desires."

I look at Raphael pleadingly.

"Is she telling the truth?" he asks.

The wind rises, and the waves get higher and higher. I have to convince him to leave.

"She..." I blink, my thoughts whirling. "No. No, she's lying. She doesn't care about her brother. She just wants you alive. She'll kill me anyway. But she won't kill you because you have her brother. And because Auberon wants you alive. You can get on that boat if you leave me behind."

Raphael's eyes soften. "Oh, Nia. For someone who spent so much time telling people what you thought they needed to hear, you're still not convincing. I thought I trained you better than this. What sort of spy lies so badly?"

Tears sting my eyes. "I can lie just fine," I say in a broken voice. "Just not to the people I care about. But you can't let her take you alive. You *can't*."

"Well, this is touching," Maertisa says, "I have to say, I just got all teary. Now, let's get this show on the road."

To my shock, she lets me go and steps back. "Go on, telepath. Before I change my mind and decide that I might actually like being a single child."

I hurry to Raphael. "Please don't," I plead desperately. "Let's go together. Take her brother with us. She won't hurt us if we have him hostage."

"She will," Raphael says. "It's true what she said. Auberon will flay her alive if he finds out she had an agent of Camelot in her grasp and let him go. Especially the so-called Guardian of the Lake."

"No, no, *listen*." I lean closer to his ear, whispering. "They don't know it, but they want *me*, not you. I'm the Lady of the Lake. I'll give myself up, and you can get out alive—"

He shakes his head. "Don't be ridiculous."

"Raphael, I swear, it's me they want—"

"I *know* that."

I stare at him, stunned.

"Of course I know that. A single person who can stop Auberon? Of course it's you. My Lady of the Lake."

"You know?" I whisper in disbelief.

"Get in the boat. Stay alive. Stop Auberon. Please. For me. End the House of Morgan and keep the Tower safe. Do this. For me."

I can see that his mind is made up. He won't get off this pier. I try to find a way for this to be different, but no matter what I think of, it ends with Raphael dead or being captured.

I think of taking control of Raphael's mind, of *making* him leave me here and take Maertisa's brother as a hostage.

But I don't. I can't do that to him.

I turn away from him. Throat thick with tears, I get in the boat and switch on the motor. I've never sailed a boat myself before. I can hardly stomach being on one. But this boat has simple controls, and I drive away from the pier.

When I look back, Raphael is watching me, his blade still on Vidal's throat. Maertisa waits patiently a few steps away, her red cloak fluttering in the wind.

My vision swims, and the figures on the pier become blurry as my eyes fill with tears.

CHAPTER 48

$\mathcal{J}$ flee in the little boat along the shoreline until I meet with British Navy ships. I'm picked up, and once I'm verified, I'm supplied with transport to rendezvous with the MI-13 agents who had evacuated Dover.

There's a war raging in the southeast of England now, and we're heading back to Camelot to see how we can help them fight the Fey.

We've already slowed Auberon's invasion and saved tens of thousands of civilian lives, but I can't get my mind off Raphael and what he's going through right now.

Sunset spreads a rusty mantle across the sky as the sun dips lower over the ocean. We're at the mouth of the river to Camelot. The river gleams in the coppery light, and the old gibbet sways in the sea wind.

We glide up the river, fog coiling around us, and

Camelot comes into view. Raphael should be here with us to see the oaks brushed with fiery shades of autumn, to feel the lure of home calling to us. And that's what Camelot is now, isn't it? Home.

When I first arrived, everything looked strange and foreign to me, like something out of a dream. No, not a dream, a fairytale that hardly seemed real, a world I was unprepared for. Now, the old Tudor-style houses and the soaring stone of Avalon Tower bathed in the ever-present mist are familiar and comforting.

Except that now, my home is missing someone very important. Jagged pain pierces me.

I have to get him back. No matter what happens, I will get Raphael back.

I cling to the railing, trying not to throw up as we sail closer to the tower. Maybe the only thing that hasn't changed about me in the past six months is that I still need to puke every time I sail. And every time I think of Raphael, I feel more nauseated. I lean over the railing, my stomach roiling.

Avalon Tower looms in the distance, the spires rising from the fog. In my mind, Raphael is there, waiting for us on the dock.

But that is a fantasy.

"I remember when you first came here with me." Tana sidles up and hands me a cup of tea. "You looked so lost."

I take it from her gratefully. As I sip it, I start to feel a little better. "I was just thinking the same thing."

"Cheer up, our Lady of the Lake." Tana lays her hand on my shoulder. "It was, all considered, a good day."

My jaw drops open. "A good day? People died. Raphael has been taken—"

"But we've slowed the darkness's progress, and we still have hope."

"Raphael doesn't."

"Doesn't he?" she asks.

Something in her tone eases the heavy weight in my chest. There's a playful smile at the corner of her mouth.

"What do you mean?" I ask. "Did you see something? Can you just tell me, for fuck's sake?"

"Calm down." She hands me her deck of cards. "Shuffle them."

I do as she says, shuffling them with trembling hands.

"Now, pick a card. Just one."

"This feels more like a magic trick than a reading."

"It's a reading."

I take one card out and flip it. The Star.

"I've checked over and over," Tana says. "Always the Star. Past and future. And that, I'm certain, is Raphael. The card represents healing and the connection to the universe, someone in tune with the creative force. If he were truly doomed, that's not what we'd see. His light would be dimmed. Raphael has been taken, that's true. But you can save him. You can get him back. And his light will return to us."

Against my better judgment, I feel hope rekindling in my heart. "Are you sure?" My throat is tight.

She touches my cheek. "You are the Lady of the Lake."

I bite my lip. "That sounds so formal."

"How about Aqua Bitch?" Serana grins, joining us. "That's better, right?"

"Aqua Bitch?" Tana asks, scandalized. "What nicknames do you have for me behind *my* back?"

"Oh, you're the life of the party, Tana, for sure."

She blinks. "I am?"

"No, pet. That was sarcasm. We could be in the middle of the wildest piss-up in the world, draped with gorgeous men and drinking and dancing, and your eyes would go glassy, and you'd tell us some poor sod was murdered on the very spot we're standing a century back. Oh, and also, that we're all going to die in a week."

Tana arches an eyebrow. "Would you rather that I kept it secret?"

I smile. "Shockingly, Tana had good news for once. Apparently, I'm going to rescue Raphael."

Serana nods. "Of course you are. No one is stopping my Aqua Bitch."

By the time we reach the dock, there's a crowd waiting for us. I recognize Amon first, by his long beard. Then other familiar faces come into focus—agents who used to be cadets with me, and a few knights I've come to know. Darius is grinning and waving at us wildly.

The Pendragons are noticeably absent.

As soon as we dock, I get off the boat, thankful to be back on solid ground. My stomach is still queasy as Amon walks up to me.

"Is there any news about the war?" I ask.

He nods gravely. "Plenty, and it will be discussed later. But before we do that, there's one thing I wish to do."

He's holding a small case, and he opens it. Inside is a torc, silver with a rosy sheen. I swallow.

"Nia Melisende," he says. "I want to welcome you again to the Agents of Camelot. You are an Avalon Steel knight."

He takes the torc from the case and slides it around my neck. All around me, people cheer, a sea of smiling faces, of friends, of comrades in arms.

I wish Raphael were here to see this, too.

But Tana says I will get him back, and I know better than to doubt her.

* * *

A CHILLY AUTUMN breeze breathes down my neck. I pull up the hood of my wool cloak and walk along the shore of the lake. I should be asleep at this time of night. Everyone else is. But Raphael isn't here, and that means I can't sleep at all. When was the last time I slept properly? Days ago, I suppose. Before Auberon captured Raphael.

The rain was hammering on my window as I was trying to fall sleep, and now that always reminds me of Raphael—being wrapped up in his bed in his tower room or kissing his rain-soaked skin in Fey France.

It's drizzling now, and the earthy scent of petrichor fills the night.

I don't know exactly why I'm heading to the bridge by

Nimuë's Tower, but something is pulling me there, maybe because it's where Raphael and I kissed that sultry summer night.

Or maybe I've lost my mind from chronic insomnia.

Fog drifts along the glassy surface of the lake, along with a few orange oak leaves, bright against the dark water.

I reach the bridge at last and climb the old stone stairs. They're slick from the rain, and I hold on to the rail. The tower looms over the lake, wrapped in mist. I pass the place where Raphael and I jumped in and feel my heart cracking at the memory. Gods, I wish I could go back in time.

Some of the ancient carvings on Nimuë's Tower are glowing faintly—the triple-spiral symbols. I walk through the arched doorway and feel the magic hum against my skin. On one side of the landing, a stairwell winds down to the lake. On the other side is a round room that looks like a temple. Peaked windows let in faint light. There's no glass in them anymore—if there ever was—and a cool breeze blows through the openings. In the center of the room is a circular altar covered in a layer of dust. Carved in the top of the stone are images of three women with long hair, holding urns. I run my fingers over the carving for a moment before pulling away again. This is too old for me to be touching.

Goosebumps rise on my skin. What did they use this for in the old days?

Going to a window, I peer out at the lake. Excitement flutters through me. A boat is waiting at the base of the tower. I've been out here a few times before, and there's never been a boat. The small vessel glows in the moonlight, and I lean out the window for a closer look. It resembles a wooden canoe with a curled bow and stern, carved with intricate knotted designs. Two oars rest across it.

My heart thrums. Some people say that the Lady of the Lake is a protector of Camelot. But that's not what Nimuë was doing. That's not why she trapped Merlin in the oak. She was a bridge between worlds and a guardian of both. And when the humans started taking too much control, she tried to restore the balance.

If I'm the new Lady of the Lake, what does it mean?

In the center of my chest, I feel a tug, as if an invisible string connects me to the boat.

I hurry from the chamber and bound down the stairs. The stairwell ends with an arched open door and a stone path that leads to the boat.

I climb in and grab the oars, damp from the rain. Ignoring the persistent drizzle, I begin to row, my breath clouding the night air.

I row faster. Surely this boat came to me for a reason. Desperately, I wonder if the reason is linked to Raphael. Tana said I would rescue him, and in the past two days, it became clear that none of the knights of the Round Table had any idea how to get him out of Auberon's grasp.

The cool air bites at my skin as I work the oars.

Nimuë sacrificed her lover for her cause.

But Raphael? He did the exact opposite. He put Camelot at risk to save me. I feel my chest cracking. The sooner I can get him out, the less likely it is they'll break him.

And then I hear it, the hum of a veil. It's so foggy out here, it's hard to see, but it's there—the opalescent sheen. It's a veil, but this one feels different. It emits a low, resonant hum that's almost musical. It's a different sort of magic, beautiful and ancient. Primal magic, perhaps.

Is this where Avalon has been all this time? My breath quickens, and I summon the red bloom of my Sentinel magic. The moment the hum goes quiet, I start to row again, faster now, moving through the veil. What if this is where they're keeping Raphael? On Avalon itself?

My oars carve into the water, and the mist thins. I keep going.

I look over my shoulder at what I'm approaching and feel the world tilt on its axis.

It's there—a rocky, moss-covered island. Avalon. A vast, rambling castle of stone perches on a craggy hilltop. Pale stone towers jut into the night sky, almost glowing. At lake level, apple trees and oak trees spread out over the island.

I can hardly breathe.

The boat touches the shoreline, and I leap onto the leafy shore, taking a moment to catch my breath. An old stone path winds up the hill toward the castle, and I charge up it, wheezing as I race up the uneven stairs. The air is heavy with the scent of apples, and red and orange leaves carpet the stone stairs.

But disappointment carves through me as I near the castle at the top. The place looks abandoned, not a single light or torch in view. The towers are crumbling, the gardens wildly overgrown. Bridges that go nowhere sprout from mossy walls. Of course they're not keeping Raphael here.

Upon closer examination, I notice the gorgeous craftsmanship of the stone, the carvings of triple spiral shapes, the phases of the moon, and faces made from the shapes of leaves.

"Nia Melisende." A deep voice stops me in my tracks.

A figure steps from the shadows of a ruined arch wearing a black cape and a pale, spiked crown. A tendril of fear coils through me. I know that crown and those dark curls. The sharp cheekbones. That crown is in paintings all over Avalon Tower. No one wanted us to forget him.

The House of Morgan...

"Mordred." My voice shakes. "You're alive."

"I am."

"Did you send that boat for me?"

He takes a step closer. "I wasn't interested in you at first. But now that I've heard about the trouble you've caused for Auberon, my curiosity is piqued."

He's going to kill me. That's why he sent for me. He wants to protect his son. Rings gleam on his fingers. He has no sword, but he doesn't need one. Mordred Kingslayer killed Arthur, the great knight and king. He can crush me with his bare hands.

I take a step back. "I thought you died." Raphael plans to kill everyone from Mordred's bloodline. He has no idea that includes Mordred himself.

His eyes are the palest blue. He shrugs. "I have been here all along. Once, every hundred years, I can break free, but only for a short time. And then I find myself back in my mother's castle. This is my curse."

I swallow hard. "Your son can't free you?"

"I have no son."

My blood pounds hot, and I can't feel the cold anymore. "Auberon. King Auberon."

His smile twists. "Is that what people think? They think that bastard is my son? No. Auberon belonged to Nimuë and Merlin. Merlin, that duplicitous, traitorous fuck, was the one who cursed me."

I clear my throat. "You murdered King Arthur, and all those people in Avalon—"

"Look at what they had planned!" he roars, gesturing at the castle. "The Fey kingdom, in ruins. It was always going to be that way. Arthur and his bitch wife were always our enemies. Any idiot could see that. Anyone except Merlin. They say we enchanted the humans. But in Merlin's case, it was the other way around."

My voice sounds distant as I say, "The House of Morgan is fated to destroy Camelot."

Mordred flashes me a dark smile. "Oh, I know. And

you are going to help me do it, Nia." Mordred stares at the sky, looking lost in thought. "I see things in dreams, and sometimes, I dream of you. There's a silver-eyed man you want to rescue from Auberon." His sharp gaze lands on me. "And I'm the only one who can help you, my daughter."

ACKNOWLEDGMENTS

Thanks to C.N. Crawford's coven, my fantastic readers' group on Facebook, and all our readers who have helped to support us over the years. We are so privileged to share our stories with you, and you have made our dreams come true!

Thanks to Liora, our brilliant beta reader, and Alex Rivers' wife.

Three amazing editors helped to refine the text, to make the writing smooth and clear: Noah Skye, Rachel Cass, and Lauren Simpson.

Rachel from Nerd Fam helped to get the word out by organizing my marketing campaigns and consulting with us.

Our fabulous cover designers are Merrybookround, who did stunning work on the ebook, paperback and dust jackets, and Coverdungeonrabbit who did beautiful work on the naked hardcover.

ALSO BY C.N. CRAWFORD AND ALEX RIVERS

If you enjoyed Avalon Tower, you can check out another action-packed, fae series by C.N. Crawford and Mike Omer.

Dark Fae FBI, starting with Agent of Enchantment.

"The fae live among us. And one of them is a serial killer."

9 781956 290196